THE KILLER WITHIN

By Gary Copeland

Published in 2012 by FeedARead Publishing

British Library C.I.P.

A CIP catalogue record for this title is available from the British Library.

WARNING

Chilling, shocking, and with scenes to make the most hardened of readers feel squeamish, this is not a book for the faint-hearted.

Because of this, I think it only fair to warn you that the opening chapters are brutal, and I urge anyone with an aversion to such horrible violence, or anyone who may have experienced such a terrible assault to begin at chapter six.

To the die-hards amongst you who risk reading the opening chapters and any similar scenes within the book, I apologise in advance for any discomfort caused.

ACKNOWLDGEMENT

In recognition of my use of their lyrics in one of my chapters, and in appreciation of their work, I'd like to give a mention to the wonderful group 'Chicago', and remind those reading this of some of their exceptional hits which include;-

Hard Habit to Break
If You Leave Me Now
Hard to Say I'm Sorry
You're The Inspiration
...and many more

DEDICATION

My thoughts and appreciation go out to the many family members and friends who make my life special simply because they are a part of it. To all of you, the biggest of thanks. You know who you are.

But on this one occasion I'd like to single out my mam, still sorely missed with each passing year, and my love for her unwaning till my own dying breath.

Prologue

The image so different from the man he'd become, the flashback played again in his mind;- the scene of a boy, hunting, his eyes narrow and his heart racing; the thought of the tortures to come filling him with excitement.

With the back of his hand, he eased an overhanging branch to one side, it's furry catkins caressing his brow as he brushed past, his eyes fixed on his prey as he stepped onto the lawn. Moving patiently. Slowly. Ever closer. His victim unaware. And his voice a rasping whisper, he began his lingering chant; eerie, like a child possessed.

"I'm going to caaaaaatch you."

He edged closer, slinking forward like a prowling cat, his pupils dilated and his heart racing a little faster.

"I'm going to huuuuuurt you."

A pause mid stride, his mouth drooling. A glance left and right before his hands reached out like claws to snatch at his prey.

"I'm going to **KILL** *you."*

Then a *pounce* and it was over; the hazy reels of time spluttering to a stop and the image gone.

A snap back to reality.

And a new victim lying at his feet… fighting for her life.

One

Her eyes taped shut, Amy lay still, the break in her torture filled with fragmented memories of a little girl dancing with her mother, a candle-lit dinner, a shower of confetti, the smile of her husband. And with the stroke of fingers across her gagged lips;- the memory of a man she'd bumped into in the café, his hair greasy, and his eyes piercing, his gaze shifting to her purse at it spilled to the floor.

"I'm sorry," she had said, fumbling to pick up her lipstick and keys. "I should have been watching where I was -"

The man had knelt opposite without answer, and as she realised he was no-longer scooping up her things, her embarrassment turned to discomfort at the sight of her drivers licence in his grubby hands, his fingers tracing the picture of her plastic face.

"Do you *mind?*" she'd asked, her open hand met with a scowl before his eyes narrowed, his attention straying to her figure and the hem of her skirt, his scowl breaking into a lecherous smile as he dragged the licence across the palm of her hand, its edge tracing the groove of her life-line before she snatched it from him, stood sharply and marched away, annoyed with herself for having bumped into him. Annoyed more so by the reactions of the man, his eyes pouring over her body as she'd picked up her things. A misconstrued smile. Her politeness mistaken for flirting as once again, some guy thinks of ulterior motives when he gets a smile from an attractive blonde.

But that was *yesterday...*

*   *   *

Now she lay on her kitchen floor, battered and bruised and covered in blood; dazed by the events that had brought her here, and fearful of how much *more* pain she would have to endure before eventually, she could feel no more.

Faintly, she cried out in a desperate bid to stem the incessant blows. Begging, "Please don't."

"Please."

"Pleeeease…"

Ignored.

Unanswered.

Unheard.

Muted screams now stifled cries, only the muffled sound of urgency escaped the tape drawn tightly across her mouth. The odiously sticky brown tape, forcing blood from her fleshy lips and pulling them tight against slackened teeth.

Her arms bound behind her back, she fought to break the seal, twisting her neck to rub at the tape with the ball of her shoulder. Contorting her jaw. Sucking and blowing, and desperately inhaling as drying blood blocked the narrowing airways of her broken nose. But like a limpet to a rock, the tape held firm, an unyielding plastic barrier to the craving of empty lungs. Her night of suffering forgotten as she was forced to face her biggest fear in life. The horror of dying slowly, being buried alive, ravaged by fire, or choking as her lungs filled with water. Nightmares she'd hoped would never be realised, yet here she was; suffocating. Drowning in a sea of air, unable to inhale a drop.

She battled with her emotions, her heart racing faster than ever as fear was replaced by panic. *'Stop it, Amy, stop it! You're only making it worse.'*

Her throat dry and tight, she fought for control, struggling to rein-in her fears, her memories plagued with images of a little girl gasping for air through a straw-width windpipe.

Two sucks on the blue and one on the brown.

Over twenty years since her last attack, yet she still remembered her 'puffers'. But this wasn't asthma. And as she vainly struggled for air, her anxiety continued to soar. Her stomach wrenching and pulling to release the despair trapped within her empty lungs. And even if she *could* breathe, *could* weep, her tears had nowhere to run, their escape blocked behind the damned tape that had caused her so much anguish. Binding her. Rendering her sightless and defenceless. Stifling her screams and sending them back to the pit of her stomach along with all hopes of rescue. And the beatings— never ending.

Countless times she had been dragged from her comatose slumber to suffer the endless barrage of torture. Kicked and punched into unconsciousness, only to wake to yet more blows raining down with brutal ferocity. And with every blow she felt his loathing, even through the numb swellings that buried her once beautiful face, his demonic hatred tearing deep into her open wounds and ripping at the core of her very soul.

Then silence…

Everything stopped bar the tick of a clock.

'The calm before the storm'

Her eyes taped shut, her ears strained at the hush. Delving. Listening beyond the ticks and probing deep into the ominous silence in search for the gruntful warning of an incoming kick.

A kick that didn't come.

A moments respite to dwell on her pain… her life ticking slowly by as her tormentor paused to rest, his laboured breathing smothering the countdown of the clock. His chest expanding as hers collapsed. Taunting her it seemed. Feasting on the oxygen, gulping it down whilst *she* could barely sip. A frightened realisation that maybe '*this'* was how he wanted her to die. Beaten by *him*. Beaten by the thin plastic layer of tape covering her mouth.

But Amy wasn't going to let that happen.

If HE wanted her dead, then HE would have to be the one to kill her. And as she fought to break the seal of the tape, he grabbed her from behind, his arm around her neck, and another layer of tape wrapped around her head. Layer after layer. Around and around. Over her eyes, mouth and ears. Leaving her blind, dumb and deaf to all around.

She lay on the floor, ignoring the ice cold shiver coursing through her body as she sensed her assailant standing over her. She *had* to fight for air. *Had* to. Her stomach tightened, pressing painfully against her empty lungs and squeezing at the last dregs of air in an effort to blow the mucus from her broken nose. A miniscule hiss, too little, too late, gone like a breath on the wind.

She cried an inaudible "*help*", knowing he couldn't hear her, but hoping nonetheless that the tape would be torn from her mouth. But as the gag held firm, the last of her hopes vanished.

His eyes were on her, she felt it. He was observing her every move. Gloating no doubt. Watching her writhing on the floor next to the bed, like a fish out of water, squirming in the throes of death. Rolling. Twisting. Wrenching. Spasmodic pauses for rest scattered with futile attempts to strip the ductile bindings from her wrists. And as her strength diminished, her efforts grew weaker.

Her time had come and she knew it.

She began to hyperventilate.

Then she stopped.

No movement.

No sound.

Two

He pushed at her limp body with his foot, and was rewarded with a stifled groan.

"Don't you fucking die on me yet, bitch!"

Oompf... A crunching kick to her stomach forced the dregs of air from her lungs and the blood-clotted mucus of her broken nose. At last, she could breathe. The unwelcome pain to her belly accepted with the return of expanding lungs, her breathing eased, and her pains announced their return. Sore, stabbing, aching pains, inflicted slowly during hours of torture. The throbbing pulses spread throughout her body, as once again, she felt the blood on her skin betraying the duration of her nightmare. Old, dried, caking blood. Cold blood. Warm blood seeping from open wounds, soaking through her night-dress and sticking it flat to her clammy skin.

How much more could she lose before eventually, her soul would relinquish her battered body.

She couldn't take any more. The pain *had* to end soon. *Had* to.

'Please... Finish it.'

Death knocked at her door and she welcomed it in. Welcomed an end to the torture and pain. And as she drifted on the edge of consciousness, her thoughts spilled over into yesterday.

A pain-free day.

A *dream* of a day...

In her customary weekday attire of black knee-length skirt and smart white blouse, Amy had returned home from work to find Sean already climbing from his car as she pulled up beside him on the gravelled drive. He stood there, suited and booted. Clean shaven, with a dimple-chinned smile, dark hair, and pale blue eyes. He looked smart in his business suit, but she preferred him in jeans. Liked his shape, *loved* his bum, which was annoyingly hidden by the cut of his jacket.

She grabbed her shoulder bag from the passenger seat, a present hidden inside. Another cigarette lighter from the Gadget shop to add to Sean's unusual collection. (made all the more unusual because he didn't smoke)

He greeted her with a kiss as she stepped from her car, his hand slipping from behind his back to reveal a beautiful bouquet of flowers richly plumped up with purple and lilac stargazers. Her favourites.

"Happy anniversary, gorgeous." he said, his arm wrapping around her trim waist and drawing her towards him to kiss her again.

"Anniversary? Today? Anniversary for what?" She struggled not to grin.

"You know very well, what. And if I *had* forgotten, I wouldn't have heard the last of it."

They shared a laugh and poked fun at one another as they walked through the hall to the kitchen. Amy stood over the sink with the flowers, the tap running as Sean brushed a stray wisp of hair from her face. "Eight years since we met," he said, "and you haven't aged a bit."

Amy cast him her pre-emptive, half exaggerated smile in anticipation of his following quip. His defence mechanism, built during a time before they had met. His displays of affection often tinged with light-hearted humour and witty remarks, sometimes masking his true feelings. But occasionally, his shell would crack open to reveal his shielded heart and leave little doubt of his sincerity.

Amy loved these moments. Loved the affection and his flattery. Loved the way he held her in his arms, even as she sorted through the flowers, cutting away at the stalks with her scissors, her grin widening with contentment as he hugged her from behind. Wrapping himself around her. Squeezing her close as he said, "I love you so much. I know I don't tell you half as often as I should, but it's true. And I love you more with each passing day."

Amy feigned retching as her fingers reached to her mouth, but inside, she was bursting, ready to pop. Swollen with the emotions of a sixteen year-old on a first date. A happy contentment as the butterflies fluttered wildly around her stomach, telling her how much she loved him. Loved being around him. Loved his happy-go-lucky attitude. Even loved his finicky ways and his sometimes quirky dress sense (or lack of it). The signs of which were echoed even now, in his banana dappled tie. Pictures of half-peeled bananas pressing into her back as she filled a second vase with water to accommodate the remaining flowers, inhaling their aroma as she arranged them. Soaking up the very essence of their being. And as she did so, Sean began to explain that he'd made arrangements for them to have the entire evening to themselves.

"No family, no callers. Just us," he said. "The phone's off the hook and you're *all* mine."

"So what are you going to do with me," she grinned.

He picked her up in his arms, leaning back and twirling as she giggled with laughter. "Well, later we are going to your favourite restaurant. The table's booked, and the taxi will be here 7:30 sharp. Until then, I'm going to make mad passionate love to you, and then I'm going to love you some more."

"What do you mean, some more?" she laughed, "You got some Viagra?"

"Well… as good as," he smiled. "I got some new batteries for your toys. Those '*extra life*' ones with the copper-coloured top."

"It's the extra *looong* battery I want, with the plum-coloured top," she smiled, her dextrous fingers tugging at his belt as he lowered her to the floor, then paused.

He kissed her on the cheek, then sensuously on the mouth, resisting the temptation to take it further. "Wait there a moment." And with a peck on her lips, he dashed upstairs, returning moments later with a "Close your eyes" before coming down.

She closed them tight, her hands over her face, resisting the twinge of temptation to peak through her fingers. Their song began to play on the music system;- '*When a man loves a woman*' and Sean joined in "*can't keep his mind on nothing else,*" And as she heard him singing along, she cried out like an excited school girl, "Can I look? Can I look?"

"Whenever you're ready, dear."

Amy slowly peeled her hands away and gasped with delight at the sight of him standing before her. Sean was smiling profusely, dressed in a white suit and matching peaked cap. It was the scene from her favourite film;- Richard Gere in 'An Officer And A Gentleman'. She wrapped her arms around him as he scooped her up, then giggled as she flicked the peak of his cap before smiling at him coyly. "I want you to take me on a pleasure cruise, sailor boy. I want you to raise your anchor, cast off, and rock my eager little boat."

And her arms draped over his shoulders, he carried her upstairs, stumbling and giggling as they went.

Three

Wednesday 28th March

Dear diary.

What an amazing day this turned out to be.

After an uneventful day at work, I had the most fantastic evening with Richard Gere (alias;- Sean in a white suit) He surprised me with a beautiful bouquet of flowers and we had the best sex in ages. It was absolutely wonderful. And what's more, he topped it off by staying awake afterwards because he'd booked a table for us at 'The Church Mouse' to celebrate our wedding anniversary. We ordered the very same meal we had there on our first date. I never dreamt he would remember. It was such a wonderful surprise, and great to have him back to his old self. I love him so much right now. Life couldn't get much better.

But it could certainly get worse.

The hard SLAP! to her face yanked her back to the present, fear gripping her instantly as the nightmare resumed. Her wrists and ankles bound, her mouth and eyes taped shut, she was helpless, struggling to break free. And her dream day was over as once more, she entered a dark world of pain.

Vainly, she struggled to scream, before her next realisation hit home. Sean had probably been killed by the psycho now sitting astride her on the floor. This evil predator who had broken into their home as they had slept, had stolen his life away. *Her* life. And stricken with grief, she sobbed uncontrollably at the thought of how he had held her that night. Hugging her close. Spooning her as he kissed the nape of her neck. And his final words before drifting off to sleep... *'I love you, Amy.'*

Then, only a few hours later, in the still dark hours of morn, her life had been shattered by the shrilling ring of the bedside telephone, Sean hardly having a chance to answer it before she had drowsily asked, "Who is it, Hun'?"

"No-one," he'd replied.

"No-one?" she asked, still half asleep, "Don't they know what time it is?" Her groan rhetorical, having failed to open her eyes to see the clock for herself.

"No, dear, I mean '*no-one'*. No answer. Wrong number I guess," he paused, the phone still pressed quizzically to his ear as he continued to listen.

"So hang up," she yawned. "I'm tired." Her sleep-laden request more a tiresome command, "If it's a wrong number, just ignore it."

"Yes, well, I thought it was a wrong number, but the line, it's gone dead."

Her patience waning, and her closed eyes seeing the mottled pink of her inner eye-lids, she rolled away from the bright light of the bedside lamp. "So hang up," she repeated, nestling her bum into him and encouraging him to spoon her. "Come on, Hun'. Switch off the lamp and cuddle in."

"No. I mean;- dead. Not the tone of someone hanging up, but '*dead'*. No tone. No sound." Then, frightened, he whispered so only she could hear, "What was that?"

Disgruntled, she moaned, "It's nothing. Just the wind and the rain. Please. Go back to sleep."

As Amy tried to cuddle closer, he kissed her on the cheek and climbed out of bed. "I won't be long," he whispered. "It's probably nothing. I'll just check the dog's okay. Maybe he was frightened by the thunder and knocked something over."

Amy drowsily protested, more with groans than with anything that could be mistaken for language. Then drifted off to sleep, sinking slowly into dreamful oblivion before waking with a sudden jolt as a crashing thud echoed loudly up the stairs.

She sat bolt-up, her eyes wide, trepidation in her voice as she cried out, "Sean...?"

"Sean?"

"Sean, answer me, what was that?"

The house had never been so quiet. The silence, haunting.

"Please, Sean, answer me. This isn't funny."

Still no reply. No sounds bar the wind and the thrashing rain.

"Sean, talk to me. Pleeease. Don't play around, Sean, I'm frightened."

She reached for the phone by the bed. Silent as an empty shell. Nothing but the sound of her own rapid breathing emanating from the hollow earpiece.

She slinked out of bed and edged toward the partially open door, peering through the crack to steal a glance to the top of the stairs before once more calling out, "Sean? What's happening? Where are you?"

Her eyes adjusted to the darkness as she strayed beyond the bedroom, relying on its light to illuminate the landing. And slowly, gripped by fear, she inched forward toward the stairs as her wandering mind went into over-drive.

What if there ***is*** an intruder in the house?

Had the light on the landing actually popped or had the bulb been removed?

Amy struggled to contain herself, shrugging-off such nonsense with 'No, it's nothing, just coincidence. Too many thrillers and not enough chick-flicks, that's all. Sean must have bumped into something in the darkness and was probably in the cellar right now, searching for a bulb. That's why he hadn't answered, he hadn't heard her.'

But why take chances?

Three stairs down, she steered beyond the fourth, careful to avoid the tell-tale creaks as one by one, she edged down the stairs, cringing with every step. All the time listening for something amiss. The most subtle of sounds betrayed by the dead-of-night silence. The wind picking up outside as she scrutinized every noise and shadow of her home. Scanning with eyes anew. Her fearful gaze flicking to doorways and shadowy corners, afraid of what she might see. Then… a knot in her stomach, her trembling hand twitched ominously at the lounge door, teasing it open as she peered inside.

"Oh god."

The words had hardly left her mouth. A heavy chill racing down her spine as she felt the presence of someone behind her. And void of thought, no time to react, her body tensed, and the heavy blow pounded hard into the back of her head.

Four

Amy lay motionless. Cold and concussed. Vaguely aware of the fine hairs on her arms standing proud, goose-pimples covering her body as she woke to a muffled whisper in her ear, the voice barely audible through the crackle of the tape.

"Are you okay, Amy?"

"Come on, Amy. Wake up."

And as her groggy confusion faded, she was snatched back to the present with a hot flash of pain across her cheek. "I said... *Wake up!*"

Another, harder slap, then her nightmare had truly begun.

Bound and gagged, she had lost all concept of time. Awoken in her bedroom to suffer all manner of pain and humiliation. Drifting in and out of consciousness as she was beaten to within an inch of her life. Time and again, punched and kicked. Prodded with a knife. Bitten. No mercies. No let up. Forever dragged from her comatose dreams to suffer the endless barrage of torture that had started with the beatings, and escalated into a frenzied attack.

Now, dazed and beyond caring, she relinquished her body to the waves of abuse, blood stained perspiration trickling down her brow as she accepted her inevitable end.

Soon, it would all be over, she thought. But she was wrong.

The phone call, the beatings, the mind games; merely a taste of what was to come. He had savoured this moment, planned it meticulously. And now he'd had a taste of her fear, he was hungry for more, and looked forward to the main course, a lick of his lips as he relished the oncoming banquet.

From the moment she was strapped into the chair, she knew worse was to come, and in that dawning instant, she was ravaged by fear, struggling to repel him. Twisting and jerking. Kicking as best she could. Lashing out with her feet as he tightened his grip around her ankles, and as her bindings grew tighter, her fears grew worse, her hollow screams echoing within her head as she felt the touch of cold metal against her fingers; pliers gripping the ends of her manicured nails. Her whole body trembling beyond her control, shaking with terror and shivering with cold as fear-induced sweat oozed from her every pore.

Then, one by one. Lingering and unhurried. Her finger-nails were torn slowly from their beds. Dragged from deep below the skin and ripping at the cuticles. The waves of excruciating pain surging throughout her body as each was pulled from its fleshy sheath.

"That's it!... Scream, bitch, screeeeam!"

As the third nail was lanced, she passed out, but the torture didn't stop.

She woke to the throbbing pulse of her fingers and the pressure of his weight on her legs as he sat astride her, salivating. Holding her head in his hands as he dragged his sodden tongue across her swollen face, then folded his arms and rested them heavily across her heaving chest as he smothered her with his warm, heavy breathing. And all the time taunting, his voice barely coherent.

"You're one sexy lady, Amy."

"Too good for *him*."

"It's a shame we didn't meet earlier, you and I. We could have been so good together."

Even through the thick layers of tape covering her ears, she could hear him drooling as he sat across her lap, his sweaty stench drifting up the narrowing airways of her broken nose to invade the privacy of her lungs, making her feel sick; nauseous at the thought of his germs infesting her from within. An odour like mould. His putrid germs contaminating the sliver of air that crept to her begging lungs.

She recoiled in repulsion as she heard him suck back the saliva escaping his mouth, allowing only the taunts to slip out as he pondered her fate, "What next, I wonder?"

Muffled and indistinct, her sobbing cries poured into the tape, "Please, stop. Please. Pleeease."

At last, her prayers were answered. He climbed from her lap, and with her brief sigh of relief came a cold shudder of dread as she felt his arousal brush against her arm. *'Oh god, no. He's getting off on this. He's going to rape me'. No. You can't. Please don't. Please god, no.*

Her fears heightened with the thought of him inside her. Lying on top of her. Thrusting. The thought of it making her want to curl up and die.

Where was he?

Why had he climbed off?

What was he going to do?

The not knowing was almost as bad as the torture, and she was almost relieved when he drifted down to her feet, her toe in the grip of his pliers. A squeeze before she felt it bent back until it snapped with an almighty crack.

"This little piggy went to market."

She screamed into her gag, sobbing as the pliers gripped another toe.

"This little piggy stayed at home." CRACK!

One after another, working from the outside in-over, he broke every one of her toes. Yanking at them. Pulling and twisting at them with the pliers before eventually hacking them off with god knows what. A slice of pain as something sharp cut through her swelling agony. And as *he* screamed with pleasure, *she* screamed for mercy, praying for the release of death as her half-empty lungs screamed out her pain. Then, at last, it was over. Time losing all meaning as she suffered the intolerable tortures until, once again, she passed out, the excruciating loss of her fourth toe, the catalyst for her slip into unconsciousness.

But her respite was brief.

Soon she would wake to her throbbing digits and his mocking taunts.

"No more dancing for you, Amy. Such a shame. You danced so beautifully."

Time and again she had passed out as the tortures continued. And every time, she was roused to suffer yet more beatings. More tortures. Her soul broken beyond repair, her body a withered husk.

She lay at his feet, numb to the pain as her body grew limp and the last of her hopes evaporated from her shattered body. Then finally; everything stopped.

Her tormentor had paused, and through her dazed exhaustion, she heard him walk across the room.

At last, this was it. She melted into the floor, tranquil and relaxed, thinking of nothing but Sean's smile as her death approached, the impending sound of shoes on the hardwood floor as her would-be killer drew closer, his pace quickening as he came towards her, almost on top of her, an almighty scream, "Let there be *light!*"

She'd never felt pain like it, and screamed out in agony as something hard and cold was rammed inside her. With the sound of glass, she felt it break. Felt the blood running down her legs… Passed out.

Then woke to the tightness of her hair in the grip of his hand, her body bouncing off the hard corners of the steps as he dragged her downstairs and left her lying on the kitchen floor, awaiting the conclusion to her nightmare, her head swooning as she slipped in and out of consciousness. Dying. Mourning the probable loss of her husband and in shock at how her night had unfolded.

Last night, she had gone to bed happier than she had been in a long time, and now, with the dawning of a new day, her life had been turned around to the point of extinction. Her life in the hands of this psycho, this madman, her 'bete noire'.

"Wakey, wakey." A rousing patter of fingers on her cheek.

Amy stirred to consciousness, her dreams fading and her pains returning with vigour.

"I said! *wakey, wakey!*" The manic voice reverberated around her head as it filtered through the ductile blindfold that covered her ears. "Don't you fucking die on me yet, bitch! I want to look into your eyes when you fucking die. But first, I want to play."

She didn't move. Didn't respond. Didn't have the energy. She was sapped from the torturous onslaught and at the mercy of her attacker, awaiting the killer blow. Wanting an end to the pain. An end to her mourning. An end to her life without Sean.

Soon she would join him in the afterlife.

She knew it.

Accepted it.

Her eyes closed, her breathing shallowed, and the long sleep beckoned.

Five

He stood looking down at her body, the ivory nightdress sticking to the contours of her slender figure and leaving little to the imagination, the satin now a swab to her wounds, damp with blood and sweat. And her face beaten beyond recognition, her identity buried beneath fractured bones, blackened eyes and missing teeth; her long blonde hair the only clue to how attractive she had once been.

He looked to her face for signs of life and pushed at her limp body with his foot, checking she hadn't already died. He wanted her attention. Wanted to see that fading look in her eyes as her soul abandoned her body. The spark of life disappearing into nothingness. And with no response, he pushed at her body again.

Still, she didn't move, even as he bent down beside her and tossed her head in his hands before tearing the tape from her eyes and ears. And for the first time since her ordeal had begun, she heard his voice, chillingly clear.

"Look at me!" he shouted, standing once again and staring down at her.

Amy's cheek remained flat to the floor, her eyes slowly opening. Squinting through swollen slits to see the shoes of her assailant standing before her.

" I said, *look* at me! Don't you care who dies next, Amy?"

Amy stirred to the sound of his voice. Groaning. Struggling to raise her head toward the psychopath looming over her, encouraging her like a father would a child.

"That's it. Come on, Amy. Just turn around. Turn around and look at me."

He stood over her tattered body as she turned towards him, the knife gripped intently in his hand. It was time for the last gouge. The last cut. The last thrust of the blade. Foreplay was over. It was time for her to die.

But as her eyes met his, there was the delay of an empty gaze.

In these final moments leading up to the killer blow, he had paused;- confused, as though waking from a coma. Standing in freeze-frame. A fleeting image from his past projected onto the screen of his mind only to be torn away as the hazy reels of time came spluttering to a stop, leaving him stood there, stunned, his senses re-awakening as he slowly roamed the spectacle before him. Smelling. Listening. Scanning. Relieved to see nothing out of place. His prey still at his feet, and the absence of light unable to mask the severity of his performance, signs of which were everywhere. Spattered drops and small pools. Dragging trails of blood smudged across the floor, and smears across the doorframe from her efforts to resist being dragged here. The carnage so extreme that he himself was drenched with the warm sinewy blood of his gasping victim.

Standing over her, he closed his eyes and slowly raised his arms out to his sides, standing like a blood spattered crucifix in the middle of the room as a splash of light bounced off crimson pools and pale skin, his chest swelling with pride as he listened to the sound of laboured breathing at his feet, her tired lungs almost smothered by the howl of the wind as it rustled through the swaying trees. Nature's orchestra raging outside. Creaks from aching branches. A flash of lightening announced by the ominous roar of thunder rumbling into the distance as leaves danced with rain to thrash against the large kitchen window and darkness seeped through its panes to swallow night's shadows, the storm reaching its thunderous crescendo to quell the subtle sound of ticking as beads of blood dripped from his hands to the hardwood floor, like a clock counting down the seconds of Amy's life.

Another flash of light. Another clap of thunder as he yelled above the roar. "Do you see that, Amy? Do you hear?!... God himself applauds my genius."

He opened his eyes for one last look over his work, appreciating the splendour of it all. A smile of satisfaction as his gaze passed over his sacrificial lamb, taking pleasure from the fact that, even now, with no chance of survival, she would attempt to fight back, just as she had done throughout the night. Her broken body battling through the pain and torment and offering what little resistance she could as she clung to the last vestige of life, unwilling to relinquish it freely.

Yet freely, he would take it. Her life was his. It always had been. And only now would she come to appreciate that.

But again, he paused… his eyes staring off into the nether.

With dark brown hair and milk-white skin, he was a boy of around nine, skinny and unkempt, his gangly form exaggerated by baggy hand-me-down clothes as he peered from behind the trunk of a weeping willow tree.

His victim in sight, he stared intently through the scattered spaces between the leaves and catkins of an overhanging branch, the excited glare of his eyes part hidden by the thick black-rimmed spectacles resting precariously on his disjointed nose.

Stealth was key, and now, like a hunting wildcat, he'd singled out his prey. Closing in on his target. Ready to pounce before his victim could know what had happened. Moving ever closer. His movements smooth and subtle, readying himself for the ambush. All the time keeping his eyes on his prey as he paused to tighten his belt and rolled up the sleeves of his dirt-white shirt, his heartbeat steady as the time to attack approached. The time... to move in for the kill.

With the back of his hand, he eased the hanging branch to one side, it's furry catkins caressing his brow as he brushed past. Moving patiently. Slowly. Ever closer. His victim unaware. Then, with a rasping whisper and his words dragged out, he began his eerie chant.

"I'm going to caaaaatch you."

"I'm going to huuuuurt you."

"I'm going to kiiiiiill you."

Thunk!...

He was snatched from his trance by the sound of the blood-soaked knife slipping from his grip and falling to his side, standing like a soldier to attention, its heavy blade embedded in the hardwood floor. His vacant gaze sparked back to the present as once again he felt the thump of his racing heart pounding on his chest like a prisoner in a bony cage, its echoed rhythm reverberating around his head. His eyes now alert, they flicked around the dimly lit kitchen, searching for unwelcome guests, and in his peripheral vision he caught a movement off to his right.

He had company.

Someone was shadowing his every move.

His heart pounding faster, harder, he spun around to see the rain crashing against the window, and there, he saw his companion in crime... watching him.

"Well, hello," he smiled. "Come to watch the show, have you?"

He looked into the eyes of his comrade, the dark cloak of night having turned the window into a ghostly mirror. "You're just in time for the juicy bits," he said, dabbing a finger to his tongue and running it across his eyebrow, his bloody reflection staring back at him, a cocky grin as he turned this way and that to check himself out in the makeshift mirror. His shoulders back and his chest thrust forward, he was barely able to recognise himself. He looked?... *stronger* somehow. Not physically, but in his manner. He exuded an air of self confidence and he liked what he saw, his whole demeanour bloating with pride and self-admiration.

It had taken him twenty nine years to get to this stage, but finally, at last, he felt important. Special even.

He combed his bloodied hand through his dishevelled hair and turned to one side to check out his profile in the makeshift mirror, musing to himself. "Hmmm, not bad. Not bad at all in fact. Though I'll have to do something about the nose."

A small dent to its bridge, and set slightly to the left, he had broken it as a child, though he had no recollection of how it had happened. Come to think of it, until the flashback, he'd had no memory of his childhood at all.

Straightening his tie and pulling the cuffs of his jacket over his protruding shirt-sleeves, his distant gaze passed through his reflection and into the darkness beyond as he thought of how he had always favoured this suit. Plain black. Well cut. Made by Armani himself, or so he liked to claim. But expensive nonetheless. A suit he only ever wore for special occasions, and this was the most special of all.

His mouth creased to a wry smile as he rubbed his thumb across his wet, sticky fingers, smearing the blood between them in appreciation of his work. Then screamed. The pain excruciating.

"Aaaaahhhh!"

In the moments of his vacuous stare, his victim had seized the opportunity to attack. His arrogant self-inspection distracting him from the matter at hand, and his guard down, the knife standing proud next to his feet, the cadaverous wretch had cut the bindings to her hands and feet, no longer a bloody carcass awaiting execution. She had seized her moment, drawing on her waning strength in her last ditch effort to escape.

Again, he screamed, filled with rage and seething with fury. Anger replacing shock at being snapped back to reality with an intense pain shooting through his foot as the serrated knife shot through leather, flesh and bone before the bloody hand released its grip on the knife and lunged for the gun at his belt, her blood-wet fingers slipping across its barrel and spilling it to the floor.

His face deep red, seething hot anger surged through every vein and artery in his body. A fireball bursting from within to explode like an overdue volcano. Its cataclysmic release giving free-reign to a force so destructive, it would reach out to consume all in it's wake. And as she reached for the gun again, he swiped her feeble hand away and made to kick her, but was off-balanced by the knife still pinning his foot to the floor, crashing him to his knees. Screaming in agony as his twisting foot lanced the blade from its fleshy sheath, and down on his hands and knees, he screamed out his rage. "I'm going to fucking kill you, you *fucking bitch!*"

His words spat out. His head shaking with anger. His eyes bulging and veins swelling at his temple, he grabbed the knife and paced towards her. Limping and hurling abuse. Hatred in his eyes and the knife gripped intently in his hand.

She dragged herself across the floor and struggled to her feet, desperate to evade him. Desperate to escape. But he was quicker and stronger, evil to the core. The gap closing between them as adrenaline pumped through her legs, but still she struggled to run. Slipping and sliding. Unable to stay on her feet as the blood oozed from the fleshy stumps where her toes had been.

"Your life is mine," he slavered, thrusting out his hand to grab at her long straggly hair and yanking her back off her feet, her legs kicking out helplessly as she fell hard to the floor, down on her knees. Vulnerable. Her attacker standing over her with her hair in the grip of his hands, her head pulled back towards him so he could whisper in her ear, "Playtimes over Amy. It's time for you to die."

Then, ripping the tape from her mouth, he asked, "Any last words?"

Amy couldn't believe what was happening. His voice full of hatred as she sobbed and begged, "Please don't, Sean. I love y-"

Her pleading was cut short by the slash of the blade across her exposed throat before he cast her body aside like meat to a rabid dog.

Discarded and uncared for, she lay where she fell, clutching her throat and choking on her own blood, her life ebbing away. Her face full of hurt, fear and bewilderment. Her final moments spent in stunned shock by the nightmare of events which had unfolded during the last few hours. The man she had loved so much, had stolen her life away, and she couldn't understand why.

She lay in the growing pool of blood, paralysed by the acceptance of her impending death, her blurring eyes focused on his well polished shoes directly in front of her face, watching helplessly as he got down on bended knee before her and spoke in a calm jocular voice, "Now isn't this appropriate, Amy. Our anniversary, and I'm on my knees to you again. But look at what you've done to my shoes."

He wiped the blood from the cut in the top of his shoe. "These were my favourites. And not a black lace in the house I might add."

He unthreaded the sliced bloody lace of his punctured shoe and replaced it with a brown one, a seemingly caring smile before he brushed her hair back from her face and bent to kiss her on the cheek. "I guess this means I'm no-longer your goody-two-shoes, but I have a little something for you," he said, reaching into his pocket to pull out a yellow rose, pausing a moment to hold it under his nose, and sighing as he deeply inhaled its aroma. "Ahhh, isn't nature wonderful," he said, before placing the flower over the ridge of her ear and adding, "Well, they do say 'a woman's place is in the kitchen'. But don't worry about breakfast dear. I plan to grab something later. Or should I say;- *some-one.*"

Again, he reached into his pocket, this time pulling out his mobile phone and holding it close to her battered face. "Smile for the camera," he chirped, a blinding flash as he took her picture. Then with a snigger in his voice as he stood up, he added, "Well. Can't stay and chat. Have to *'cut',* and *run*, so to speak."

He turned on his heels and walked away, a limping spring to his step. The sound of the catch on the door, the last thing Amy would ever hear.

She felt the cold of darkness draw in.

Her vacant eyes welled with tears.

And her life drained away.

Six

With the loud irritable ringing next to his bed, Ben rolled over to squint at his alarm clock; the red digits displaying 10:24pm.

"You've got to be kidding me."

He buried his head deep into his pillow to soften the deafening shrill, his hand fumbling blindly across the bedside cabinet in its search for the source of the infernal noise, and still half asleep, his mouth dry as paper, he croaked into the receiver, "Ben Miller."

A gabble of words flew back at him. "Sorry to wake you, Ben. It's D.S.I. Brandt. We need you down here, pronto. There's a -"

Groggily, Ben cut him short, "Jesus, Jim. I've only been home two hours. I'm back in at 5a.m. Can't it wait?"

"Listen Ben, we've had a call, not ten minutes ago. The sick bastard's laughing at us, thinks it's a fucking game. The date, Ben. Are you aware of the date?"

"Please, just tell me. I'm too tired for trick questions."

"It's the 29th, Ben. The 29th of March. And that call came in at 10:15."

In that instant Ben's tiredness was snatched away. The words echoing through his mind, he repeated them under his breath, "10:15…? Can't be".

"We've checked it out, Ben. The core officer's down there now. Just radioed in. Matches the m.o., Ben. Matches the sick bastard in every way. *Everything*. She's been dead around twelve hours and…" The pause was long, drawn out to the extreme.

"And *what,* Jim?"

His reply barely audible, Brandt uttered, "The body, Ben. There's a yellow rose on the body."

During the next few hazy moments, Ben scribbled down the address of the crime scene and got dressed in record time. *A yellow rose on the body*. It had to be a mistake. Everything came flooding back to him. A once distant memory he'd buried deep in the back of his mind had resurfaced to become his living nightmare once more.

Not much more than a mile from where he lived on the opposite side of town, he'd be there in five minutes, and as he drove en route to the crime scene, all manner of possibilities came to mind;- Coincidence maybe? A botched burglary perhaps. Or at worst, a copycat. Speculative conjectures fringed on the verge of wishful thinking as he raced down the A167 heading north, his thoughts sifting through each of the alternatives and crossing them out in his mind as he skirted around the edge of Chester-le-Street to arrive on its outskirts.

No matter how much he thought about it, something wasn't right. The yellow rose had been the killer's signature throughout a spate of gruesome murders seven years ago. The flower had been a closely guarded secret, withheld from the media in order to avoid the likelihood of other random murders being attributed to the same killer. But the call, the time, the date, the flower. All too accurate to be counted as anything other than a copycat. But if that were true, then this meant that the killer had to have access to the case-files, or had been involved at some point throughout the investigation. He may even be on the force.

Still in denial, he persuaded himself that even this was unlikely as he sped down the quiet, amber-lit roads.

Then another possibility sprung to mind. Probably the worst scenario of all. Maybe Ben had shot and killed the wrong person all those years ago. All the evidence indicated that they had got their man, but evidence can be tampered with. Especially if it's by someone on the inside trying to cover his tracks. What if the killer was a cop all along, and now, after almost seven years since his last murder, he had come out of hiding to continue where he had left off.

But why now? It didn't make sense.

He exited the roundabout at the junction headed for Birtley and followed the length of the tree-lined wall on his right, until eventually, its length was interrupted by the entrance to North Lodge and the secluded grounds beyond.

He entered the hidden enclave and drove slowly down the narrow lane past the large gated driveways branching off on either side of its length, every one of them leading to large individualistic homes with landscaped gardens, the houses varying in size and design, and each surrounded by cropped shrubbery, trimmed hedges and manicured lawns. Even at this time of night, the setting was of an idyllic hamlet, secluded from the sleepy town on one side and the hedge-lined fields on the other. Unattached neighbours with unattached lifestyles, he imagined. Each giving little more than the nod of recognition as they passed one-another in their cars.

About half way down the lane, he paused and turned right onto the gravel drive of a large stone-built house, the shifting stones beneath his wheels announcing his arrival.

Two uniformed officers stood guard at the door, and from his conversation with D.S.I. Brandt, he knew that they had been the first officers on the scene. The core officers. He paced up the steps towards them, reaching into his pocket for his I.D. and flashing it to the younger officer who gave a brief glance and a nod before waving him on through.

"I have to ask, did you boys touch anything in there?"

The slovenly older officer was quick to assert himself. "No, sir. I checked the woman in-case she needed medical attention, but didn't need to touch her to see that there was nothing I could do. From then on in, I just followed procedure. Radioed in and secured the scene until you and D.C.I Rainer got here."

Ben caught his breath, his throat giving an involuntary gulp, "Rainer did you say?"

"Yes, sir. She's in there now, with the body."

Shit, thought Ben, *As if things weren't bad enough already.*

The older officer continued with obvious discomfort at what he'd seen, "I have to say sir, I've never seen anything like it," he said, scratching at his protruding belly as it fought to break free of his shirt. "The young lad here couldn't handle it. Threw up all over the place, he did. Though he did manage to hold it off till he got outside I s'pose."

Flushed with embarrassment, the younger officer piped up. "It was bad, sir. No denying it. But it wasn't that that made me sick. Was a dodgy burger, that's all."

"What's your name, officer?" Ben asked the younger one.

"Jason, sir. I mean, p.c. Trevors, sir."

"You a rookie, Trevors?"

"Yes, sir. Three months out of training, sir."

Ben noted the devious smirk of the older officer as he continued, "And you went to that grubby little van down the road, did you?"

Rubbing his stomach, Trevors gave an affirmative nod as the older officer answered his radio.

Ben's thought's slipped back for a moment, to a time he himself had eaten at *Fur-ball Frank's*. A nickname earned on account of the amount of times people had found hair in their food. "Yeah, well, of the few cesspits you could have chosen, you certainly picked the worst. And if he's been moved along or had a ticket, you can be sure it's *us* that gets it in the stomach. Literally."

The older officer cut in, "Just had word sir. The C.S.I.'s on his way. Be about five minutes."

Half ignoring the interruption, Ben continued talking to p.c. Trevors, "Listen, constable. Anyone'd be sick, seeing what you've just seen shortly after having one of those thick-o-grease fry-ups. And murder's never like they show you on television. It's the smell that gets you. And it hits you right in the stomach."

"Yes, sir," said the young officer, his head bowed to hide his embarrassment.

Ben continued, "An old partner of mine once told me that the best way to do myself and the victim any justice, was to always look at the body objectively. As evidence, rather than as a person. And search for the clues that put that evidence there. Works for me," Ben smiled, "Best advice I ever got as a matter of fact."

Then, with a look of warning to the older officer and thanked for his second-hand advice, Ben took leave of himself and headed for the door to the house, realising that, if this had been any other case, he'd have merely flashed his badge and carried on through without once breaking stride. But this wasn't *'any other case'*. And so, he had given the advice, more for his own benefit than for that of p.c. Trevors. A moments distraction as he steadied his nerves. Preparing himself. Building up his courage and delaying the inevitable until he could put it off no-longer.

He stepped up to the door, stretched his hand into a latex glove and took a deep breath before gripping the brass handle and tentatively pushing it open like a child entering a haunted house.

Yes. Ben remembered exactly what it was like to witness the horrors of his first murder victim. And now, his nightmare realised, he was about to witness a repeat performance.

Seven

At thirty-two, Ben had never been married, never had kids, and never been in a relationship for more than a couple of months, except once.

Two birds with one stone, he told himself.

Quietly, he walked down the hall to the light from the half-open door, peering into the kitchen to see detective Rainer looking over the body, down on her hunkers as she scrutinised the various wounds, unaware of his presence as she immersed herself in her work.

Even in the cold air of death, he felt a warm tug at the knot in his stomach as he watched her mentally taking notes and methodically checking the wounds in her search for clues. She was good at her job. Efficient. And Ben stood mesmerised, watching her as she removed her gloves to gather up her loose wisps of hair and tease them back into a pony-tail with the snap of a band.

He gathered his composure, wondering how best to break the silence, and as Meg looked at the rose over the victim's ear, he surprised her by asking, "Is it fresh?"

In one swift movement, Meg whipped around, a gun in her hand, and it was pointed at Ben's head, his nerves already fractured as he stumbled backwards and bumped into the breakfast-bar, a vase of flowers falling to the polished marble surface, then spilling to the floor with a shattering crash.

"Fuck me," he gasped, "Where'd you get that?"

"You fucking *idiot!*" Meg snapped back at him, her eyes wild with anger, "You should've known better than to sneak up on me like that. Haven't you heard of friendly fire?"

"Oh. So we're still friends then?" Ben asked, his arms still raised in surrender.

"After our last little tete-a-tete, I think *'acquaintance'* would be more appropriate," she answered, her eyes narrowing and her pistol picking it's spot. She honed her aim between his eyes.

"You wouldn't," he said.

"Oh, wouldn't I?"

"It's not loaded," he answered, trying to sound confident.

"Tell me, Ben. What's the point of carrying a gun if you're not prepared to use it."

"Come on, Meg. Don't muck about. Regardless of what happened between us, I don't deserve this."

"You think?"

"Don't be stupid, Meg. There are officers outside. They'll know you did it."

"You were the one who was stupid, Ben. You surprised me. You didn't follow procedure. And in fear for my life I acted accordingly."

"They won't believe you."

"Why not? It was instinct. A reflex action, with no time to think."

Her eyes focused sharply on an imaginary dot between his eyes as they squinted towards closure, his head turning away from the dark hole of the barrel as her finger squeezed slowly on the trigger. "Meg. No. What are you doing?" Then came the click as the hammer struck the pin, and a small orange flame flickered innocuously from the end of the 'gun'.

"Does this mean you've quit smoking?" she smirked.

"You *fucking* bitch."

Meg slipped the lighter into a plastic evidence bag. "Come now, Ben. Did you really think I'd shoot you?" she asked, before bending to examine the affect the spilled flowers might have had on the crime scene. "But then again, you know what they say about a woman scorned."

"I only asked if the rose was fresh."

Meg snapped back at him, "But that's not all you did, Ben. IS it. And now you've gone and made a mess of the crime scene."

"You're right. I'm sorry. I made a mistake. Then, and now. I guess I'm tired and in need of a coffee."

"Not a cigarette?" Meg asked sarcastically as she examined the broken vase.

His hands to his chest, he feigned being wounded, "Again, Meg. You got me."

"If only," she sniped back at him.

His attempt at making light of the situation had blown back in his face, BIG time, because he'd been fool enough to think they could still be friends, even after what had happened between them. But Meg obviously didn't forgive and forget so easily. And she wasn't about to let *him* forget either.

"At least she wasn't stabbed in the back," Meg said, looking down at the victim's body.

"Listen, Meg, I'm sorry. How many more times can I say it. I never meant to hurt you. Really I didn't. It was a mistake. A one-off. And it will never happen again."

"You're damned right it won't," she said, her voice low and assured, "Because 'I' won't let it."

Ben already knew that Meg would never take him back, but still, the blow struck deep. He swallowed the lump in his throat as he attempted to disguise his hurt and diffuse the air of hostility. "I know that, Meg. And I'm not asking you to forget what I did, but we need to get our priorities right here. We need to put our differences behind us and concentrate on nailing the bastard who did this."

Meg drew back a little, having bitten his head off, more for the shock he had given her than for what he had done to her eleven months ago. The pent-up ammunition had been ready and loaded long before he had shown up to trigger it's release, and her shots fired, her anger subsided and her thoughts switched back to the case. "I suppose I'd guessed you'd be here," she said, "But listen, Ben. If this means we're going to be working together, let's get one thing straight. I'm not happy about this. I transferred to Aykley Heads to put my past behind me. This is the last thing I want. So please, let's just make the best of a bum deal."

"If we can be civil to one another, then that's fine by me. And besides, if the bastard who's done this is half as bad as his role model, then we've got plenty to deal with as it is."

"So you already assume it's a copycat?" Meg asked.

"We got our guy seven years ago. What else could it be?"

"Then it's likely the perp was her husband. There's no sign of a break-in, and he's nowhere to be found." Meg turned her attention back to the body and looked at the fingertips, the nails avulsed, a few of them still hanging loose from their beds.

"What you looking for?" Ben asked.

"Finger-nails."

Ben looked down at the victim's hands, "If he's done his homework, some'll be ingested and on their way to her stomach, and the others'll be at the scene where they were lanced. Judging by the trails of blood, that'll be upstairs."

"I'm fully aware of all that," Meg paused and checked her tone, "But if we *do* have a copycat on our hands, I want to know just how meticulous he is. How many nails have been removed, swallowed, left at the primary scene, etc. If he dots all the 'I's' and crosses his 'T's' then he's going to follow a path we've already tread. And if that's so, then maybe we can take a short-cut and get ahead of him."

"So you're on the same train as me then?" With her questioning glance, he continued. "Train of thought, I mean. You're thinking it's a copycat?"

"Has to be." She glanced at the victim's neck, "And besides, wasn't our killer left handed?"

"Yes. Why?"

"Look at her throat," she answered.

"What about it?"

"The original killer;- Inkleman, he was left handed, right. And obviously, like Inkleman, our killer stood behind her. Otherwise the cut would more likely be a small puncture wound, but look at it."

Ben glanced at the victim, then back to Meg as she tilted her head back and swept her hand around her own throat, her pointed finger starting just below her left ear and finishing lower on the other side.

"And this one's a righty," Ben declared.

Meg rose to her feet. "The autopsy will confirm my suspicions one way or another. In the meantime, we need to prepare for a bumpy ride. If this son of a bitch IS copying Inkleman, we have to act fast."

"Nine dead in seven days, Meg. We need to be quicker than that."

"Listen, Ben. I'm sorry for biting. I know we had our problems, ships passing in the night and, well, you know what else. But, I'm over it. It's just that, seeing you like that. Out of the blue. Well, it's the first time I've seen you in a while, and it brought it all back to me. I never expected you to hurt me, Ben. I never thought you had it in you."

His feelings of guilt making him uneasy with her eye-contact, Ben diverted his gaze as she continued.

"Ben! Are you listening to me?"

His attention shot back to her. His eyes meeting hers with an angry glare as he lunged towards her.

"What are you doing, Ben!" she shouted, instinctively twisting away from him before realising he had been looking beyond her. Snatching at something. A framed photograph from the nearby shelf.

He stood staring at it.

"What is it, Ben? What's wrong?"

Ben turned the picture towards her. It was a picture of the dead woman, smiling. A man standing at her side with his arm around her in cheerful pose. And a beautiful little girl stood in front of them, each parent with a hand on her shoulder.

"Fuck! They have a daughter."

Ben shouted for the officers outside as he and Meg raced to the bottom of the stairs, shouting to them as they burst through the door. "Look for a little girl! Quickly! You take downstairs, we'll go up!"

The simultaneous banging of doors could be heard on both floors as they checked one room after another until eventually, Ben and Meg stood either side of a door marked 'Abigail's room'.

Meg called out motherly, "Abigail?" as Ben slowly pushed the door open and reached around the wall in search of the light-switch.

"Abby… it's okay, sweetheart, we're the police," Meg continued, "We just want to check you're okay."

With a click of the switch, the room was illuminated with night-lights projecting stars onto the ceiling. Another click, and on came the main light as they focused their eyes on the child's empty bed, the Barbie doll quilt pulled to one side, a clump of hair on the pillow… and a faint trace of blood on the sheets.

Eight

11:04 p.m.

In a quiet country lane, a lone car stands at traffic lights, flecks of rain illuminated in its headlights.

With the jar of his neck as his head dropped, and a startled snap to attention, Sean Edwards awoke at the wheel of his Mercedes, his panic subsiding with the realisation he hadn't fallen asleep whilst driving.

The car was in neutral and idly ticking over, the wipers sweeping faster across the windscreen as the drizzle became a downpour, and through blurred eyes he watched them swipe to and fro whilst rubbing the tiredness from his eyes and slowly becoming aware of his surroundings, the grip of the seatbelt fastened tight across his chest. The sharp pain in his foot. The rain beating down heavily on the roof of the car to match the volume of the music on the radio, playing classical undertones of long dead composers he'd never liked.

'Where am I? What happened? How did I get here?'

Ignoring the pain in his foot, and the glare of the green traffic light, he whipped his head around in every direction, staring out into the darkness of the surrounding countryside. No landmarks. No buildings. No signage or discernible shapes. Nothing looked familiar. And consumed by fear, his mouth dry as paper, he gulped on the lump in his throat as he fought back his tears. "Please, god, no. Not again… Not again."

Distraught.

Confused and disorientated.

Alone, with only the lights of the abandoned road-works for company, nervous sweat settled on his brow as the panic took hold of him and his frightened eyes flicked around the car in search of his phone, his hands dipping urgently into his pockets, rifling through his trousers and jacket.

'Where was it?'

A bead of sweat trickled from his brow, past his eye and down his cheek, his anxiety soaring, and then he noticed it, merging into the darkened interior of the car, sitting in the holder on the dash, and reaching for it, he cried out, recoiling at the sight of his hands. "Oh god, what have I done?" He turned them over, the palms as bloody as their backs. His eyes open wide as he stared down at them, burying himself into his seat. Blood everywhere he looked. His hands, his sleeves, his trousers. *Everywhere.* And the glow of the traffic-lights had changed as if to emphasise its ominous presence. Red, glowing through the rain, bouncing off the windows and the dashboard. And dried blood, caked and cracking in the folds of his skin.

Red. Red. Red.

Fear gnawed away at him as he checked his hands for open wounds. Scanned his clothing. Padded down his body, arms and legs. Checked his face in the rear view mirror in his search for cuts, until finally, his fears were confirmed.

The blood was not his own.

He screamed like a wounded animal, "Nooooo!" his fists banging hard on the steering wheel in unison with his cursing, "FUCK! FUCK! FUCK!"

Filled with self-loathing, his heart sank to his stomach's abyss as the tears welled within him, "Oh god, no. Not Amy. Please god, not Amy."

He grabbed at the phone, snatching it from its holder. 11:06 flashing on its screen and the date shown underneath;- Thursday 29th March.

"No, it can't be. Not a day. Not a **full** day."

He had only ever lost minutes. A couple of hours once. But never a day.

His finger punched at the fluorescent numbers in an effort to dial home, and though his signal was strong, the dial-tone was dead, his fears escalating as he looked at the display, checking he'd rang the right number, and about to try again when he noticed the 'missed call' icon blinking in the corner of the screen.

'Maybe it's Amy. Her mobile. Maybe she rang from her mobile.'

He checked through his list of missed calls and the number unfamiliar to him, his heart sank. It wasn't Amy. Unless, that is, she had called from another phone. Maybe from a hospital. The caller had tried to make contact several times during the last fifteen minutes, so it had to be important. Maybe she was trying to get in touch with him. Worrying about him, just as he worried about her. He stared down at his bloody hands, fearing the worst. Frightened to ring back. Crying inconsolably as he thought of the possibility that Amy had died at his hands. "What's happening to me? What have I done? I couldn't have hurt Amy, I just couldn't."

But how could he be sure? How could he possibly know what he was capable of if he couldn't remember what he'd done since their meal together last night.

He rang Amy's mobile and was rewarded with the sound of her voice, polite and friendly. "Hello?"

"Thank god. Amy, listen, I don't know what's –"

"Hello?" … A short pause before she continued. "Hello?... I'm sorry, I can't hear you. Could you just hold on a moment."

There was the sound of distortion and missing syllables, her voice breaking up before a tear rolled down Sean's cheek at the sound of her mischievous giggle. "Sorry about that. Just kidding. This is an answering machine, but if you could please leave a message, I'll get back to you as soon as possible. See ya."

It was her first practical joke in ages, and unwittingly, she had played it on Sean; the sound of her voice lifting his spirits then knocking them down again. His fears unabated. His heart sunk as he listened to her message again and left a message of his own, crying as he did so. "Please, Amy. Get in touch. I need to know you're okay. Whatever I've done, please don't punish me with your silence. I love you more than you could ever know. I always have." He sobbed, his tears streaming down his face. "And I always will."

Nine

Meg had spotted a mobile phone on a coffee table in the living room and from the pink casing, surmised it belonged to the victim. She resisted the temptation to pick it up and switch it on. The clues it could hold. Its records of calls made and received. Text messages, videos, a list of contacts and e-mails. But first, it would have to be checked for latents and trace elements. Fortunately, close by, she had found what she was searching for and flicked through the address book, past the remnants of a missing page until she had found the number for Sean Edwards mobile, and using her own, rang him several times without reply until eventually, Edwards rang back.

"Hello?" Meg answered, her voice calm and relaxed, "Mr. Edwards?"

Ben was standing nearby browsing over the bookshelves, his finger running along the titles, trying to get a feel for their owners. He paused to listen in on the conversation.

"Mr. Edwards, I think we should talk."

The line went dead and Meg turned to Ben with a shake of her head.

"Not a word?" Ben asked.

"Nothing. I don't get it. Why did he ring? He killed his wife and scarpered, right. And then this. It doesn't add up."

"Add up how? What are you getting at?"

"If you had killed someone, would you ring a number you didn't recognise?"

"Curiosity got the better of him," Ben said. "Or maybe he guessed it was us and wanted to hand himself in, then had second thoughts."

"Or maybe," Meg replied "there's a piece of the jigsaw missing."

"What piece?" Ben asked, again looking through the books and then pausing at what he recognised to be a safe-keeping box designed to look like a dictionary. "Maybe this piece," he answered himself, taking it from the shelf and opening it to reveal a girlish diary inside. He passed it to Meg, uncomfortable with the idea of invading a dead woman's personal secrets if he could avoid it.

Meg leafed through the diary to the last entry. "Does this sound to you like he was about to kill her," she asked, passing the diary back to him and pointing to yesterday's entry. "They sound happy and in love. It just doesn't make sense."

"Yeah, well. Domestic bliss can soon turn awry."

"But this wasn't a heat of the moment killing, Ben. It's drawn-out. Deliberate. And what's more, it matches the m.o. of a serial. Something doesn't fit."

Ben snapped the diary shut, "And maybe, after seven years of marriage, he'd decided to call it a day."

"By killing his wife?"

"Maybe it wasn't about his wife. Maybe it was about him. He flipped. He wanted to go out in style and this was his way. Who knows how the minds of some of these psychos work. They want to be remembered. To go out a somebody, rather than a nobody. That's just how it is sometimes."

"Say that again," said Meg.

"What? To go out a somebody, rather than a nobody?"

"No. You said 'they want to be remembered'."

In an instant the cogs of Ben's mind clicked into place and his mouth along with it, "And we're back to the yellow rose. Shit, Meg. What the hell's going on here?"

Ten

11:11 p.m.

This was bad. Sean had hurt, possibly even killed his wife, and the police were looking for him. They would find things out about him. About his past. His problems. His 'doctor'. And there lay another problem. They would talk to him and discover things about him that even his wife didn't know. Personal things. Some would say *'dark secrets'*. They would say he was insane and lock him up.

He wondered if there was such a thing as '*Patient confidentiality',* and in the light of an investigation, just how confidential those things would be, regardless of their bearing on a case.

In his sessions with his psychiatrist, Sean had been told that he may never regain the memory of his adolescence. It seemed his minds instinctive self-preservation had denied all access to memories too traumatic to recount. His doctor adding that maybe this was the reason behind his 'missing-time' episodes. That there was a possibility they were triggered by an incident of some kind. A connection to his past perhaps. And this was his minds way of protecting him. Blocking out resurfacing memories from his forgotten childhood. Memories his doctor had attempted to tap into using psychoanalysis and various regression techniques.

Two months had passed since his last session, but at the end of it, he had awoken from his trance on the outstretched black leather couch feeling revitalised, almost euphoric. Feeling at last, that he was in control of his life. That his problems were behind him. That maybe it was time to forget about his past and move forward. Time at last, to look to his future and move on. And so, no-longer feeling the need for his doctor's guidance, and against his advice, Sean had stopped attending the sessions. Thinking he was fine. Felt great. Didn't need to go anymore. But now, all that had changed.

'I have to call him, before it happens again,' he thought, 'He can help me. He *has* to.'

He rang his doctor's office; No answer. His home; Still no answer.

Maybe he was busy. Maybe it was because it was late or because the police were there now, asking him questions. Interrogating him.

Still in need of help, unsure of what to do next, he decided to ring the police, desperate to get some answers.

Meg answered, "Hello?"

"My name's Sean. Sean Edwards. I'd like to speak to my wife."

"Your wife, Sean?" Meg remembered her training. Establish a first name basis to gain the confidence and trust of the suspect.

"Yes. My wife. I want to speak to her."

Was he unaware of his wife's death? she wondered. Hadn't he realised he'd killed her? Was it possible that Edwards wasn't involved?

Unsure of how to respond, she had to think quickly, "You'll need to come to the station, Sean. We can talk about things there."

"I don't *want* to come to the station. I want to speak to my wife."

"That's not possible right now. She's being attended to."

Sean choked. "Please. Tell me I haven't hurt her."

"If you come to the sta-"

"She's dead! *isn't* she. She's dead, and you think **'I'** did it."

"Let me assure you, Sean. Until I know all the facts, I don't assume anything. But it's important that we clear up a few details. That's why I'd like you to come to the station. Just to answer a few questions."

"You mean to lock me up. Put me behind bars. With criminals. I couldn't survive in there. I don't deserve to be in there. It's not my fault."

"Please, Sean. If you come down to the station we can do what's right and sort out all this confusion."

"I would never harm Amy. I couldn't. I love her."

"I know you do, Sean. The signs are all around us. I can see that you do." Meg was speaking truthfully. The bunches of flowers. The diary entry explaining the meal and the love-making. She had somehow managed to see beyond the cruel depravity of the calculated slaughtering of his wife. He was madly in love with her. But now, he was just mad. Now, she was concerned for his daughter.

"And what about Abigail, Sean? Do you love her too?"

"Of course I love my daughter. What are you getting at?"

"You wouldn't hurt her, Sean, would you?"

"No. Never... Never."

"So please, Sean, tell me. Where is she? Is she with you now? Can I talk to her?"

"She's…" he paused, thinking to himself; *My daughter? Why are they asking about my daughter?* He needed to think. He hung up the phone and sat a moment, looking at his hands again, covered in dry blood. The blood of his wife, and maybe;- the blood of his child.

He flung the car door open and ran out into the rain, dragging his hands across the film of water on the bonnet to wash away the blood as the tears streamed down his face. "They *can't* be dead. They *can't* be."

He dropped to his knees by the side of the road, splashing into a puddle of water. Sobbing. His head bowed and the rain lashing down hard, soaking his suit and diluting the blood into the very fabric of his clothes. Somehow, he knew his wife was dead. He felt it. But his daughter was a different matter. She was missing. The police had blatantly told him so. And if she *was* missing, then where could she be?

He jumped into the car with the intention of going to the police. It seemed his only option. The only way he could live with what he'd done was to help them find her, though in his heart of hearts he knew they wouldn't listen to him. And why should they? To them, he was a murderer. They would arrest him and he would never see his daughter again. Denied all access, his little girl growing up a stranger, hating him for what he'd done, not knowing the truth or understanding that he was ill. Not knowing that he couldn't live with that, he couldn't bear it. And in a heartbeat, he knew he would have to find her himself. But first, he needed help, and there was only one person he could possibly turn to. Probably the only person who *could* help. And if he wasn't going to answer his phone, then he would have to risk driving to his house.

For the umpteenth time, the lights changed to green, and as they did so, a vehicle pulled up behind him, Sean squinting nervously into his rear view mirror, blinded by its headlights as he looked for motifs, expecting to see a flashing blur of blue. A sudden blast of the horn forcing him to dip his clutch, snap the car into gear and stall, the silence betraying the sound of something behind him. A feint whimper and scratching from the rear of his car behind the seats.

Something was moving in the boot.

Eleven

Beeeeeeeeep!

With another blast of the horn from the car behind, Sean was startled into action, his foot slamming hard on the accelerator to screech away from the lights and race past the orange and white barricades until the road opened up again, the car weaving behind him, the glare of its headlights, flash, flash, flashing in his rear-view mirror before racing to pull alongside him, the driver shaking his fist before speeding off with another loud blast of his horn, leaving Sean itching to chase after him. Itching to get out of his car and ram that fucking horn down his fucking throat, but afraid of the consequences. Afraid, not because he was a coward, but because he preferred to negotiate his way out of trouble rather than suffer the guilt of having hurt someone, however deserving they may be.

His stomach churned as he resisted the urge to chase after him, battling with his emotions, his thoughts shooting back to Abigail and forcing him to pull sharply into a lay-by, his hands gripped tightly around the steering wheel, shaking with both anger and fear as he watched the tail lights fade quickly into the distance, his mind now focused solely on the absence of sound from the rear of his car. No more scratching in the boot. No more whimpers. The radio already silenced, he switched off the ignition and demisters to hear nothing but the random pitter-patter of rain on the car's roof, and the sound of his own anxious thoughts, fretting for his family and gripped by a sense of urgency, his grip loosening on the wheel to click off his seatbelt and pull the door release, only to be stopped by the ring of his phone vibrating across the passenger seat, the light from its screen shining bright in the darkness of the car. Not a call, but a reminder. The time flashing; *11:15 p.m.* He reached over to pick it up and read the message;-

Not all is as it seems.

'What?'

He looked to the back seats, wondering what was behind them. Wondering who had set the reminder, and if it was connected to what was happening to him. He hadn't set it himself, he was sure of it. But then, who else would tamper with his phone. It didn't make sense. He was about to toss the phone back onto the seat when he was startled into almost dropping it as the reminder rang again. Another message, set to follow a minute later.

You have an ally.
Listen to your voice mail.

A cold shiver ran through to his bones, frightened at the idea that someone else had access to his phone and that that someone could be involved in what was happening. Possibly even responsible for it. And if that were so, then Sean would use every ounce of his being to seek his revenge.

He dialled into his messages to hear a voice, bitter and twisted, a cruel inflection to his tone, "Hello, Sean."

He hung up instantly, shaking and frightened, unable to believe what he was hearing. "It can't be. It's not possible."

But it *was* possible. And no matter how inconceivable it may have seemed, it was happening. His wife was dead and his daughter missing, her life in the hands of a madman. A man they had mistakenly trusted, and now that man stood with his hand gripped tightly around the phone, stricken by fear and disbelief as he pressed it to his ear and tentatively played the message again, the voice cold and deliberate. A voice he recognised as his own.

"Hello, Sean. This is you. Or should I say… *'me'*. Now, before you go wimping out on us, listen to me carefully, and do *exactly* as I say. Your life may depend on it."

Sean continued to listen, his mind frantically searching for answers and finding none as his alter-ego gave his instructions, "In your inside jacket pocket you will find a key."

Apprehensive, he reached slowly into his pocket.

"The number on that key corresponds to the number of a room at the Travel Lodge hotel on Washington Highway, registered in the name of Inkleman. It is obscured from plain view and should be relatively simple for you to sneak into without being noticed. The room is yours for a week. But before you go there, there's something I want you to do for me. For you even. Remember, Sean; '*Not all is as it seems'*, so bear with me on this, and everything will turn out just fine."

He listened to the instructions from his other self;- his polar opposite, cold and calculating. The killer within, interested only in achieving his own aims and using his reluctant host to run his errands.

"First of all, I want you to get rid of our guest in the boot of the car."

His thoughts shot back to the scratching.

"Dump the body. Dump the car. And dump the phone. They can all be used to track you down. And no matter what happens, do not contact anyone. Not the police, not your doctor;- *no-one*. If you are to get through this with what matters to you most, you must follow my instructions to the letter. All will become clear in due course. Just do as I say, then get back to your room, and stay there. You will receive a call in the morning, at 9:15a.m. In the meantime, try to get some sleep... We're going to need it."

He couldn't believe what he was hearing as he listened to the self addressed instructions (left during one of his lost-time moments no doubt). What had once been blank episodes, sometimes stretching into minutes, had now become spells of madness stretching into hours, his problems blown out of all proportion. He was out of control. A present day Jekyll and Hyde. It seemed his alter-ego was ending the lives of others and ruining his own life into the bargain. But what could he do about it and how could he regain control. The parasite within seemed to anticipate his every thought, and finished his message with a warning.

"One last word of caution, Sean. If you've listened to this message, then for now, your body's your own. But I'm warning you, don't fuck with me. If you go getting any ideas about ending this, about handing yourself in or going to the extreme of killing yourself, you will be making a very dangerous mistake. Just remember that when you open the boot of the car. And trust me, my time will come soon. So take great care to follow my instructions, or suffer the consequences if you do not."

Sean stood nervously at the rear of the car, building up his courage to check the boot. Not wanting to look, but having to.

Dump the body.

But whose body?

He had no way of knowing what he had done during his blackouts, and now, nervously, he held his breath, afraid of the horrors he was about to confront, the car-keys gripped tightly in his hand as he edged closer, no sounds from within. But dead or alive, someone was inside, he was sure of it.

His entire body shook rigid, his heart torn between racing to open the boot and find his wife or daughter alive, and opening it slowly to find her dead.

He called out for a response, "Hello?... Amy?.... Abby? Are you in there?"

With no reply, he urged himself to press the key-fob, and with the click of the catch release, slowly raised the lid, his eyes wide with terror as he caught sight of its contents and his hand shot to his mouth.

He stood frozen to the spot. Unable to move. Unable to tear his eyes away from the battered body, so badly mutilated that the image would be engrained into his mind forever, his eyes drawn to the head-wound, golden hair meshed into the cracked-open skull as blood oozed from the gaping wound, the lifeless body lying crumpled next to the blood-spattered spade. And his stomach retching, he turned his head to the kerbside and vomited into the long tufts of grass.

Twelve

Friday, 30th March, 7:30 a.m.

Facing the entering entourage, Meg and Ben sat side-by-side behind a desk at the head of the parade room as it became a hive of activity with the sounds of gathered papers, bustling chairs and feet shifting across the linoleum floor.

Meg had had to prove herself more capable than her male counterparts to be given this opportunity. Ruffling some well plumed feathers and constantly harassing her superiors before eventually, doors had begun to open for her, her way to the top marginally impeded by bureaucracy and back-biting as she impatiently forged her way through the last few years; each a slippery stepping-stone grooming her for this one chance to prove herself. This one defining moment which could make or break her career.

She began to wonder if this was payback. If she were being used as a scapegoat. Finally given the lead in a case too hot to handle. Fresh meat thrown to the lions whilst the hierarchy watched from the other side of the cage, expecting her to fail. Maybe even *wanting* her to fail. She hoped she could disappoint them and save some lives into the bargain. Problem was, if Edwards stayed true to form, there was about to be another murder, and there was almost nothing she could do to prevent it.

She looked around the crowd of faces, some familiar and some not. Old friends and new strangers. *Some initiation this was going to be.*

Rising through the ranks to the position of D.C.I. at breakneck speed, she had earned her right to be here. She had gained the qualifications, the experience and the know-how. And she had assisted in more than her fair share of murder investigations too. Some of them high profile. But she had never actually led one. This was to be her first. Her one and only chance of success rested on her ability to gain the trust and respect of the team she was about to lead through the investigation. Trust and respect, she reminded herself, were qualities easier to tear down than to build up. Yet here she was, right in the thick of it. D.C.I. Megan Rainer. Head of the investigation. Head of protocol. Head of diddly-squat.

She stared out into the gathering hordes, butterflies fluttering wildly in her stomach, and as if sensing her trepidation, Ben gave her hand a comforting squeeze below the boxed-in desk. "You're the right person for this, Meg. Don't let anyone tell you otherwise."

Her tensions eased a little with the grip of his hand and her recognition of a few friendly faces drifting in to join the masses;- some of them from her time here last year. A sergeant, whose name escaped her, and a press officer by the name of Jack Roberts, and two guys she knew from forensics at Aykley Heads. But the majority of the team were Ben's colleagues. Experienced officers. Most of whom had probably been on the force longer than she had. Nearly all of them had worked on the initial inquiry seven years ago. Key officers from various departments of the County Durham Police Force (or Constabulary as they like to call it nowadays) joined by the draftees from surrounding divisions and the occasional civilian expert.

She leaned closer to Ben, so only he could hear. The two of them bouncing ideas off one-another as the last of the stragglers weaved his way to one of the few remaining seats.

"It's not him, Ben, is it? Inkleman, I mean. I know everything points to Edwards, but something doesn't fit."

"Edwards is our man, Meg, you know it as well as I do. But until we know more, I think we should treat the investigation as though we are still on Inklemans trail. The majority of our evidence is derived from that case. I think it's our best way forward."

In her heart she wanted to agree with him, but in her head she wasn't so sure. Eventually, it had all come down to trust and relying on her instincts. She had made her decision. She just needed to be sure it was the right one.

"I listened to the tapes, Ben."

"Of Inkleman?"

"Yes. And Edwards sounds the same. Not just in his voice but in his manner. His characteristics. But what I don't understand is, if we have a copycat here, how the hell does he know so much about the Mutilator case, and where's he getting his information?"

Ben had asked himself those very same questions.

“I don’t know,” he answered, racking his brains. “But it will all come together, Meg, trust me, you’re ready for this. The only person you need to convince of it is you.”

“But what if it doesn’t come together, Ben? He’s used the same m.o. The same signatures. Even the same fucking piss-taking rhyme for christ’s sake. And what if he already knows our strategy before we start? Our next move even. Everything points to Edwards, but everything says it’s Inkleman. He even started his call the same way. *‘Remember me’.* That’s what he said. But his voice was definitely different.

After all.

It had to be.

Inkleman’s dead...Isn’t he?”

Thirteen

Meg was stirred into action by a coaxing cough from one of the higher ranking officers at the back of the room, the stern expression across D.S.I. Brandt's face indicating its source. The hierarchy, here, supposedly to oversee the investigation. Covering their arses more like, thought Meg. No real involvement, just sitting there, waiting in the wings, as if their presence amplified the importance of the case. Hovering like vultures, waiting to pick the meat from the bones. Quick to take the credit for the work done by their minions, and quicker still to throw the blame if things went pear-shaped, in which case, minions became fall guys. Problem was, she and Ben were the ones perched on the edge of the damned precipice ready to bungee without a rope.

Her stomach turning, she stood to address the assembly with the believable yet false impression of confidence as she began her authoritative delivery.

"None of you know yet why you are here, but all will soon become clear. For those of you familiar with the case I am about to present to you, please bear with me. Those of you dragged in at a moments notice, thank you for your patience. Soon, you will all understand the importance of your being here. For the un-initiated amongst you, it is important that you give this briefing your full and undivided attention in order to appreciate the scale of the task before you. I can not stress this enough, other than by telling you that we have a copycat killer on our hands, and his chosen archetype was the most heinous of murderers. His name, some of you will remember, was Joseph Inkleman, though most of you will know him best as he was dubbed by the media." Her mouth dried up as she told them his nom de guerre, "They called him… The Mutilator."

With the mention of the archetype's moniker, papers stopped rustling and hushed whispering fell silent.

"So, people, we need to hit the ground running."

As sporadic arms raised for attention, she shot them down, saying, "It is likely that some of your questions will be answered during the briefing, and others may arise because of it, so can you please keep your queries until the end. Thank you. Now, as some of you will already know, The Mutilator was sometimes referred to as 'The Time-Waster'. The reason being that he always killed his victims at 10:15a.m. and then called later that night, at 10:15 ***'P.M.'*** to report the murder, just as our copycat has done. Unfortunately, thanks to the media of the time, this became common knowledge. But an example of how in depth our suspect's knowledge is, lies, not only in the fact that he killed his wife in the same slow and deliberate manner as Inkleman, but that he was accurate, right down to the type of flower he left on her body, the knowledge of which was withheld from the media. And yet, our copycat was all too well aware of it. This gives us cause for concern, and because of it, we have to beg the question;- How does he know so much?"

All eyes were focused intently on Meg as she relaxed into her role.

"As I've mentioned already, The Mutilator of seven years ago was a man named Joseph Inkleman. And, like our suspect, he was married with a seven year old daughter. A generally placid man with no criminal record, he went on a sickening murder spree, starting with his wife and killing a total of seven women, one man, and his own seven year-old daughter before eventually being killed himself at the scene of her murder. All of this, ladies and gentlemen, within the space of a week. So as you can see, time is of the essence. Because of this, and in order to limit our chances of getting bogged down, we have sifted through the records from the original case and provided each of you with a broken down copy of the information found to be most relevant to the investigation so far. These will be updated with any further developments that transpire from the material gathered at yesterdays homicide. In the meantime, I expect you all to be vigilant."

Meg's captive audience looked on as she pointed to the lists on the board behind her. "You will each find a copy of this list in front of you, along with a list of all the victims, past and present, and a transcript of every phone-call."

JOSEPH INKLEMAN	SEAN EDWARDS
29th March 2000 to 4th April 2000	29th March 2007
D.O.B. 27/6/1962	D.O.B. 4/8/1978
Deceased 4/4/2000	
Status;- married	Status;- married
Children;- daughter aged 7	Children;- daughter aged 7
Profession;- Bank manager	Profession;- Self employed (network marketing)
S.O.C. / M.O.	S.O.C. / M.O.
Duct tape.	Duct tape.
Yellow rose;- Remember Me.	Yellow rose;-Remember Me
A broken watch, set at 10:15.	
Finger nails, severed toes.	Finger nails, severed toes.
Severed limbs, bodies lying cruciform.	
	Address-book, page missing for letter M
Polaroid camera.	
A yellow ribbon	
10:15 a.m. murders	10:15 a.m. murder
10:15 p.m called police	10:15 p.m called police
Pliers, knife,	Pliers, knife
Hacksaw, pistol;- Luger.	Light bulb
Severing of limbs progressively worse from one victim to the next	Severed toes, avulsed finger nails.
First and last victim had their throats slashed. All died of blood loss.	Victim's throat slashed.

Meg continued. "As you can see, on the left we have a list of the known signatures and details of Joseph Inkleman. And highlighted on the right, the similarities and signatures used by our suspect thus far, though this by no means makes him predictable."

"There's also the possibility that Edwards may have taken photographic souvenirs of his work, just as Inkleman was thought to have done using a Polaroid camera found at his last crime-scene, though no photographs have ever been recovered."

She looked around the faces, checking she still had their attention. "So, on the one hand we have an idea of Sean Edwards's m.o., depending on his knowledge of the case and his attention to detail, in which case we can deduce his likely pattern. And on the other hand, there's the possibility he could stray from this, or use this knowledge to mislead us. But some things I ***do*** expect to remain the same. The times for example. The methods of killing, the phone-calls, and the yellow rose on the body. All of which were adhered to in the case of the first victim. And the rose. Not just *any* yellow rose. But a 'bush rose' of the Hybrid Tea variety. And our killer chose the exact same genus."

Having been involved in the original case as a gofer, Meg probably knew more about the yellow rose than anyone, because, in those days, she had done a lot of the leg work for the more experienced officers. She'd visited florists, garden centres, experts in horticulture, etc. She had even taken fresh cuttings home, keeping them in various conditions and identifying their rates of deterioration once cut. And over time, she had developed a theory of her own which had never been aired, the case closed before she'd had a chance to put it forward. A theory she now shared with her team.

"The reasoning behind these signatures was never discovered, but the significance of the flower most probably lies in how it is referred to by those in the know. The likes of horticulturists call it the 'Remember Me' rose. A term Inkleman used over and over again, and a term Edwards used at the beginning of last night's call. We figure it's a message of some kind, but as yet, we haven't been able to decipher it. We can, however, surmise that these signatures had some personal relevance to Inkleman, though the only relevance they are likely to hold for Edwards is the enactment of copying the crimes verbatim."

Meg placed both of her hands on the desk and leaned towards her audience, her voice an octave higher. "Lives are at stake here, people. And to complicate matters further, the suspect's daughter is missing. You all have a copy of her last known photograph amongst your papers and the m.o. suggests she's still alive, so I want teamwork on this. And nothing missed. Every little detail is important. Every single question *has* to be answered. Don't blind yourselves with the fact that she's his daughter, she is every bit as at risk as any other victim he may have chosen. Maybe more so. So, if at any time you find yourselves unfocused, I want you to imagine that it is your own little girl out there, and think about how you would feel knowing a mistake could cost her her life." Meg paused a moment, allowing them to think about this before continuing. "I'll finish by saying I want diligence at all times on this. No excuses will be tolerated. No mistakes will go unpunished. I want up to the minute reports on any new information, and I want *everyone* to be held accountable for any failure to perform their duties. But most of all, I want this son of a bitch caught, and fast."

Meg's determined gaze spread out across her audience as they listened to her, hanging on her every word. They had been prepared, and now they were about to discover just how sick The Mutilator really was. If the next few minutes didn't kick their arses into gear, nothing would.

"Now. I'll hand you over to D.S. Miller who was one of the key detectives in solving the original case… The floor's yours Ben."

Fourteen

Rekindled whispers were quickly silenced as Ben rose from his chair to make his presence felt, "Can we have quiet please!"

An oblivious young officer continued speaking quietly into his mobile phone until Ben singled him out.

"*You!* Officer. Is that call related to this case?"

Almost stuttering with the realisation he was the centre of attention, he hung up and replied. "Nnno, sir. It's my-."

"Never mind what it is, I'm not interested. Leave the room."

"But sir, I –"

"Immediately!"

The embarrassed young officer fumbled to gather his things, and as the door closed behind him, Ben continued, "For those of you who were not involved in the 10:15's of seven years ago, let me forewarn you;- this is going to be a traumatic time for many of you. If at any time you feel the need for counselling or wish to exclude yourself from the investigation, then please, do not hesitate to do so. As detective Rainer has already said, we can not afford the distraction of anyone being unfocused. Now. Pay close attention. You are about to listen to a recording of the call we received last night at 22:15. The caller's number is registered to Sean Edwards."

With the flick of a switch and a brief hiss of static, the tape began to play, its volume turned up to room filling capacity as a man's quietly rasping voice seeped through the surrounding speakers, "Remember me?"

There was a long lingering pause before he continued, "Killing time again, Ben. Doesn't time fly these days. And as I'm sure you're already aware, you're on the clock. Can you hear it, Ben? Tick, tick, ticking. Your time's running out fast, so I have a little something for you. Something you might find… useful. I hope you remember it. I know I'm not exactly your Keats or Byron, but hey, I thought it might give you something to ponder over. A reminder if you will. After all, the clues are there, Ben, if only you would listen to them. Problem is, you don't listen, do you. If you did, you could have stopped all of this from happening. So I suggest you *listen* this time, Ben… In fact, I suggest *all* of you listen. And those of you who know the words, sing along if you wish. Because the game begins again, Ben… The game begins again."

Edwards began his poem, the pleasure evident in his voice as his drawling speech dragged slowly through every sentence.

Fingers and toes... in exchange for my rose.
Hands and feet... now we're getting to the meat.
Elbows and knees... I'm their killer disease.
Arms and leg... hack them off while she begs.
Killer's surprise… when I gouge out their eyes.
Tits and cock… nicely sends them into shock.
Then it's off with the head… once again she is dead.
Because all closed their eyes to the killer's surprise.

His rendition finished, the pitch of his voice grew a little deeper and his pace quickened, his deranged excitement spilling over, "Wish I could say that the poem was my own work, Ben, but I can't I'm afraid. Oops, did I let a clue slip out there. I forget myself sometimes. Oh look, I've done it again. One clue after another."

He let out a laugh before his voice sank close to a whisper, "Had you forgotten her, Ben? The little girl?"

Ben hadn't forgotten. How could he.

"I'm here to remind you, Ben. *Everyone closed their eyes to the killer's surprise.* You included. And that is why she died?"

His pace picked up again, chopping and changing like a warped tape, his tone friendly to the extreme. "Come on, Ben. *Think* about it. Look around you and *see.* We're simply playing mind-games you and I. The problem for you is;- **'I'** always win. You see, you should never have closed the case back then, Ben. The game wasn't over. So this time. When you find the victims. By all means remember me, but most importantly, remember ***you*** are the one to blame for all of this. The one to blame for not putting a stop to it when you had the chance. But you'll stop me this time, Ben. Won't you. Even if you have to die trying."

Ben's jaw clenched tightly, his teeth grinding together as the tape of Sean Edwards' call wound to an end.

“Well. Must dash. As I’m sure you’re already aware; I have a busy day ahead of me. Early bird catches the worm, as they say. Maybe next time we can talk one on one. But in the meantime, catch you later, Ben. If you don’t catch me first.”

His cackling laughter echoed throughout the room to stop midstream as the recording was switched off and a mixture of expressions stared back at Ben.

Fifteen

Ben stood from his chair, topped up his glass of water from a jug on the table, then broke the air of silence, his words blunt and to the point.

"Seven years ago, Joseph Inkleman callously tortured and murdered his wife. Twenty-four hours later, her sister was found dead, butchered in her bed. Inkleman then went on a seemingly random killing spree before finally killing his seven year-old daughter whom he had held captive throughout. So believe me when I say, ladies and gentleman, that this man was as cold and calculating a murderer as you are *ever* likely to come across. And now it seems we have a carbon-copy in Sean Edwards, who, as your handouts will tell you, is twenty-nine years of age, 6'2", with dark-brown hair, and on the athletic side of approximately one hundred and ninety pounds. Intelligent too, it would seem. Some sort of network-marketing whiz-kid or other. And because of it, a member of the millionaires club too. He has no priors, and up until now, was a seemingly well respected, law-abiding citizen. But all of that has changed, and he is out there, an organised, cold-blooded killer, stalking his next victim."

He paused to take a sip of his water before continuing, "In the first instance, Edwards was uncannily accurate and just as callous in the copying of his brutal archetype. The victim;- his wife, suffered unbelievable cruelty over a duration of several hours before eventually, he slit her throat. The signatures, the call, the poem and so forth, all match Inkleman's modus operandi to a T, and it is my hope that this will work in our favour. Make him predictable almost. But, because of this 'predictability', we fear he aims to kill another eight people in the course of the next six days. And all within a ten mile radius."

"In the original case, the first two victims were related. Therefore, the tracing of relatives is our primary concern and our first line of inquiry. We have officers working on this as I speak. Time is against us, ladies and gentlemen. We must act fast on any new leads and take care to avoid any costly mistakes. Lives depend on it."

Watching from the wings, Colin Morton was a weed of a man in his early forties with freckles all year round. His ginger hair cropped short and thinning on top, he was a senior officer during the original case and couldn't resist his chance to have a sly dig at Ben in front of a large crowd. He spoke with an arrogance as he broke into Ben's pause, "Could it be that this is the original killer? That we made a mistake the first time around? That maybe, we killed the wrong man? Or should I say, that *you* killed the wrong man, and now, your mistake has come back to haunt us?"

Ben checked his tongue before responding, "Dead men don't kill people."

"My point exactly," came the reply.

It had seemed that from the moment Ben and D.I. Morton had met, there was a clash of personalities, their mutual dislike for one-another increasing more so, ever since Ben's influence in solving the mutilator killings of seven years ago. And to make matters worse, the powers-that-be had decided against Morton's objections that Ben should be at the forefront of this investigation too, as back-up to D.C.I. Rainer. And once again, they were crossing swords, their heckles raised.

Unwavering, Ben fired back, "We have already established that Sean Edwards killed his wife, and because of his method, we know he is right handed. And Inkleman was without doubt, a lefty."

Again, Morton butted in, "What if you're wrong? What if it wasn't Inkleman's body we dug from the fire and he survived? He could have changed his identity. He could be ambidextrous and the rose could be his way of saying 'I'm still here' or 'don't forget me'."

Ben's frustration filtered into his voice as he replied with a touch of sarcasm, "A valid point, if it weren't for the dental records, but I deal in *facts, not* what ifs. And if his agenda *was* merely to be remembered as you say, then why not use a more commonly known alternative, like 'forget-me-nots'."

Without waiting for an answer, Ben spread his gaze across the assembly, his voice a little louder, "To the laymen amongst us, a rose is just a rose, the connection wouldn't exist. But to Inkleman, it probably meant something more personal. Important to him in a way we never established. To Edwards however, the flower is purely for the purpose of authenticity and has little relevance to anything else. He is merely copying every detail. Dotting the I's and crossing his T's so to speak."

Morton interrupted again, "One more thing. What did Edwards mean by you closing your eyes? Was there something you missed that could have prevented all of this?"

A chink appeared in Ben's armour, his cool exterior melting away, "He's a psycho. He flipped. It happens. What could Edwards possibly know about what was going on at that time? *HE* wasn't there. ***'I'*** was"

"He obviously knows something," Morton countered, "Otherwise, how could he replicate the m.o. so accurately?"

This wasn't the time or place for Ben to lose his temper, and fighting to regain his composure, he held Morton's gaze, "Reporters, police officers, leaked files, there are any number of possibilities. And that is something we need to look into."

As Morton stood up to fire yet another question, Meg also stood, her eyes pressing him back into his seat as she intervened, "It has to be said that mistakes *were* made during the initial investigation. There's no denying that Inkleman was underestimated by practically everyone back then. You included Colin. But it was Ben who saw what most of us did not. And if it wasn't for him, countless more people may have died."

With the hint of a nod from Meg, Ben returned to his seat as she continued.

"This IS a different killer. A copycat. Not Inkleman under a new guise or anything to that effect. I have no doubt of that. But as we have already explained, he knows a great deal about the original case. The intro, the verse, the m.o. *Everything*. So we have to ask ourselves;- what's going on here?" She paused, allowing them to ponder her question.

"Also, during the original investigation, we had initially thought that Inkleman was trying to disguise his voice because of the way he spoke in his calls, and maybe that was the case. But the fact that Edwards is doing the same just doesn't make sense. His wife is dead. *He* is missing. And he rang from his mobile phone to leave that message, making no attempt to conceal his number. So again, why disguise his voice?"

"But what I find really strange is the fact that he's acting as though he IS Inkleman, rather than merely copying him. And he has that same lullfull tone. Slow, as though he's drugged, or had a few drinks too many." She pointed to an officer off to her right, "Check his medical records just in-case. See if he's had a stroke, or some kind of speech therapy. It may come to nothing, but until we can rule it out, my guess is that he is simply copying everything, right down to the trailing speech. There must be a reason for all of this and I want to know what it is."

Gaining in confidence and shifting into auto-drive, Meg began dishing out her instructions, "Right, I need details of every major factor in this case, as, and when it happens. Names, dates, times, deaths, times between deaths, witnesses, places, you name it. And I want all the facts broken down into chronological order. I want to know where it happened, how it happened, any possible links between Inkleman and Edwards, and any irregularities or deviations in this guy's format so far."

Her pre-emptive worries now behind her, she was on a roll.

"Time is of the essence people. And if he ***is*** operating verbatim, then he will call, tonight, at 10:15 to report another murder. When he does, I want us to be ready."

"If we can't prevent the death of a second victim, then I want us to find the body before he calls so we can turn it against him. Even in death, a victim can fight back. So let's make it happen everyone. Let's force him into making a mistake. And when it happens, let's be there to make him pay for it. In the meantime, I want *all* there is to know about him;- Not just *where* he works, but *what* his work entails. Is he punctual? How does he get on with his colleagues? Does he eat out for lunch or does he take sandwiches to work, and if he does;- what's in them? Also, what does he do in his spare time, other than kill people, that is."

"Who are his friends? What are his habits? And where are his favourite haunts?"

"In short, I want to know what makes him tick."

"I want to know where he drinks, where he goes for a piss. *Everything*. And I want bank details too. Check if he has made any unusual transactions lately. Large withdrawals, deposits, anything out of the norm'. Also, I want his picture sent to the special branch divisions of every airport. And I want all of this *yesterday*. Any questions, ask the co-ordinator. Now, come on people, what are you waiting for? Let's move!"

As the room reached fever-pitch with the swapping of information and the delegations of responsibility, Morton sat in his chair, calmly gathering his papers. His gaze fixed on Ben and Meg as they stood talking, ignoring him. Ignoring his ideas.

Watch your back, Ben, Morton thought to himself... *Closed their eyes to the killer's surprise.*

Sixteen

8:34 a.m.

Sean's eyes were heavy in their reluctance to open. Heavy from crying to sleep, reluctant to see the truth of what he'd done, tiredness draining his resolve as the empty void returned, and already, he missed her smell, her touch, the way she lay her head on his chest, her ear to his heart as he stroked the groove of her naked back.

"Why is this happening to me? I don't deserve this… *WE* don't deserve this," his heart bursting as he cried out for an answer, "Why, Amy, why!?"

An empty pill bottle by his side and his head in his hands, he rocked back and forth, sitting on the edge of the bed in the sparsely furnished room, his suit badly creased from a night spent in the foetal position as he'd struggled to get to sleep, the solace of unconsciousness his only escape from the images bombarding his mind. Scenes of him spooning Amy. His blood-soaked hands. The digging of a shallow grave in the dark of night. And the message on his phone, playing over and over in his head;- *Not all is as it seems.*

Zombie-like, he trudged into the en-suite bathroom and again, he washed his hands. Double figures now. Scrubbing away at the blood engrained in his skin. Blood only he could see. He looked into the bathroom mirror, and with a splash of water onto his face, goaded himself into action, "I have to do something. I have to put an end to this, one way or another. *Think,* damn it, *think*!"

Brooding over his dilemma and obvious he needed help, there was only one person he could turn to. Only *one* who would actually listen and understand.

Don't call anyone, the message had said, *Not the police, not your doctor, NO-ONE.*

His hand hovered over the bedside telephone before he snatched it up and made the call, then crumbled as the prolonged ringing ended with the intervention of an answering machine, a high-pitched tone whining in his ear, a frozen moment as he stood on the verge of hanging-up, then stopped and pleaded into the phone, "Please, doctor, you have to help me, I'm desperate. I've done something terrible... I... I don't know what exactly, but-," the image from the boot of the car still haunting him, he choked, "there was blood everywhere."

Stifling his tears as he thought of his wife and child, he continued, "I didn't mean to kill them, I couldn't help it. It's the time-lapses. They're back. And they're getting worse." And as the tears came flooding, he cried out once more, "*Please,* doctor. You've got to help me."

Every second like a minute, every minute like an hour, he'd sat for what seemed like an eternity, anxiously stroking his wedding band, his thoughts of his wedding day and his daughter's christening. Despair turning to anger as his tears ran dry with an overwhelming feeling he had to do something to end this now before it happened again. And then, with a feeling of déjà vu, it dawned on him that he'd sat here before; on this very bed. A sudden feeling of familiarity with his surroundings as he glanced at the cheap prints on the wall and realised that the room wasn't just a stop-over, it was 'lived-in', and he had been its tenant. The toiletries in the bathroom were clearly his. Deodorants and aftershaves he had bought himself, all lying hap-hazard rather than in the neat arrangement of a new lodger. But how long had he been coming here? And how often?

He paced to the set of drawers and raked through them, searching for clues to his time here. All bar one were empty, its contents leading to yet more questions. A collection of items he wouldn't normally wear. A curious selection of hats, scarves, gloves, bandages, and an old pair of spectacles he'd stopped wearing after having converted to using contacts. All could be used to disguise himself. To conceal his identity.

With very little to go on, he reached into the fitted wardrobes, plucking out a t-shirt and a fresh pair of jeans before pausing, "These are my clothes. How did-?"

Quickly, he flicked through the hangers, his hands dipping into the shirts and trousers, checking their labels and sizes. Everything hanging in readiness along with underwear, socks and shoes. A realisation that this had all been planned. His wife's murder. The room. The clothes. Everything. All planned without his knowing, and yet, it seemed that he himself had done the planning.

His mind now racing, he rifled through all the pockets and shoes and balled-up pairs of socks. All of them empty, not so much as a hint of what was to come. His shoulders slumping to defeat, despondent, as he watched a dark blue tie slip from its hanger to the cupboard floor, its tongue pointing like an arrow to scratches in the MDF panelling. Something was hidden underneath.

Within seconds he was struggling to prise away the panel with the only tool he had available to him. But to no avail. The scissors weren't up to it. Time for something more drastic, he switched on the television and turned the volume up high before his foot kicked like a mule into the stubborn flooring, until at last, the panelling broke apart.

He sat on the bed with the shoe-box on his lap, his gaze fixed on the elastic bands securing its lid, hesitant to reveal its secrets, until, eventually, curiosity over-rode his fear of the unknown, and slowly, he removed the lid to find the box full to the brim, an envelope at the top of the pile with his name typed boldly across its seal.

He tore it open to read the letter within.

> *Sir John Lubbock once said, 'What we see depends mainly on what we look for'. So congratulations, Sean. Your search has been rewarded. But I expect you're confused right now, so let me clear up a few things for you.*
>
> *First of all;- you're a murderer, plain and simple. GET OVER IT.*
>
> *Secondly;- You have no choice in the matter. You* ***will*** *kill again, and there is nothing you can do to prevent it.*
>
> *And thirdly, if you do not follow my instructions to the letter, the one person left that means anything to you will be dead within a week. But here's where things get a bit more interesting, because we are going to play a game you and I. And to add a little twist, I have left a series of clues for both you and the police. Some of them simple, and some not so simple. How you play the game is up to you. My one and only rule is;- for* ***her*** *to live, others must die, and like it or not,* ***you*** *will be the one doing the killing. So get ready for the ride of your life, Sean. And remember:- your only chance to save her depends on your ability to stay alive and avoid being captured. The moment you fail either of these requirements;- she dies. I'm sure you can appreciate my sincerity when I tell you this. Especially after the quickie divorce I arranged for you yesterday. Great timing too. Right on your anniversary. So let the game commence, and for*

the sake of fair play, help yourself to the contents of the box. But first of all, if you wish to have even the slightest chance of getting through this, I suggest you follow these instructions;-

ONE;- *Bin all the plastic and use cash only for any transactions.*

TWO;- *From this point forward, don't call ANYONE, unless* ***I*** *instruct you to do so.*

And THREE;- *the mobile phone you already own and the one in this box are to remain switched off until you receive further instructions.*

JH (JB)

Fearful of what it all meant, Sean put the letter to one side and looked through the contents of the box, placing them side-by-side on the bed and listing them in his head.

A mobile phone, obviously brand new.

A roll of money wrapped tight in an elastic band. Ten and twenty-pound notes with a pound coin wedged inside. He counted it to the total of £1,951.

Next, was a full bottle of pills, his own prescription and his name across the label. Probably taken from his medicine cabinet at home.

There were a number of receipts too. Most of them inconsequential, but one in the name of Inkleman was dated six weeks ago. It showed the room had been paid for in advance, using cash, and only one weeks lodging remained. But most disturbing of all were the newspapers featuring headlines of the murders from seven years ago. The first victim, a woman, had been tortured and raped by her own husband before finally having her throat cut. The second, dated seven years ago to the day, told of another victim who had bled to death after having her hands and feet removed. And as Sean flicked from one paper to the next, the murders grew ever more sadistic until finally ending with the gruesome murder of a child.

Sean remembered the murders distinctly, as did everyone from the area. A blight on the northeast, no-one had felt safe. A killer in their midst and everyone a potential victim. Neighbours afraid to trust one another, the papers spreading fear and panic with their stories of the killer, his nick-name an epithet he'd rather forget, conjuring up all kinds of ghastly images. 'The Mutilator' would never be forgotten.

Sean lay the papers to one side, and the television still broadcasting in the background, his thoughts were distracted by the introductory music of a newsflash cutting into the mornings talk-show, the anchorman expressionless. "News just in. A woman has been found brutally murdered in her home in Chester-le-Street, County Durham, and as yet, we have unconfirmed reports that a child is missing too. The whereabouts of the victim's husband, a Mr Sean Edwards, seen here in this family portrait, is unknown at this time, and police have warned that this man may be extremely dangerous and should not be approached. Anyone knowing of his whereabouts should contact the police immediately on 0800 227 8873."

Sean looked on as the scene switched from the studio to a local reporter being filmed live, standing outside the cordoned-off area surrounding his home, the drizzling rain unable to dampen his spirits as he struggled to compose himself in front of camera. A reporter more used to giving reports on the weather and fronting the pleasant, more mediocre stories, he was hardly able to contain his excitement at being the one to front this breaking news as he was asked by the anchorman, "Is there anything else you can tell us, Mark?"

"Very little, Alan. But I have unconfirmed reports that events seem to mirror those of seven years ago, reflecting the beginnings of the Mutilator killings."

"So this is a copycat?"

"Police are refusing to speculate on the possibility of a copycat slaying at this time, saying that they are currently following up all leads and stating that domestic violence can occasionally escalate to homicide and the corresponding snatching of a child. Other than that, I'm afraid we have no further information at this stage. This is Mark Jakes, live in Chester-le-Street, County Durham, handing you back to the studio."

His nightmares realised, Sean switched off the t.v. with the remote.

He *was* a murderer. His wife *was* dead. And the reporter had said that his daughter was missing too. And to top it all, his face was being plastered all over t.v.

Distraught and consumed with self-loathing, he swiped at the newspapers, scattering them from the bed as he screamed out, "What's happening to me?!"

In a matter of days his life had been turned upside-down, but as he buried his face into the pillow, it was about to get a whole lot worse, his cries stopped short by the shrill of the bedside telephone.

Seventeen

Ben entered his office with two stale coffees from the vending machine, puffing and blowing to vent the heat from his scalding fingers as he searched for a space on the desk whilst Meg sat raking through the Inkleman file. She looked up at him with a smile, "That's some personality clash you and Morton have got going there, Ben."

"I might agree with you," said Ben, "if Morton *had* a personality."

"Yeah, well, sometimes he can be a pain, I know that. But he's a good cop, Ben. One of the best. He's just too busy trying to prove it."

Ben wasn't so sure, but kept his thoughts to himself. What mattered most was that Meg was still in his corner, and he wanted to keep it that way. *Building bridges.* Maybe she no-longer loved him, but even with their past differences she had shown her support for him, and admonished Morton in the process. He put the cups down, sucked the froth from his fingers, and pulled his note-pad from his pocket, tearing out a page and passing it to Meg.

"Same old Ben," she smiled. "Still got the memory of a goldfish."

"Only when it comes to names," he said with a half serious smile. "The truth is, I like the note-pads. Things look different somehow when you write them down. You can see things at a glance. Whereas on a computer screen you can skim right over stuff and miss what's right in front of you. Miss what's really important, if you know what I mean." Ben took a sip from his coffee, thinking to himself;- Stop waffling and say what you really mean for god's sake.

"So this is a list of what exactly?" she asked, struggling to read his writing and pretending she hadn't picked up on his double entendre.

"It's a list of the evidence from the mutilator case that we should have in the lock-up, but it's missing."

"Missing? How?"

Short as it was, Meg struggled to read the untidily written list;- A yellow ribbon, a knife, and an old Luger pistol with two unused bullets. All of them Inkleman's.

"I don't know," Ben answered. "I've got someone checking it out now to make sure there's nothing else unaccounted for, from this or any other case."

"You think this is someone helping himself to mementos?"

"This isn't a coincidence, Meg. There's a connection here. I can feel it."

"You may be right, but until we get a full inventory, I want us to concentrate on finding Edwards. *He's* the one doing the killing."

"Yeah. And someone at our end's involved in it."

"I'm not ignoring the possibility, Ben. But until we know more, Edwards is our primary concern. Though I do have something else you can help me with."

"Name it."

"I know this is changing the subject a little, but, since this case began, I've been reminded of a question I didn't like to ask you during the Inkleman case."

Ben's demeanour quickly changed. He picked up the Edwards file, skimming through it, apparently oblivious to Meg's mutterings, pretending not to hear in order to avoid the ominous question.

Meg continued, "Listen, Ben. When we were down there that day; the house ablaze and the flames gushing out of the windows. We were all watching the house going up in smoke, thinking there was nothing we could do as we were forced back by the searing heat."

"Please Meg, don't," Ben begged, placing the file on the desk, his eyes distant.

"I have to, Ben. That sound. I'll never forget it. The screaming as a little girl was being burned alive. Or so we had thought. But it was all a smoke screen. Literally. And only you spotted it." She looked at him for an answer. "Whilst we were blindly risking our lives to save a damned recording of his daughter's screams, you were the only one who had the presence of mind to see what we could not. But *how* Ben? How did you know?"

Ben's sorrow lay heavy in his voice, "I lost my partner in that fire, Meg."

"I know you did, Ben." Meg's voice was sympathetic, "He was a good man. He knew the risks, just as we all did. You mustn't blame yourself for something that wasn't your fault. It was Inkleman who lay that trap. And if it wasn't for you, Ben, others would have died too. But I still don't understand. What did you see that no-one else did? How did you know they were in the house next door?"

Ben's eyes full of hurt, he sat with his elbows on his knees and his head in his hands, the scene playing over in his head. "I'll never forget it as long as I live. I still see her, Meg. In my dreams. I was too late." His eyes were distant. Tortured. "He cut off her head. That's what I saw. His own fucking daughter and he cut off her head. If I'd had a gun I could have stopped him, but it all happened so fast. And I was *too... fucking... late*."

Meg's hand settled gently on his shoulder, "I know, Ben. But there was nothing you could have done."

His eyes glazed over with the feeling of guilt. "It's not right, Meg. *They* carry guns. They can shoot at us and we'd be dead by the time armed response got to the scene. It makes me angry. *Everything* makes me angry. People here respect me and I hate it. They think I'm some kind of hero because I tangled with Inkleman before he died. They think I shot him, but I've never been more angry than at that moment when it was over. Not because I wanted him to live, but because I wanted him to suffer. And in prison he *would* have suffered. There are ways to make sure of it. That's what pisses me off, Meg. He got off light. As the fire spread to engulf us, he raised that fucking gun to his head, smiling at me as I shouted for him to stop. And his last words, just before he pulled the trigger. He was laughing at me as he said it. '*Closed their eyes to the killer surprise*'.

With that image conjured up in Meg's head, she was slightly startled by a knock on the office door as it was pushed ajar and a young officer popped his head around, giving her a brief glance before his eyes fixed on Ben. "Sorry to interrupt you, sir. There's a doctor Schmidt on the phone. Says he wants to speak to you."

"Who?"

"Doctor Schmidt, sir. Well, he's not your regular doctor. He's a psychiatrist. Thinks he may be able to help in some way."

"Bloody quacks. Always after another test-case. How do they get their information so damned quick? Tell him thanks, but no thanks. Tell him we've got all the psychologists and profilers we need."

"I already did, sir. But he was adamant. He said that it was important. He said Sean Edwards was his patient."

Eighteen

Ben got off the phone from talking to Schmidt, and looking at Meg, pointed the remote at the small t.v. in the corner of his office, "You'd better take a look at this."

Meg closed the file as the screen sparked to life and couldn't believe what she was seeing. "So that's how Schmidt knew to contact us."

"Yeah, *that*, and the fact that Edwards tried to contact him last night. He said he had sounded agitated."

"But, what about the media? How'd they get their information so fast?" She had scarcely finished asking her question when she remembered the evicted officer. "The briefing. The young guy on the phone."

"I don't think so," said Ben. "He collared me at the vending machine and apologised saying it was his partner running late for the briefing. It all checked out.

"Do you think it was Edwards then?"

"No, Meg, I don't. Even a psycho wouldn't be stupid enough to make things more difficult for himself. We've got a leak. And though I'm no plumber, I know exactly where it's coming from."

Another knock at the door and Morton entered the room.

"Speak of the devil," Ben sneered.

Morton glanced at Meg then turned to Ben. "I came to apologise."

"You stupid *fuck*. You've jeopardised the whole operation. What good are apologies now."

"You're blowing this out of all proportion, I only said my piece to make things clear to everyone."

Ben pointed to the t.v. "Yeah, well, you can't get much clearer than that."

Morton turned to the broadcast in bewilderment as a photograph of Sean Edwards appeared on the screen and the anchorman continued. "This man is presumed armed and dangerous and must not be approached. If you have seen him or know of his whereabouts, then please contact the authorities on 0800 CAPTURE. That's 0800 2278873."

"How the fuck?... That's not me. I don't know anything about that."

"I suppose you don't know anything about any missing evidence either."

"No. I don't. Since the briefing ended, I've spent the time chasing up leads and going through the files with sergeant Dawson. Ask him if you don't believe me."

"And you haven't used your phone?" Ben asked sceptically.

"I don't believe this. I came in here to apologise for fronting up to you in the briefing, and you try pinning this on me."

"Mud sticks, Morton. You undermined me in there. Raised doubts about my ability to share the lead in this investigation."

"No, Ben. I stood up to you and was shot down. I showed them how serious this investigation is. I asked the questions that they may have been thinking themselves but dared not ask. I thought it was better to put our cards on the table and start with a clean slate."

"And so you used the briefing to rock my boat?"

"I said a clean slate, Ben. Put our differences behind us. This is going to be bad. Worse than most of them can imagine. I raised questions that needed answering. About you, Inkleman, Edwards, the whole damn lot. I did it to make them concentrate on what really matters, and that's catching this sick bastard, before he kills anyone else."

While Ben and Morton argued, Meg was on the phone to the head honcho at Tyne Tees studios, and as their voices rose, she hushed them quiet before continuing, "And the picture of Sean Edwards arrived in this morning's post you say?"

"Yes," the director replied. "We got an anonymous tip off this morning by phone, just after eight, alerting us to the police presence at North Lodge and telling us of your suspicions."

"What suspicions?"

"I think you know what I'm talking about," he answered, annoyed he was being played for a fool. "The copycat mutilator. We were sceptical ourselves at first, but the caller seemed to know what he was talking about. And when he told us to check our mail and we discovered he'd sent us a picture of the suspect. Well, then we had to follow it up."

"And when did you say this call took place?"

"It was just after eight. That's why we used Mark Jakes to do the report. Our link-up was set for 8:15 and he was the only reporter we had in the area."

"Is there anything you can tell us about the caller?"

"I heard he used our intro."

"Your intro?"

"You don't know it?" he asked surprised, regardless of the fact they'd stopped using it some seven years ago. "The voiceover we used to use at the start of the show. The girl who took the call said the guy had said it all strange like. *Cold* is what she said. Like he was twisted."

"Said what exactly?"

"'Tyne Tees. The news team at the heart of the north east, it's finger on the pulse' The way he said it shook her up a bit. That's part of the reason we followed it up."

"Is there anything else you can tell us about him?"

"No. Nothing. Like I said;- the girl took the call. She'll be here till 3:30 if you'd like to interview her."

"I'll send someone over immediately to debrief her. Thank you. One more thing."

"Yes?"

"The number you gave on air for contacting us. It's the one we used seven years ago. What made you come up with it?"

"The informant said you would be using it."

"I guess now we have little option," she conceded. "This caller? Did he give a name?"

"Weird that," the director answered with a sound of puzzlement, "he didn't. But apparently, his last words before he hung up were 'remember me'. I mean, how can we remember someone if he doesn't give us a name?"

Meg hung up and was at the point of explaining what she'd discovered when she was interrupted by the ringing phone. The men remained silent whilst she answered it. The call brief and to the point. When she hung up, the investigation had stepped up a gear.

"They've found Sean Edward's car near Waldridge Fells."

Nineteen

The rain had fizzled out, the sun buried behind an overcast sky as Morton drove to Schmidt's address with Meg sat quietly in the passenger seat, seemingly pondering through the updates but her mind elsewhere. She wondered if she had done the right thing in sending Ben to the site of the suspect's car. Edwards's daughter was missing. If she were found dead at the scene, then Ben would be forced to face his demons.

* * *

Just off the winding country road, Ben pulled alongside the stationary police cars parked on a square patch of tarmac with foot-trodden pathways shooting off in every direction, the heather swamped fells stretching for miles around and interspersed with the occasional copse or lone tree. Approximately a dozen officers had beaten him to the scene, including an officer he recognised as detective Christopher Bolden from forensics who was already taking samples from the drivers foot-well as Ben approached the car only to be stopped by a voice coming from his left.

"Hold on a minute, sir. I need you to sign this." A thick-set constable with a clip-board in hand broke into a heavy jog, rushing to greet Ben with a shake of the hand before passing him the security log, "P.C. Mathews, sir. Drafted in from Stanley. Wish we could have met under better circumstances, but it's an honour to meet you nonetheless."

Taken aback by the over zealous handshake, Ben asked, "We sure it's his?", his eyes looking across the open fells for anyone coming back towards the car.

"The car's registered to the perp' alright, sir. Been here all morning. It seems a walker reported it whilst out with her dog. She said the dog went crazy, wouldn't stop barking. That's when she spotted the blood on the rear bumper, got scared and called it in."

"Anyone other than detective Bolden been near the car?"

"Not while I've been here, sir."

As another police car pulled in behind them, Ben handed the constable his clip-board and off he went as Ben strolled over to the Mercedes and peered through the passenger window to see Bolden huddled under the steering wheel, deftly using his tweezers to place scarcely visible fibres into a plastic wallet.

"So what we got?" Ben asked.

Bolden recognised Ben's voice, and his focus still fixed on what he was doing, he answered without looking his way, "Pretty much what you'd expect. There are hairs on the front and back seats matching the description of the known family, as well as a few unknowns. And some fibres to be analysed."

"Anything substantial?"

Bolden had checked the outside of the vehicle first in case it started to rain again, and had scarcely begun on the interior. "No quick fix, if that's what yer mean. I'll tell yer better when I get back to the lab, but I've got all I need from the boot-lid if you want me to pop it and see what's inside."

Ben's stomach churned as they walked to the back of the car, frightened of what he might find, his thoughts of seven years ago.

He cut off her head.

He shook away the memory, his eyes gliding along the silver body of the car, remembering it was Meg's favourite model. The sporty version Mercedes SLK. "Smooth like silk," he muttered as he looked along its sleek lines, remembering how she'd described it, her comments borne out in its name.

"Sir?"

Ben dropped the formalities, "Tell me, Chris. This guy's young, loaded, seemingly happily married, and not had so much as a parking ticket. Then this. A major felony, with no apparent motive and no 'get out of jail free' card."

Though Chris was listening, he was focused on avoiding contact with the smear of blood on the boot of the car as he readied to pop it open.

Ben continued, "Doesn't it strike you as strange that a guy with no criminal record should go to being top of our list in a matter of days?"

"The love and money side o' things must be nice." Chris answered, "I wouldn't mind some of it myself. But nothing surprises me much these days."

Ben looked to the lid of the boot, worrying about what surprises lay in store as Chris rambled on, "Life's never a bed of roses, if yer pardon the pun. Worries at work cause problems at home, and visa versa. The shifts I work I'm always getting it in the neck off the missus. Sometimes, for some people, I guess it's too much, and when that happens, as they say in America;- *shit* happens, if yer know what I mean."

Ben knew exactly what he meant. *Shit happens.* And as Chris looked at him for the okay to open the boot, Ben held his breath and gave a hesitant nod, taking a step back as he heard the click of the release and watched Chris's gloved hand slowly raise the lid on what he expected to be a body.

Instead, they found the more usual items. A torch, a jack, a wheel-brace, a tow-rope and a not so usual spade;- a clump of blonde hair stuck to congealed blood on the shoulder of its muddy blade.

Ben stood there, frozen a moment, his thoughts of Edwards butchering his daughter just as he had butchered his wife. He had become unpredictable. The pattern in disarray, his daughter was meant to be last.

With a heightened sense of urgency, Ben turned and shouted to the gathering team, "Quickly! She's here somewhere. We have to find her."

Stirring them into action, he pointed to various officers and the areas he wanted them to search, "Start working on the embankment down to the right," he ordered, his knowledge of what the criminal would do instinctively clicking into place. Easier to carry a body downhill than up.

A hurried glance at his watch. 9:02a.m. His mind raced ahead of himself as the officers searched through the fringes of dense heather, aware that, in little over an hour, Edwards would be butchering someone else while they were searching for the body of his daughter.

"Over here!" Came the shout from an officer on the fringes of the group, all of them quickly converging on a mound of fresh earth, poorly disguised with the scatterings of uprooted heather.

Twenty

Morton pulled the car to a stop as Meg put the latest report into the glove compartment and delved into her pocket for her ringing phone, "D.C.I. Rainer."

Ben's voice was sombre, "We've got a problem."

"Another body?"

"Looks that way. We've found a grave. I think it's the girl's."

Meg lowered her voice as she climbed from the car, "You okay with this, Ben?"

"Of course I'm okay damn it! Why wouldn't I be."

"Just hold it right there, Ben. There's no need for you to go jumping down my throat like that. You know I want you on this. But if you can't handle it."

Ben checked his tone to mask his discomfort, "Listen, Meg. I'm fine. Honestly. But there's something you need to know."

"What is it?"

"The grave. It's shallow. Not well hidden. I think he *wanted* us to find it. We're processing it now. But even with the shortcuts, its gonna take some time."

Time we can ill afford, thought Meg, "Just take care, Ben. We can't allow shortcuts to become slip-ups."

"Trust me, Meg. I'm on it. We'll get everything we can from this. I promise."

"Okay, Ben. Got to go. We'll be over there as soon as we're done. In the mean time, call if you need me."

Pedestrian-worn cobbles under foot, Meg and Morton wound their way through the old narrow streets of Durham city, filtering their way through the congested traffic of people as they headed for the townhouses sat on the south side of the river-bank. Elegant old buildings converted into modern-day office space, their doorways leading directly onto the street and a canopy of oak trees their backdrop, the view from the houses spellbinding. Like stepping back and forth in time to witness an encapsulated shimmer of romance destined for canvass and camera alike.

On the opposite side of the river stood an old boathouse, weathered and tired looking, with dirty stonework and blistering forest-green doors hanging on antique hinges. Nearby, a string of small boats fastened to their moorings rocked gently as another boat pushed off onto the river, a young couple giggling as their oars splashed to the water and a lone canoeist skimmed narrowly past them, sliding effortlessly over the smooth silvery surface that gently wound its way through the heart of the city.

With a break in the clouds, reflections of old and new buildings bounced off sun-dappled ripples as seagulls swooped overhead to then dive and glide under the ancient bridge; built during a time of knights and horse drawn-carriages. A fleeting glimpse of history marred only by the streak of a jet-trail reaching to the heavens as a once battle-scarred castle towered majestically over its outcrop, the neighbouring cathedral standing proudly at its side to announce that this truly was *'The Land of the Prince Bishops'*.

Meg and Morton walked briskly toward the end of the terraced townhouses, too objective to note the beauty of their surroundings as they came to a doorway with polished brass name-plates pinned to the surrounding brickwork. One of which, belonged to Dr. J.H. Schmidt BA, MSc, FBPsS.

Meg pushed on the glossy royal-blue door as Morton stubbed out his cigarette on the step and followed her lead down a narrow hallway to a small reception room where an attractive young receptionist with impishly short brown hair sat smart and assured at her desk, the obligatory telephone and intercom system close at hand. Her fingers dancing across the keyboard as she looked up and smiled, "Can I help you?"

Meg flashed her badge, "D.C.I. Rainer. Here to see Doctor Schmidt."

A glance at the I.D. and the receptionist pressed a button on the intercom, "Your guests are here, doctor. Shall I send them up?"

"Just be a few minutes," came the tinny reply.

"He's just finishing off with a client," she smiled. "Would you like a tea or coffee while you are waiting?... I'm having one."

The detectives declined almost in unison before the receptionist disappeared behind a wall of glass bricks to the sound of a boiling kettle.

Morton picked up a magazine and dispassionately leafed through its pages as Meg stood fidgeting, keen to get on with the interview, her eyes impatiently shifting from wall-mounted certificates and diplomas to the small empty chairs and the occasional flash of shrubbery that brightened up an otherwise dull but adequate waiting room.

With the tinging of a stirring spoon came the chatter of two men coming down the stairs and passing by the reception door. One of them spoke with a heavy accent, rolling his 'R's and pronouncing his 'W's as 'V's. Moments later, his head peeked around the door. A short, balding old man, with silver hair framing his face, half-circle spectacles and a slightly dated suit. "Good morning," he said, looking to each of the officers before fully entering the room to shake their hands, "I am Doctor Schmidt."

"Good morning, sir," Meg said reaching out her hand. "I'm detective Rainer, and this is detective Morton. I believe you're expecting us."

"Indeed. Indeed," he answered. "I had always thought something like this might happen some day, but had hoped that I vas wrong."

"You expected this to happen?" Meg asked, surprised.

"Vell, not *this* exactly," he answered, removing his spectacles to exhale on them, give them a wipe and return them to his face. "But something *like* this, sooner or later. Troubled minds lead to troubled times, detective. And troubled times to troubled minds. But who knows who or ven."

"So there were no signs that Mr. Edwards was on the verge of a breakdown?"

Schmidt looked apologetically over his spectacles, "I vould like to help you detective, but as I am sure you are already avare;- I can not betray a patients confidentiality."

"Then why call us, doctor? We need information. *Useful* information. And fast. Before *your* patient, Sean Edwards, kills again."

Doctor Schmidt caught sight of the shock in his receptionist's eyes as she returned to her desk with her tea, and ushered the detectives from reception, "Maybe we should discuss this in my office."

He led them up three flights of stairs at a surprisingly nimble pace. "My office is on the top floor," he said, adding proudly, "fifty-three steps from top to bottom. That is vhy I chose it. That and the view. Helps keep me active in the body as vell as the mind."

It was at times like this when Morton wished he'd given up smoking years ago. Last in line and a slight wheeze to his cough as they reached the top.

There was the automated hiss of an air-freshener as they entered the large open-plan office with its sumptuous black leather couch, extensive bookshelves and scatterings of well pruned foliage. Meg inhaled the fresh aroma of jasmine and couldn't help but feel that the overall effect was welcoming, almost relaxing, as Schmidt sank into an oversized black-leather chair behind a desk and gestured for Meg and Morton to sit on the couch opposite.

"I rang you because Mr. Edwards left a message on my answering machine last night. He sounded as though he vas in trouble."

"He IS in trouble," Morton interjected, still a little breathless from the stairs. "Serious trouble. And up to his neck in it."

"I understand that now. But I vas in bed ven he rang."

Meg took charge of the questioning, "And what time was that, sir?"

"It vould be just after eleven o'clock."

"You sure of that?"

"For sure. For sure. Creature of habit you see. Always retire to bed at 10:30. Read a good book until I drift off, then it is lights out. For the lamp, and for myself." His attempted humour wasted, he continued, "Anyvay, the telephone voke me. I heard it distinctly. Just a few rings before the answering machine took his message."

"You said he sounded as though he were in trouble. What did he say in his message?"

"He vas frightened. He thought he'd killed his vife."

"What do you mean, he *thought* he'd killed his wife?"

"He vas confused. He is not a vell man."

"How did you respond to his message?"

"I tried to call him only this morning, but could not get an answer. Then I saw the news broadcast and rang you."

"How long has Mr. Edwards been a patient of yours, doctor."

"Ummm, about eight months I vould say. I can check my records if you vish."

He swivelled in his chair and without leaving it, reached into a filing cabinet and thumbed through to 'E'.

"And what were you treating him for exactly?"

"He suffers from a sleeping disorder called Parasomnia. Have you heard of it?"

"No. I can't say that I have."

"It's a condition that includes sleepwalking, and, although he had memory lapses too, his main concern vas obviously his attacks on his vife."

"So he has a history? He had already shown acts of violence toward his wife before he killed her and you didn't think to report it?"

"As I said earlier, there are ethics involved here, detective. He vas seeking treatment for his condition. There were signs he vas beginning to improve. They had even begun sleeping together again."

Morton grumbled. "Fucking nutters. They are always given the benefit of the doubt. Only when something bad happens, only then do we hear 'I told you so.'"

"But he is not a '*nutter*' as you so eloquently put it, detective. As I have said already, he suffers from parasomnia. A condition that includes sleepwalking, night terrors, and occasionally, acts of violence among its symptoms."

"And how does this help us exactly?" asked Meg.

"I am trying to help you understand him. Sufferers are found to have an increased likelihood of sleepwalking episodes if suffering from sleep-deprivation, stress, or the consumption of alcohol shortly before sleep. It is a condition that has become increasingly more common in todays society as we adjust to the introduction of artificial light and varied shift patterns. I suppose, vat I am trying to say, is that stress may have caused him to kill, and it may cause him to kill again."

"Are you suggesting that we allow him to have a good night's sleep doctor, and then everything will be hunky dory?"

"No. Indeed not. I am not trying to justify vat he has done, detective. I am merely trying to explain the reason behind it. Please, let me ask you. Before today, had you ever heard of people who have killed whilst asleep?"

"Load of nonsense, if you ask me," said Morton, before Meg hushed him quiet and asked the doctor to continue.

"Von case in particular comes to mind. A very recent von as a matter of fact. A Manchester man by the name of Jules Lowe beat his 82 year-old father to death von night in October 2003. There vas no doubt of his guilt, but he vas acquitted of murder on the grounds that he vas asleep at the time of the attack. It turned out that Mr. Lowe's case vas an extreme example of parasomnia."

"And you think Edwards did the same?" Meg asked.

"I think Mr. Edwards loved his vife very much. He told me himself, his life revolved around her. Or, as he put it;- she vas the centre of his universe. Because of this, I find it difficult to accept that he killed her intentionally."

Morton snapped, "What? Of course it was deliberate! He tortured her for Christ's sake. Raped her. Slashed her fucking throat. He didn't simply fall onto her with a knife in his fucking hand."

Meg shot a glance at Morton, "This isn't helping. Why don't you go downstairs and have yourself a coffee."

"Just fucking vunderbar!" Morton growled, resisting the temptation to give a Nazi salute as he jumped to attention and clicked his heels together before marching out of the door.

"Allow me to apologise for my colleague, doctor."

Doctor Schmidt's face an expression of shock, he replied, "It is not that I am refusing to help you, detective. It is simply that, there are ethics involved here. I can offer my help vithin the boundaries of character definition and the likelihood of how Mr. Edwards' mind vill perceive and deal with certain events. But it vould be unethical of me to divulge information relating to the personal matters and state of mind of a particular patient. I vant to help. Believe me I do. But already I have said too much. It is a matter of ethics. A matter of patient confidentiality."

"To hell with confidentiality, doctor. People's lives are at stake here. And if we don't …" she paused to compose herself, "If we don't catch this man. Others will die. So please, answer me this one last question. Would such a sufferer, supposedly killing without intent, copy a serial killer and then go on to call the police twelve hours later and inform us of his intention to kill again?"

"Vell, no. But, I did not know that he had-"

Meg cut him short, "As I'm sure you're already aware, doctor, Sean Edwards has a daughter. And as yet, we have no idea of her whereabouts. Now. Let me give you something else to ponder over. I received a call, not ten minutes ago, from a colleague of mine at the scene of Sean Edwards' car. Forensics are going over it right now as we speak. Nearby they have found a shallow grave. It could be his daughter's. It could be someone else. But one way or another, we have a second victim. So answer me this, doctor. Do you think he is capable of killing his own daughter?"

Schmidt didn't answer verbally. He didn't have to. The lowering of his eyes gave their affirmation.

"So where do you stand on this, doctor? Can I assume you are going to help us to stop him before he kills anyone else?"

"Yes. I.., I'm sorry. I did not know. It is just that, I put two and two together and got five. He alvays seemed such a nice man."

"Is that why you gave him your home number? Or are you in the habit of giving patients an alternative way to contact you?"

"Mr. Edwards vas an exception. He knows where I live. Three months ago he came banging on my door in the early hours of the morning, demanding that I see him. He had just hurt his vife and called at my home after leaving her at the hospital. He vas deeply upset. That night I gave him my home number, but this is the first time he has ever used it."

"Why didn't you answer your telephone when he rang?"

"I did not know it vas him. I live alone. I have no family. Since my vife passed away, I think it best not to answer the telephone so late. And besides, von usually finds that these things can vait until morning." He paused before adding, "At least, that is vat I thought until I saw the news. It made me feel responsible in some vay. Like I failed them both. I should have seen the signs. I could have taken measures to prevent all of this from happening."

"It's too late to concern yourself with that now, doctor. There is nothing you can do for his first victim. But I want you to give serious thought to the next one."

"The next von?"

"Yes, doctor. The next one. This isn't over… And as I've already explained, he's copying a serial killer, and the signs are, he is going to kill again. His victims die a slow and agonising death. He cuts off their limbs as they live and breathe. And if she's not already dead, an innocent child could be next. Do you want that on your conscience, doctor?"

"Okay, okay. Spare me the details already. Like I said;- I should have known this vould happen. My vife always told me so. *'Jahn,'* She said *'be careful vat you get into and keep your nose out of other peoples business, it vill come to no good'*. But do I listen. No. Not me. That is my job I tell her." He stood from his chair, "I didn't take my vife's advice ven she vas alive, and I rarely take my own. So tell me detective. Confidentiality aside. Vat do you need to know?"

"Everything."

Twenty One

Meg dipped under the yellow crime-tape, passed the Mercedes and sidled down the incline toward the group of officers encircling a patch of earth. One of them in paper overalls was down on his knees taking samples. Another stood nearby, camera in hand. And Ben stood with the rest of the team, silent and still, gathered like the blocks of Stonehenge around an alter.

The soft scraping of Meg's trousers brushing against the damp heather was enough to turn Ben's head as she approached.

"Where's Morton?" Ben asked.

"Updating the file back at headquarters," Meg replied.

Though Meg was leading the investigation, she felt obliged to address Ben's concerns. Not that she minded. After all, it wasn't as though he was questioning her authority. He wouldn't do that. It was simply his way. A man who got so wrapped up in a case, everything else became a blur. His tone and manners inadvertently forgotten as he strove to find answers. Every snippet of information;- there to be consumed and digested. Every morsel a possible clue. Nothing taken for granted and trusting no-one bar himself to do the job properly. And Colin Morton, well, Ben had made it perfectly clear how he felt about Colin Morton. *If he's not within sight, he's not to be trusted, and less so since the leak to the news-hounds.*

But Meg's instincts told her different. Morton was a loner, and without doubt, a man who got people riled, there was no getting away from it. But there was something else about him. Something she liked. Something... *'familiar'*. He was, like Ben in a way. A man to get the job done. Dependable. No fooling around. No heirs or graces. Just the 'find him and nail him' kind.

"So, tell me," she said, standing next to Ben, "What have we got so far?"

"Nothing much," Ben answered, his mind wandering. "There's more evidence in the boot of the car than there is around here. Until we get to the body, that is."

"*Nothing much* tells me exactly that, Ben. Don't keep me guessing. I want details."

Ben's eyes were drawn back to the mound of earth as he absent-mindedly described the contents of the boot. "A blood-spattered spade. Blonde hair. Some trace evidence. Everything points to the kid."

Meg's heart sank at his choice of word.

It was over a year since they had lived together, but during that time, when they had spoke of having children, Ben had confided in Meg that 'kid' was his emotional cut-off switch. A word he used to disconnect himself from a situation rather than using the terms child, daughter, or son. Their connections too clear. Their meanings too heart rendering. Less involvement, he had said, less hurt. But as Meg herself was all too well aware, some emotions just can't be turned off, no matter how hard you try. But they *can* be bottled up.

She stood shoulder to shoulder with him, and although he wasn't showing it, she knew he was struggling to deal with the unfolding scene, both of them staring down at the mound of earth and imagining the horrors of what lay beneath.

During his time on the force, Ben had dealt with all manner of violent crime, including murder, rape and child abuse, and those cases had taken their toll, each in their own way. Scenes he had joked and laughed about, but never forgotten. Sick humour used to cancel out the sickening acts of others, their cruelty incomprehensible. His mind struggled to block it out, even now, as he stood before this tiny gravesite, unable to forget the horrors of the past. The suffering of innocent children. He sank within himself, fighting to hide his emotions, his anger kept on a leash until the time came to let it go. *'Not a good trait in this job'* he'd once admitted to the one person he could confide in. The only one he had ever truly opened up to. He had loved her and lost her. And now, once again, she was by his side, at the time when he needed her most.

As it started to rain again, Meg looked to Ben's face, seemingly devoid of emotion, his pain buried deep. She wanted to hold his hand. Wanted to put her arms around him, but couldn't. She was there for him but couldn't show it. Too many people around. Too many tongues and ears. She wanted to say something meaningful to him, but instead she asked "Did you see the sticker in the rear window of his Merc'?"

Ben raised his bowed head, "Driven by the best dad in the world. Yeah, right. If Edwards was such a great dad, we wouldn't be here."

"It seems he *was* a great dad," said Meg. "And a good husband too. Up until a few months ago at least."

"Schmidt tell you that?"

"That and a whole lot more. It seems we've got our hands full here, Ben. This guy's smart, *and* twisted."

"Details, Meg. I want details."

Touche, she thought, before saying, "The good doctor was vague at first. He started by telling me about Sean Edwards's sleep disorder. Parasomnia he called it. In layman's terms, it's the act of involuntary movement or actions during sleep."

"What?"

"Sleepwalking, night terrors, violence, you name it. Sean Edwards was beating his wife whilst he slept. It got to the point they slept in separate rooms, he beat her so bad. It seems he was leading up to this."

"You're forgetting something, Meg. He copied Inkleman."

"Schmidt had his hypothesis for that too. He said our memories and dreams are interlinked, and in his subconscious mind, Sean Edwards was acting out those dreams. Whether it be things he'd seen or heard, real or fictitious, he'd follow them through. Lashing out in his sleep to a mishmash of images, regardless of the fact that most dreams don't seem to make much sense."

"That still doesn't explain how he knew about the rose," said Ben.

"My thoughts exactly. But if you think that's strange, hang on to your hat, because this'll blow your mind;- It turns out that Edwards is also suffering from blackouts, or 'time-lapses' as the good doctor likes to call them. And therein lies another problem."

"What problem?"

"It's during these so-called time-lapses that Sean Edwards' normal self gives way to an alter-ego. A split personality if you will."

"That's just fucking great. As if it's not bad enough having a psycho on our hands, we get two for the price of one."

"There's more," said Meg, pausing to gather her thoughts as if to be sure of what she was about to say. "It seems that, when Edwards first started visiting Schmidt, he was an amiable, friendly sort. A regular Joe, so to speak. Except for the sleep disorder that is. Then, just when he seemed to be on the mend, Edwards sprang the alter ego thing on Schmidt. The doctor says it's possible that he had been expressing his *other* 'violent' self all along. Through his dreams. One condition counteracting the other. And as one condition improved, the other deteriorated."

Like most women, Ben thought, Meg tended to ramble on a bit, regardless of the situation. "You're losing me."

"What I'm saying is;- it's likely that Sean Edwards no longer suffers from Parasomnia. Maybe he never did. And now, we have a full blown psychopath on our hands."

"No, Meg. What you're saying is;- when we bring this bastard down, he's going to plead insane. He's going to say *'it wasn't me your honour, it was the dreams.'* Or *'it was the other guy.'* Or, any other load of bull-shit he can think of to get him off with it."

"A split personality would explain a few things," she countered. "His call to my mobile phone. His state of confusion. Maybe even the girl being snatched. Maybe a part of him was trying to save her from himself."

"He murdered his wife and then turned from psycho Edwards to good guy Sean. Is that what you think?"

"I don't know what to think," Meg answered, remembering what doctor Schmidt had said about the possibility of Edwards having had homicidal tendencies from the outset. That he may have been subconsciously covering them up, and now, the subconscious barrier down, he was out there, killing with a purpose. She thought too, about how Schmidt's perspectives had changed from being a doctor concerned for the welfare of his patient to those of a feeble old man more concerned for his own safety once he had discovered the facts.

Meg's thoughts switched to Abby Edwards as detective Bolden used a pencil-sized brush to delicately sweep away the dirt. And as the exhumation continued, her gaze fixed firmly on the child's coat, the wishbone pattern of the jacket slowly materialising before her eyes. Her mind absorbed by the revelation to come, oblivious to all else and unaware that Ben was watching her, admiring her strength and beauty as he stood beside her, his eyes averted from the emerging body.

"What did you make of him?" Ben asked.

The trigger of Ben's voice clicked her mind back into gear and her tongue along with it, "Huh?"

"Schmidt. What did you make of him?"

"He's frightened," she answered. "He's offered to help us in return for protection. After receiving that call from Edwards last night, and knowing what he knows now, he thinks that *he* may be the next target."

"Unlikely," said Ben. "It's not his m.o."

"I agree. But I'm thinking of bringing him in anyway, to help on the case. Take advantage of his familiarity with the perp'."

"Makes sense. He understands how Edwards' mind works better than any of our profilers could ever hope to."

"Ahum," Detective Bolden cut in with a clearing of his throat. "We're there. But I think I should warn yer. If there *is* a body under here, it's not very big."

"Do you think it's the girl?" Meg asked.

"Don't know what to think. Didn't yer say she was aged seven?"

"Yes," Ben answered edgily.

"Well, if it is the girl. She's smaller than I would expect."

He was right, thought Ben. The shape under the coat was way too small. "He's dismembered her, Meg. Hasn't he?"

"It's what we should expect," Meg answered.

Hands and feet, now we are getting to the meat.

Carefully, detective Bolden brushed the remainder of the loose dirt from the little girl's overcoat to reveal it was tucked tightly around a small form. Maybe as a sign of respect, shielding her from the elements. A small gesture of thoughtfulness from a once caring father. Or maybe a moments guilt, felt after the deed was done. A deed Ben and Meg were about to witness as they looked down at the now visible coat with the realisation that such a small jacket couldn't possibly cover her entire body.

Ben wondered if Meg felt like this; his tongue dry like sand against his pallet, his throat closing up, and the knot in his stomach growing ever tighter, his insides churning as he watched detective Bolden delicately brush the remaining earth from the fringes of the collar to reveal wisps of golden hair feather from underneath. And with it, a hushed whisper slipped from Meg's tongue, "Oh god."

Her mind was working overtime, fearful of what was about to be revealed. Fearful they were moving too quickly as they worked beyond the restrictions of procedure. It had started raining. Short-cuts had been taken. The photographs. The bagging and tagging. All hurried. Normally, forensic needs would have delayed this moment until much later, but with the prevailing weather and on a tight schedule, they had hurried everything along, unable to afford the luxury of waiting any longer than necessary.

Meg inched closer to Ben, hoping, if she were going to faint, that he would steady her or break her fall. '*Stay on your feet*' she told herself, her body tensing as detective Bolden nipped the lapels of the coat between his fingers and thumbs. "You ready for this?" he asked, looking up to Meg for confirmation. And with a tentative nod, he peeled the coat away from the body.

Ben stole a breath and turned his head away, unable to watch.

"The *evil* bastard," Meg cursed. "The *sly… evil… bastard.*" She rested her hand on Ben's shoulder, her voice soft and gentle, "It's okay, Ben. Take a look."

Ben half turned, and still wary of what he might see, he asked, "What is it?"

"It's okay, Ben. It's not her."

"What do you mean, *It's not her*?"

"It's not blonde *hair* under the coat. It's *fur*."

Ben turned his gaze to the grave, "What the-. He's been playing us all along. Winding down the clock and wasting our fucking time. The blood. The coat. The hair on the fucking spade. All of it to mislead us."

"That photograph, Ben. In the kitchen. There were four in the picture. The couple, their daughter. And a dog."

Ben looked down at the corpse of the golden retriever, uttering, "And the sly bastard used it against us. He left the battered body of his wife in plain view for all to see. Then he buried his fucking pet."

A sudden shout from Meg, "Hold it!" and Ben turned to see she was staring at detective Bolden who almost dropped the coat in shock as he stood with it partially submerged in the awaiting evidence bag.

"Check the pockets," she ordered.

Discarding the plastic evidence-bag, Bolden did as instructed. His gloved hand reaching into each of the pockets until eventually, he found two pieces of note-paper, neatly folded, stapled together, and BEN MILLER written on the outer surface.

Twenty Two

Meg was acting almost on impulse, not knowing what had made her think to check the pockets. Maybe it was instinct, or maybe it was some kind of woman's intuition, but whatever it was, it was important. She felt she was beginning to understand how his mind worked. The mind, not of a man on the run, frightened by what he had done. But the mind of a killer who had left clues. Teasing them. Taunting them. Challenging them to catch him. Two minds trapped in one body and each with its own agenda.

There are *always* clues.

Wearing gloves, Meg carefully unfolded the note, and read it with Ben looking over her shoulder.

You did it again, Ben, didn't you. You closed your eyes to the killer surprise. How many more times must I tell you;- Don't just remember ME, Ben. Remember 'Not all is as it seems.'

Nevertheless, I suppose congratulations are in order. After all, it's not every day you end up with a new pet now, is it? But did you find him in time, Ben?

Though Ben already knew the answer, he checked his watch for confirmation;- 12:47p.m.

I'm guessing it wasn't what you expected, but better the dog than the girl, don't you think? Spins the game out a little. Gives you reason to 'PAWS' for thought, so to speak. Such a nice dog, too. We called him Lucky on account of the fact we saved him from certain death the day we brought him home. Ironic don't you think. Not so lucky now though, is he. But we did love him. He was beautifully trained, and as you can see, brilliant at playing dead.

But back to what matters, Ben. I know you are a busy man, but are you a 'lucky' man? I suppose we all have elements of good and bad luck at some point in our lives, but have you ever won anything important or substantial, like a holiday, or a car, or a lot of money perhaps. If not, here's your chance, because I've left something for you at big momma's house. A clue to help you save the life of tomorrow's playmate. Does that seem like a prize worth winning, Ben? Find the clue by 10:15 *tonight and you win the prize.*

One more thing. I'm sure you noticed there was a page missing from the address-book when you searched my home. I thought it a little unfair to keep it from you, so I've attached it here. We'll talk later about victim number two, but don't get your hopes up, Ben. The dog doesn't count.

Catch you later
The Mutilator

Meg flicked to the adjoining page.

Mum	0191 372527
HANDS AND FEET, NOW WE'RE GETTING TO THE MEAT	
E-mail	
Marie	0191 371972
E-mail	
Mary	0191 376359
E-mail	
Melissa	0191 323021
E-mail	
Macie's Hair + Design	0191 327416
E-mail	

M

Twenty Three

With a call from Meg, Morton had arrived on the housing estate in the north-west suburbs of Chester-le-Street, the houses in the midst of transition with scatterings of one house after another being re-modernised or upgraded as council tenants became home-owners.

He stood outside one of the older looking houses on the corner juncture of the street, the name-plate on the gable-end confirming he was on Bullion Lane. The last in a long row of houses dating back to the 1950's, it was a small two bedroomed property with a character all its own, with a plastic squirrel climbing a trellis on one of its walls and garden gnomes sat on mushrooms with their rods dipped into a murky pond. The house faced an out-dated primary school on the opposite side of the road.

No whisper of a breeze, Morton looked up to the overcast sky, his mood reflected in its atmosphere. The dull blanket of grey hung heavy with billowing clouds threatening to empty their bowels on those below. Like Morton, everything appearing calm on the surface, a storm brewing underneath. He was still brooding over what had happened earlier, angrily mulling over the leak to the press and how suspicion had fallen on him almost instantly. Suspicions he needed to deflect after Ben had planted the seed of doubt in Meg's otherwise trusting mind, and that, more than anything, had annoyed him.

The problem of damage control now a major concern, he wanted to make them feel they could count on him. Wanted their respect. And the two of them only a few short miles up the road, they'd be here in minutes, meaning he had to move quickly. Had to take this opportunity to prove that he was as good as them, if not better. It should have been *him* leading this investigation. If anyone had deserved such an opportunity, it was himself. And he would show them. He would show *everyone*.

With three lower ranking officers trailing behind him, he paced down the short garden path to the front door and stood to the side of a rumpled-up welcome mat, his patience dwindling as he rang the doorbell for a second time as constable Harper stood next to him, looking curiously at the request on the doormat. '**please wipe your feet.'**

"Move that out of the way," said Morton, more a command than a request.

Harper bent down, and taking care not to contaminate it, nipped at a corner of the mat and dragged it to one side before jumping back in shock, his feet almost leaving the ground as he backed away from it, pointing as though something were about to attack him.

"What is it?" Morton growled.

Harper was practically stuttering, "There was sssomething bobbling along underneath, sir. I-, I think I saw blood."

Morton slowly peeled back the edge of the doormat until a pair of pink corduroy slippers tumbled from beneath. One of them still worn on a severed foot.

"Shit," Morton uttered, staring at the protruding flesh. The foot cut off at the ankle and the cartilage clearly visible, scarcely a trace of blood to mask the pink of the gristly flesh against the whiteness of the surrounding skin.

He raised the mat still further and found what appeared to be its partner, with painted toe-nails and flesh hanging from the bone, a moment's hesitation before he looked up at his stunned subordinates, shouting, "Harper! You stay with me. Quickly. You two. Round to the back of the house. See that no-one comes out."

Morton tried the door and found it locked. "We'll have to break it in."

"I'll get the Enforcer," Harper shouted, turning toward the car for the battering ram, but stopped in his tracks by the thud of Morton's foot kicking hard against the wooden door.

"No time to waste," Morton blurted, this time shoulder-charging it. And with the sound of splintering wood, the lock of the door broke away and they raced into the house, the two of them rushing through the short hallway and branching off into adjoining rooms, shouting. "Mrs Armstrong? Mrs Armstrong?"

Then Morton heard Harper cry out, "Sir! Come quick!"

Morton rushed to find him at the foot of the stairs, standing, his mouth agape. Staring at a dismembered hand stood on the base of its wrist. A woman's hand, pointing to the top of the stairs. Then came the sound of another door clattering open as the other two officers came bursting through the back to join them.

"Wait here," Morton ordered, then gingerly stepping over the hand, made his way quickly though cautiously to the top of the stairs, wary that Edwards may still be lurking, and listening for any tell-tale sounds. He mentally cursed the sound of Harper radioing for back-up as he strained to hear the faint sound of music coming from the last of the doors at the end of the landing, his hand gripping the banister for support as he found himself staring at the other severed hand clasped around the door-handle. Just hanging there, embellished with gold rings and peppered with liver spots. Like the carpet beneath, with dark red dots against a light creamy beige. The last drops of blood to have dripped from her severed wrist.

Morton's eyes stayed fixed there, even as he heard the hurried rush of more officers coming into the house, the cacophony of sound drowning out the tune from beyond the door as one pair of feet continued its race up the stairs to stop closely behind him, a whisper of reassurance coming from Ben, "I'm right behind you."

"That's handy," Morton whispered, using humour to counter his fear, the tinkle of music now a little louder as they approached the door with baited breath, Morton thanking god it was slightly ajar. No need to touch the hand as he slowly pushed it open to witness the assault on his senses.

A deluge of brutality swept throughout the room in snap-shots as the door opened wider. A dressing table swiped clean, bits and pieces strewn everywhere. A broken frame smashed against a wall, shards of mirror lying next to scattered jewellery and an open music-box, its ballerina turning a last dance as its battery ran low. And as the door opened wider, they saw the empty bed with its blood-soaked sheets. And next to it, the body of an elderly woman, her lifeless eyes staring up at the ceiling and her tongue lolling from her mouth as she lay on her back in the middle of the floor, the carpet stained with traces of blood from her severed extremities, a sign she was already dead when put into position. And she lay there, a dull pink dressing gown over a long floral nightdress, surrounded by her littering horde of beauty products, eye-shadows, lipsticks, hairbrushes and skin-creams, never to be used again. Her expression pale, no make-up to mask the colourless tone of death.

Yet there was a strange sense of order in the mayhem.

The scene was set, her body placed cruciform. Staged for their arrival, no doubt. Her legs strapped together with tape and her arms out to her sides.

And the signature of the yellow rose dropped casually onto her dismembered body.

"Jesus," said Ben, as Meg came up the stairs to join them, "I hope the kid wasn't witness to this."

"The child!" Meg repeated, "Quickly. Do a full sweep of the house." And once again, the house was a flurry of activity, everyone searching whilst Ben stood alone with the body of the victim. An old, excessively large woman, with heavy bags under her vacant eyes, and a few remaining curlers hanging limp in her grey-black hair, her efforts to look presentable wasted on her killer.

"She's Amy Edwards' mother," Ben said on Morton's return. "How come we didn't find her sooner? There should have been something to lead us here hours ago."

Prior to the call from Meg telling him to attend the scene, Morton had been investigating Sean Edwards' background and the documentation from his home. The only connection to relatives he had found was a letter from the suspects estranged mother whom he'd had checked out. She lived about twelve miles away, in Consett. And apparently, she had had no contact from her son in over a year.

"There was nothing," Morton answered. "All evidence relating to the deceased was erased from the Edwards home."

Meg cut in as she too looked around the room, "Erased?"

"Yes," Morton replied. "As though she never existed. We found nothing that could have led us here within the time-frame we had."

"Amy Edwards' birth certificate?" Ben asked. "It would have given her mothers name."

"Not one lead," insisted Morton. "We were working on it when you rang with the telephone number that led us here. Until then, we had nothing."

Ben turned away from him and began visually scanning the room, searching for the clue to the next victim, saying to himself, 'What is it, Edwards? Where have you left it?'

Closed their eyes to the killer surprise.

Twenty Four

Back at the incident room, Meg found herself watching Ben as he looked to the clock on the wall and she too looked at the time.

10:02p.m. In just thirteen minutes Edwards would be calling.

Meg looked back to Ben, wondering what he was thinking as he sat studiously, his chin in his hand and his elbow on the desk, his thoughts a million miles away until he turned to catch her blush of embarrassment, their gaze holding for a moment, until, with a sheepish blink of her eyes, the connection was broken, her attention shifting to the papers on her desk, tapping them on the desktop and shuffling them into shape as Ben behaved like an embarrassed schoolboy, making as though he were looking for a misplaced snapshot amongst his pile of forensic photographs.

Forget him, Meg, she told herself. He's no good for you.

She shook away the thoughts of how she felt and looked back to the sheets in front of her, sifting through the evidence, collating it and re-shuffling it in the hope of finding something different. Something that didn't fit.

It was now known that on the morning of Cordelia Armstrong's murder, she had dropped her granddaughter off at the school across the road, and a short time later she was seen by one of her neighbours as she returned home, a little wet from the rain. She had then taken a bath, and was probably getting ready for her coffee morning at Bullion Hall, but never made it. Less than two hours later, she was dead, and Abigail had been picked up by her father; all whilst the police were processing the gravesite on Waldridge fells, and a note left there by Edwards hinted of a clue at 'big momma's house.' Something that may lead them to the next victim, his daughter, or maybe even Edwards himself.

In their search of the house, they had discovered the victim's damp shoes in the rack by the door, but they had failed to find her overcoat and brolly, and other than the missing items, nothing stood out.

Now, as 10:15 fast approached, their likelihood of finding the clue seemed remote at best.

"What the hell are we looking for, Ben? Clues and evidence, they're one-in-the-same."

Ben looked up from the batch of photographs spread out in front of him, the picture of the old woman rested in his open hands, "We'll know when we find it," he said unconvincingly.

"We have to stop him, Ben, before he kills anyone else."

"Before it's time for him to kill the girl," Ben said sombrely, his own frustrations growing with the prospect of finding more bodies and ending finally with the death of a child.

Meg could see Ben was flagging, his fidgeting legs and shortening attention span; signs of his exhaustion as he fought to stay awake. He had hardly slept a wink in two days, and in his weakness she was drawn to him. Wanted to wrap her arms around him as he fell asleep, the way she used to when they were together. Her head on his chest, listening to the slowing of his heart as he drifted off.

"After the call, Ben," she said, "Go home and get some rest."

Ben faintly grunted in the affirmative, resigned to the fact that he needed to recharge his batteries if he was to be of any use to the investigation. A fact re-iterated by his quest for answers. His probing thoughts coming to dead ends. His ideas slipping away to nothing as he struggled with his questions, going over and over them in his head.

Tyne Tees Television had received their information about the first murder, even before the police briefing;- *why?* And from what they now knew, it was probable that it was Edwards who had made the call. Again;- *why?* It didn't make sense. Edwards was making it harder for himself. So what was he up to? What did it all mean?

Ben considered what he had learned earlier about Sean Edwards. The fact that he was morphing. Slipping in and out of character. Sometimes copying Inkleman's m.o. to the letter. Sometimes not. And, just as with the last spate of murders, the first two victims were mothers, as were the majority of Inkleman's victims. But how did this factor into what they had so far?

The questions had become his stumbling blocks and he was tired of falling over them.

The fact that Edwards was a copycat made him no more predictable. He was deceptive. Constantly misleading them with false trails and missing evidence. The girl's abduction from his home had been staged. The hair and blood on the girl's bed had been her mother's, put there deliberately to deceive them. And then there was the grave and the note. From the moment Ben had read of a clue at 'big momma's house' he had wondered if it too was a hoax, and looking across the desk, he said as much to Meg.

"Remember the diary entry? The mention of the flowers. The sex. The romantic meal, etc. There was no mention of their daughter per se. They were having a night alone. Remember?"

"What of it?" asked Meg, "The child was with her grandmother. We know that now."

Ben pondered, then said. "Her night-bag, school books, trace evidence, etcetera, all show she was there, I agree. My problem is, we didn't spot this at the Edwards house, and we wasted time following up other leads and standing around a bogus gravesite. Why?"

"Because everything happened so fast," she answered. "He misled us. We didn't know what to expect."

"*Exactly*. That's what I'm getting at. This was all part of his plan, and we did exactly what he wanted us to do. He's controlling us, Meg. And leading us astray.

"And you think he's controlling us now, with the mention of a clue at big momma's house?"

"I think he's been controlling us from the very start. Right down to convincing Schmidt of his Parasomnia."

"You think he intended to kill his wife?"

"I do. And he wanted to get it right. The method. The staging, etc. It all had to be perfect. So he bought himself some time by making sure his daughter was out of the way at her grandmother's house."

"And then he spent that time alone with her," Meg added. "spoiling her, scaring her, and then killing her?"

"He's calculated, Meg. And his daughter is the main objective in all of this, I'm sure of it. It wasn't until we dug up his dog that we discovered she was at Bullion Lane, almost within our grasp all along. He's toying with us. Misleading us at every juncture. And while we concentrate our efforts where he wants us to, he's already making his next move. Always one step ahead of us."

"So what are you trying to say, Ben? Where's all this leading to?"

"The same place Inkleman took it. He's going to murder his daughter. And god only knows who else on the way."

Though Meg agreed the promise of a clue at 'big momma's house' could be a diversion, there was still a lot to consider, and in the end, they decided they couldn't afford NOT to take the possibility of a clue seriously. But Ben thought that there was more to it than that.

"I think he is misleading us in order to divert our attention away from something more important," Ben said.

"Like what?"

"I don't know. Maybe a mistake. Or maybe something he inadvertently left at one of the crime scenes and doesn't want us to find. Might be nothing. Might be everything. Like a magician plays tricks with the mind to deceive the eye.

"Go on," She prompted.

"He misled his wife. Made out he was okay. Got back to sharing her bed. '*Back to his old self*' is what the diary said."

"And the romantic meal?"

"Turned out it was her last meal. Maybe, in that twisted head of his, he wasn't celebrating their anniversary at all. Maybe he was giving her a final send off."

"So even if we find the clue, you think it will be of no use to us? Just another false trail?"

"I think that by the time we find it, it will already be too late. I think we need to concentrate our efforts more on what we find for ourselves and give less priority to anything volunteered."

Meg thought Ben had a point. Edwards was proving himself to be a tricky son-of-a-bitch. And having more evidence, more clues, and another body, was adding to their problems rather than alleviating them. The more they knew, the more questions they needed answering. Where's Edwards? Where's his daughter. Who's next? How can we stop him?

"We still have to look into everything he offers up," said Meg, "But let's delve deeper into how he knows so much about the m.o. and see if there's a connection between him and Inkleman. Maybe they knew one another." Another glance at the clock and once again she buried her head into her seemingly fruitless search, trawling through the evidence as Ben read the poem for the umpteenth time. The words engrained into his skull. Mulling over and over in his head.

Fingers and toes, in exchange for my rose.

Hands and feet, now we're getting to the meat.

Ben sat staring at his notes, thinking aloud, "I'm missing something… there, on the page right in front of me. I know it, but what?" Something in the last line, he thought, and verse only, listened to the tape again, transcribing it to paper as it played out. Ignoring the writer's cramp running through his arm as he wrote it down yet again, one copy after another. Each interpretation a little different from the last.

And all closed their eyes;- to the killer surprise.

What did he mean by that? he asked himself.

Who closed their eyes?

The victims?... The police?... Both?

What the hell is he trying to tell us? And what ***is*** the 'killer surprise'?

Now fumbling to grip his pen, Ben slipped back into the comfort of his chair as Morton weaved his way through the desks of the incident room, heading in his direction, and passed a paper bag to Meg. "Ham and cheese, coffee, no sugar." Said Morton.

"What. No cookies?" Joked Meg, looking into the bag.

With a slight shake of his head, Morton turned away, miffed at her lack of gratitude. He had rang on his way to work asking if Meg needed anything. He hadn't expected her to order a takeaway, let alone get one for Ben as well as herself. And as Meg touched the paper cup to her lips and slurped at the scalding drink, Morton grudgingly slid the other paper bag across the desk towards Ben, who grunted his thanks with a look of contempt.

Almost everything about Morton had a tendency to get under Ben's skin. A runt with a self-righteous attitude, he wore the symbol of a saint and carried the manners of a heathen. Up until yesterday that is, when all of a sudden he'd become the perfect gentleman, turning up at the station in his civvies, with perfect manners and a false show of etiquette. Pussy-footing around Meg and saying how glad he was to have her back. A dweeb in tatty jeans and a buttoned down shirt, wearing a cross around his neck like it was a medallion, entangled in sprigs of red chest hair. Skinny as a bean pole and prancing about like some kind of macho man. A hypocritical atheist, Ben had thought, and probably the least religious person he had ever known. There *had* to be a connection between him and Edwards.

Had to be.

"Colin," Meg called, "Take a look at this and tell me what you think, would you."

It was the first time Meg had openly called Morton by his Christian name since they had met, and Ben hated hearing it like he hated watching a perp leave a courtroom with a slap on the wrists. She was warming to him, he thought, and Morton thought so too. He looked at Ben with a cocky arrogance as he took the folder from Meg's hand and began to read it, his expression changing to an angry frown, "What's this?" he asked.

"It's a list." Meg answered, "of all the B&B's, guest houses, hotels and bunkhouses in the area."

He passed it back to her with a sharpness to his tone. "Yes, well, I can see that. What I want to know is;- what do you expect *me* to do with it? There's way too many to check within the time-frame available to us. And it's not like he's going to check in under his own bloody name, is it."

"This isn't open for discussion," said Meg, "I want you on it. Immediately."

startled by the ring of the telephone, Ben, Meg and Morton stood swapping glances before finally, Meg shouted, "We're on." And the few officers that were not already at their stations, slid off desks into seats, donning headphones and monitoring computer screens. Recording equipment ready to trace the call.

Ben lifted the receiver and held it to his ear, "D.S. Miller."

Sean Edwards spoke slow and deliberate, his tongue wrapping around every syllable. Salaciously slavering. His voice like the hiss of a snake, "Fingers and toes, in exchange for my rose." His voice echoed into the incident room as Ben switched to speaker-phone. "Do you remember me, Ben?"

A pause before he continued, "Hands and feet, now we're getting to the meat. Do you remember the rhyme, Ben? It's there to help you, if only you'll listen."

"Tell me," Ben said calmly, "Why should I remember you?"

Like a malevolent child acting the super-villain, Edwards's voice boomed through the speakers, "I aaaaaaam 'THE MUTILATORRR'." His exaggerated laughter like that of the Joker from Batman, fading down through the echo of the speakers, before, sarcastically, he said, "Sorry about that folks. I sometimes forget myself. But life can be too serious sometimes, don't you think?"

"I think you're a sick piece of shit. That's what I think," said Ben.

"You're wrong, Ben. I'm an artist. It takes a certain amount of skill and patience to turn a bed-chamber into a torture chamber. And you should have seen her face, Ben, when I told her her daughter was dead. It was as though I'd ripped her beating heart from her sagging chest."

"That was your mother-in-law god damn it. What's wrong with you, Edwards? Have you got something against mothers. Weren't you loved as a child?"

"*fuck you!*" Edwards burst out down the telephone. "Why should I care about one woman more than any other. That's all they are. *Women.* Mother is just a title we give to someone who's supposed to care for you. Supposed to look after you. *And* your sister."

"But, you don't have a sister, Sean. You're an only child."

"I… I… Oh, I see what you're doing, Ben. Playing for time. Clever boy. Taking your work seriously at last. Well, I have to admit, I used to take *my* work seriously too. But this," his voice now buoyant, "This is all just a game."

Ben struggled to control his anger, "A game to you maybe, but in *your* game people die."

"Those aren't people, Ben. Not *real* people. Not like your Gacys, Bundys and Sutcliffes. Now they are what I call people. Those we kill, they're just the unfortunate by-products. The pieces needed to play the game. Just like you, Ben. The pieces within the game of life and death. And it is I who hold the dice. Or should I say 'die'."

"You can say whatever the hell you like. You've had your last throw, Edwards. The game's almost over."

"Oh, it's far from over, Ben. Though it could have been, if you had played your cards right. But it seems that once again *you closed your eyes to the killer surprise.* And you closed them more than once, Ben, didn't you."

Ben maintained his composure, "So tell me. If you're 'The Mutilator', where's Sean Edwards? I'd like to speak to him."

"Oh, you can't right now. I'm afraid he's indisposed."

"What do you mean, indisposed?"

"Don't be fucking stupid, Ben. There is no Mutilator…. No Mutilator. No Inkleman. And no fucking Sean Edwards either if I decide it. You're hearing *them,* but you're not listening to *me*. You're not *seeing* it. Open your fucking eyes you condescending piece of shit with your fucking psychological profilers. Coming to me with that split personality crap. I know exactly who I am. And I know exactly what I'm doing."

"And what *are* you doing? Couldn't you think of anything original? Is that why you copied Inkleman?"

"You're not listening, Ben. You never.. fucking.. listen. Not then, and not now. If you did, we wouldn't be having this conversation. But did you really think it was all over, Ben? That it could all end so easily? Can't you see; life doesn't always end the way you expect it to. And as I talk to you now, I am living proof of that. If you had done your job properly back then, none of this would be happening."

"What do you mean, back then?"

Edwards' patience was growing thinner, "Come on, Ben. Get with it for fuck sake. Seven years ago, during the Inkleman saga, you made the mistake of closing the book on this when it wasn't over. It was merely the end of a chapter. So here's what I'm gonna' do, Ben, just for you. I'm gonna' give you a chance to redeem yourself. My next call should be a little more, '*informative*' shall we say. But I'm warning you, Ben. Make the most of it. You're the only one to get a second chance."

"Now you listen to me, Edwards. And mark my words. We're going to catch you, and sooner than you think. This time, we got to the body before you called, and we'll get quicker. Next time, we might be there waiting for you, before you even have a chance to strike."

Edwards burst out with anger, "Yeah, well, *fuck you*! You had to get there sooner. It's taken you this long to realise there's a plan. A sequence even. This one was the easiest for you to find, being related and all. But who's next, Ben? WHO'S… FUCKING… NEXT?

Twenty Five

Ben could see from Meg's expression that her back was up and turned to avoid her outburst only to feel a yank on his arm.

"What the hell was all that about?" she asked angrily. "You were meant to get him talking, not piss him off. There was no mention of the clue. The next victim. *Nothing*. I hope you realise just how much you've set us back, Ben. I've got a good mind to-"

"A good mind to what?" he interrupted sharply.

Meg didn't reply, though her eyes held his gaze as he said calmly, "Listen, Meg. I told you earlier. We won't find *anything* until it's too late. I did what I felt I had to, and, well, I hope it paid off. I think he made a mistake."

"You're wrong, Ben," she said, staring intently into his eyes. "*You* were the one who made the mistake. He asked if you were listening, and I'm beginning to think you weren't."

Just then, Morton got off the phone to interrupt their stand-off, "We got his location. He's at the Holiday Inn, Washington. Just off the A1. We can be there in minutes."

"At least we got *something* out of this," Meg said, grabbing her jacket from the back of the chair and giving Ben a stern look before turning to Morton and barking at him to take her there.

* * *

Just a short way down the road, Meg's thoughts were plagued by Ben's stupidity, and for a moment, she wondered if she'd thought out loud as Morton said "I've got to say, ma'am. I think detective Miller was way out of line back there."

Meg gave no reply as Morton turned off the roundabout and onto the A1. "Yeah, pigheaded as usual," he continued.

Meg looked beyond her reflection and out into the darkness as they picked up speed. She was angry at Ben. She felt he'd let her down. She had trusted him to be professional and instead he'd allowed his emotions to get the better of him, acting on impulse, without a thought of the consequences and what was at stake. And the annoying thing was, she had no-one to blame but herself.

It was at a moments notice, on the night Amy Edwards' body had been discovered, and following a call from Jim Brandt to his commanding officer, that Meg had been given the reigns of the case, and instinct overriding her reluctance, she had asked her boss to arrange for Ben to be included in her team, though initially, she had thought of using his experience in other areas. Out of the firing-line so to speak. He was a time-bomb waiting to explode and *she* had lit the fuse.

'I should have known better,' she thought.

'I should have expected him to lose it on the phone.'

'I should have dealt with it myself.'

Seven years ago this case had almost broken Ben, and during their time together, he'd confided in Meg that, occasionally, he still suffered nightmares.

'The girl, Meg. He cut off her head.'

Her anger turned to guilt at the thought of having involved him in the case, though she knew he would have it no other way. He had the tenacity of a Pit-bull. Better to keep him close, she had thought, where she could keep an eye on him and make use of his experience, than to have him on the fringes making ripples in her pond. And besides, she needed every option available to her, and although she'd had her doubts about his frame of mind, when she'd confronted him with her concerns, he had told her he needed this. Needed to face his demons. And in her selfish wisdom, she'd agreed.

It was an agreement she now regretted. Made on the spur of the moment during a conversation in which she was reminded of his gentler, more caring side. She had buckled to the almost pitiful request of a man passionate about his job, and at one time;- passionate about her.

She began to wonder about what had happened between them. Why they had drifted apart. Not much more than a year ago they had been deeply in love and seemed destined to spend the rest of their lives together. They had spoken of getting married and having children, though they'd decided against the latter. *'Not yet'* they had said, Ben getting tongue-tied, though she herself had felt they would make wonderful parents. And a child the only piece missing from their jigsaw, she had longed for that space to be filled.

Then, she was reminded that life was no fairytale. That sometimes it was better to anticipate the worst for fear it actually happened.

Her hands clasped, her palms resting on her empty womb, she recalled how Ben had started acting suspiciously, occasionally going missing for a couple of hours with no explanation of where he'd been or what he had done. She had overheard a phone call and the mention of flowers, the calls becoming more secretive. And when she had finally smelled perfume on his clothes and confronted him with her suspicions, he had laughed it off, accusing her of being paranoid to the point she had even begun to doubt herself, wondering if she were imagining it. Telling herself she was reading into things, but wary of trusting him as she had edged through the latter part of their relationship, waiting for the almost inevitable pitfall. Anticipating that, eventually, it would all come to an explosive end. And even when it did, she had thought she'd be able to handle it. Thought she was prepared. But the pain was like having him bury a grenade into her chest and yanking out the pin, her heart exploding into a thousand pieces, one rainy night, as they were drenched in a torrential downpour. Meg standing in a darkened doorway. And Ben across the street with another woman, sharing an umbrella as Meg stood soaked to the skin.

She'd sat at home for over an hour that night, waiting to confront him as he came through the door, her stomach churning with thoughts of what they were doing together, before, finally, she had booked a taxi and packed her bags, just moments before he'd returned.

"Just bare with me, Meg," he'd said, "It's not what you think."

"It never is!" She'd screamed back at him, struggling with her bags and refusing to put them down. Ignoring his pleas for her to stay. Ignoring his excuses as she climbed into the taxi and slammed the door in his face, her expression one of fortitude, a tear rolling down her cheek and her gaze looking straight ahead, away from Ben as he pounded on the window.

She'd been on the force long enough to know the usual outcome an affair had on a relationship, and hard as it was, she had turned her back on him. No excuse good enough, she had stormed out, ignoring his pleas to wait. His belated offer of an explanation. She was having none of it. He'd deceived her. End of. Better to suffer a life alone, she had thought, safe in the knowledge that there was no-one to hurt her. No-one to let her down.

But now that he was back in her life she found herself inexorably drawn to him. The fact that he was close yet beyond reach making her feel lonelier than ever. Why hadn't she listened to him. Given him a chance to explain. Why hadn't she answered his calls. Not *all* men were liars. At times, Ben could be infuriating, no doubting it, but there was another side to him, and only a short time ago, in the build up to Sean Edward's call, things had been better between them. There was a semblance of them being capable of working together without their personal history being a problem. They had shared a laugh together as she playfully teased him about his thinning hair, and then the topic had changed to Morton, and Ben's manner had changed along with it. His comments laced with jealousy, trickled through her mind, "Watch out for him," Ben had warned, "He's so far up the bosses arse, what the gaffer chews, Morton swallows."

Meg's body leaned toward Morton as they sped around another roundabout, her daydream disrupted by him waffling on, "If you don't mind me saying so ma'am. I think you should reconsider his position on the case."

"As a matter of fact, I *do* mind," she snapped. And as Morton clammed up, she adjusted the rear-view mirror to see Bens' headlights following close behind....

Ben kept his eyes on the car in front. His need to catch Edwards prevalent in his mind as Morton exited the roundabout and Ben followed, his eyes on his tail-lights, his mind on the call. His tete-a-tete with Edwards had raised further questions and on his journey here, he'd gotten in touch with records.

"Thanks Andrea," he said, "I owe you one." And as the radio clicked off, he pulled into the car park of the Holiday Inn Express, a flurry of vehicles screeching to a halt and a multitude of doors slamming as officers jumped out of cars and ran into the building...

Meg and the team stood in the hallway outside room 101, some with their backs against the wall, others crouched, waiting for the 'okay' to come from armed response after they had burst into the room before them, *"Move! Move! Move!"*

Only one room with an adjoining bathroom, it was over in seconds, their voices shouting from room to room, "Clear. Clear." And safeties clicked, weapons holstered, Meg walked into the room.

They were too late.

Edwards had obviously expected them to trace his call and was gone.

"He was alone." Meg said out loud, airing the thoughts of the team as they looked around the room. There was no sign of the girl and no signs she'd ever been there. If she were still alive, then she was being held somewhere else, making it easier for him to leave in a hurry, and that's exactly what he'd done, his mobile-phone left on the cabinet by the bed, still switched on. But Edwards was no fool. He was intelligent and organised. He would have left it there deliberately, allowing them to pinpoint his location. A method to his madness. Another plot to delay them. And whilst they were working this scene, he'd be preparing the next.

Ben snapped on a pair of latex gloves and picked up an empty pill bottle from the bedside cabinet whilst Meg flicked through the newspapers on the bed, the clippings from all the major tabloids and some from the local freebies. Almost all of them were from seven years ago. All related to the merciless killings of The Mutilator and told in a way that allowed the mind to picture the worst without giving any of the gory details. She reached for the shoebox and browsed through the receipts to find one for the rental of the room, and one only three days old, showing the purchase of two mobile-phones. She looked to Ben, his eyes scouring the room, then she turned to Morton. "We've lost him," she said, passing Morton the receipts. "We need to find out the details and numbers of those phones," she said, "And if they're switched on, I want their location."

"Yes, ma'am."

As Morton made a call and read out the details of the receipts over the phone, Meg noticed something written on the reverse side of one of them and gestured for him to pass it back.

She read the short message.

Detective Rainer.
Please help me.
I don't know what to do.

I need to save my daughter.
She's all I have left.

Meg remembered the statements of eyewitnesses who'd seen the Edwards's in the local park walking their dog. How they'd seemed like a loving family without a care in the world. Sean walking with his daughter up on his shoulders as his wife teased and tickled her. But sometimes, as Sean Edwards had already proven, life could be deceptive. You know what they say, she thought, If walls could talk. Or as her father used to say, long before he ever knew he had cancer;- things can look fine on the outside, but you never really know what's going on on the *inside* until something goes wrong.

Ben came over as Meg stood with the note still in her hands. She showed it to him.

"He's trying to mislead us again, Meg. Trying to come between us. Disrupting the investigation in order to throw us off the scent."

"I don't think so," Meg said, "The writing's different somehow. It's softer. More caring. I think it's genuine."

"Like we thought the grave was genuine?" said Ben.

"I know how it sounds," she answered. "He has a split personality. He's a killer. But he's also a father."

"Yes, Meg. He has a daughter. She trusted him too. As did his wife. And look what happened to them."

Meg thought about the methods of contact between Sean Edwards and Ben. In each case;- the phone calls and the note in the pocket, Edwards had addressed Ben by his forename. But on the night they discovered Amy's body, Edwards had rang home sounding confused and unsure of what was happening. Meg had been the one to take his call and it was to her that he had addressed the note. Written more formally, as a sign of respect or politeness maybe. His decent persona in a desperate bid to be heard;- crying out for help.

"I told him my name, Ben. That night at the house, when he rang. This is not at all how I would expect him to behave from what I've seen so far. We need to have another chat with Schmidt. This may be our way to break him down. Before the return of his alter-ego."

"Be careful, Meg. Don't forget, he wanted us to find this room. That's why he left his phone switched on."

"He could be an unwilling participant in all of this, Ben. Don't you think it's strange? His m.o.'s the same, but everything else seems different."

"I don't know what to think."

"Doesn't any of this seem familiar to you, compared with Inkleman I mean?"

"Speaking of which," Ben said, looking at the hotel records as they were passed to him by another detective, "Inkleman's the name he used to book this room."

"Shit. If this gets out, the press'll have a field day."

Ben mumbled under his breath, "You're the only one to get a second chance."

"What?" Meg asked, unsure if she'd heard him right.

"That's what he said to me in his call. He mentioned a sister, and he said I'm the only one to get a second chance. I tried to tell you back at the station."

"What do you think he meant by it?"

"It's possible he thinks *he* did the original killings. Maybe he thinks he's Inkleman, or maybe he meant I got a second chance where as the victims didn't. But I think it's something more than that."

"Any ideas?"

"I'm waiting for Andrea to get back to me. I know he had no siblings at the time of the murders. But maybe he had a sister when he was younger and she died or was put into care or something. Until I hear from Andrea, there's no way of knowing whether that's what he was hinting at, or if he was just feeding us another load of crap."

"That's *it!*" Meg exclaimed, "He fed her it."

"What?"

"The clue we were searching for at big momma's house."

"What of it?"

"The victim. Cordelia Armstrong. *That's* where the clue's hidden. Like he forced his wife to swallow her nails, he forced his mother-in-law to swallow the clue."

Twenty Six

"Business or pleasure, sir?" asked the driver.

Sean rubbed his brow, mumbling as he got his bearings, "What?"

"At the train station. Business or pleasure?"

"Erm, Business," he answered weakly.

The driver continued making small-talk as Sean vaguely came to his senses. The bright LED display of the clock showed 10:27 p.m. And next to it, the fare showed £7.80 and rising.

He looked out of the window as they travelled down the A1 motorway to Newcastle, a sports-bag held firmly on his lap, its contents now his soul possessions. Its familiarity giving him little comfort as he stared at the destination signs whizzing past the window, the driver still rambling on, oblivious to his anxiety.

"You work shifts, do you?" asked the driver.

Sean's thoughts were a million miles away, fearful of the horrors he may have committed during his latest time-lapse.

"Of course you do," said the driver, fishing for answers and trying to make small talk in an effort to increase his likelihood of a tip. "Why else would you be going to town so late."

Not thinking straight, Sean was at the point of asking the driver to pull over, then thought better of it. They were on a motorway. And besides, there'd be a reason he was going to Newcastle. The journey arranged during his time-lapse, he *had* to follow it through in the hope that that reason would present itself. Maybe he was going to meet someone who could help him, or better yet, it would lead him to his daughter. With few other options available to him, where else could he go.

He stepped from the taxi outside Central station to the sound of a train rumbling slowly along the track on its journey out of town, the taxi pulling off too as he stood at the kerbside, leaving him feeling lost and abandoned in a town he was more than familiar with.

Why am I here? he asked himself.

Where do I go?

He wandered around the train station to find it almost empty, then, sure no-one was paying him any attention, returned to his drop-off point and sat there, on a bench, for almost two hours, his time filled with thoughts of Amy and Abby as he watched people coming to and fro, hoping that someone would approach him and tell him where his daughter was, his gaze shifting from a workman emptying the bins to a young woman exiting the hotel across the street, pale, yet reasonably attractive. Intelligent looking too, with an air of sophistication. A businesswoman he surmised. With chestnut, shoulder length hair, she wore a grey pinstriped jacket and matching knee-length skirt along with a little black shoulder bag and elegant high-heeled shoes. Very demure, he thought as she walked towards him. Probably on her way for a train. An important business meeting in London perhaps. But, if that were so, then surely she would be carrying some baggage or a case of some kind.

To Sean's surprise she sat at the other end of the bench, and getting a cigarette from her bag, turned to him with a smile, "Excuse me. Do you have a light?"

Sean turned away and carried on looking across the road to the hotel, avoiding her eye contact as he watched the odd person drifting in and out of the building. People that knew why they were here, or where they were going. "No," he answered, still avoiding her eye contact. "Sorry. I don't smoke."

"You waitin' for someone?" she asked in a soft northern accent.

He was here because of his daughter, but unsure how to answer.

"Might be," he said.

"Anyone… *special*?"

There was something in her tone that made him wary as he turned to face her. She was smartly dressed and self-assured, looking at him as if she knew something he did not. As though she knew exactly what she wanted. And what *he* wanted for that matter, making him wonder if she were the person he was here to meet.

He would have to play it by ear, taking care how he answered her questions. If they *had* met before, there was a chance she would pick up on changes in his persona. As his alter ego, he would *think* differently. *Act* differently. Maybe even *talk* differently. And he may have pre-warned her not to divulge anything to him under certain circumstances.

"Maybe it's me you're waitin' for?" she asked.

"Maybe," he answered, trying to keep his answers short while he sussed out her intentions.

"We are all waitin' for someone," she said. "It's a matter of being in the right place at the right time, to find that someone special."

"So what brings you here?" he asked.

"Circumstance," she answered.

"Yeah, you and me both," he mumbled.

"You in some kinda trouble?"

Sean didn't answer. He didn't know how to. He wondered if she already knew the answer to her question. He was a bad liar and was sure she would pick up on any deceit.

She slid along the seat to sit next to him. "You lookin' for a room?" she asked.

"I hadn't thought about it."

"It'll be hard traipsin' the streets for somewhere to stay at this time of night," she said, looking across to the hotel, "And it's quite expensive in there."

"I've got money," Sean said, holding his bag closer and looking across the street. Problem was, he didn't want to draw attention to himself by going into a hotel so late at night. He'd been on the news. Someone might recognise him.

"I've got a nice bottle of wine back at my place. You can share it with me if you like."

Though she didn't seem drunk, something in the way she smiled told him she'd already had a few. "Are you in the habit of picking up strangers?" he asked.

"Well, let's just say I'm in the habit of bein' in the *company* of strangers."

He began to ask her a question, warily, trying not to offend, "Are you a-"

"Prostitute?" she half laughed, though not sounding overly insulted. "God, no. I'm an escort. You know;- extravagant meals and trips to the theatre. Company for loners and out-of-towners, that's me."

"Don't you have a *date* for tonight?"

"Did have. But his wife turned up. It got a bit out of hand. Are you married?" she asked, seemingly hoping the answer was 'no'.

His face solemn, he answered with a heavy sigh, “Widowed.”

“Oh. Sorry.”

For the briefest of moments, Sean felt a compulsion to open up to her, but stopped himself short as she shuffled a little closer and rested her hand on his thigh. “You in need of some company tonight, are yer?”

He looked into her eyes, unsure of how to answer, and saw a police car over her shoulder, hugging the kerb as it ambled towards them. His body tensed, readying to make a run for it, and in that same instant she kissed him, her lips pressed gently to his as he nervously watched the car carry on by.

Twenty minutes later he was back at her place; a small but nice apartment on the banks of the river Tyne. A request to use her shower as they entered, he stood there now, his head back and his eyes closed as he immersed himself in the spray of the water washing over his face and body. For the first time in days he felt safe. No-one would think to look for him here. He had paid her £200 up front and it was worth every penny for another night of freedom. Another chance to rest before resuming his search for his daughter.

“You from round here?” the escort shouted from the bedroom, her voice pitched above the sound of the shower as she rifled through his pockets and bag. She heard him mumble something inaudible and replied conjecturally, “Oh, that’s nice” as she splayed a wad of twenty-pound notes between her fingers, pilfering a few into her purse before jumping onto her bed.

Sean came out of the bathroom to find her lying there in a see-through negligee, patting the bed and gesturing for him to lie beside her. Making him feel uncomfortable. He’d never slept with anyone other than his wife since they’d married, and although sex wasn’t on his agenda, he still felt as though he were being unfaithful.

“It’s alright, I won’t bite. At least, not unless you want me to.”

A towel wrapped round his middle, he sat on the bed beside her. “Don’t take this the wrong way, erm…”

“Rachel.”

“Don’t take this the wrong way, Rachel. You’re a beautiful woman. It’s just that, I’m not here for sex.”

“Then why *are* you here?” she asked curiously.

“I can’t say. I… I needed somewhere to stay. Somewhere safe.”

She put her arm around him as he lay back on the bed next to her, "You're safe here, darlin'," she said, holding him close, her soft skin pressed against his chest.

Sean fantasised that he were in Amy's arms. "Please. Just hold me," he said, "Hold me until I fall asleep and tell me everything's going to be okay."

She did as she was asked. *At last,* she thought. How many times had she heard tales of easy punters. The ones who would just lie there, telling you their problems. Weirdos just wanting to be hugged and feel cared for. Easy money for a single nights stay. Weirdos who pay you, just to listen to them jabbering on about their miserable lives. And better still; this one was quiet. Most of them don't know how good they've got it, she thought. They should try living in her shoes for a while, see how difficult life *really* is. Still, this was the easiest money she had ever made.

Sean was almost asleep, his voice a little croaky as he drifted off, mumbling, "Please. Call me Seany. My wife called me Seany."

Twenty Seven

Saturday 31st March. 7:32a.m.
Police Headquarters, Aykley Heads. Durham.

Ben was at the station earlier than most, and Meg had barely had a chance to get her bearings before he popped his head around her office door, "There's something I need you to see," he said, turning on his heels and heading down the corridor.

Meg grabbed her bag and chased after him, "And what would that be?"

"You're not going to like it," he answered. "I've made some calls to check out a few theories, and something came up."

"Where are we going?" she asked, catching up.

"Forensics lab," he answered, both of them walking briskly, their stride almost in sync. "Remember the knife Inkleman used to kill his wife?"

"A hunting knife, with a serrated edge. Are you saying Edwards used the same type of knife?"

"Not the same *type*," Ben answered. "The blade of Inkleman's knife was worn and had flaws in its cutting edge, leaving a distinctive mark on the bones of his victims, and those same marks were found on the neck vertebrae of Amy Edwards."

"He used the *same knife?*" Meg asked, her stunned expression checking Ben was deadly serious. "How is that possible?"

"I don't know," said Ben, his pace quickening. "But I intend to find out."

As they marched down the corridor, Meg remembered the mystery of the knife during the last spate of murders. All of the victims had been killed with weapons from their own homes. All, that is, except for Inkleman's immediate family. His wife, and eventually his daughter, had both been murdered with the same knife, which, it turned out, was not from the Inkleman household, and its provenance had never been discovered. Now, the knife threw up a new mystery. It had been stolen from police custody and used in the first two murders. Would it finally turn up again with the death of Sean Edwards' daughter?

"The audit from the lock-up," Meg asked, "Have we got it yet?"

"We're still working on a list of those who've had access, but for now, there's nothing else unaccounted for other than the items used by Inkleman."

"We have to find out who took that knife," Meg said.

"I told you. We have a leak. Someone with access to the evidence and case files. Someone who could benefit from making us look like fools."

"You think it's Morton, don't you?"

"I have my suspicions, you know I do. Someone's gunning for me and it pisses me off to think that you could be dragged down with me in this."

In her two-inch heels, Meg struggled to keep up with Ben's pace as they passed through the fire-doors and continued down another corridor. "There's more to it than that, isn't there?"

"I've seen how he looks at you," Ben answered. "He likes you. He likes you a lot."

Meg normally wore flat shoes for work, but for the sake of appearance in a meeting with superiors, she had slipped on something less comfortable. Now, losing patience with them, she broke stride to whip them off, and in bare feet, caught up to Ben again. "That's stupid, Ben. If he likes me as much as you seem to think, then why would he undermine me?"

"Who knows. Maybe to get you demoted. Maybe to get you on a level playing field and make you more approachable."

With a shake of her head and a roll of her eyes, she dismissed his reasoning, "We haven't got time for this. *Morton* hasn't got time for this. It's all in your head."

She was right, thought Ben. For now, it *was* all in his head. But he was more determined than ever to prove that Morton had more than the dubious interests of the case at heart, and that, in her naivety, Meg had failed to spot the obvious. Morton was besotted with her. And to Ben's annoyance, he had nothing to tell her other than the jealous suspicions of a man in love himself, desperate to tell her how he felt. How he had *always* felt. How he had never stopped loving her since the night he'd returned home to a full blown argument, and her bags already packed, she had left him. Alone. To spend the whole of the following week locked away in his home. No-one to console him as he poured over their torturing display of photographs, mementos, and romantic little love-notes. All from the only woman whose trinkets he'd ever actually kept. Every day, pouring over his collection and hanging around his telephone, trying to call her from the moment he woke till the moment he fell asleep. His calls going unanswered, and in his despair, his soul broken apart a little more with each passing night after lonely night, until, through time, he had learned to merely exist through one eternal day after another.

I can't go through that again, he thought. If she does develop an interest in Morton, then so be it. Difficult as it would be, he would learn to live with it. Learn to get on with his life. And with a little luck, maybe she would do him a favour and wreck Morton's life too.

But it wasn't as simple as that. And as they carried on walking down the corridor, he asked himself who he was trying to kid. The thought of Meg with another man would drive him crazy. And if that man were Morton, then God only knows how he would cope with it. His sense of loss dredged up again. The lesson of its pain learned last year when he and Meg had split up, and soon after, that lesson amplified with the death of his mother.

Yes. Ben now knew better than most just how much the loss of a loved one could hurt a man. He had felt it first hand. And he had seen what it had done to his father. Torn down, like a building reduced to rubble. Ben unable to ease his suffering as he looked on, swearing never to leave himself open to that much hurt ever again.

Easier to bear the pain of being alone through choice, he had thought, than to be alone through loss.

Another set of fire-doors, they were almost at the other end of the complex when Ben said, "We got word from Sean Edwards' bank. Everything run-of the-mill until a few days ago. Then the day before he killed his wife, he withdrew £1,951."

Meg was both surprised and puzzled by the amount, having seen Edwards's home, his car, and his lifestyle, "That's all he had?"

"On the contrary. He's a very wealthy man. His account's bursting at the seams, and all of it legitimate."

"So why such a specific amount?" she asked, "It doesn't make sense. Doesn't that strike you as odd?"

"And his plastic," Ben added. "All cut up and accounted for. His cards were found in a bullet-bin in his kitchen."

"So why are we going to forensics?" she asked.

"It's the clue from the second crime scene. You were right. It was in the victim's stomach all along. It's a coin of some sort. We'll know more when we get down there."

"Did Inkleman do anything like this?" Meg asked.

"Not as far as we know. But then, this isn't Inkleman."

Ben punched the code into the door-lock and they entered a small sealed room with a window to the adjoining forensics lab where Meg could see a man in his mid forties with grey-black hair examining a small metal disc and flicking through the pages of a book. The Encyclopaedia of Coins snapped shut as he sensed their presence and came to join them.

"You've met detective Bolden," Ben said, realising they hadn't been properly introduced when at the gravesite.

"Please. Call me Chris," he said unsmiling, the seriousness of his work dispelling any further pleasantries. "I believe this is what yer were looking for, detective." He passed her the coin, and as she turned it through her fingers, he added, "It's from Denmark. And as yer can see, it's dated 1958."

"Is that all you can tell me?" she asked.

"There's not much else to tell, other than it's a 2 Kroner coin issued to commemorate the declaration of princess Margrethe as heir to the throne. It has her portrait on one side, and her father, King Frederick IX on the other. That's pretty much it I'm afraid."

"He was right," Meg blurted out suddenly. "Schmidt. He's next."

Something in his name and the way he spoke had made her assume Schmidt was German, but then, from what she knew of other languages, he could just as easily be Danish, Dutch, or any other neighbouring nationality for that matter, and still she'd be none the wiser.

Just a short while later, in another part of headquarters, Ben and Meg sat with Schmidt to confirm his nationality, and then explained his plight and the reasoning behind their suspicions.

"You can protect me, yes?"

"You're safe here, doctor," Meg said reassuringly, though uncertain if that were true.

"I don't understand. I'm his doctor. His confidant. Why would he vant to kill me?"

"We think you're a target because he feels betrayed by you, or let down, or maybe because he knows you're helping us."

"Is it possible that you are wrong?"

"Anything is possible, doctor," said Meg. "When it comes down to how his mind works, you're the expert here, not us. So please, if we are off the mark here, steer us right. We need all the help you can give us."

Schmidt looked across to Ben taking notes, then back to Meg, "You have a good hypothesis, I think. Time spent with forensic profilers no doubt. But Mr. Edwards is an intelligent man. He vill not do vat you expect of him. I fear my life is already at an end."

"Have faith, doctor. We can protect you. But we need your help on this. As you're already aware, Sean Edwards has a daughter. We need to find her. In doing so, we may have a chance of finding *him.* Is there anything you can tell us to help us locate her whereabouts?"

"I'm afraid not," Schmidt answered bowing his head.

"No hidden retreat? No place he goes to get away from it all? A favourite hotel maybe, or a caravan by the coast?"

"No. I am sorry. I do not know of these things."

"The morning you discovered the message from Mr. Edwards on your answering machine, did you attempt to call him?"

"Yes. Shortly before I called you. On numerous occasions. But in each case I vas unable to get in touch. It seems his phone is alvays switched off."

"Not always," said Meg. "We have a window. Or should I say;- we *had* a window. His phone was switched on four times a day, and each time for only thirty seconds. We had thought of putting a block on it, but it was our only way to keep in touch with him. If we had cut him off, he may have stopped contacting us altogether."

"Vat do you mean by 'had' a window, detective? Doesn't he switch on his phone anymore?"

"He swapped it for another," Meg answered. "We'll have his new number soon enough, and when we do, we're hoping we can still keep tabs on him. But most importantly, we'd like you to ring him for us. That is, if you feel there's anything you can say to persuade him to give himself up?"

"If you are correct, and I am indeed his next target, then it is unlikely he vill be villing to listen to me. But I vill help you vherever I can, detective. I assume you have tried calling him yourselves during these times?"

"We have. Several times. But he won't answer our calls. We're hoping he'll recognise your number and pick up. Though I'd prefer it if you didn't speak to him without our being present."

"Of course not, detective. You have my vord."

"There's one more thing. Another request. If you're able, we'd also like you to assist us in the incident room. Especially during the 10:15 calls."

"Indeed, indeed. I vould be only too glad to help. Tell me. The times you say he has his phone switched on, are these at any specific times of the day?"

"Yes," Ben jumped in. "An hour either side of 10:15, both morning and night."

"Uhmm, curious," said Schmidt.

"What do you make of it?" Meg asked.

"9:15 and 11:15, morning and night you say. Does he make any calls during these times?"

"Occasionally, yes. To another mobile phone. Also registered under his name. But the majority of the time, he *receives* the calls rather than makes them."

Meg wondered how best to divulge what they knew. How could she expect Schmidt to trust them with his safety if he knew of their suspicions that there was a rogue cop in the camp. It was time to bend the truth a little. "We now believe that he only has one of those phones and his accomplice has the other."

"Accomplice, you say?"

"We think that he may be romantically involved with another woman. That he killed his wife out of passion and tried to blame it on a copycat. But it all went wrong. And now he's cracked and continuing with the charade. We also think that the accomplice may be the one holding his daughter."

"He hasn't 'cracked', detective. He has M.P.D."

Meg had heard of the term before. Multiple Personality Disorder.

Schmidt continued, "Or, as you may like to refer to it, a split personality. And to take it to the extreme, it is possible that each of those personalities has a phone of his own. Though unlikely I might add.” His fingers on his lips, his eyes drifting away in thought, he added, “It pains me to say this, but I suspect you may be correct about there being somevon else involved. Though my guess vould be that it is most probably another man rather than a mistress. After all, it is not unheard of for killers to hunt in pairs.”

Ben and Meg looked at one-another, Ben thinking of Morton, and Meg reading his mind.

“I think it a good idea not to put a block on his phone,” said Schmidt. “Though highly unlikely, it is possible that Mr. Edwards vill try to contact me again to ask for my help. I may even receive a call from his alter ego, threatening me. Either vay, this may be of help to you. Maybe you can do that bugging thing you people do, or you might like to record my calls. Or maybe there is something in particular you vould like me to say to him.”

“Thank you, doctor,” said Meg “Your assistance is much appreciated.”

“Not at all,” said Schmidt. “That is vhy I called you in the first place. I felt it my duty. To the public, *and* my patient.”

Ben grew angry, his voice raised, “Screw your patient, doctor. There are people dying out there, at the hands of your so-called patient. And in case it’s escaped your attention, allow me to remind you, we think *you’re* next. So *please*,” Ben stressed, “Don’t go anywhere without our say so.”

Twenty Eight

Sean lay awake, his eyes still closed as he bathed in his own self awareness, listening to the whisper of his breathing. Appreciative of the soft cotton caress of the plumped up pillow against the skin of his cheek and his arm resting across Amy as she lay at his side. It was the best he'd slept in ages. No dreams or nightmares to wake him through the night. No sweat-laden panic attacks brought on by his nightly lashings out. A feeling of serenity and comfort in his surroundings, refreshed as he lay near the edge of the bed, the sensation of slightly cooler air feathering his skin where the quilt failed to cover his back.

He shuffled a little closer to Amy and dragged the quilt up to his neck, basking in his contentment before the neurons of his brain fired on all cylinders and electric pulses shot through to his senses.

'''Amy was dead.'''

The woman sharing his bed was a stranger, still asleep and a little cold. And as the mattress squelched beneath him, his eyes flashed open to find himself staring into her open eyes, her empty gaze staring back at him.

"Ahhhhhh!"

He fell from the bed, screaming out in horror. His legs tangled in the sheets as he scuttled backwards across the floor to sit with his back pressed hard against the wall, his arms out to his sides like rigid props to support his weight. His hands flat to the floor to prevent them from buckling beneath him as he looked up to the bed, eyes wide with terror. His gaze fixed firmly on bloody stumps and blood-spattered thighs;- arms hacked off at the elbows and once slender legs now ending at the knees. The blood still glistening wet where the missing limbs had been ripped from their sockets, leaving a mass of raw flesh hanging like meat from the protruding bone.

For a moment, everything blurred, a huge lump welling within his throat and his stomach tightening before he almost choked on his own vomit, retching till there was nothing more to spew. His stomach pulling on empty and his nose running like water, his vision blurred with tears of exertion as he turned onto all fours to be sick once again, the colour draining from his face and a string of saliva drooling from his mouth to the floor as he fought to regain control.

He had never seen a corpse before.

Not like this.

A relative in a funeral parlour once, made to look like he was asleep, but *this* was different, the scene terrifying. And in the horror of it all, he knew that *he'd* been the one to murder her. His third victim in three days. The first time he'd witnessed the horrifying truth of what he'd done, and he was smacked with an urgency to put an end to it all.

He made to stand up, his body shaking, fighting for control of his senses and the movement of his limbs, his hand clumsily grasping for the handle of a nearby wardrobe as he struggled to steady himself. Rising to his feet. The sheet still tangled around his ankles, trailing blood across the floor and back to the bed, his feet lashing out at it as he fought to escape its grip. His face twisted in revulsion as it flailed about his legs, tying him in knots and forcing him to stumble on something beneath, his eyes drawn to the severed limbs laid out on the floor in the shape of a cross;- stump to stump, leg to leg, and arm to arm. An intermingling mesh of flesh causing him to retch again as he staggered to the bathroom, turned on the shower and ran his head under the cold gush of water.

11:09a.m.

Still dripping wet, Sean sat on the edge of the bath away from the horrors of the other room, the cable of the telephone pulled tight as it stretched from the adjoining bloodbath, his finger wavering over the last number before he pressed the button and committed himself to calling the police.

Eventually, he was put through to Meg, his voice trembling, his words spluttered out in quick succession. Panicking and flustered. "There's been another murder. I… I've killed her."

"Calm down Mr. Edwards. Take it slowly."

"Please. Help me," Sean pleaded. "I don't want to do this."

"Do what, Sean? Where are you? What have you done?"

"She's dead," he cried.

"Who's dead, Sean? Tell me. Tell me where you are so I can help."

Sean tried to think of a way out of his mess. "I want us to make a deal," he said. "I want us to come to some arrangement."

"I don't know if I can do that," said Meg, trying to sound sympathetic.

"I need your help," he cried. "My daughter needs your help. Tell me we can make a deal, and together, we can save her."

"I want to help you, Sean. Really I do. Your daughter's life is very important to us. But we have to put an end to this, Sean. You *have* to turn yourself in."

"That's not an option," he said. "If I'm caught she dies."

"Not if you hand yourself in," Meg repeated.

"You don't understand. None of you understand. It's not my fault. It's the time-lapses. I can't give myself up. I can't let you catch him. Catch ***me*** I mean. If he's caught he'll let her die, and there's nothing I can do to stop him."

"You and the killer, you're one and the same," said Meg. "And if we don't have you in custody, then there's every chance you will take her life."

"Fuck me! Don't you think I already know that! Why do you think I'm calling. The only way to save her is to follow him. To follow ***me*** I mean. To find out where he's hiding and follow him to my baby."

"And where *are* you hiding her, Sean?"

"How many more times do I have to tell you. I don't know for Christ's sake. If I did I'd tell you."

"How can I be sure you're telling the truth? How can you convince me you're in the right frame of mind right now, and that you're talking as a father, not a killer."

"Don't mess me around, detective. Don't mess with my head. I'm asking for your help, but I'm prepared to work alone. Whatever it takes to save my baby."

No price too high to save his daughter, Sean had already contemplated suicide. How could he kill Abby if he killed himself first? But self sacrifice was an option unavailable to him. His alter-ego would have hidden her somewhere safe. In a place no-one could find her. Not even the police. He had to make them aware of that.

"If you catch me she dies," he said to Meg. "And if ***I*** die, Abby will be lost forever. We have only one choice."

"I'm listening."

"We make a deal and I'll do whatever I can to help you keep track of me, but there's a catch." He paused before continuing, anticipating a negative response. "Whatever happens, you mustn't try to stop me."

"You know I can't agree to that."

"I'm not asking you to allow me to kill people. Just allow me to go free. If not, then I'll have to do this alone."

The pause too long, he was at the point of hanging up. "Well, if that's your answer."

"No. Wait!" Meg shouted, her mind racing through the alternatives. "Tell me. What's your plan?"

"You have to follow me," he answered. "You have to track my every movement and follow me to my daughter. With any luck I'll lead you to her before anyone else is killed."

"If such a situation arises, Sean, I have to intervene. I can not allow you to kill anyone else."

"I understand that, detective. All I'm asking is that you make allowances. But then, I'm sure you can understand that I must do everything I can to save my daughter."

"So tell me," said Meg, "Where are you?"

"First. There's something I need to ask you."

"What is it?"

"Do you believe that someone like me could commit such atrocities. Without the time-lapses I mean."

"It doesn't matter what I believe," said Meg. "What matters is that I do my job. No presumptions, no regrets, and if possible, no mistakes."

"To serve and protect," said Sean. "That's your job, right? To protect her. I want you to promise me you'll do your best to save her from me."

"I'll do everything I can, Sean. I give you my word."

"I know you will," he said, his voice saddened with doubt. "But please, watch your back. There's no-one else I can trust."

Sean flicked through the victim's purse and read out the address.

"You'll wait there for us, Sean… won't you? You'll be there when we arrive?"

"No," he said dolefully. "I won't."

"I thought you wanted to save your daughter, Sean. I thought you trusted me."

"I do, detective. Believe me I do. I'm putting every ounce of my faith in you."

“Then why won’t you wait?” she asked.

“You’ll know when you get here, detective. In the meantime, keep your friends close and your enemies closer. And remember;- it’s not always easy to distinguish between the two.”

Twenty Nine

"He gave me an address," Meg said, hanging up the phone. "I think it's kosher."

"Don't count on it," said Ben.

"I don't count on anything, or *anyone* for that matter. But I think he's counting on us. He asked for my help."

"Yeah, well, let's not disappoint. *I'll* give it to him, from the end of a barrel given half a chance."

"And what good would that do?"

"It would make me feel a whole lot better for a start," Ben answered.

"Maybe it would. But we'd be a lot less likely to find out who else is involved in all of this. And besides, I think he's being straight with us."

"You *think* whatever you want," said Ben. "The simple fact is;- I don't trust him. He's done nothing but throw us off track with delaying tactics and false trails since this thing began, so who's to say this is any different."

Against her better judgement, Meg had raised her hopes that the nightmare would soon be over, and though she hated to admit it; Ben was probably right. The hair and blood on the girl's bed had been her mother's, the illusion amplified with the dog's blood on the spade and the coat in the grave. All eating into their valuable time. And now, knowing where the body was so soon after death, she had to consider the possibility of it being another trick. Another kick in the teeth. *Three dead in three days*. Maybe more were to follow. Maybe the deceptions would continue. Until she had Sean Edwards in cuffs, she could take no chances.

"Anything he gives us is too little too late," Ben continued.

"That doesn't alter the fact that we have to find him. Not just for the sake of the girl, but before he gets to anyone else he may have in his sights."

She knew that Ben wasn't trying to be difficult. He was merely looking out for her, aware that she'd made waves amongst the hierarchy to be given this chance, and her superiors were watching her, waiting for her to slip up. Nevertheless, she hoped Ben was wrong about Edwards and that she had finally made a breakthrough. That the killings would stop and an arrest was imminent. But to achieve this, her interaction with Edwards could be pivotal, and the longer it dragged out, the more her career hung in the balance.

She thought back to the first time she had spoken to Edwards, his call short and to the point. He had wanted to speak with his wife. He had wanted to know what had happened and how she was, and his call had ended with his realisation of her death.

But this last time had been different.

Meg had spoken with a man desperate to save his daughter. A loving father mourning his murdered wife and the death of another victim. He was frightened and confused, reaching out for help from someone not prepared to give it, and only when he had threatened to go it alone, only then did she buckle to his requests. A distraught father, pleading for help to find his daughter, she had found herself feeling sorry for him, and cursing herself for being so weak. Cursing herself more so… once she got to the apartment.

Another woman dead. Another child deprived of his mother.

Working long days in a factory, and as an escort by night, Rachel Earnshaw had been working every hour she could to pay for her autistic son to have specialised treatment in an overseas clinic, and she only ever worked during the three month stints that he was away. Only, this time, she would not be there for his return.

Meg stood on the balcony of the apartment composing herself, her hand shielding her eyes from the sun as it broke through the dispersing clouds. She had been wrong earlier and hated herself for it. She had allowed her concerns to waiver on the side of Sean Edwards for a moment, imagining how she herself would feel if she were in his position, his wife dead and his daughter missing, with no memory of what he had done.

But on entering the apartment, Meg's empathy shrivelled like a poisoned weed as she was forced to face up to the reality that Sean Edwards was sick in the head, his degenerate acts of cruelty turning her stomach; his dismembered victim suffering the cruellest of tortures before dying at his butchering hands. The carnage forcing Meg to realise she'd made the mistake of forgetting her contempt for this cold and callous killer. That mistake rectified with the discovery of Rachel's body and knowing that her four year old would end up in care, her thoughts had turned, not just to the victims of Sean Edwards, but also to the families of those victims suffering their irreplaceable loss, the affect on their lives with them always. And because of it, any pity she had once felt for Sean Edwards was now long gone, along with all thoughts of helping him. She guessed he'd expected as much. Guessed that this would have been the real reason he'd decided not to wait for her at the apartment. And so, again, he was on the run, searching for his daughter and his next intended victim. No-one to help him. All out to stop him. And Meg with a murderer to catch, determined that nothing would get in her way.

She looked down to the busy road below, thinking, one way or another, it would be all over within a week. But at what cost?

She turned to the sound of Ben coming through the French doors to join her on the balcony. "It's not your fault," he said.

"I know it isn't," she answered. "But I can't help feeling I could have done more."

She turned away from him, avoiding his eye-contact for fear he would see the guilt eating away at her soul. "We were close, Ben," she said, looking down at the traffic and wondering if Edwards was down there, stuck amongst the slow-moving vehicles as drivers eased on their brakes to stare with curiosity at the heavy police presence, the road into the development sealed off. Officers knocking on doors and radio frequencies crackling over one another with the comings and goings of information. "He's on the move," she said. "Chester. The hotel at Washington. And now here."

"That could work in our favour," said Ben. "More districts, more back up."

Meg turned to him, "I need a drink, Ben. You're buying."

His eyes traced her features. Her exquisitely formed lips, her delicate little nose, and the sad expression of her eyes. It was an invitation he was glad to accept and he hoped he was reading her correctly. Hoped she wanted to be around him just as he wanted to be around her. Hoped she wasn't just using him as a distraction from her feelings of guilt. But how could he tell her that he loved her? The timing was all wrong. The setting inappropriate. And worst of all;- how would he deal with the hurt if she said the feeling wasn't mutual?

He plucked up his courage and decided to give it a shot. "Did you... erm. Did you notice there wasn't a rose?" he said, disgusted at his own cowardice.

"I figured it was because she wasn't the intended target," said Meg. "He's keeping it for Schmidt."

"Yes, well, I... I'll go get the car. Meet you around front in two minutes."

*   *   *

Meg smiled as she watched Ben tuck into his chicken kiev.

"What?" he asked, looking up from his plate.

"You're doing it," she said.

"Doing what?"

"That humming thing," she answered.

Meg had always insisted on dating guys who ate with their mouths closed and it was a category she was pleased Ben had fallen into, sort of. Problem was, Ben had a category all his own. An annoying little habit that emerged only around people he was comfortable with, and it wasn't until a few months into their relationship that she had discovered his propensity. At first, she had found it funny. Then it had bugged the life out of her. And then she found it just plain embarrassing. Like a cat purring with contentment, only, instead of purring, he had this scarcely audible hum as he ate. A mildly infuriating drone she had eventually gotten used to, and now, to her surprise, its familiarity made her smile.

"I like to see you smile," Ben said, thinking how nice it was to see a glimpse of the old Meg. It was something she hadn't done much of lately. Even with the pressures of the case and the extra responsibility she had taken on, he thought she'd seemed more tense than he'd remembered. "It's just occurred to me," he continued, "During our whole time together, before we broke up, there's something I never asked you."

"And what might that be?" she asked.

"Though I hate to admit it," he said, a wry smile forming at the corner of his mouth, "you're an intelligent woman. So, of all the professions you could have chosen, why did you choose to become a cop?"

"It was more like the profession chose me," she answered. "I was studying psychology. I wanted to be a psychiatrist."

"Like Schmidt?"

"I s'pose," Meg reflected. "Then, during study, we covered criminal psychology, and at first I found it intriguing. Then the Jill Dando murder happened and I took a particular interest in the case. I remember thinking about how someone so nice, so harmless, could be killed in such a way."

"And you wanted to do something about it," Ben said assumingly.

"It made me wonder," she continued, "How safe was I in a world where the mentally ill were locked in hospitals, and the *'real'* crazies were out there roaming the streets to unleash their psychopathic tendencies on an unsuspecting public. I thought I would feel a whole lot safer in myself if I were the one chasing after them rather than the other way around."

Ben nodded his agreement.

"And what about you?" she asked.

"Ah, you know boys. Or at least;- boys from my days as a child. Nowadays it's all computer games and ipods, but when I was a kid, if you weren't playing football, it was 'cowboys and Indians' or 'cops and robbers'."

"And you were a cop were you?"

"And proud of it," he said smiling. "I was small for my age, but I was the only one with a sheriff's badge. It made me feel '*important*' if you know what I mean. Like I was a somebody. Anyway, it just seemed like a natural progression from there. I watched all the cop shows. The re-runs of Hawaii-five-o, Kojak, Starsky and Hutch, The Sweeny, Magnum, Van Der Valk-"

"Okay, okay," she laughed, "I get the message. You were addicted."

"You might say," he laughed. "But my favourite was Columbo."

"That explains a lot," she said, her grin broadening.

"What do you mean?" he asked, half expecting a leg pulling about what he was wearing as she looked him up and down.

"Just kidding," she answered. "You're dressed okay, but..., never mind."

"Never mind what?"

Her glance shifted to the top of his head with a smile, "Looks to me like you're getting the first signs of a sunroof up there." She laughed as his hand shot to his hair. "Showing signs of a merging Telly Sevalas," she continued, laughing as he checked himself out in the reflection of his cutlery.

"How come we've never spoke about things like this before?" he asked.

"Because you had more hair back then," she smirked.

"No, seriously. Why didn't we ever really talk about *us*?"

Meg shrugged.

"We used to talk about finding a project together," said Ben. "We used to talk about finding a bigger home or doing a church conversion like the one in Lumley."

"Come off it, Ben. That was all your idea. Lets face it, we never really talked much about anything. What we had was more a relationship of sex and convenience than love and allegiance."

"Oh." Ben slumped, his smile deserting him. "I'd always thought there was more to it than that."

Meg did too, but she didn't want him to know that. She was testing the water to see how he'd react, and with his slip into silence, she changed the subject. "I'm gonna have Schmidt present during the call tonight. See what he can offer."

Ben emerged from his thoughts of what Meg had said about their relationship and tried to hide his disappointment. "You want him to talk to Edwards?"

"No. That's your job. I want him to help us get as much information as possible out of him. Help you to ask the right questions."

"Don't you think I'm capable of conducting an interrogation?"

"This isn't about your capabilities, Ben. It's about getting answers. Schmidt knows him better than anyone. We have to take advantage of that."

Ben shifted in his seat, and after washing down the last of his food with a sip of coke, dabbed a serviette to the corners of his mouth, saying, "One of the best bar meals around here, don't you agree?"

She could neither confirm nor deny his appraisal, having had only a small sandwich herself. "It was nice," she said as she took in her surroundings, her mind preoccupied by the events of three nights ago. It wasn't the food and drink that had brought her here; it was the place. "Let's kill two birds with one stone," she had said in the car. "I want to see where Sean Edwards took his wife the night before she was murdered."

They had pulled into the car park of the Church Mouse and entered through its rustic porch, it's roof trailing with ivy and colourful foliage, and first things first, Ben had spoken to the middle aged woman behind the bar and learned where Edwards and his wife had been sitting.

"What did you think of them?" Ben had asked.

"They seemed like a nice couple," the barmaid answered, adding studiously, "Happy."

"Did you notice anything out of the ordinary?"

"No. They just seemed… nice. Like regular people."

"Who served them their meals?"

"That would be David."

"David?"

"David Hetherington. Nice lad. Quiet. Studying to be a doctor. Works here part time to make ends meet." She looked over to where the Edwards had sat. "That's one of his tables."

"And where do I get hold of this… David?"

The woman had checked through a note book and wrote down an address and contact number which Ben put in his pocket before he and Meg sat in the pleasant pub-come-restaurant, soaking up the atmosphere. Sitting where Sean and Amy Edwards had sat during their last night of normality. A small table close to the large open fireplace with bare stone walls and a cosy kind of ambience, the twisted bespoke wooden struts and matching gnarled beams across the low ceiling adding to the character of the place.

Some thirty minutes later they still sat there, more for the benefit of hindsight, discussing Sean Edwards' frame of mind and whether Amy had been brought here by a doting husband or a devious killer in his guise. A modern day Jekyll and Hyde.

Ben pushed his empty plate to one side and put his glass of coke in its place. "There are things here that don't make sense," he said.

Meg agreed, trying to figure it out. "Sometimes organised, sometimes not," she said, "But it's the inconsistencies I don't understand. Like the lack of a rose on Rachel Earnshaw's body, and yet, like Inkleman, Edwards killed his third victim with her own kitchen knife and left it at the crime scene."

"And the missing evidence," said Ben. "Why take the ribbon, and what makes it different to any other yellow ribbon he could buy over a counter?"

"One thing's for sure. He's not recycling for the sake of it. These items have some meaning to him, and someone at the station made sure that Edwards got the chance to use them again in his re-enactments of the original crimes."

"The knife to kill his victims," said Ben. "The gun to kill himself."

"And the same ribbon to bind his daughter," Meg said studiously. "The m.o. is almost exactly the same. Edwards wasn't suffering from parasomnia when he killed his wife. I doubt he ever was. It was a ruse. He had to have planned this months ago. He had to have planned *all* of it."

"Or our guy on the inside did," said Ben.

Ben requested the bill, and as it was placed in front of them, they both reached for it at the same time, their hands touching, and a frozen pause with the contact of their skin. Meg looked down at his hand as she felt a connection pass between them, their bodies fused and his fingers lightly stroking the back of her hand before she looked into his eyes, about to say something. The moment snatched away with the bleep of her phone and the quick withdrawal of her hand.

"I'll get this," he said, looking at the bill.

"No," she said, an urgency filtering into her voice as she checked her message. "I'll get my own."

She took some money from her purse and placed it next to the bill as she stood up, her chair falling to the floor and her discomfort evident in her voice as she hurriedly picked it up. "I have to go," she said, searching for an excuse to leave. "There's something I need to do."

Ben rose to his feet with the intention of giving her a lift.

"Please, Ben, no," she said, her hand gesturing for him to stay in his seat. "I'll find my own way. I need to be alone. I need some time to think." And sounding unnerved, she hurried toward the exit with her phone pressed to her ear.

Five minutes later, Ben stood from his seat and checked the address on the paper he'd gotten from the barmaid.

She happened to look over as he read it.

"I don't know what good that'll do you," she said. "But if you see him, tell him to get in touch, will you. He didn't show up for work last night, and when I tried to ring him earlier I couldn't get an answer."

"He didn't show for work?"

"That's right. It's not like him. He's normally so reliable. I tried to ring him earlier to see if he was intending coming in tonight in case I need to arrange cover for his shift."

Ben slipped the paper in his pocket and made for the door, the barmaid's voice trailing after him, "Tell him he can't go dropping shifts without.."

Thirty

Thomas sat halfway up the stairs, his blonde, almost white basin-cut hair making him stand out sharply as he peered at the guest through the spindles of the banister.

"Thomas. Come down from there," his father said impatiently. "And bring your toys with you."

"But dad."

"No 'buts' Thomas. You're not to play on the stairs."

Thomas gathered up his aeroplane and action-figures and trundled down the stairs to join his father behind the reception desk, climbing onto his vacant stool and peering shyly from behind him as his father smiled his 'guest smile'.

"It will be £80 per night sir, including breakfast, towels, and a daily change of bed-linen."

"That's fine," the guest said, trying to disguise his apprehension as the proprietor turned the checking-in book to read his name.

"Do you mind if I ask how long you will be staying Mr… Waders?"

"Three, maybe four days I guess." Sean flicked his wallet open and paid for the room in advance, a fourth day onwards to be decided later.

"Thank you, sir. Your room's up the stairs, second on the left. Breakfast is between eight and ten in the dining area, and if there's anything you need, just-"

Thomas had watched the man count out £240 then tugged on his father's shirt, "Daddy. Can we go get an Aston Martin now?"

"Excuse me a moment," said the proprietor, before turning on the boy. "Thomas! How many more times must I tell you;- Don't interrupt me when I'm busy with a guest."

Thomas looked up at his father's pointing finger, puppy-eyed, his bottom lip showing the first signs of quivering as his father rattled on, "I've told you before; it's *rude*. You know the rule. If you can't hold your tongue, you can't have your fun."

Sean stood convincing himself to keep out of it but couldn't help himself, and masking his feelings behind friendly conversation, he interrupted the admonishment with a clearing of his throat. "Ahum… An Aston Martin did you say?"

"Yeah," said the disinterested father. "One-eighteenth scale. This week, he's going through a 'James Bond' phase. Who knows what it'll be next week."

His back half-turned to his father, Thomas focused his attention on his aeroplane, spinning the propellers with his finger before turning to the sound of Sean's voice, "You ever been on a *real* aeroplane, Thomas?"

Rocking himself side to side, Thomas replied, "Daddy says I went on an aeroplane to Spain once, when I was little, but I can't remember it because I'm big now."

"Yes, you are," Sean laughed. "And how old would such a big boy be?"

"I'm almost seven-and-a-half," Thomas answered.

Sean smiled, "I've got a daughter aged seven. Not quite as big as you though."

"I'm older," Thomas boasted, "And I don't like girls. They wear *dresses*."

"Great kid," Sean said, his smile aimed at the father.

"He has his moments," came the dispassionate reply, the proprietor's hand resting on Thomas's head and acting the proud parent before he added, "but I wouldn't be without him."

The boy's innocent eyes broke into a smile with the show of affection, and reminding Sean of his own daughter, he choked in his response, "Yes. I know exactly what you mean."

Once in his room, Sean threw his bag onto the bed, angry and frustrated, his face reddening as he looked at himself in the upright mirror and a stranger in black stared back at him, convincing him he'd done the right thing. Done what he'd had to.

On his arrival at the B&B, Sean had felt anxious, unsure of how to behave. His normally confident swagger giving way to a slumped, defeatist sort of amble, hoping not to draw attention to himself, shrinking in his demeanour and the way he spoke. Then, with the signing of the book, his anxiety had fallen away with his identity, erased with a stroke of the pen, his thoughts of self-preservation forgotten and his pretence evaporating as his attentions strayed to the boy, an itch to lash out at the father with some of his own angry opinions and show him exactly how it felt to be bullied.

Instead, he had opted for a different tack. His usual way out. The way of distraction and manipulation. The way of '*Winning Without Intimidation*'. The self help book that had helped him earn his riches and guided him through everything bar his illness, had also helped him deal with a man who felt safe and secure in his own little shell of a world, oblivious to the threat that had entered his home. A paying guest, submissive, and normally mild mannered when faced with confrontation, was in control of himself. But then, there was another side to Sean. *Better watch out.*

His thoughts strayed from the boy and his father to his own appearance as he looked at himself in the mirror, everything black, like a burglar awaiting nightfall.

In his attempt to go incognito, he wore a tracksuit, trainers and a thick woollen hat. A total amateur, he thought, removing the dysfunctional spectacles that were the finishing touch to the deception of his new portrait, and peeling off the thick woollen hat to reveal his shaven head, a dark cranial shadow where there was once a thick black mane. His head rough as Velcro, his hand ran over it to scratch at the irritable itch of the razor cuts, and relieved he hadn't been recognised, continued down his face to rub at the choking skin of his stubbled chin.

Earlier, when he had spoken to the police, he had threatened to go it alone, then had second thoughts. He'd returned to Chester-le-Street intent on handing himself in. A police station close to home, he had thought, and hopefully, close to his daughter too, his thoughts dwelling on his chances of saving her as he walked along the footpath just twenty yards from the front of the building where he saw a female officer opening a window for fresh air. Police officers getting in and out of cars by the side of the building. Two constables sitting in a smoking-zone, chatting. And not *one* of them noticing him.

How could he put his trust in them, he had thought. How could he expect them to care the way *he* cared. And with a last minute change of heart, unsure of what to do next, he had walked on by until he'd ambled upon the white-fronted B&B, almost walking right past it. A large converted house with a white cat sat inside the window, a living, breathing ornament, taking in everything around, its eyes alert and its body still. Where better to hide, he had thought, than under their very noses. And so, his nerves fraying, he had entered the B&B, gambling on its proximity to the police station. So close, he had hoped, that the proprietor would be less than suspicious. And the police, well, their attentions were obviously focused in other areas.

This was to be his *safe-house*.

His coming back to Chester-le-Street had been vindicated with the realisation that the police needed *him* as much as he needed *them*, and in his quest to save his daughter he would enlist their help. All be it without their knowledge. He would call them. Follow them. Milk them for information. And one way or another, as they strove to find him, he would find his little girl.

He stood a little taller, his hopes resurrected and his new found confidence giving rise to another idea, another option. Something he had once been taught by his doctor, though up until now, he had not dared contemplate it.

There were dangers involved.

He was unaccomplished and it was risky. And he was scared of dredging up the memories of what he had done to his victims. Most frightening of all, the memories of what he had done to Amy. But to save his daughter, it was a chance he would have to take.

The door locked and the room quiet, he lay on the bed, focusing on his breathing. The rise and fall of his chest… Slow and shallow… In and out, trying to relax as he slowly counted backwards and the tension slipped from his body. And slowly. Quietly, he drifted into a state of self hypnosis, a blurred image becoming clearer, a dream of something real…

His dark hair accentuating his milk-white skin, he was a boy of around nine, skinny and unkempt, his spindly form swamped in baggy clothes as he peered from behind the trunk of a weeping willow tree, his pupils dilated, and the excited focus of his eyes part hidden by the thick black-rimmed spectacles resting precariously on his disjointed nose.

The boy was to become a hunter.

Having spent countless hours watching wildlife documentaries from the confines of his bedroom, he knew that stealth was key. And now, like a hunting wildcat, he had singled out his prey. His target less than ten yards away, oblivious to the adversary lurking close by; staring intently through the small scattered spaces between the leaves and catkins of an overhanging branch.

Everything falling into place; it was time to move in for the kill.

With the back of his hand, he eased a hanging branch to one side, it's furry catkins caressing his brow as he brushed past. His movements smooth and subtle as he inched forward, ever closer, as if replicating a scene from the plains of Africa. Readying himself for the ambush as he closed in on his target to pounce with the element of surprise. A pause as he drew closer. All the time keeping his eyes on his prey as he tightened his belt and rolled up the sleeves of his dirt-white shirt before edging forward. Moving patiently. Slowly. Purposefully. His victim unaware. And his voice a rasping whisper, he began his eerie chant.

"I'm going to caaaaaaatch you."

"I'm going to huuuuuurt you."

"I'm going to kiiiiiiill you."

Thirty One

Sean woke in a sweat to the sound of the room's telephone ringing, thoughts of being caught rushing through his head. He had made a mistake. He had gotten involved in a conversation with the proprietor and told him something personal. Told him he had a daughter, relaxing with the realisation they hadn't recognised him. Let his guard down. And because of it, he now he worried he may have let something else slip too. Something important. Maybe something that would help them recognise him from the newspapers or t.v. Or worse still, maybe the proprietor already knew who he was, and like Sean, was acting as though nothing was wrong.

The telephone stopped ringing, and so close to the police station, Sean worried they could be downstairs right now, readying themselves for an assault.

He stood with his back against the wardrobe, nervously rubbing his hands together, his heart racing as he panicked over what he should do and then *jumped* with the ring of the telephone. Again, his body rigid, his eyes fixed firmly on the phone, waiting for it to stop. But unable to let it go unanswered, he warily picked it up.

"Sorry to disturb you, sir. I hope you don't mind. The boy's on his way up with some flowers for your room. Wants to make himself useful for a change."

Just then, there was a knock at his door, Sean's eyes darting between one side of the room and the other. The door and the window. The proprietor's voice distant in his ear, "Sir?... Sir?"

"Sorry," Sean answered, trying to sound calm, "He's at the door right now. Thank you."

He hung up the phone and looked out of the first-floor window. Too difficult. Too visible. He had to take a chance. And nervously, he opened the door. A sigh of relief at the sight of the boy with his cheeky grin and cocky little walk as he sauntered into the room and put the small vase of flowers on the dressing table next to the window Sean had almost climbed through.

"Mum usually brings the flowers," said Thomas, part embarrassed, part pleased to be doing something less boring than playing on his own.

Sean's shoulders dropped as he relaxed, "And where is your mum?"

"She's taking care of Nan," Thomas answered sadly. "Nan's not well."

"And you're left with your dad, huh?"

"He's not my *real* dad," said Thomas. "I never knew my *real* dad. But he's been my pretendy dad ever since I can remember."

"Funny thing;- memory," said Sean, thinking out loud as the boy looked at him curiously. "Memories are like bubbles, floating through the air," Sean said, wiggling his fingers like a mime artist to illustrate bubbles floating by Thomas's face. "Sometimes… they just float away, way out of reach."

Thomas watched his mimicking hands, transfixed.

"And sometimes they just suddenly go ***'POP'*** the moment you reach for them." Sean smiled and Thomas giggled at the fact that he'd jumped to the sound of the 'POP', finding humour in his own momentary fright.

'You're loopy', Thomas thought to himself, wary of saying such things to an adult. But already, he liked Mr. Waders. He was strange.

As Thomas left the room, he turned back to Sean and aimed an imaginary pistol at him. "Pow. Pow," then scampered off to the end of the hallway before looking back to see Sean smiling, his finger pointed right back at him, "Pow."

As Thomas took another shot at him, Sean reached into his pocket for an imaginary grenade, putting it to his mouth and pretending to pull the pin out with his teeth before throwing it at Thomas and covering his ears to protect them from the imaginary bang.

Thomas giggled, eyes bright and dimples in his cheeks as he took a few steps forward. "Do you want to play soldiers?" he asked.

Sean crouched to sit on the floor in his doorway, bringing himself down to Thomas's level before answering, "I'd rather play spies."

"Me too," Thomas said excitedly and stepping closer to Sean. "Tell me how to play."

"Have you heard of James Bond?" Sean asked, expectantly.

"Of course, silly. Everyone's heard of James Bond double-o-seven."

"Well, how would you like to play the most important spy game ever?"

As if realising he were doing something wrong, Thomas answered woefully, "Mummy says I shouldn't talk to strangers."

"And your mummy's right," said Sean. "Which is great, because it means you already know the first and most important rule of the game."

"I do?" asked Thomas. "But, *you're* a stranger."

"Well, not really. Didn't you hear your father say my name?"

"Yes, well, sort of," Thomas answered, recollecting his father down in reception. "It's Mr. Waiters."

"Waders," Sean corrected. "Mr. **D.** Waders. The D stands for David. But if we're to play the spy-game, you must promise to keep this a secret."

"Oh, I will Mr. Waders, I will, I promise I will."

"Good. Now we know one-another, it's okay for you to play the game. But this is no ordinary game. This is real life. And as a real life spy, you will be paid five *whole* pounds, every.. single.. day. Of course, that is assuming you do want to play."

"Yes, I do. I do want to play."

"Good. Now, first, you have to promise me three things," Sean said, noticing Thomas' cheap, grey-faced digital wrist-watch. "First, you mustn't tell *anyone* about our mission, otherwise, the game will end, and the payments will stop."

"I promise, I promise," said Thomas, his eyes lit up.

"Secondly, no matter how tempted, you mustn't spend any of your earnings until after I have checked out of my room."

"Not even on an Aston Martin?" asked Thomas.

"*Especially* not on an Aston Martin," said Sean. "Not *one* penny is to be spent until the day after I leave."

Thomas didn't like this rule, but replied, "Okay."

"And thirdly, but most important of all, there's the matter of your mission. I want you to spy on me, Thomas. I want you to write down the times you see me leave or return to my room." Sean looked hopefully to Thomas, "You *can* tell the time, can't you?"

Thomas looked at his watch and with an animated nod, held out his wrist so Sean could see the time. "Two-forty-four," he beamed triumphantly as though he had just passed a test. "On my other watch, that's nearly quarter to three."

"Excellent," said Sean, having confirmed that the boy was correct. "Now, remember, no-one must know that you're doing this, and each night, before you go to bed, you are to put a note of those times under my door. Do you understand?"

"Yes." Thomas answered, nodding his head excitedly.

Sean gave a warm smile before continuing, "Tell me, Thomas. Have you heard of the tooth-fairy?"

"Yes, I have. She's sneaky. Just like James Bond. Why? Is *she* a spy too?"

"No, Thomas, she's not. But just like the tooth fairy, we have to be sneaky too. Do you think we can do that?"

"Easy peasy, lemon squeezy," said Thomas, before proudly announcing, "I heard her once. The fairy, I mean. I heard her leaving my room."

"Did she put a silver coin under your pillow in place of your tooth?"

"She used to. When I was little. But now, it's a *whole* pound."

"Wow. That's great," said Sean. "Now. Tell me. Where is your room? And just like the tooth-fairy, I'll leave your money under your pillow."

"It's down past the kitchen. Down the hall, on the left."

"That's good, Thomas. But there's one more thing. Something I forgot to mention. There's a rule. A *special* rule that only you and I will know about. It was created especially for this mission and must be adhered to at all times. Are we understood?"

Thomas nodded, "What is it? What is it?"

"I am now your honorary secret best friend, so you mustn't break this rule. If you do, we can no-longer be friends, and the game will be over."

"I won't break it. I promise I won't."

"This will be the most difficult rule you have ever known, Thomas. And no matter what, you *must* stick to it."

"I will, I will. Tell me what it is."

Sean spoke quietly, building up the tension, "You must never be seen speaking to me, Thomas. No matter what happens. No matter what I may say. You are to stay well away from me, do you understand?"

Thomas nodded furiously.

"We are on a top secret mission and it is vitally important that we are not discovered. If we are, your life could be in great danger," Sean winked, "So tell me Thomas, do you accept the mission."

"Yes, I do," he said excitedly.

"Now, before I can confirm your acceptance into the agency, I have to ask you one more time, what is the *special* rule?"

As Thomas opened his mouth to answer, Sean stopped him short, putting his finger to his lips to remind him of his vow of silence. "This is very important, Thomas. You must get this right if we are to succeed in our mission. You must remember, no matter what, that you can only ever speak to me if I salute, no matter how hard that may be. If you fail to follow this rule, you will not be paid £5, the game will be over, and we will no-longer be friends. Are we agreed?"

Thomas almost spoke before stopping himself, then gave a deeply affirmative nod.

"Good," said Sean, "Now we have to do the secret handshake."

Thirty Two

Ben pulled the notepaper from his pocket and checked the address. Number 27 Horesham flats. He knocked on the door and it half opened to reveal an unshaven young man of about twenty, squinting into the light.

"David Hetherington? Ben asked.

"Who's asking?" the young man asked, half yawning.

Ben showed his I.D. and the door opened a little wider.

"He's not here," said the man.

"And you are?"

"Andrew."

Ben raised an eyebrow in question.

"Andrew Sparks. I'm one of El creepo's flatmates."

Ben mentally noted the reference. "And where *is* Mr. Hetherington?"

"Why? What do you want with him? What's he done?"

"I'll ask the questions if you don't mind," said Ben, stepping forward and imposing himself in the doorway. "I think it's better if we talk about this indoors, don't you?"

Andrew stepped aside and turned to lead the way into the flat, his shoulders slouched, his walk lazy. He wore dirty jeans and a scruffy shirt that hung open, and his hair looked like it had never seen a comb his entire life. "Please yourself," he grunted, "But like I said;- I don't know where he is."

"When did you see him last?"

"A few days ago I guess."

"Is that the norm'?"

"Not exactly. But normal and David don't exactly go together."

"Just the two of you share this place?" Ben asked, walking down the hall with its badly fitted carpet and a poster of some rock-band or other, peeling off the wall.

"Three of us," Andrew grunted.

They entered a poky living room, dark and murky. Clothes scattered everywhere. The curtains drawn against the light of mid afternoon, and the television lighting up a corner of the room.

"This is Mouse," said Andrew, glancing over to his friend.

With his thick mop of curly brown hair, long shorts and a baggy T-shirt, Mouse sat on an old couch, an overflowing ashtray by his side and a cigarette hanging loosely from his lips as he kept his focus on the screen, and joystick in hand, carried on playing his game.

"Do you mind turning that off," Ben said assertively.

Instead, Mouse paused his game and looked at Ben with a degree of boredom.

"When was the last time *you* saw Mr. Hetherington?" Ben asked.

"Like Andy said," Mouse nodded a glance over to his friend, "A few days ago."

Ben's thoughts logged into a list of what he called 'No Hopers' such as these. His 'Be' list. The 'Be' meaning has beens, wannabe's, and never will be's. These two fell into the latter category. Ben stared Mouse square in the eye, goading him into something more definite, "Wednesday? Thursday?"

"Friday I guess."

"Yesterday then? You saw him yesterday. What time?"

"'Bout nine, half past. Something like that."

"*A.M? P.M?*" Ben badgered. "I need to know *exactly*."

"Nine's about right," Andrew butted in. "Yesterday morning. I was getting ready to go and see my girlfriend and Mouse was playing on the Playstation. I remember 'cos he's never normally up that early but it was giro day. He was up waiting for the posty."

Ben's thoughts switched to Cordelia Armstrong and the fact that David Hetherington was last seen just an hour before she was murdered, just as he had been at the Church Mouse before Sean Edwards had murdered his wife.

"Did Mr. Hetherington say where he was going when he left?"

"No," Andrew answered. "He never does. But it's always the same."

"What is?"

Andrew looked uncomfortable. El creepo wasn't exactly his friend but he paid towards the rent. "The skulking around. The secrecy. He thinks I haven't noticed it, but I've seen him trying to hide it."

"Hide what?"

"That fancy camera of his. Not a cheap one either mind. But he hides it, like I'm going to nick it or something. I mean, like, what good is it to me."

"What kind of camera?"

"Don't know. Not really interested to be honest. One of those digital things I think."

"What's he use it for, do you know?"

"No. Like I said;- I'm not interested. A lot of what he does doesn't make sense anyway."

"Like?"

"Well, he's got an old phone that he never uses. And when I say old, I *mean 'old'*. A black and white screen and no gadgets. But like I said, he never uses it."

"He doesn't call anyone?"

"No-one. And he only ever gets calls from The Church Mouse, like, when they change his shifts or something. But he's got that camera, like;- really posh. It's weird. *He's* weird. I could certainly think of better things to spend my money on."

Yes, thought Ben, I bet you could, the smell of happy backy wafting up his nostrils.

"Help me out here," said Ben. "The two of you are sharing a flat with Mr. Hetherington, and yet, I get the distinct impression you don't like him."

"Well, I wouldn't say *that* exactly. It's just that, he's always in his room. He studies a lot I guess."

"So, he's not a friend?"

"He's a bit weird, that's all."

"So why do you share a flat with him?"

"We were thinking of asking him to leave, weren't we Mouse."

Mouse's thoughts were of his game, the picture of a blood-spattered zombie frozen on the screen. He grunted in the affirmative and lit another cigarette.

A complete waste of space, Ben thought, and continued directing his questions at Andrew, "But he pays towards the rent, right?"

"I s'pose."

"Show me his room."

Ben stood outside a plain door, made strange by the fitted clasp. "There was a padlock on this?" he asked.

Andrew looked down at the clasp and shrugged his shoulders, "Doesn't trust us I guess. Don't think he trusts anyone. But the landlord said it was a fire hazard and ordered him to remove it."

Ben opened the door.

"Hey. Don't you need some kinda' warrant to do that?"

"You already invited me onto the premises," Ben answered, looking over to Mouse sucking on his roll-up. "But if you want me to get a warrant and give this place a thorough going over, then I'm sure I can oblige."

Andrew stuttered in his response, "I only asked 'cos I don't want him thinkin' we were in there. Especially if anything goes missin'."

Andrew stood in the doorway as Ben entered the room, surprised to find it so clean and tidy. Much more organised than the rest of the flat. The only extravagance appeared to be an old p.c. at the bottom end of a single bed, and stacked high next to it, was book upon book on human anatomy.

Thirty Three

10:02 p.m.

Ben had been at the station for almost three hours and Meg not much less, yet they'd hardly spoken a word. And even allowing for the busy distractions of the case, there had been long moments of uncomfortable silence between them. But for almost an hour now, he hadn't seen hide-nor-hair of her, and wondered if she was avoiding him altogether.

With less than fifteen minutes to the call, his gaze swept the filling room as more and more officers converged on the incident room from their various departments. Forensics were joined by C.I.D. and S.O.C.O., along with those responsible for house-to-house enquiries and tracing the perp's known associates, each with their own findings to add to the cooking pot. All and more, adding their ingredients to the thick soup of information. And then of course, there was Schmidt. Ben had already explained what he wanted from him. His need to find the girl, but most importantly, his need to track down Edwards and put an end to this never ending bloodshed.

"It vill not be easy," said Schmidt.

"I don't expect it to be easy. But I do expect you to give me your all."

Schmidt could see that Ben was otherwise distracted, something heavy weighing on his mind. "Might I ask, ver is detective Rainer?"

"Busy elsewhere I guess," Ben answered, rummaging through his pockets for a pen.

"Vill she be here for the call?"

Ben looked around the filling incident room, wondering where she'd got to and answering unconvincingly, "She'll be here."

"Does it not cause you problems?" asked Schmidt, "Vorking together."

“Cause problems?” Ben asked, unwillingly being drawn into a conversation he neither instigated nor wanted.

“I mean, you and detective Rainer. Your relationship so to speak.”

“Our *working* relationship, you mean?”

“Your personal relationship,” said Schmidt, pushing the subject.

“Listen, doctor. You’re not here to analyse me, Meg, or any other officer for that matter. Just go through your file and wait for the call. Concentrate your efforts on Edwards, no-one else.”

Schmidt was unable to help himself. Asking questions wasn’t just his job, it was his nature. Always had been. He found people interesting. Their minds. Their habits. Their interpersonal relationships. Sometimes causing him to overstep the mark, just as he had done here. Unwittingly hitting on a sore point whilst intruding into the life of a man suffering an unrequited love, tetchy and not in the mood for conversation. Wisely, he decided to steer clear and sit quietly, waiting to see what he could add to the fold.

Ben turned away from Schmidt to see Morton sitting on a desk with his feet on the seat of a chair. He was handing out A4’s to gathering officers.

“Morton. What you got?”

Reluctantly, Morton came over and passed Ben a copy of the handouts. “It’s the updates from forensics and the latest on the phones. Times of use and so on.”

“And I was going to get these *when*?” Ben asked, his irritable mood showing no sign of let up since he’d arrived this morning.

Morton didn’t bite. Instead, he gave a smirk that clearly annoyed Ben, then turned to pass out the remainder of the handouts amongst the empty desks, thinking to himself, Strike 2, though Ben was still ignorant of the first that was struck against him only a few hours earlier when Meg had almost bumped into Morton as she’d entered through the main entrance, the two of them mirroring one-another as they did the dodge-dance. Morton had made light of the situation by gesturing towards Ben in the corridor as he spoke innocently with a W.P.C.

‘*It seems we’re not the only ones getting up close and personal,*’ Morton had laughed falsely, ‘*Ben’s been laying it on thick and heavy over there for some time now.*’

The look on Meg's face had brought a smile of pure contentment to Morton's as she'd paced down the corridor to the loneliness of her office, walking straight past Ben without a word. *(Strike 1)*

Ben looked through the handouts. The first was a report on a coat found to be missing from Cordelia Armstrong's home. A neighbour had seen her wearing it the morning she had taken Abby to school. Described as a long, wishbone patterned overcoat like that of her granddaughter's, it hadn't been seen since her murder.

The next report was on David Hetherington. Aged twenty-one, he had been studying to be a doctor but had dropped out of university only a couple of months ago. His family lived in Leeds and had been unaware of this until the police had contacted them. He had been missing since Friday morning and thus far, his whereabouts at the time of the murders was unknown.

The remaining reports showed that the various departments of forensics had been exceptionally busy during the past few days, as had everyone else. The evidence of which lay in his hands.

The first sheet was from the forensic botanist and verified little more than they already knew. At present all they could add was that the two roses left at the crime scenes had most likely come from the same bunch, and this they had deduced from the signature of the cut stalks, the nutrients absorbed from the water in which they had been kept, and the rate of deterioration. They were still searching for the supplier in the hope of finding a delivery address, though it was more likely the flowers had been collected at source.

The next report was from the document examiner confirming that the note found in the girl's coat pocket had been written in Sean Edwards's own hand. It went on to mention that there was a firmer pressure of the pen against the paper than samples of his 'normal' writing, and other slight changes would appear to back-up Schmidts diagnosis of multiple personality disorder.

The pathologist's report however, though harder to stomach, was a lot more revealing. Briefly, it explained that, in the case of Amy Edwards, transit suggested she had been forced to swallow her nails approximately two hours before her death, and both she and the third victim had also suffered vaginal injuries. The first being the violent insertion of a light-bulb and the other having been circumcised after death, the labia placed within her mouth. Victim 2 however, had no such injuries, and trace evidence suggested that she may have been killed by someone else using the same modus operandi and the same knife. Either that, or Edwards was in fact, as Morton had suggested;-ambidextrous. But in all, Ben noted the dismemberments stayed true to the poem.

The pathologist went on to explain in great detail how the killer had used a serrated blade to cut through the flesh and peeled it back to gain access to the joint, cutting through the synovial sheath and ligaments then bending and twisting the limbs to cut further into the sinewy tissue, until, eventually, the limbs became separated from the body altogether. In each case, the victim was alive at the start of dismemberment. Curiously, the first two victims had been killed with the same knife which had still not been recovered, whereas, the third victim had been killed with a knife found to be from her own kitchen, and this was left at the scene.

But it was the last sheet that threw up the most intriguing questions.

He read through the analogy of countless calls deemed significant, starting with Edwards attempting to call his wife after she was murdered and followed by his calls to Schmidt and Meg and the '10:15's to the police station. But more importantly, evidence suggested that one of the new phones bought by Edwards (number 07741762063) was in the possession of an unknown subject even before the murders began, and this threw new light onto everything. And with the surrender of Sean Edwards' old phone, it seemed a pattern was emerging. The first indication of which took place this morning when both of the new phones were switched on simultaneously at 10:15 a.m.

Now, reading the last few lines of the report again, everything began to make sense.

Sean Edwards has been contacted by the unknown subject an hour before each murder, but Sean Edwards himself has only ever contacted the unsub twice via the phones monitored, and in each case, the kb output suggests he sent a picture message from the murder scenes of both Amy Edwards and Rachel Earnshaw.

A picture message, Ben thought. Edwards is sending picture messages of the victims to the unsub.

As the pieces clicked together in his mind he now felt he understood what was meant by *'closed their eyes to the killer surprise'*.

That's why we never recovered the photographs taken by Inkleman. There was an accomplice, even back then. Probably the same man who is helping Edwards right now. *He* had the photographs, and that's why Edwards was able to copy the m.o. so fucking accurately.

Only a few more minutes to the call, Ben called Meg to tell her of his discovery. Her phone ringing endlessly as once more, he pondered the possibility of putting a block on the phones. But it was a risk that needed weighing up. In breaking contact between Edwards and the unsub, he would also be severing one of their few remaining advantages;- their ability to monitor the interaction between the perp and his accomplice. And who was to say they hadn't already arranged an alternative route of contact if such a problem arose, in which case, they could cut the police out of the loop altogether.

"Meg Rainer?"

The moment she answered, Ben blurted down the phone, "There have been some developments, Meg. Where are you?"

"Not now, Ben, I'm busy."

"Busy with what? Don't you know what time it is? He'll be calling in less than five minutes."

"Deal with it, Ben. I'll get there when I get there."

"Did you sign off on the handouts?" Ben asked.

"If they're in circulation, then yes, I did. Why?"

"We should have kept this to ourselves, Meg. When the unsub gets wind that we're onto him, it could scare him off before we can I.D. him."

"If he's in here as deep as I think he is, then he'll find out soon enough, no matter what we do. You know what it's like with these things. Info gets shared, whether you want it to be or not. At least, this way, he doesn't know we suspect one of our own. And by the time he does, hopefully, it will be too late for him to do anything about it."

"Why? What have you got?"

"I'm not sure. I'm going through the tapes now. The one from the T Mobile shop was filmed just two days before Edwards killed his wife. It shows nothing out of the ordinary, and when he purchased the phones he was alone, just as he was when he left the Holiday Inn on the night he picked up Rachel Earnshaw. There though, the tape shows him deliberately looking up to the camera. Posing for us. His fingers crossed, like we are vampires or something. And the bastard's smiling at us, Ben. But there's another tape;- more baffling. It was taken on Friday morning from Chester-le-Street train station."

Meg had been over the footage countless times, and on every occasion, she had come to the same dead end.

"So what's on it?" Ben asked, knowing that the station was only five minutes walk from the home of Cordelia Armstrong.

Meg skipped through the images again and relayed her findings to Ben, describing the old station as being not much longer than the length of a single train-carriage, and less than a dozen people stood waiting on the platform.

"He's just sitting there, Ben, on a bench, acting unusual, even by *his* standards. And Ben," her mouth dry, she swallowed before continuing, "he's not alone."

"The accomplice?" Ben asked.

"No, Ben. His daughter."

"*Alive*? What time?"

"That's where it gets stranger. It's 9:50 a.m. Twenty-five minutes before the murder of Cordelia Armstrong. And he's just sitting there, with his daughter. Waiting."

"Waiting for what?"

"Not a train, that's for sure. At least, not for himself. I've watched it over and over again, Ben. And he just sits there, staring out towards the track, with scarcely a word to his daughter. He sits there until 10:28."

"The pathologist," said Ben, "He was right. Someone else killed the old woman. It all makes sense. That's why Edwards didn't send a picture message from the crime scene. The unsub was there to see the body for himself. Because *he* was the one who killed her."

"What?"

Ben's mind was racing through what they now knew had happened that morning after Cordelia Armstrong had dropped Abigail off at school. The teachers doing what teachers do, and closed in from the outside world, they'd be unaware of the newsflash that morning and the impending danger to Abby when her father had arrived to collect her at 9:30 saying there was a family emergency.

"We've got two killers out there, Meg. Working together. Both of them following the same m.o."

As the revelation sank in, Ben interrupted Meg's silence, "The tape, Meg. At the train station. What happens to his daughter? Where does he take her?"

"That's what I'm having trouble with," Meg answered. "He didn't leave with her. He put her on a train and that's the last we see of her. Then he left, without so much as a wave and not once looking back."

10:15 p.m.

With the inevitable ring of the telephone, Sean Edwards' drawling speech rang out over the speakers.

"Fingers and toes... in exchange for my rose."

"Hands and feet... now we're getting to the meat."

"Elbows and knees... I'm their killer disease."

"And the coffins are getting smaller, Ben. Soon, they'll be small enough to fit a child."

"Why are you doing this?" Ben asked. "This can't go on. For Abby's sake, stop this and hand yourself in."

Edwards carried on talking as though Ben hadn't uttered a word. "Lovely girl, Rachel. Attractive. Not my type though. And she did have her 'limb'-itations shall we say."

"What about your daughter, Sean? Are you going to cut her into pieces too?"

"Don't waste your time, Ben. I don't care about the girl. She means nothing to me. None of them mean anything to me."

"Then why did you call?"

"I rang to help you, Ben. As I always do. I rang to tell you where Rachel is."

Schmidt leaned to whisper in Ben's ear, "He needs to feel in control. Take it avay from him. Make him feel like *you* are pulling *his* strings and it is possible he vill make a mistake."

"But we don't need your help," Ben said to Edwards. "We've got officers down there now."

"Pull the other one, Ben. She's a prostitute. People like that aren't missed by the authorities. They are expected to go missing. Who would report her absence? Who would notice? And for that matter, who would care?"

"Her son will care. I care. And better still, Sean;- *you* care.... The *real* you that is. So you see, we already know all there is to know about Rachel. And she told us a lot about you too."

"She didn't tell you *anything*! She's *dead*."

"The dead have a way of speaking to us. And no matter how hard you try, you can't shut them up. So sooner or later, we *are* going to stop you. And when we do, your whole world is going to fall apart."

"*Fuck you,* Miller! I call all the shots. I decide *who* dies. And I decide *when* they die."

Ben remained calm. "Oh. Sorry, I must have made a mistake. I thought it was someone else who made all the decisions. Someone else that killed your mother-in-law. But you see. We know more than you think. You said last night that *you* killed Cordelia Armstrong, but now I know different. So why should I believe you killed Rachel? You didn't even sign your work, Sean. Why is that? Why didn't you leave her a rose? Didn't she deserve one?"

"You're not being very efficient, Ben. I suggest you check her body again."

With a nod from Ben, an officer rang through to the coroner to check it out.

"You think you know me, don't you," Edwards continued. "You think you've got it all worked out. Well… work this out, Ben. I'm going to kill someone close to you. Someone *really* close. And there's not a damned thing you can do to stop me."

Ben bit back, "Don't you believe it, Edwards. I'll stop you. If it's the last thing I ever do. If there is one thing you can count on, it's *that*."

Ben's rant finished with him slamming down the phone, seething and frightened. He wanted Edwards right in front of him, right now. Wanted to hurt him the way *he* had hurt his victims. But most of all, he wanted to make sure that those he loved and cared for were safe from harm.

"I want blues and twos around my dad's house, *now!*" he shouted to a sergeant, his eyes sweeping the room as he thought to himself;- He's toying with us. With me. He's trying to get under my skin. Trying to mislead me. But what if he meant it? Who would he be aiming to kill? My family? A friend? A colleague? *'Someone close'* he'd said, but what kind of close.

"It vould seem that I vas of little use," said Schmidt, interrupting Ben's thoughts.

"On the contrary, doctor," Ben said absent-mindedly, his eyes still wandering the room. "You've been very helpful." Then he saw the door to the incident room swing open and Meg rushing in with a handful of papers, looking frustrated as she crossed to join him.

My god, thought Ben, Was he going to kill Meg?

"Sir.."

"Sir!" The young detective called out louder to grab Ben's attention. "It's the coroner, sir. He's down in the lab. He's just checked the body of Rachel Earnshaw."

"And?"

"He says there was no flower found during the post mortem, sir. But now, there's a yellow rose in her hair."

Thirty Four

Sunday 1st April, 9:08 a.m.

Even with his pills, Sean hadn't slept too well. He'd had another time-lapse last night and had come out of it some time after eleven, wondering if he had killed someone else. Wondering if the police were about to break through his door. And all the time, his thoughts plagued with worries for his little girl, wondering how he was going to find her.

He mulled over what little he knew of what had happened during the last few days, trying to think of how he could find her, but unsure where to begin. He was new to this. He wasn't a policeman. He didn't know the first thing about how to go about tracing a missing person. And to make matters worse, *'HE'* was the likely kidnapper. The only positive in all of this, if it could be construed as a positive, was that the information was buried somewhere inside his head. In an alternate mind. And he'd have to dig deep for it to share its secrets.

He thought of places he had visited throughout his life, picturing old childhood haunts and places he was familiar with. Anywhere a child might be hidden. Like the old farm where he had once played as a boy, with its various barns and out-buildings. Or the skeletal remains of a coal-pit with its sealed shaft, boarded-up offices, and the shell of a garage works. One memory leading to another;- of an old, half-submerged bomb-shelter on the edge of a secluded field high on the hills of Sacriston. And then to the tunnels of Daisy Hill, hidden amongst the dozens of grassy mini-craters that looked like the remnants of a bygone bombing raid. All of these places he would have to check, and except for the still working farm, most of them would be secluded and safe from prying eyes. But to check them, he had to cover a distance of approximately twenty square miles, and this had its risks. The police would be on high alert, and it was likely that all taxi firms were now being monitored, along with the public transport system, and many towns now had c.c.t.v. in built-up areas. His only option was to buy a cheap run-around, either privately, from someone who wouldn't ask too many questions, or from a breakers yard, and hopefully something reliable that wouldn't draw too much attention. He reckoned on spending no more than a thousand pounds, having to keep money back for essentials like fuel, food, and unforeseen circumstances.

The majority of his planning had been done during the night, his head full of ideas on how to go about everything. How to avoid capture. How to find the one person left that made his life worth living. And all of this interspersed with bouts of dozing. His restless sleep disturbed by bloody flashes of harrowing scenes that he prayed were not the recurrence of memories or the forewarning of nightmares to come. His morning tainted with thoughts of what he might do here in the B & B, and who he might kill next, if anyone. He had taken a disliking to the proprietor, but even so, he would not want his death on his hands, and nor would he want to hurt the boy who in ways reminded him of his daughter. His age, his innocence, the colour of his hair. How he imagined himself to have been when he was that age.

I have to get out of here, he thought. I have to stay away as much as possible.

He looked at the clock. The breakers yards would now be open. It was time to pluck up the courage to leave the security of his room. Time to face Joe-public and hope he wouldn't be recognised. Time to face his greatest fear of all in his search for his daughter. The fear of not being able to find her at all, or worse yet, finding her dead. He was sure the police expected as much. He had sensed it in their tone when he had rang for help. They despised him. They thought he had killed his own daughter and disposed of her body. But what if they were correct in their assumptions? What if he *never* found her, and she was trapped somewhere, starving. In a cold dark place, with no-one to help her.

He needed to retrace his steps. Go over old ground. Trigger his memory by referring back to the last thing he could remember doing before each of his time-lapses, taking care to be extra vigilant. His daughter's life depending on it. If he were caught, there would be no chance of him finding her. And even in their custody, something in his gut told him the police were not to be trusted.

No, he thought. If anyone was to save his daughter, then it had to be him.

His motivation spiked, he picked up his room key and was stopped by the ring of the telephone.

He turned to look at the clock. It was 9:15a.m. And tentatively, he picked up the phone, “Hello?” A moments pause before his gaze drifted to the vase on top of the nest of drawers. “Yes,” he said, staring blankly at the bunch of flowers as he listened intently.

“Yes………. I understand………………… One flower.”

Thirty Five

9:23a.m.

Ben and Schmidt sat at a table in the corner of the deserted police-canteen drinking black coffee, Ben picking Schmidt's brain for every ounce of information he could get on Edwards, eager to understand how his mind worked and discover any weaknesses he could turn against him.

"How did you become acquainted with Sean Edwards?" Ben asked.

"I don't understand?"

"I mean, how did he become a patient of yours? Of all the experts he could have chosen, why you?"

"Curious thing, that," said Schmidt. "It vas by chance, I think."

"You think?"

"Mr. Edwards had this rule. The 'three foot' rule he called it. Anyvon he came into contact vith, he gave a business card. It vas how he grew his network and built on his success. We bumped into von-another in a restaurant. He gave me his business card and I gave him mine."

"And that was it?"

"No. I met him there again a few weeks later. I vas viewing some property nearby, and ven I called in for brunch, he vas sitting at the bar having a drink."

"And where did these meetings take place?"

"Didn't I say? It vas The Church Mouse, just outside-."

"I know where it is, doctor."

"Anyway," said Schmidt. "it vas then that I found out about his sleep disorder, and soon after, he had his first consultation."

"So, tell me, doctor, what drives him?"

"The past drives him," Schmidt answered, "Along with the love of his family and his fear of being alone."

Ben urged him to elaborate and Schmidt went on to explain that Sean Edwards had lost his father in a house fire when he was eleven years old. Soon after, his mother had turned her back on him and put him into care, blaming him for his father's death.

"What caused the fire?" Ben asked.

"It vas an electrical fault. His father died trying to save him, thinking he vas in his bedroom, but Sean had sneaked out to go camping vith some friends. From then on, he vas on a downward spiral. Until, that is, he met his vife. He said she had turned his life around. Given him new hope."

"If that was the case, why kill her?"

"That is a mystery I'm afraid. Even to me. He vas alvays haunted by the fear of losing her, and I believe this, along vith the history of his childhood, may have been the trigger for his sleep disorder. His parasomnia. Even now, I still find it difficult to believe he could have done such a thing."

"You mentioned his mother. Do you know if their relationship was rekindled once Edwards turned his life around?"

"I know she moved into the area on discovering she had a granddaughter. Consett I think."

Ben gave a knowing nod. Morton had already checked her out and come up with nothing. Edwards had cut all ties.

Schmidt continued, "She had vanted to patch things up with him but he cut her off completely and denied her access to her granddaughter. And though she still sends birthday and Christmas cards to Abby along with presents, they're usually returned."

"The first three victims were mothers," said Ben. "Do you think it's possible that the murders could be construed as an attack on his own mother for abandoning him, and that maybe, that's why he chose to copy the 10:15's? Because they fit his purpose."

"To be honest, detective, I do not know vat to think. I never for von moment thought his behaviour could digress to such depravities. It's not like him."

"But it *is him*," said Ben. "And the bodies just keep on coming."

Doctor Schmidt couldn't make sense of it all. Nor could he justify the reasoning or motives behind Sean Edwards' behaviour.

"Can you think why Edwards should mention a sister?" Ben asked.

"As I have said already. As vell as the parasomina, Mr. Edwards is suffering from Multiple Personality Disorder. And up to now, we have only seen von of his alter-egos. But it is not uncommon to have a series of differing personalities and I vould not be surprised if we see signs of this at some stage. Von of those personalities could vell have a whole other family in his own eyes. His parallel personalities coming from different backgrounds, a different era, and in some cases, a different vorld even."

"So Edwards isn't a schizophrenic?"

"No. He is not. You heard the tape of his calls to me, did you not?"

"I did."

"And did you not hear how frightened he sounded? He vas panicking, like an innocent child caught up in a vorld he did not understand."

"Does he know about these alternative personalities?"

"It is more likely he knows the consequences of those personalities from the trails they leave during his missing time episodes."

"What about his daughter? Do you think he has her with him?"

"I do not. I think she vill be held somewhere safe. In a place chosen by the ego responsible for these crimes. And that alter-ego vould not vant to run the risk of you tracing his call and finding her. It vill be a place that even Mr. Edvards' true self may not be avare of."

"One more thing, doctor. Deception seems to be a trait of his. Is it possible that Edwards deceived you into believing that he suffers from parasomnia and MPD, when in fact, he does not?"

"Anything is possible," Schmidt answered. "The mind is an intelligent tool, but if the blood pumped to it is from an evil heart, then surely, it vill be contaminated."

His coffee finished, and with his new insight into the workings of Edwards' mind, Ben rang to check on the police guard at his father's house.

Two officers were sitting in a car outside his bungalow, and another sat in his kitchen. No doubt being stuffed full of bacon sandwiches, thought Ben, followed by Rington's tea and biscuits as his father proudly told stories of Ben's achievements. Stories that Ben would find embarrassing; like the day he'd achieved his bronze badge for swimming. His father exaggerating as he joked about Ben not having to swim below the depths of the water to retrieve the rubber brick because he'd already swallowed half the pool. These and other anecdotes were the signs of a changed man. A man, who, until the latter part of last year, was unable to openly express his emotions, but now, to Ben's embarrassment, they flowed freely. Sometimes, Ben thought, *Too* freely.

The change in his father's ways had come about last year when he'd climbed from the deep hole of depression after mourning the loss of his wife. Up until then, Ben's mother had been the doting affectionate one, and his father the opposite. An emotional recluse who had always had difficulty showing his softer side. Especially in public. It seemed it was a 'man' thing. A problem Ben and his father had shared due to the way they had been raised;- the role model that was his father, and his father's father before him, with any displays of emotion resigned to the 'sign-offs' in a birthday or Christmas card. Then, last year, everything had changed between them as Ben's mum lay dying in a hospital bed, his father a once strong and emotionless man, crumbling with the fading of his wife, crying as he told her just how much he loved her. That he didn't want her to die. Ben and his father growing closer than ever during those final moments, the two of them sitting on either side of her bed. And even through the ravaging pain of cancer, his mum had held their hands and brought them together, resting them on her stomach with the last of her strength, and saying how much it meant to have them there. The two most important men in her life, together. Each of them holding a hand as she slipped away. Both of them staying there for hours after she had died, her hands still warm as her arms grew cold. And as each of them gave her a final kiss goodbye, they turned to hold one-another in deep embrace, squeezing out the empty space of detachment between them as they held one-another closer than they had ever done before.

'No,' Ben thought, he couldn't lose his father now. He had only just found him. And his ear to the phone, he was relieved to hear the officer's packed mouth mumbling something along the lines of "Everything's A-okay, sir. I won't let him out of my sight."

"Make sure you don't," Ben said, thinking how, even under their very noses, a rose had been left on the body of Rachel Earnshaw.

With his worries eased a little, his concerns switched to Meg. She had not left the station until almost five this morning, and already, he was late with her wake-up call. Or rather, her '*make sure I'm out of bed'* call, as she had put it. And though she had wanted to be woken earlier, he had left it as late as he'd dared, allowing her to sleep as long as possible before another long day / late night.

Meg answered his call with the hopeful presumption that they had found something. Either some useful information that would lead to Sean Edwards' capture, or better yet, the announcement that he was already in custody.

Unfortunately, it was neither.

"Okay," she yawned, "Give me half an hour, and if you can't make it yourself, have someone pick me up, would you. First though, I need some breakfast and a shower."

Thirty Six

9:43a.m.

Sunday morning and only a few shops open, he had thought it would be quiet, but the café was filling fast as visitors popped in for a bite to eat before going to the cricket ground, and weekend shoppers stopped off for breakfast en-route to the Metro Centre, greasy fry-ups and stale cake the order of the day as Sean hid his annoyance behind downcast eyes and took a sip from his milky tea, his appearance that of a workman so as not to draw attention to himself, wearing old jeans, a baggy top and a black woollen hat rolled up above his ears, blending into the background. Just another punter at the greasy spoon. Or so it would seem.

Full of pretence, the woman behind the counter made him want to strangle her, her voice grating on his every nerve, finishing every sentence with;-*Love, Pet, Darlin'* or *Sweetheart.* "What would you like, *love?* Okay *pet.* Do you want chips with that, *darlin'?* That'll be £6, *sweetheart.* She was a short, fat woman with amazingly skinny legs. And not in a good way. Her appearance so repulsive he couldn't take his eyes off her, and unwillingly, found himself studying her. A woman of about fifty with a black knee-length skirt, a cheap white blouse and her hair flicked back to the early eighties.

Sumo Gran with a tan.

He fantasised about walking up to her, snatching the bread-knife from her hand and slashing her throat with it to see her blood spurt everywhere. There'd be no more fucking 'darlings' *then*, would there, sweetheart.

He thought too about how the customers might react. Would they scream in panicked shock? Or would they cheer and applaud him, giving him pats on the back and shaking his hand.

He dragged his eyes from her to a girl verging on womanhood, her jet-black hair too long at the front and her every blink exaggerated by the movement of her fringe. He guessed she was in her mid teens and watched her dab a napkin to her tongue and wipe the sauce from her 2 year-old's face. The parent little more than a child herself, grumbling to her non-existent partner, "Kids. Who'd have 'em," as she fussed over her child, oblivious to her scruffy pushchair blocking the entrance as another blue-rinse struggled with the spring-loaded door.

Sumo Gran loudly greeted the old woman as she entered, her lips working overtime to shape the words that everyone bar the old woman could hear, "Hello, Mavis. How yer doin' darlin'. What can I get yer love? The usual is it, sweetheart?"

Struggling to make herself heard, the old woman gave a Parkinsons-laden nod and shuffled to the nearest available table as Sean sat fantasizing about his next victim, wondering what it would be like to kill someone here and now as he looked around the grimy café for a likely candidate. No-one here to offer any real resistance. The old lady would be too easy, and probably grateful. No fun in that.

He looked at the messy two year-old. Better, he thought. A deep slash across his soft little belly and his entrails would spill to the floor. Not much a napkin could do about that, he thought, pondering over how the mother would react to protect her child. Would she stand frozen to the spot or step in his way, sacrificing herself for her baby?

And what about the two girls on the table next to the window? How would *they* like to die?

He watched them with their over emphatic smattering of gums, their chewing exaggerated with the occasional clacking of chewing gum. They were about fourteen years old, wearing way too much make-up and not enough clothing.

"Yeah, Steven's dad is a *real* piece of FILTH," he heard one of the girls say.

"What do you mean?" asked the other.

"Oh, Helen. You're just *so* not with it," her friend answered, then explained with an emphatic gesture and the bluntness of a rough up-bringing, "Father-I'd-Like-To-Hump, *silly*." The two of them giggling that 'aren't-we-naughty' laugh as Sean took a sip of his tea and his attentions strayed to a young woman just a few tables away. She was alone and engrossed in her magazine. Pouring over it, yet absorbing nothing. Mindlessly flicking through one page after another in her search for that eye-catching headline or a recent photograph of the latest 'Wannabe'.

'If she played her cards right,' he thought, '*She* could be the next headline grabber, her face next to his on tomorrow's front pages.'

He watched as she sat there, blissfully unaware of the danger she was in. Death all around going unnoticed; the bag of bones with the blue rinse on the adjoining table. The background noise of the radio churning out the local news with an up to the minute report of six dead on the A1, only two miles from this very spot. And here in the very same café where she was aimlessly picking at what could well be her very last meal, a murderer in her midst as she continued to read her girlie mag', ignorant to the suffering of others and her close encounter with death.

Maybe it was time to wake her up, he thought, watching her as she swept back her hair and pinned it in place with her sunglasses, her fingers combing through stray wisps and teasing them over the ridge of her ears. So beautiful. So feminine. So young. An almost faultless complexion unspoilt by the heavy layers of make-up which so often buried the faces of immature girls or women past their sell-by date. But not this girl. *She* had an air of self-confidence and used only the subtlest hint of make-up to highlight her expressive, yet beautifully innocent eyes. *Perfect.*

Her head buried in her magazine, he thought about how amusing it would be to see the reaction of the other customers, the shock in their faces as they looked on in frightened disbelief whilst a customer died right in front of them.

It would be so easy. She wouldn't even see it coming.

His piercing eyes scanned his prey, his sadistic thoughts outside the realm of the devil himself as his fingers toyed with his belt buckle. *'I could do her right now. Just casually walk up behind her and throttle the life out of her.'*

He pictured the scene, the shock on her face priceless. A mixture of horror and fear as she realised that someone was trying to kill her. His exhilaration building, he was getting a hard-on just thinking about it. And as his thoughts delved deeper into the macabre possibilities, an ejaculation beckoning, he hurried to the toilet so as not to mess his trousers, wary of drawing attention to himself.

When he came out, the need to take a life had subsided. All be it, temporarily.

He checked his watch and glanced at the 'almost girl', thinking to himself; *'Some other time perhaps'.* But today, he had an appointment with a slightly older woman.

Thirty Seven

9:51a.m.

Meg had received a call from Ben before breakfast to say he'd pick her up shortly after ten, and as she slipped out of her dressing gown and jumped into the shower, she was reminded of a time he had been out jogging from his home on the riverside estate, his route taking him up Ropery Lane and on to Waldridge village. From there he would have beared left along the road to Chester Moor and headed back alongside the dual carriageway. A long haul for Meg, a canter for Ben. She knew his route almost as well as he did, having joined him on the odd occasion, though she preferred to cycle alongside him so she could keep up.

On this particular occasion however, he had gone out on his own, and Meg had let herself in with her key shortly before his return.

His body a sheen of perspiration, she had felt a stir at the sight of him. If anything got her going, it was the rough-and-ready look or the tanned-and-sweaty one. Ben fell into both categories, his stubble prickling her face as he greeted her with a kiss then headed for the shower, Meg following close behind with small talk as he peeled off his top to reveal his well toned body, his lungs still panting for breath and her heart beating a little faster as he removed his shorts, turned on the shower, and held his hand under the water to check its temperature.

Even now, as she stood in the shower herself, she felt that same heated stirring within her loins. The thought of his toned back glistening with sweat as he reached into the shower. His pertly toned bum good enough to bite into. She had stroked her finger down his back, tracing the curve of his spine and her hand brushing across his bum to cup a cheek as he'd turned to kiss her, and moments later, they were in the shower together, she still fully clothed.

Long gone were the inexperienced fumblings of her earliest sexual encounters, with their slobbering kisses, the groping of her breasts, and a quick rush for goal. Not Ben. Ben was in another league.

His sensuality displayed in every action, he was patient and had known exactly how to please her. Nothing rushed. Nothing predictable. Spontaneity the key and her lock eager to be opened he had taken his time. Allowed her to live in the moment. Made her feel loved and appreciated, his affection oozing from his every touch. His kisses drifting randomly from one part of her body to the next in search of hidden erogenous zones waiting anxiously to be discovered. The gentle warmth of his breathe across her ear. The light suck and nibble of her neck. Soft kisses trailing down her body to her inner thighs, lingering over the areas that made her squirm with delight. A teasing flick of the tongue before penetration. And in the heat of the water, her orgasm had washed through her and over her, flooding her senses as the shuddering tremors of ecstasy ripped throughout her body.

She had found herself thinking about him a lot lately. She had tried to block it out but was drawn to him. Attracted to him all over again. Maybe she had never stopped being attracted to him. There was a chemistry between them that she had never felt with anyone else, and whether it was love, or lust, or a mixture of both, she could not be sure until she acted upon her feelings.

She stepped out of the shower. He would be picking her up soon. It would be a chance for them to chat and for her to explain things to him, tell him how she felt. Explain that she didn't have time in her life for another relationship, her life was already complicated enough. But that was another story. Something she was learning to live with. It would get better, she told herself. Easier. Only then could she consider her life with someone else in it, and by then, Ben was sure to find someone else. Someone more homely, less ambitious and more forgiving.

Maybe she could never be that person.

Maybe she never wanted to be.

Thirty Eight

10:02a.m.

Sean stood at the front door, to all extents, just a regular guy, his knock accompanied by the sound of water flushing down the drain as he looked around the quiet cul-de-sac, no-one watching and everything still.

A perfect Sunday morning was about to get better, and with the sound of someone approaching from within, he whispered his ominous chant, "I'm going to caaaaaatch you."

A cheery voice called out from the other side of the door, "Just a minute."

His whispering grew a little louder, "I'm going to huuuuuurt you."

With the loosening of the chain she reassured him she was coming, "I'll not be a second." Then the key turned in the lock and the door opened to his smile.

"I'm going to **KILL** you."

He burst through the open door, the palms of his hands thrusting hard into her chest and sending her sprawling to the floor.

She lay on her back in the hall, perched on her elbows, looking up to her attacker in frightened shock, her dressing gown falling high on her thighs to reveal her shapely legs and her cries drowned out by the spinning of the washing-machine as he rushed towards her and kicked her hard in the stomach, a crack of ribs stealing her breath away, her arms hugging her stomach as her attacker closed the door.

"Good morning, Olivia. How were *you* today?"

She recognised him instantly from the news bulletins and consumed by panic, she choked on her words, "Oh god. You're the man who-," she stopped mid-sentence, as if her denial would dispel the truth of what was happening. A murderer was here, in her home.

Even in his guise, his glare affirmed her fears and her stare shot to the bottle she had been holding when she had answered the door. Her babies bottle, lying where she had dropped it. And her pains forgotten, she scrambled to her feet, darting through the neighbouring door into the living-room and snatching her baby from his cradle, scarcely breaking stride as she ran through the kitchen to the back door, the killer close behind. Her baby held tight to her chest as she fumbled to turn the key in the lock, and as it clicked, she felt the kick like a mule hard into the base of her back, pushing her headlong into the opening door, and somehow, in that split second, she threw herself further off balance so she alone would take the brunt of the impact; a mother's instinctive reaction to shield her baby from the force of the blow, her head smacking hard against the door before she fell to her knees, still clutching her baby. The dizzying blow forcing her to collapse yet further as she screamed for him to stop, her jaw met with the crunching blow of his fist and her head banging hard against the corner of the table, her limp body collapsing into a heap and her baby spilling from her grasp as she lay unconscious, unable to hear the cries of her child.

"Olivia."

A man's voice gently roused her, "Olivvvviaaaaa."

Her eyes flickered open to the sound of his voice and the blur sharpened to a chilling image of a killer cradling her baby in his arm, the glint of a knife in his other hand. He used it as a pointer as her tears spilled down her cheeks.

"You or him, Olivia? Who's it going to be?"

She clambered to her feet, "Please don't hurt my baby."

"I guess that means you, then," he said, smiling.

The baby reached up for the knife, smiling at the shiny object just beyond his reach as it was teased near to his fingers.

"He seems to want it. You sure you don't want me to give it to him?"

"No!" she cried, reaching out for her child only to feel the slap of the blade against her hand. "Wait, Olivia. Be patient. I have to explain the rules."

Holding her stricken hand, she watched him baby-talk to her child, "Who's a naughty mummy, then?" he said, smiling down at her baby. "Yes. She is, isn't she."

Her baby gurgled and smiled back at him, his little legs kicking with glee.

"Tell me, Olivia. Would you want to live if you were unable to perform your motherly duties? Or to be more specific, if you were unable to hold your baby in your arms."

"Yes," she sobbed, "I would."

"Even if you were unable to change him? Unable to feed him or pick him up when he falls. Unable to nurse him when he is ill. Would you want to live if you were unable to do any of those things?"

"I want to be there for him always," she cried. "I love him. I love him more than anything."

"More than life itself?"

"Yes," she cried. "He *is* my life."

"Which is a good thing," he said, an evil glint in his eye, "But tell me, though I've never seen it for myself, I hear there's no greater bond than a mother's love for her child. Is that true?"

"Yes," she cried, frightened of how her answers might affect what he'd do.

He looked at her with disdain, "That bond is about to be broken, Olivia. And it is up to you *how*?"

"Please," she begged, "Don't do this."

She reached out for her baby, desperate to hold him in her arms, away from the killer who just smiled at her, enjoying his control and feeding off her desperation. Her arms held out imploringly, until, to her surprise, he passed her her son.

"You see," he said, watching her as she cradled her baby, "I'm not *totally* heartless. But make the most of this moment, because you will never hold your baby again."

She held him close, a minute seeming like seconds as she rocked him in her arms and drew comfort from his warmth. Moments she had treasured and expected to last for years were to be denied her forever.

"Now, give me the child," he said, his voice gentle, his eyes narrowing.

She drew away, crying, "Please, no, don't hurt him. Don't take him away from me."

"I have to, before you drop him."

"I *won't* drop him. *Never*."

"Oh, but you will," he said, his face leaning close to hers and the knife held between them, his voice pure evil, "when I cut off your arms."

Her eyes filled with terror, she ached to scream, but for the sake of her son, she did not dare.

He held her baby in his arms once more as she looked at him imploringly. Looked into his cold eyes as he turned and twisted the knife, this way and that, teasing her with the horrors of what he might do.

"Shall I remove his legs?"

"No," she cried.

"It will be so easy. They are small and weak, with no muscle to slice through. Just soft skin and feeble bones."

"Pleeease," she pleaded, "Don't do this. I'll do anything." She fumbled with the cord of her dressing gown, crying as it dropped to the floor.

"Anything?" he asked. "Will you refrain from screaming?"

"*Anything*," she submitted, standing naked before him.

"I normally put tape over the mouths of my subjects." He paused before telling her why. "They scream you see." He looked her in the eye, his expression one of concern, "You're not going to scream, are you?"

She shook her head.

"For your child's sake, I hope not. Because I'm offering you a chance to save his life. Would you like that, Olivia?"

She nodded as the tears rolled down her cheeks.

"Good. Because this is going to hurt a little." He grinned like the devil and sighed as if full of regret, mocking, "Actually, it's going to hurt a lot."

He turned to put her baby on the sofa and motioned for her to sit beside him on the floor, their backs against the sofa, his arm across her shoulders and hugging her as if she were a friend as he began to explain, "First, I am going to cut through the skin around each of your shoulders." He teased the point of the knife along her shoulders, his eyes lusting after her skin. "I am going to cut through to the bone, Olivia. There will be lots of blood. And remember, if you resist or scream, your baby dies."

Through tear-filled eyes, Olivia looked over her shoulder to her baby as he gurgled a smile at her.

"Then, I'm going to peel back your flesh and cut through the ligaments and cartilage around your joints, severing your arms from your body." He trailed the knife up and down her arm. "It is likely that you will pass out or die from blood-loss long before we get that far, but if you can endure my teachings up until either of those moments arrive, your baby will live. If you cry out however, or if you scream. I will ensure that you witness the slow and painful death of your child before your life is at an end."

She cried as he turned her to face him, her face scrunched up in tears as she watched his focus shift to the knife resting on the ball of her shoulder, his hand gripping tight around its handle, and her head whipping away with a grimace as it cut through her skin, her fists clenched and her legs thrashing, her head rocking back and forth, and her lips nipped tight between her teeth as the cut swiped around her shoulders and sliced up through her armpits, her screams buried deep in the chasms of her throat.

"You're doing well, Olivia. You must love your baby very much."

She was panting and sweating. Swooning with the pain. Her eyes closed tight as he shifted to her other shoulder. The cut slower this time. The blade sluggish on its journey as it sliced through her skin, dragging through every long second as he watched her fight against the torture. Biting hard through the flesh of her lips. The taste of blood in her mouth as she swallowed her screams, and her back arching with the pain as she looked through tear-filled eyes at her baby drifting off to sleep, his face a picture of tranquillity as she writhed in agony. "Please don't do this," she cried softly, her head swimming as the blood flowed down her arms. "Please don't leave my child without a mother."

He paused to look at her, surprised she was still conscious, let alone able to speak, "Would you like to take him with you, Olivia? To the other side, as they say? Would you like my blade to taste his flesh?"

She shook her head, "No." And felt the blade press harder, her gums bleeding with the force of pressure as she clenched her teeth and the blade dug deeper. And then she did it. Unable to withstand the pain any longer, she screamed.

His eyes lit up as she fought to stay conscious and cried to him, her head swooning, "Please. I won't do it again. I promise."

"Too late," he chirped, standing to lift the baby from the sofa and holding it by the ankle, dangling him upside down. "What a pity," he said, "And you were doing so well."

"Please, put him down," she mustered.

Her baby started to cry, his face reddening as Sean raised his arm above his head until they were face to face. "Would you just look at him. Such a cute baby. And what strong lungs he has. What's his name?"

"Please don't hurt him."

"I *asked* you his name."

"Michael," she said weakly.

"Michael, huh." Still holding the baby upside down, he brought his face closer to his own, "Well, look at you, Micky boy."

Olivia grew paler, her voice weaker, "You said you'd spare him if I didn't scream, and I won't. Do whatever you like to me. I promise, I won't scream again."

He lowered the child onto the sofa and Olivia heaved a sigh of relief as he sat down beside her on the floor, the knife pointed towards her face. "Look at you," he snarled, "You couldn't scream now, even if you wanted to. If I want to hurt your baby, there's not a god damned thing you can do about it."

"Why are you doing this?" she asked, her strength fading with the cries of her baby. "Why me?"

"Right place, right time, I guess," he answered, looking at his watch. "Speaking of which, what time is it by you?"

He'd asked knowing full well she couldn't raise her arm even if she'd wanted to. "Time to continue where we cut off, I guess," he said, pleased with his little pun, his smile growing wider, more sinister. A rock and jump to his feet before he delved into his pocket and pulled out a crumpled yellow rose, holding it in front of her face. "Nice, isn't it. It's for you."

She looked up at him from the floor, raw pain at her shoulders, her arms numb and her body cold. "Please," she cried, remembering something she had seen on television, "Don't *you* have a child?"

Like a bullet to his brain he paused and Olivia saw a glimmer of hope, a chance to save her son. Sean Edwards had a daughter. She was missing, but maybe she was alive. Maybe there was an ounce of compassion somewhere inside that twisted brain of his. And with her fading strength, she gave it one last try, appealing to his paternal instincts, "Don't you have a daughter called Abby?"

Thirty Nine

Sean stood over her, his gaze distant as he stared off into the nether reaches of his mind.

Once again, the image was of a young boy wearing a dirt-white shirt with rolled up sleeves and slack, shabby grey trousers, their hems almost obscuring his badly scuffed shoes fastened with knotty, mismatched laces.

His quarry some twenty yards away, he began his eerie chant; a rasping whisper and his words dragged out.

"I'm going to caaaaaaatch you."

"I'm going to huuuuuurt you."

"I'm going to kiiiiiiiill you."

Like a hunting wildcat, he'd mentally singled out his prey. A slow moving target capable of sudden bursts of speed and the ability to change direction in an instant. A victim that, if threatened, could hurt him, and would do so without hesitation.

It was time to move in for the kill, the thrill all consuming. He relished the challenge and began stealthily closing in on his prey as if recreating a scene from the plains of Africa. Except, his hunting ground was a rural back garden. And his target;- a lowly bumble bee.

With the back of his hand, he eased an overhanging branch to one side, its catkins softly caressing his brow as he brushed past with his trap at the ready, glass jar in one hand, its pierced lid in the other. Moving ever closer. The bees droning buzz of activity growing louder with every stride.

"I'm going to pull your leeeeegs off."

"I'm going to pull your wiiiings off."

Then slowly, as the bee trawled over the yellow rose, he carefully eased the lip of the jar over it from above, and in that same instant, the bee made to fly off, then;- ***SNAP!...*** Sean was whipped back to reality.

Awoken from his trance, the rose slipped from his fingers and his gaze shot to his victim, the flesh stripped from her shoulders, his eyes fixed there, oblivious to the feint movement of her lips, her voice down to a whisper as she slipped closer to death, pleading for the life of her baby. Too weak to move as she looked at the killer looking down at her. Looking at her with an expression she was unsure of.

Looking at the bloody knife in his hand.

Looking at her baby before moving towards him, his hands reaching for his throat.

Forty

"Oh god, what have I done."

Sean stood looking down at the infant, his fingers on the little one's neck, and breathing a sigh of relief as he felt the throb of the baby's pulse, "You're alive," he said, "Thank god, you're alive."

He picked up the baby in his arms, his back turned to the bloody scene on the floor, shielding him from waking to the sight of his dead mother. So much blood, it was hard to believe it came from one person. And guilt ridden tears welling within him, he looked to the heavens and cried, "What's happening to me?"

"My baby?" came the reply, his question answered with a groaning whisper.

He turned to see the woman was still alive, her grey-white body, pale against the scarlet stain of the carpet. And her baby still in his arms, he knelt down in front of her, crying out his remorse, "I didn't want to do this. *Please*. You have to believe me. I can't help it. I can't control it. I don't know what I'm doing."

Olivia was too weak to move as Sean remained kneeling in front of her, repentfully rocking, his eyes fixed on her injuries as she looked to her baby stirring in his arms. Only four months old and sucking his thumb, he woke with a stretch and a kick, blissfully unaware of what was happening. His mother clinging to life, wanting to hold him one last time. Wanting to feed him when he woke. Wanting to blow ripples into his belly and hear his infectious gurgle of laughter. Each a treasured moment, never to be experienced again. Her life over as his began. And a tear in her eye, knowing she wouldn't be there to see his first tooth nor witness his first step. And she'd never hear him say '*mummy, I love you*'.

Sean wiped his tears on the back of his hand and began to panic.

He wanted to help her. He wanted to stop the bleeding. He wanted to reassure her that everything was going to be alright. That she was safe now. That her baby was safe too. He wanted to comfort her but felt sick at the thought of touching her, repulsed at the sight of what he'd done. Frightened that any contact might trigger the return of his alter-ego and he'd continue where he'd left off. Exercising his cruelty. Torturing and dismembering. Killing both her and her baby. And his panic set in deeper as he watched her slipping away, his eyes flicking around the room in search of a phone. Knowing it was already too late, but having to do something nonetheless. Then finally, he spotted it on a nest of drawers by the lamp, with its antique dial and old fashioned handset.

"My baby?" she said weakly, "I can't see my baby."

"He's here. He's okay."

Sean sat next to her and held her baby close, holding him so she could see his little cherub face. So close she could smell the perfume of his skin and the milk on his breath. And through her pain, she squeezed out a smile with his name, "Michael."

Sean's panic escalating, he dialled 999, his call answered with the voice of indifference, "Emergency services."

"Ambulance. Quickly. She's losing blood fast."

"Name please."

"I don't know her fucking name," he snapped down the phone, his anxiety growing.

The telephonist tried to calm him and asked for more details before Sean lost his patience, "I don't know the fucking address either. Just trace the fucking call god damn it."

He put the phone to one side and hugged the baby closer, rocking back and forth, watching Olivia's eyes drift towards closure.

"You have a beautiful son," he said.

Olivia felt cold and tired, and so so weak. Not an ounce of energy, she was desperate to close her eyes, wanting to sleep for the longest time and wake up afresh to find that everything was alright. But not yet, she thought. Her maternal instincts telling her to hold on. That her baby wasn't safe. And her words no more than a whisper, she said it again. "Please don't hurt him."

"I won't," said Sean. "I promise I won't."

Her eyes heavy, she fought to stay awake until help arrived.

"Stay with me," he pleaded. "Stay awake. The ambulance is on its way."

Her focus fading and her eyes slowly closing, he knew the ambulance would be too late, and swallowing the lump in his throat, he held her baby closer to her face, watching her eyes flicker open and her lips purse to kiss him one last time, the slightest of smiles crossing her lips as her eyes rolled white and her head collapsed to her chest. And with it, as if sensing she was gone, her baby began to wail, his tiny lungs bursting out with an ear-splitting cry. A cry waiting to be silenced. A cry that said he wanted to be with his mum. And with a heart full of regret, Sean turned to him before he left…

"I'm sorry, Michael. Truly I am."

Forty One

Ben had arrived at Meg's just as she had received a call from Morton, her mobile to her ear as she climbed into the car.

"We've got another one, Ma'am," said Morton.

"Where?"

"5a, Lindom Avenue. But this time, we've got a pulse."

"She's alive?"

"Just about. The paramedics are working on her now. It seems Edwards gave them a call before he left."

The moment Meg told Ben the address, his face filled with concern, his foot slamming hard on the accelerator. Urgency taking prevalence over professionalism. His driving faster and more erratic than ever before, even as he wound his way through the estate and into the street where the police cars and ambulance were parked. A bump of the chassis against concrete as he pulled sharply onto the neighbouring driveway.

HIS driveway.

'Someone close, Ben. Someone ***really*** *close.'*

There had been no shortage of rain during the past week, yet the neighbours were out in force;- watering their gardens, washing their cars, emptying their rubbish bins. The least obvious of them twitching at their curtains. All of them snooping.

Ben jumped from his car as two ambulancemen wheeled a gurney from his neighbour's house, a body under a white sheet and black straps holding everything in place as the wheels juddered over the ridge of the path. One of them opened the doors to the ambulance as Ben rushed across, shouting for them to stop. He flashed his badge and stood to the side of the gurney, looking at the contours of the sheet, the petite figure of a woman lying underneath. He nipped at its corner and hesitated, preparing himself for the worst, before, woefully, he peeled it back from her face.

Olivia had been a nurse at a home for the elderly, and Ben's neighbour for some six years, having moved here with her husband, Joe, soon after they were married. The day they had moved in, she had knocked on his door to introduce herself. "We're the Cromptons." She had said, rather proud of her new name, and invited him round for coffee. Less than an hour later, the cup of coffee was a can of lager, and Ben was inviting her husband Joe to a round of golf at Lumley Castle. From then on, they had been what Ben had thought of as 'ideal neighbours'. Casual friends who were there if he'd needed them, and at the same time;- respecting his privacy, rather than knocking on his door every five minutes like his previous neighbour had done. But now, Ben was calling at *their* door, and in a context he'd never imagined.

Olivia was dead, maybe because of *him*. And Ben would have to find it within himself to break the news to her husband. His familiar face turning up at the cricket club where Joe worked as a groundsman, happy in his work, and even happier at home with his wife and son. His grin etched into his face ever since Olivia had fallen pregnant and given birth to their baby after five years of trying.

It was a pregnancy they had fought long and hard for, jumping through hoops to qualify for I.V.F. treatment on the N.H.S. And then, when that course had failed, they'd had to work extra shifts and longer hours to have it done privately, before, finally, their persistence had paid off, Olivia falling pregnant, and Joe happier this past year than he had ever been.

But with a call from Ben, all of that was about to change.

He gently replaced the sheet over Olivia's face, and thinking of Joe, turned toward the house, desperately hoping this wasn't a double homicide, his hand tapping nervously against his leg as he marched past Meg talking to officers at the foot of the garden, and approaching the open door, paused at the sight of a man in green overalls coming from inside the house, his heart skipping a beat as he stood staring.

The paramedic was holding a tiny bundle in his arms, his expression blank as he looked down at the infant, quiet and unmoving, Ben fearing the worst as he watched him gather up the loose corners of the powder-blue blanket and tuck them tight around the baby. And then a smile as he saw a small hand reached up to squeeze it's tiny fingers tight around the paramedics nostril, and with his wince of pain came a gargle of laughter.

Forty Two

Unable to shake the images from his mind, Sean paced his room with his hands behind his back. His eyes down to the floor. His strides short and fast between each turn of direction, back and forth over the length of the room, muttering to himself, "I killed her. I killed her," over and over again. The television just a drone in the background as the horror of what he had done ate away at him. The picture engrained into his brain like a concentrated snapshot, sharp as a full colour photograph before his very eyes. An innocent woman. The flesh stripped from her shoulders, he had sliced to the bone. The sharp line of the cut;- straight and neat as it passed through the thin outer-layer of skin and disappeared into a thick red mass of blood, muscle and fat interwoven with a multitude of veins, its colour contrasting brightly against the pale pallor of her skin as the blood ran down her arms.

Up until yesterday he had never seen anything like it. Or if he had, he couldn't remember it. At least, not as himself. And then it came back to him how, before she had died, she had woken him as if from a dream, her voice haunting him still, '*Don't you have a daughter?*' his flashback coming to a sudden stop as something crucial was about to be revealed. The image of him as a boy, in a place he didn't know, doing things he couldn't remember. His own fear coupled with the excitement of his alter ego as he had watched the scene play out in his head. And throughout it all, he had felt some kind of affinity with what was happening. A distant connection;- broken the moment she had mentioned his having a daughter.

Now, somehow, he knew that all of this had played a part in what he had done. In some way, the murders and the flashback were connected. And so, this meant, was his daughter's disappearance.

He closed his eyes in an effort to remember more, hoping for a replay of the flashback. Knowing that if he could make sense of it all and unravel the clues within, as you would a dream, then maybe he could find his daughter and the reasoning behind what he had done.

Instead, he remembered his plans to check his childhood haunts. His plan to get a car. And the interruption of a phone call as he was about to leave his room. And that was all. No flashback. No memory of who he had spoken to on the phone, what was said, or when he had left. His alter-ego had played out the next hour onwards of his life, and in that time, his mind was void of what he had done. Not a thing until that poor woman had uttered something of his daughter, and then, his nightmare had begun all over again with another death. Another tragedy. Another chunk of his day unaccounted for, and still no closer to finding his little girl.

He thought about the possibilities of who could have called him in his room. *Who* knew he was there? The proprietor? The police? Or was the call from someone else? Or **FOR** someone else for that matter. That 'someone' being his alter-ego.

"Sean Edwards has claimed a fourth victim."

With the mention of his name, the news bulletin drowned out his thoughts. There was a photograph being shown of him on television, taken by Amy. Pre-disguise. Not a good one, he couldn't help thinking. Why was that? Why were criminals or wanted men always shown in a bad light with unflattering photographs. Surely there were better pictures. Pictures of them with a baby or smiling at the camera, like those you'd see of a politician digging for votes. But then, maybe that was the point. Why flatter someone suspected of bad deeds, or as was thought in *his* case; hideous crimes of murder.

The news broadcast continued with Mark Jakes reporting from a street called Lindom Avenue, the excitable reporter giving his overview of the developments so far as he stood next to Jack Roberts, press liaison officer for the police.

The reporter looked straight into camera, "As we now know, on Thursday morning, at approximately 10am, Sean Edwards tortured and brutally murdered his wife." He paused for affect, milking his moment, a chance to further his career. "The following day, he also killed his mother-in-law, Cordelia Armstrong, cutting off her hands and feet, and leaving her to bleed to death. And soon after, kidnapped his daughter, who, as far as we know, may also be dead." Another pause, allowing the images to sink into the viewers minds. "Then he killed Rachel Earnshaw, a young single mum, trying to do her best for her handicapped son. And *now*, it seems he has murdered another innocent woman in her own home, and *still*, the police are no closer to stopping him."

With his account of events leading up to this latest incident, he turned to Jack Roberts, shifting the microphone back and forth between them.

"Because of a lack of information from the police so far, I can only speculate that these murders have continued to follow the same pattern as the mutilator killings. Is that correct?"

Jack Roberts looked nervously between the camera and the reporter. He had never been involved in such a high profile case and the strain was beginning to show as once again, he tried to curb his emotions, "I cannot divulge anything of that nature at this stage in the investigation."

"We have just heard the latest announcement of another murder," said the reporter, "And we have also heard your advice to the public to be more vigilant until this man is caught. But what more can you tell us about the mention of an accomplice?"

"I never said there was an accomplice," Jack Roberts replied, an air of caution to his wording. "There are elements of this case which are being investigated further, including the *possibility* of an accomplice. This is not to say that an accomplice exists. We are merely exploring all avenues, and this is a precautionary measure put in place to ascertain the reasoning behind Sean Edwards' behaviour."

"So you're not ruling out an accomplice?" the reporter asked.

"Mr. Edwards is an unknown quantity. He has no prior convictions and no prior knowledge of the details of the original killings other than those known to the general public. Yet, for some reason not known to us at this stage, he has been shown to have a deeper understanding of what took place during those killings than we would anticipate, and copied them meticulously. Because of this, we have to look further a field. We have to find out *where* he got his information. And we have to look at all the possibilities available to us, no matter how extreme or unlikely they may seem."

The reporter turned to the camera, "So there you have it. A brutal and callous murderer is still at large in the northeast… his whereabouts unknown… and the likelihood that he'll strike again, almost a certainty. And now we have a new threat. It would seem that Sean Edwards isn't alone in this. He has an accomplice and –"

Jack Roberts grabbed at the microphone, "That's *not* what I said –"

His voice was muffled by the crackle of the microphone as the two of them tussled for control, the pressure of the situation evidently getting to even the most professional of men, and as their scuffle continued, the broadcast cut back to the studio and an embarrassed anchorman with his fingers pressed to his earpiece as he tried to re-establish contact with his fellow reporter, before, coolly, he slipped into auto-pilot and spoke into camera, "I'm sorry. There seems to be a technical fault of some kind. We hope to get back to our reporter at some point later in the programme, but in the meantime – "

A loud knock on his door, Sean whipped his head around, his heart in a racing panic as he tried to sound calm. "Yes? Who is it?" he called out, frightened that the police had tracked him from the woman's house.

"It's me, Mr. Waders," the proprietor called from the other side of the door. "A letter has just arrived for you."

Sean stood nervously looking around the room, unsure of what to do. Wondering who could possibly know his pseudonym and where he was staying. It's a trick, he thought. It has to be. No one knows I'm here. Unless? Sean remembered the letter from the shoe box and the messages on his mobile phone. And on the news there had been mention of an unknown accomplice.

'Not all is as it seems.'

The proprietor knocked again, "There's no stamp on it, sir. Someone must have left it whilst I was out back."

Sean slowly opened the door to find the proprietor leaning his shoulder against the doorframe, his face a picture of embarrassment as he was caught curiously studying the envelope, turning it in his hands as he repeated, "There's no stamp on it. No address either. Just your name. That's what made me figure it must have been delivered by hand." With a puzzled expression, he passed it to Sean. "Curious thing, though. That letter I mean."

"Why's that?" Sean asked, keen to close the door.

"It's just that, I always lock the front door when I go out back. It's a habit. You know, in case of undesirables. Only, the door ***is*** locked, and I'm sure the letter wasn't there beforehand."

"I have days like that too," said Sean, slowly closing the door and trying not to appear rude or suspicious. "Thank you," he said, "It was good of you to bring it up."

Just like the letter from the shoebox, his name, or rather, an anagram of his name, was printed boldly across the seal.

Sean ripped it open.

READ ALL ABOUT IT! READ ALL ABOUT IT!

Read the papers, Sean. Listen to the news. See what you have done and what you have become. Because like it or not, The Mutilator has risen like a phoenix from the flames, and YOU'RE ***IT****.*

By now, I expect you are wondering how you got into this mess. And out of the goodness of my heart, I'm going to tell you. You are here because you are mentally unbalanced. Or as the locals might say;-. Your head's a shed, Sean. It's all messed up. And I'm going to help you to sort it out. But first of all, I need to warn you to watch your back. The police are getting closer. And we can't have them interfering with our little game now, because that would spoil things. It could even bring an end to your daughter's life before the time is right, and we don't want that now, do we. You see;- we both want the same thing you and I. Though for very different reasons. Your daughter, Sean, she's been crying for you. Such a shame. And such a cute little thing too. At the end of all this, if you fail to live up to my expectations, I might just keep her for myself. Or some small part of her at least. As a keepsake perhaps. Maybe I'll take her sweet little head and leave the rest of her body for you, to do with as you please. But if you can find her before your time runs out, then you can change all of that. That's why I've left you this letter, Sean. To remind you;- You have just three days left.

But here's where things get a little more interesting, Sean. I want you to take heart in the fact that you are a good killer. Probably the best so far. And because of this, I have made it so much easier for you than I did for the others. You see, I've come to like you. And that's why I'm giving you this chance to save your daughter. Not because I care whether she lives or dies, but because you deserve it. But the rules of the game say that I can only help you so much. The rest is up to you. So make the most of each and every clue. And remember;-

every woman you have killed has played her part in all of this. And it is up to you to find the connection before it is too late.

JH (JB)

I close my eyes in order to see;- St. Augustine.

Forty Three

From the black void of the cellar echoed the sad little voice of a child murmuring a nursery rhyme.

"Star light, star bright, first star I see tonight… I wish I may, I wish I might, have the wish I wish tonight."

Her wish was her secret, never to be spoken out loud, like the blowing out of candles on a birthday cake. Kept secret from everyone, so that it might one day come true. She hoped that this wish more than any other would come truest of all. She wanted to be back in her bed with her bears and Mr. Flopsy. But most of all, she wanted to be with her mummy and daddy, the two of them giving her a great big hug, never to ever leave her again.

Blindfolded, with goose-pimples on her arms and her knees drawn to her chest for warmth, she lay on her side on the dusty wooden floor, her ankles bound and her hands tied behind her back. Shaking and frightened to move. Not knowing where she was, or what was going to happen to her. Her mind left to wander through the sounds of the dank and murky cellar. The constant dripping from a leaking pipe off to her right. The sounds of rats foraging for food, scuttling across the floor and the overhead beams, the noise of their claws scratching against the wood accompanied with their nerve jangling squeaks, echoing into the emptiness of her solitude.

She flinched as something crawled on her skin, small like insects, her mind exaggerating their size and monstrosity as she imagined them nibbling away at her. Eating her. Bite after tiny bite. Big black beetles and hungry spiders, covering her in webs. And though she had shouted for all she was worth, no-one had ever come. No-one, except, that is, the horrible man. Or at least, she assumed it was a man, because it was men she had always been warned about.

*'Don't play too long in the snow or **Jack Frost** will get you'*

*'Don't go out on your own in the dark or the **bogey-man** will get you.'*

Earlier, Abby had tried to put such thoughts out of her mind by singing and humming every song she could possibly think of, from 'The Cheeky Girls' to 'Chico', from 'Girls Aloud' to 'The Pussycat Dolls.' All in an attempt to forget what was happening to her. Trying to block out her fears and the loneliness, and the sounds of the squeaking rats. But in her sadness, the songs hung heavy in her heart and didn't sound right. And so, instead, she had taken to repeating a nursery rhyme her father would say with her every night as he tucked her up in bed. The thought of the tightly tucked blankets and a kiss on her brow 'goodnight' making her feel better. Her door left open with the light filtering into her room until she fell asleep, waking in the morning to a hug from her mother. *'Wake up, sleepy head. Time to dance.'* She'd say, teasing her from her bed. Dancing all around her. Sometimes all around the house. She loved her mum so much and began to wonder if she would ever see her again. And in her loneliness, she began to cry, just as a key turned in a lock behind her, almost out of earshot.

With the sound of the door creaking open, Abby stopped crying and attempted to open her eyes, the blindfold so tight, she could scarcely move her eyelids. Then, slowly, with a faint click of a switch, artificial light filtered through the edges of the coarse cloth, a bleaching white blur seeping through the shroud to her green-blue eyes as she listened to the footsteps coming down the wooden stairway.

The horrible man was back.

Her eyes scrunched closed again in fear of the unknown, the rats and insects forgotten as she shrunk back within herself and curled up tight like a hedgehog into a ball.

She had been taught by her parents never to talk to strangers. She had been told that nasty people weren't just on television, that some of them were real, and sometimes they hurt children for no reason at all. The more Abby thought about that, the more she became afraid. Lying here, all alone except for this nasty man, unable to see or move. Alone with a stranger she was sure was going to hurt her.

She flinched at the touch of his fingers stroking across her brow, slow and gentle, his silence scary and un-nerving. A smell of her hair before he sat her up, and just as before, placed his hand on top of her head, holding a glass of water to her lips as she gulped it down, frightened she'd have to wait as long again before she got any more. Then her thirst quenched, she opened her mouth to the sound of tearing foil, anticipating the food to follow. A sandwich held under her nose for her appraisal. (Tuna fish and cucumber again.) She took a bite, wondering if this was the only sort of sandwich he could make, or did he somehow know that it was her favourite and lacked the inclination to offer her anything else. Either way, she dared not complain. He scarcely fed her enough as it was. And so she ate the remainder of the sandwiches, neither of them speaking a word, her pleading wasted on him earlier when she had begged him to let her go, and without an utterance, he'd untied her wrists and allowed her to squat over a plastic bucket. Then he had bound her once again and left her alone.

But this time was to be different.

He stood her up, untied her hands and ankles, then slowly started removing her clothes; first pulling her t-shirt over her head, her fears growing as she crossed her arms over her chest and hugged herself against the cold, doing everything as she was motioned, too scared to resist, shivering and crying as he unfastened the buttons of her jeans and tugged them from her legs, then tossed them aside.

Twice she had almost fallen over, and in the darkness of her blindfold, he had steadied her, putting her arms by her sides and standing her straight, then fussed and cursed, struggling with something, his breathing a little faster as she heard the ruffle of some clothing and the sound of a zip.

"I have something for you," he said, his cold hands resting on her shoulders and staying there a moment before sliding down her arms and holding her hands, rubbing them affectionately. "I think you're going to like it."

Her hands still in his, he raised them in the air and slipped a large piece of material over her head, then turned her away from him, the zip drawing tight up her back from the waist to the base of her neck before he turned her to face him again, fussing over the dress, sometimes giving tugs to its hem or re-arranging the shoulders. And when he was finished, he paused and held her hand above her head, turning her in pirouette, one clumsy twirl after another, then stopped and released her hand, the sound of his breathing betraying his position as he walked full circle around her. Studying her. His plaything. Like a cat studies a mouse. Her frightened mind imagining him as a monster like the horrible looking rats with their beady eyes, long whiskers, and even longer, worm-like tail.

A cold shiver coursing through her body, she tried to change the picture in her head to one of her parents. Her thoughts on happier times. The smell of the dampness hanging in the air like the whiff of her daddy's socks after a long day at work. Her thoughts of how he would tickle her, the giggles and the hugs to follow his threat of rubbing them in her face. And then, as if on cue, Abby felt something soft brush against the tip of her nose, making her itch a little. Making her want to sneeze. And then again, for a moment longer. The sweet smell of perfume reminding her of her mother. Its floral aroma so fresh in the cold damp air, she inhaled it deep into her lungs before his fingers stroked across her cheek and brushed up through her hair, his hand lingering a while before she felt the stalk being fed over her ear. Then a kiss on the brow and he was gone.

Forty Four

Morton had spent the last twenty-five minutes going over old ground as it were, interviewing a horticulturist and gleaning all he could about roses. In that time he had learned the basics about the various categorisations, hybrids, origins, and usage according to occasions, etc., along with the fact that some flowers were named after places, events, emotions, and even people. But there were other things to remember too. The do's and don'ts for example. A single red rose, as most people know, signifies love for instance, whereas, a bouquet of red and white roses taken into a hospital is considered an ill omen;- likened to bloodied bandages in times of war.

The expert's insight deviating, Morton steered him back to the rose in question, showing him a photograph of a flower taken from a victim. "What can you tell me about this particular flower?" he asked.

The expert looked at the photo and smiled his appreciation, "This, my friend, is a bush rose, also known as a Hybrid Tea. It has thirty-five petals and is generally recognisable by the large size of the flower. This particular specimen is more fondly known as the 'Remember Me' rose." Passing the photo back to Morton, he added. "A beautiful example of an unusual flower I might add."

"Unusual, how?" Morton asked. He liked unusual, unusual meant uncommon, easier to narrow down the possibilities of origin.

"Well, I mean unusual by its colouration. Yellow, yes, but with a unique mixture of copper and bronze. And easily singled out from other, more common roses. Not the most hardy of plants though. Won't grow well in cold regions, and needs a little shade from intense sunlight."

"Are they easy to come by?"

"Well, you could probably order them from most florists I suppose, if they haven't already got them in stock."

Morton's hopes dashed, he asked, "Why leave this particular flower? Why not 'forget-me-nots' for example."

"Honestly, I don't know. But the Myosotis, or 'forget-me-not' as you so rightly called it, is thought to be a symbol of true love, never to be forgotten. It is a totally different genus to the rose. Maybe your answer lies there."

Morton pondered the thought of a message hidden in the type of flower used, along with its name. A double-edged sword? he wondered.

Soon after the expert left, Morton pondered his notes. The flower was important. He knew it. Solve the problem and the pieces would begin to fall into place. 'Remember Me' he thought. An instruction, a request, or a query? And the fact that it was a rose rather than any other type of flower had to mean something. Connected to the killer personally perhaps. If he could find the answer, then he could show D.S.I. Brandt what a huge mistake he and the board had made when choosing Ben over himself for promotion. A mistake that chewed into Morton's very soul.

When the position of D.S. had come up five months ago, there had been two officers in the running for the position. The decision for the selectors was to decide whether the job should go to the best qualified or the most experienced. Morton had felt he was a shoe-in. He had been at the station five years longer than Ben and that had to count for something. But, as it had turned out, it had counted for nothing.

He had found out later that he had missed out on promotion thanks to his people skills. Or rather, his lack of them. His work record and success rate were exemplary, but come the end of the day, success depends on teamwork. And he had been told that if he were serious about progressing through the ranks, then he needed to learn how to delegate. "You can't always go it alone." He had been told. But he would show them. Sometimes you needed to do things yourself to get things done properly, and at this, there was no-one better.

Morton's thoughts were disrupted by the sound of someone's knuckles rapping on his open door, and he looked up to see the old psychiatrist entering his office.

"Yes, doctor," he snapped impatiently, "What is it?"

Schmidt was becoming a part of the furniture. From the outset of the murders he had asked for protection, and though he was now considered low risk, Meg had decided to take advantage of his familiarity with Sean Edwards. 'We need every available resource' she had said, and so, had come to an arrangement with the doctor. For his own peace of mind, he would be given the use of a small office at the station on condition that he only received calls from his patients by phone rather than in person. His calls were being monitored and re-routed to the station from his office. This was agreed on the understanding that Schmidt would be on hand if ever his services were needed throughout the case, including his presence during the 10:15 calls. Beyond this, he could come and go as he pleased, and when he returned home at night, a police escort would first check his premises before he went in.

Schmidt spoke in his croaky, heavy accent, "I am looking for detective Miller, or detective Rainer. Could you tell me ver they are?"

"They are out on police business," said Morton, "Maybe I can help."

Schmidt looked doubtful of whether he should speak to Morton or wait until Meg or Ben returned. "Vell, I think I may have something of use to you."

"Go on."

Schmidt produced an audiotape from his jacket pocket and placed it on Morton's desk. "This is from a session I had vith Mr. Edvards some months ago. It vas recorded during a stage of regression. You might like to listen to it."

"Why? What's on it?"

"Information about his past. It has details of ver he lived and played as a boy. It might give you an idea of ver to find his daughter. But it vill also give you an insight into the man."

"And why didn't you give us this sooner?" Morton asked.

"Vell, I hear things. I vorry that there is somevon helping Mr. Edwards. Somevon on the police force perhaps. I fear I should be careful."

"Careful indeed," said Morton. "A split personality and an accomplice. Effectively, that makes three of them we are looking for."

Schmidt looked at him quizzically, unsure how to respond, and in that moment a WPC rushed into the room from the adjoining office. "Doctor Schmidt. There's a call. It's Edwards."

Morton told her to transfer it through to his office and moments later listened in as Schmidt took the call on speaker-phone.

"You've heard what they're saying about me?" Sean asked. "About me killing people? About my daughter?"

"Yes," Schmidt answered with an air of regret. "Yes, I have."

"I need your help, doctor. I've looked for her *everywhere*. My baby, Abby. You have to help me find her."

Schmidt spoke in a soft, soothing voice, "Sean, you need to stay calm. But if you *are* to find your daughter, you need the help of the police. You must hand yourself in, Sean."

"I can't. I daren't. If I do, I may never see her again."

"And if you do not, you may never see her again," said Schmidt. "You know vat it is like, Sean. The time-lapses. The memory loss. You have to come in, before it's too late."

"There's something you need to know, doctor. I remembered something. I had a flashback. There was a boy, about nine, sneaking up on some-one. Only, well, it wasn't someone, it was a bee. But it means something, I know it does. I need you to help me remember the rest of it. To figure it out."

"Come to the station. We can vork on it together. We can find out ver Abby is and bring her home."

"The station?" Sean asked. "I don't understand." Then everything clicked into place. "They are there, aren't they? The police. They're there. You're helping them." His voice rose with his anger, "You're supposed to be helping *me!* Remember? Not the police."

"And I *vill* help you, Sean. We can find her, together. Before it is too late."

"She's alive, doctor. I feel it. No. I know it. Don't ask me how. Besides, I wouldn't kill her. I couldn't." He paused, the silence dragging on forever before he asked the question on the edge of his lips, "Could I?"

"But it is not you doing these things," said Schmidt. "Not the *real* you. That is vhy you have to come in."

Sean was silent as Schmidt waited for his response and Morton listened intently, the pause ending with a click and the drone of the dial-tone as Sean hung up.

Forty Five

From the moment the case had hit the front pages of the national newspapers and the t.v. stations clambered for information, Chief Superintendent Jim Brandt had seen to it that he was the one at the forefront of the investigation. But now, all of that was about to change. The hierarchy were breathing heavily down his neck for results, and he'd had enough of getting hot under the collar.

With an increased body-count and no sign of any let-up, the media thronged for information, and Jim Brandt sat at the desk in the conference room, acting the chaperone to Meg as she was forced to face a barrage of questions. If anyone was going to crash and burn, he'd decided, it was to be acting S.I.O. Meg Rainer. From now on, *she* would be the focal point in all of this. *The scapegoat*. And Ben was the failsafe on hand for any backlash, sitting to Meg's left with an earpiece linking him to the incident room should there be any further developments.

Like a bursting firework, blinding flashes merged into an explosion of white light as reporters bustled and cajoled for a response, shouting out their questions as they vied for attention. Questions fired from all angles. Notebooks at the ready.

"Is it true that you are no closer to catching Sean Edwards now, than you were at the start of the investigation?" shouted one of them.

Meg was calm in her response, "At this moment in time we have a number of ongoing leads and expect to reap the benefits of those in due course."

Raised voices merging into a gaggle, Brandt pointed to a reporter on the left.

"As we are all too well aware, Detective Rainer, Edwards is replicating the killings of Joseph Inkleman who went on to kill nine people in the space of seven days, ending with the brutal murder of his own daughter. Do you think it's possible that Edwards is aiming for the same death toll as his counterpart, and if so, do you expect it to also culminate with the death of his own little girl?"

"As I'm sure you are well aware, I can not make assumptions as to the intentions or mindset of Sean Edwards. However, we are pooling all available resources into this case and hope to bring it to a quick and effective conclusion."

"What can you tell us about Sean Edwards' movements?" asked another.

"I can not divulge that information at this time."

"Do you have any further evidence of an accomplice?"

"I can not say," Meg replied.

"What ***can*** you say, detective?"

"We are keeping an open mind at this stage. Some of our questions remain unanswered, and because of this, nothing can be ruled out."

"What can you do to assure the general public of their safety, and how soon do you expect to apprehend Sean Edwards and put an end to these killings?"

"I would appeal to the public to be vigilant. We are doing all we can to bring this matter to its conclusion, but in the meantime, I urge the general public to err on the side of caution. Do not open your doors to strangers. Do not leave yourself vulnerable to attack. If you do have to go out on your own, please make sure you can be seen. Avoid dark or secluded areas. And if you see this man, do not approach him. He is considered to be armed and dangerous and any sightings should be reported to the police immediately."

Ben felt like a Christian watching his inamorata being thrown to the lions. He wanted to stand up and draw her tormentors away. He wanted to defer the questioning back to the superintendent, the grilling relentless as Brandt pointed to one after another from the horde of inquisitors. And when the inquisition finally came to its end, he saw Meg pulled to one side as they exited through the door of the conference room.

"What the hell did you think you were playing at back there?" barked Brandt.

Meg remained calm, "I was preparing them, sir. I was trying to save lives."

"You were scare-mongering, that's what you were doing. Driving them into a panic with your 'do's and don'ts'. They didn't need to hear all that. It's all common sense."

Ben knew Meg was more than capable of fending for herself, but he couldn't take this any longer and squared up to the superintendent, "Forgive me for saying so, ***sir***, but 'common sense' isn't so common anymore," his restraint bursting at the seams, he continued, "If it were, then you would have stood up to *your* responsibilities back there, instead of looking for a patsy to soak up the furore surrounding this."

"Shut it, Ben. You've got no idea what kind of shit I'm dealing with right now, so get this into your thick skull. We're *all* patsies here. So unless you want to be taken off this case, I advise you to take a good long walk and cool off, before one of us does something we might regret."

Ben's temper rising, he opened his mouth to vent more of his frustrations, but with a look from Meg, stopped himself short.

Brandt turned to Meg, looking for the honesty in her eyes as he repeated a question thrown up by one of the reporters. "I want to know, in no uncertain terms;- are we any nearer to putting an end to all of this?"

"We're closing the net, sir," she answered. "It's only a matter of time."

"We haven't **got** time, detective. Didn't you see the frenzy out there?"

See it? Thought Meg, I was in the thick of it for fuck sake.

For the first time since the media became involved, Brandt had shied away from the publicity and Meg could see why. The limelight more of a shitty brown as the tabloids pointed the finger at the police with accusations of inadequacies and incompetence. "We'll get him, sir," she said. "You have my word."

"Your word isn't good enough, detective. I want results. And for all our sakes, they had better come quick."

Following a threat of disciplinary action, Meg and Ben sat quietly in her office as their news conference was broadcast nationwide, the coverage of their grilling followed by a rundown of what had happened so far, and pictures of the victims shown along with a photograph of Sean Edwards. This, they knew, would result in the call-centre being flooded with calls from so-called witnesses spread over the length and breadth of the country. And because of this, and the timescale involved, it had already been decided to filter out those calls *not* from the Northeast, as this was Sean Edwards's hunting ground, and he was still suspected of being in the area. From this nucleus of valid callers, some would be mistaken identities, and others would be timewasters or attention-seekers. This left approximately sixty-five percent of the remaining calls to be narrowed down yet further, and although the majority of them would be viable, only a handful could be expected to have any real chance of being authentic. All of which had to be checked. And there was still the matter of finding David Hetherington.

When the broadcast finished, Meg felt a mixture of emotions, her angry gaze hidden from Ben as she stood looking out of the window onto the expanse of lawns bordering the staff car park. She was still fuming at the way Brandt had spoken to her after having heaped the extra burden of the interview onto her already buckling shoulders, the pressure growing more intense as one lead after another came to a dead end. And to top it all, she was torn between her waning ambitions and her propensity to make a move on Ben, desperate for a hug and wanting to feel the strength of his arms around her. Wanting some affection and companionship. Maybe even some emotional involvement. Yet, earlier in the day she had wanted none of these things, her emotions in turmoil, her heart saying one thing and her head saying another, unable to make sense of how she felt.

Her shower this morning had brought back memories of a time they had made love, causing her to contemplate putting a proposal to Ben and telling him that she had needs just like anyone else. That she would like to have a casual relationship with him. Nothing more, and nothing less. Now, she wasn't sure what she wanted, her thoughts of how quickly things had changed throughout the day, everything conspiring against them to push and pull them apart. It seemed it had always been that way between them. That it might be that way forever. The two of them, never meant to be 'together' in the *real* sense of the word.

She walked over to where he was sitting and stood behind him, resting her hand on his shoulder. Comforting him, and in turn, drawing comfort from his touch, his hand resting on hers as he sat with his back to her, staring down at the desk. His thoughts of Joe and Olivia Crompton. To his superiors, just another statistic on Sean Edwards' record. A woman in the wrong place at the wrong time. But *they* hadn't seen her husband crumble into a heap, his life shattered when Ben broke the news of what had happened.

"It's one of the hardest things I've ever done, Meg," said Ben. "Telling a friend his wife is dead, and knowing I could have done something to prevent it."

"You mustn't blame yourself, Ben. There's nothing you could have done."

"I should have realised, Meg. Edwards told me. He said 'someone close'. And I failed to pick up on that. I thought he meant my family." His heart sank with the guilty feeling of relief that that wasn't the case, and he turned to look into Meg's eyes. "I was blinded, Meg. The red haze fell over my eyes as I feared the worst."

Meg wanted to kiss him and hold him close. "It's not your fault, Ben. He could have meant anyone."

Ben stood from his chair and held her hand loosely in his own, "I didn't see it. I allowed my emotions to cloud my judgement. I-," He wavered on the verge of spilling his guts before the words trickled from his lips, "I thought he meant you. I thought he was going to take you away from me, Meg. I thought he was going to kill you."

Meg moved nearer and held him close, her head against his cheek. "He'd be a fool to try," she said, "With you shadowing my every move, he would never have stood a chance."

The sweet smell of her hair drifting to his nose, Ben remembered a time he had seen the Cromptons locked in a similar embrace, the day they found out they were pregnant.

"Maybe that's the reason he chose Olivia," he sighed. "She was accessible. He wasn't after just any victim. This time, it was personal. He did this to prove a point. He did it to show me who's in charge."

With a bolt from the blue, Meg broke away from him, "Maybe that's just it, Ben. Maybe he's not in charge. Maybe it's the accomplice we need to focus our attention on. Maybe he's holding Edwards to ransom. And using his daughter as bait."

"That doesn't make sense. He surrendered her to this so called accomplice. Remember? At the train station. And she went willingly."

"So maybe it's not your regular accomplice," said Meg, her thoughts spinning off in all directions as she tried to make sense of it all. "We've been assuming it's a cop, and probably a man. But who's to say it's not a woman. Maybe we were right earlier when we told Schmidt that Edwards had a mistress. Only, maybe she's the alter ego's mistress. And maybe his daughter knows her as a friend, and that's why she went so willingly."

Forty Six

During the news conference, Morton had left Schmidt's tape in Meg's tray, but not before making a list of the places mentioned on it and heading out to check them for himself.

So far, all had come to nothing.

Fyndoune bank, Sacriston, County Durham. Approximately six miles from Chester-le-Street.

Morton had parked his car at the roadside and crossed to the hedgerow, its gaps bridged with fencing, and a ditch on the other side bordering a fallow field. He climbed over, jumped the ditch, and stumbled through the clumpy thatches of long grass before heading for the upper end of the field, walking until he could eventually see the old stonework of a long disused bomb-shelter. A pause to survey the landscape around him, looking in every direction. Not for the first time today, he felt as though he was being watched.

He closed on the shelter slowly, wary that Edwards might be lurking inside. Possibly with his daughter. Possibly alone. Watching him as he inched forward, out in the open, looking all around, checking there was nowhere else to hide. Suddenly aware of his own vulnerability as he approached the shelter, his eyes watching for any movement, the wind brushing past his ears and muffling any sounds as he listened for voices, and his footing unsteady as he crossed the uneven surface, realising too late that he'd made a mistake in coming alone. That this was dangerous. Thinking; if something should happen to him, how long would it be before he was found.

Just yards from the shelter, he called out, "Edwards?"

No reply.

He edged forwards, almost at a crouch. Ready to react if he was attacked, "Mr. Edwards, it's the police. We'd like to talk to you."

The wind muffling his ears he listened for an answer, and just feet away from the shelter, he tried one last time, "Mr. Edwards. I have colleagues hidden nearby. There are weapons trained on the shelter. If there are any sudden movements, they'll shoot, but I don't want that. So please, come out peacefully with your arms raised, and we can talk about where this is going."

Still feeling he was being watched, the adrenalin pumped hot through his veins and his hands balled into fists ready to lash out. And then, stealing a breath, he did it, without a moment for second thoughts. He darted through the entrance of the shelter only to find it empty, the ravages of time turning it into nothing more than a square patch of dirt sunken four feet below the level of the field, its walls and entrance lined with stone. No windows, no door, and no-longer a roof to shield it from the elements. The last of his leads had turned up nothing.

He stepped from the shelter, angry and disappointed, a reflection of sunlight catching his eye as it bounced off glass in the distance. A car parked behind his own and a man standing between them, watching him through binoculars. Watching Morton picking up his pace as he headed towards him. The man merely a silhouette, turned to get into his car as Morton drew closer, breaking into a run as he shouted, "Hey, you!" Trying to make him out. Trying to identify the car. The ignition starting and the engine revving. A screech of the tires as he sped away.

Forty Seven

Sean stood at the self-service pump, apprehensive as he watched two young men in football shirts come out of the garage-shop, get into a car, and drive off, his thoughts of how much easier it had been buying the old Nissan from the breakers yard. An out-of-the-way flea pit ran by a gypsy-like one-man team of owner, mechanic and salesman, standing in a tacky suit with patter to match, and more interested in the £600 Sean was waving in front of him for the old banger than he was in the person holding it. But in the shop he was more likely to get attention. People being people, customers could be nosy or the patron the suspicious type, watching for shoplifters and possibly noticing more about Sean than he would like him to.

The tank full, the fuel nozzle clicked off and Sean nervously rubbed his hand over his shaven head, trying to build up the courage to walk the dozen or so strides to the shop, thankful to find it quiet, only a few people wandering around the rows of shelves to pick up an odd item whilst an old man with tar-stained fingers stood at the till collecting his change for a pack of cigarettes. Sean, in his casual jeans and T-shirt, was scarcely given a glance as he headed for the rack of newspapers where he feigned browsing until the shop grew quieter, awaiting his moment before picking up a selection of tabloids and hurrying them to the counter where the cashier barely made eye-contact, his interest focused between the items being put through the till and a dusty old portable, a vividly coloured movie playing in a language Sean could only guess at as being of Indian/Asian origin.

Sean threw the papers onto the passenger seat, and starting the ignition, heaved a sigh of relief. He needed the papers as much as he needed the fuel. His search for Abby had been fruitless and he hoped that the papers would tell him something useful. Perhaps a thread of information that would provide him with clues to her whereabouts, or better yet, tell him his daughter had been found safe and well. Either way, he needed to know what was happening, and ten minutes later he sat in a quiet lay-by, flicking through the pages to find the public outcry huge and the headlines tugging at his heartstrings.

'Doomed to Die'

'The Sacrificial Lamb'

'Missing or Murdered?'

The front pages were plastered with a photograph of his daughter cuddling her favourite toy, standing with her arms wrapped around a rabbit that was almost as big as she was, its ears draped over her shoulders as she smiled for the camera. It was a copy of another of Amy's photographs. Abby and Flopsy. Taken last year after Sean had won the toy at the fair.

He looked into her smiling eyes, a lump in his throat as he remembered the day of his anniversary, his happiness tinged with a pang of guilt for leaving her, though she was more than happy to spend the night with her gran, and laughed as he said goodbye; pinching her nose and crossing his eyes before giving her a hug and a kiss as she had held onto the rabbit, the scene the same as the photo.

"See you tomorrow, sugar bun." Another hug and kiss before tearing himself away.

"And Flopsy too," she had said.

And his hands mimicking ears on top of his head, his nose twitching and a goofy expression, he gave the rabbit a kiss, "And Flopsy too," he had said, Abby beaming a smile as she watched him leaving.

Now he was confronted with the papers telling him he had played a part in her disappearance;-

---

POLICE APPEAL FOR HELP

Late last night, in a dramatic call to our editor, Senior investigating officer Megan Rainer revealed that on Friday, 30th March, their prime suspect in the Mutilator killings, Mr. Sean Edwards, also wanted in connection with the abduction and disappearance of his daughter, was seen at Chester-le-Street train station between the times of 9:50a.m. and 10:28a.m.

Mr. Edwards is known to have seen his daughter onto a train before leaving the station himself on foot, and at the time of this report, the whereabouts of both are unknown. Anyone with information of their whereabouts, or anyone who was in the area at the time stated above is asked to contact the police immediately on 0800 2278873.

Sean remembered none of it.

Another time-lapse during a time with his daughter, she had been with him at his most dangerous. An unpredictable killer strolling along with an innocent, trusting little girl.

He battled with his questions, wondering why he had put her on a train. Wondering if he had met up with her later, or worse still; had he sent her to her death at the hands of his so-called accomplice, and if so, how could he find out?

He turned on his phone and looked at the only three numbers saved to its memory. Dr. Schmidt, who was now helping the police. Durham police headquarters, whom he felt he couldn't trust, and Detective Meg Rainer, the police-woman who had taken his call when he'd attempted to contact Amy.

* * *

Meg was at home, multi-tasking, her microwave bleeping her meal was ready as she fastened her fresh white blouse and tripped into a pair of trousers. She pinged open the door to her bolognaise pasta and was stirring it with a fork when her phone rang.

"Detective Rainer," she answered.

His voice low, his tone troubled, Sean said, "It's me. I need your help."

Her stirring stopped cold, "You're killing people Mr. Edwards. Or should I say, you're *butchering* people. So give me one good reason why I should help you?"

Sean spoke with an air of regret and desperation. “Because I don’t want to kill these people. Because I have a daughter, and I think the only chance we have of saving her is to work together.”

“Then come to the station,” she said.

“That’s not an option.”

“Why isn’t it an option?”

“Because if I do, he’ll kill her.”

“Who’ll kill her, Sean? Tell me. I need to know.”

“I don’t know,” Sean answered, despondent and confused. “Maybe the accomplice, maybe me. Not ***me***, I mean;- the other me. The killer. I think we are working together. I think we are both connected somehow, during my time-lapses.”

“You’re not making sense, Sean. You’re playing games with me. How can I be expected to help you if you won’t tell me anything.”

“I’m telling you, I don’t know who he is. But I can tell you other things. Stuff that might help you find Abby. He sends me letters. He tells me there are rules.”

“What letters? What rules?”

“He says he has my daughter and that he’ll kill her. He said there are only three days left, and then, he’s going to cut her head off.” He froze at the thought, then continued, “And he knows things.”

“What things?”

“All kinds of things. He said that the victims were all connected in some way. He said that the others had had to try harder to find the clues.”

“What clues, Sean? And what others? What are you talking about?”

“I don’t know,” he answered, his throat closing up.

“You have to come in, Sean. We have to put a stop to this.”

“You’re not *listening!* I can’t come in. He told me he’ll kill my daughter. If I’m caught or hand myself in, he’ll kill her.”

“It doesn’t have to be that way.”

“You don’t understand. He knows everything about us. About me, about you, about everything that’s happening. And he warned me you were getting closer. It’s not safe for me there. That’s why I had to ring you. If you catch me, he’ll kill her, and I can’t let that happen. Please, you have to help me. You can’t allow that to happen.”

“We’re doing all we can, Sean. But I need to know everything *you* know if I’m to have any chance of saving Abby. I need the letters, Sean.”

"I'll post them to you. On one condition."

"Which is?"

"When you find out who the accomplice is, you let me know."

"I can't do that."

"You have to," said Sean, desperate. "He'll know when you're onto him, but I can get close to him. And if I can convince him I'm my other self when I'm not, I can be of use to you. I may be your only option."

As Meg pondered his request, Sean's thoughts were of the danger his daughter was in, the dismemberments getting progressively worse, until, finally, it would end with the death of his little girl. The most gruesome killing of all, decapitated after a slow and painful torture.

Meg's voice interrupted his thinking, "When we know who it is, I'll get in touch," she said.

"And you'll tell me?" he asked.

"We'll talk," said Meg. "But what about tonight? Does this mean you won't be calling the station?"

"I can't answer that," said Sean, his voice fading with his hopes. "I don't know what I'll be doing. I never do."

Forty Eight

As darkness fell, the scene from his father's conservatory became a montage of silhouettes against the dulling sky. The flowering borders, rocky water feature, and green-stained shed at the bottom of the enclosed garden, now a jumble of shapes without colour. Ben was sat on a lounger, mid-call on his mobile, when he heard Meg's voice as she was shown through by his father, and quickly, cut short his conversation, "I can't talk right now. Have to go. Speak to you later," and snapped his phone closed, slipping it into his pocket before she entered the room.

"Nothing better to do?" she asked with a joking hint of sarcasm.

Ben sat leaning his head back into his hands and yawned as he stretched, "That depends. What's the latest?"

"I've just had a call from Edwards. He's asking for help again."

"And you said?"

Meg flexed her eyebrows in a 'what do *you* think' expression.

Ben didn't like to think she'd entertained the idea. "You can't, Meg. He's dangerous."

"He was different, Ben. There wasn't that mean streak of before. He's frightened and confused."

"Of course he's confused. He has a split personality. Remember?"

How could I forget, she thought. But it seemed everyone else had forgotten that Sean Edwards had lost his wife, and his child was missing. And there was a side to him, who, in his innocence, had been caught up in all of this. He himself a victim of his own illness. Meg felt that there may be times when it would pay to remember that.

Ben continued, "Don't forget, Meg. He may have seemed scared, but he can be cold and calculating too. When you talk with him, how can you be sure which is which? He fooled his wife. He can fool you too."

Throughout the case, Meg, like Schmidt, had pointed out that Edwards had actually loved his wife and child. "It may have been premeditated," she said, "But it wasn't voluntary. He killed her because of his illness. It's not like she was having an *affair* or anything."

"I can't believe you're defending him. He didn't need an excuse to kill her. He's a psycho. Simple as."

"He says he wants to save his daughter. I have to believe that, deep down inside, there is an element of truth to what he's saying."

"Ahum," Ben's father interrupted with a cough to remind them he was there, and an excuse for him to leave them to it, "Coffee anyone?"

"I could murder a cup of tea, please." Meg answered, her pun unintended.

Harry looked to his son for an answer, "Coffee?"

Ben tried to make light of the situation, and with a rye grin, shook his head as he answered, "Yes." The two of them sharing a smile as Meg looked from one to the other in confusion. And as Harry left for the kitchen, Ben explained, "It's something I used to do as a kid. Answer one way and gesture the opposite. Dad knows what I mean. It's just a matter of listening to what I say and ignoring the head action."

"Yeah, right," said Meg, "I bet *you* couldn't ignore a little head action."

Ben smiled, asking if that was an offer, and Meg struggled to imitate his childish prank, her awkward nodding over-exaggerated as she said, "No."

Their disagreements on the back-burner, the two of them joked and flirted a little more before Meg excused herself to go to the bathroom and Ben's father returned with the beverages and biscuits.

"You worry about her, don't you?" his father asked.

"All the time," Ben replied.

"Listen, son. You don't have to tell me how you feel about Meg, I can see it plain as day. But can *she* see it. Does she know how you feel?"

"I'm not sure I want her to know, dad. I don't know if I could burden her with that."

Harry's expression was one of sadness and understanding. Up until his wife had died, he himself had always had difficulty explaining his feelings and could see some of his own failings in his son, buried amongst the strengths of his dear departed wife. "You've got to tell her, son."

Though it had been a long time coming, the floodgates opened with a whoosh, Ben telling his father *everything* in one mad rush, trying to give good reason for his split with Meg. Explaining how he had intended to marry her. How it had all fallen apart. How, for weeks she had failed to return his calls. And then, one night while on duty, he'd had a close call with a perp', narrowly escaping with his life as he dived out of the way of an oncoming car. He explained how it had made him think. How he worried about Meg being caught up in a similar situation and found it difficult to do his job properly knowing she was out there, taking the same sort of life-threatening risks. How could he live with that? How could he expect Meg to give up a career that he himself was a part of. And hard as it was, he'd decided, regretfully, that maybe it was best that he and Meg didn't get back together after all.

"You boys talking about me by any chance?" asked Meg, coming back into the conservatory.

"I was just saying," said Harry, "how much Mary thought of you. You know she loved you, don't you? You were the daughter she never had."

Meg tried to disguise her flattered, slightly embarrassed expression before saying with a fond smile, "She was a wonderful woman, Harry. I miss her greatly."

"Me too," Harry said, a tear welling as he puffed up a cushion on a wicker chair for Meg to sit next to him and choked, "Come on, brew's up. Help yourselves before it gets cold, and you two can't stay here and chat all day. You have work to do."

The three of them sat a while longer, Ben drifting off into his own private thoughts as Meg and Harry spoke of times past and lessons learned. The two of them catching up on a lost friendship as Ben caught up with his memories of his plans to marry Meg, remembering how he had spent weeks of surreptitiously scheming with one of her former colleagues. The woman acting as go between and reporting back to Ben with her discoveries of Meg's ideal marriage proposal. Filling in the blanks to what Ben had found out for himself. The two of them slowly gathering snippets of information and piecing them together, bit by bit, so as not to arouse her suspicions. Meg was, after all, a detective.

Then, one rainy night, after making the final arrangements, Ben had returned home struggling to wipe the grin from his face to hide how happy he was, everything set to take place a week to the day. The day of Meg's birthday. Everything booked and organised, the plan was as intricate as planning a wedding itself, and all being well, that would be the next step. His hope being that she would be so happy, so blown away by it all, that she would have no alternative other than to say "*Yes*" to him there and then.

But his plans were to take an ominous turn.

On that final night of planning, he had been bursting with excitement, the thrashing rain unable to dampen his spirits as he'd returned home to find a taxi parked outside his home, its meter running and Meg struggling with the last of her cases.

She had let the driver take it from her grasp as she turned to see Ben approaching, and with venom, spat out her curses, saying how sly and devious he had been. Saying how she couldn't trust him again, *ever.* Stomping around to the passenger door as he tried to bar her way, pleading for her to let him explain. To wait. But enraged and hurt, she had barged past him with a hateful stare, and blinded by anger, stormed into the taxi, deaf to his pleas for her to listen to him. Ignoring his shouting out, "But I love you" as the taxi pulled away. Its tail-lights becoming a blur as he stood there soaked, his arms slumped to his sides. His tears and the rain, trickling down his face.

It was almost a month before Ben's life had regained some kind of normality. He'd figured she had found out about his plan and was scared off, not yet ready for such a commitment. And, as he sat in the conservatory, contemplating how he had wanted to spend the rest of his life with her, he thought of how frightened he was of getting that close to anyone ever again. Frightened of falling at that same final hurdle. Afraid to make the jump in case there was another deep chasm on the other side.

"Too many things are left unsaid until it is too late. Isn't that right, Ben," said his father.

"Huh?" Ben snapped out of his daydream.

"Never mind," Harry said, turning his attention back to Meg. "Better to have loved and lost than to have never loved at all. Isn't that what they say?"

"I guess," Meg replied, taking a bite of her biscuit.

"I never really understood what it meant until my Mary was taken," Harry said, standing to take away the crockery and placing his hand on Meg's shoulder, telling her again, "Loved you like a daughter, she did," a heavy sigh before he added, "Loved us all as a matter of fact."

As his father left the room, Ben turned to her, "It's true, Meg. She did love you. And I loved you too." And with obvious sincerity in his voice, he held her eyes, afraid of what they might tell him as he added, "I still do."

Meg's heart skipped a beat and landed like the bang of a drum. She almost leapt from her seat with the urge to jump on his lap. She wanted to wrap her arms around him and feel his arms wrapped around her in return. She wanted his affection. Wanted to feel loved. And yet, all of these feelings she kept hidden within her bursting heart. Afraid to open up to him. Afraid to show weakness. She bit at her lip and stayed in her seat, without moving an inch to reveal a clue to her true feelings. "Ahum… Errr, let's not do this, shall we," she said, "There are more important matters at hand right now."

She had struggled to control herself, but had had to. Ben was acting out of character. Saying the sort of things his mother would have wanted him to say. Saying what his father had already hinted at. Maybe even saying what he thought Meg wanted to hear rather than what was really on his mind. But this time, she wasn't going to play along. Never again would she allow him to take her on that emotional rollercoaster to be derailed yet again.

"Why did you leave me, Meg?"

"It's in the past, Ben. Forget it."

"I need to know. I'm trying to understand."

"Understand this, Ben. There's a killer out there. A little girl's missing and could be dead within the next three days if we don't find her. And then there's an accomplice out there who may well be on the force. And as if things aren't complicated enough, you throw this at me."

Ben backed down and apologised, saying that she was right. That from now on the case came first. And with an air of discomfort, the two of them awkwardly changed the subject. No more flirting. No more laughing. The two of them sitting together, yet miles apart. Neither of them thinking about the case as each of them made their excuses to leave in opposite directions with the understanding that they'd meet up at headquarters within the hour. Each thinking they had made a mistake. That they had spoken out of turn. That they had said the wrong thing.

Each with regrets.

And each feeling alone when they needed each other most.

Forty Nine

Back in the solitude of his room, Sean sat on his bed with a note-book and pen, his back against the headboard as the television played away to itself on mute. Over and over again, the news channel flashing up one picture after another of the victims when they were alive, their homes now shown as crime scenes with neighbours giving their input into what they knew of them. The report concluding with a picture of Sean and his missing daughter.

He closed his eyes to the haunting images and listened to the cheap portable radio sat next to him on the chest of drawers, the tinny echo of its speakers vibrating against its casing. A BBC news reporter with a slight northern accent told of the latest developments and appealed to the public for help, ending his broadcast with the offer of a reward for information leading to Sean's arrest. And throughout, Sean continued to take notes. The steady influx of evidence streaming in from all angles as he sat compiling, analysing and cross-referencing every little detail against the piles of pages he'd collated from his selection of newspapers, leaving a mess all around him. Paper strewn everywhere. The room looking like it had been struck by a mini-tornado, with discarded broadsheets and crumpled up pages torn from his note-book, Sean sitting in the middle of it as though in the eye of a storm; his face sullen and his complexion pale, the lack of sleep draining his resolve, and his hopes waning after a long day of searching for his daughter.

He had searched everywhere he could, keeping a low profile whilst checking anywhere that looked like a possible hideaway, avoiding the populace and trying to look inconspicuous as he wandered around old childhood haunts, derelict buildings, farms and barns and disused factories. All to no avail. If he had thought Abby was dead, he'd end his life right now and not care one iota, but instead, he convinced himself to carry on. Convinced himself that *'no news'* as they say *'was good news.'* As long as there was a chance she was alive, there was hope, and ironically, that hope was given to him by the very tabloids that persecuted him. The tabloids that had portrayed him as a cold blooded killer, public enemy number one, their comments and statements limiting his movements and confining him to the perimeters of the guest house, his room fast becoming a prison cell in its own right. But, from those very same tabloids, Sean had discovered that he had put Abby on a train at Chester-le-Street.

The odds stacking against him, he rang customer services to find the train travelled south, all the way to London, making countless stops and connections en route, his frustration growing as he sank into the deep hole of despair, angry at his own incompetence. His inability to remember anything of importance. Angry that, no matter which way he had turned, every lead came to a dead end. Each slap in the face bringing him closer to his nightmare's end and reminding him how useless he was. Reminding him he wasn't a policeman, he was a network marketer. A jumped up, over-the-top salesman, who only got where he was by making the most of other peoples skills. And.., he froze as it dawned on him, thinking to himself, *Other people.* Use *their* skills. *If he* couldn't investigate, then he would learn from those who could. And whether they wanted to help him or not, tomorrow he would shadow the police in the hope that, by retracing his steps, something would jog in his memory.

He climbed from the bed to gather up the mess of scrunched up papers, down on hands and knees, and only then did he see a note had been slipped under his door;- *Mr. Waders* written sloppily on its outer surface.

He had all but forgotten his arrangement with Thomas, and his time-lapses unaccounted for, he hoped that the note would shed some light on what he had been doing.

Tentatively, he unfolded the note-paper and read through the childish writing.

today was like this
at qorter past nine I herd your fone ring in your room and you were torking and then you come out of your room and you had a flower in your pocket
at ten past three you came back to your room and you have a new car and it is a vorxall astra
at four aclock my daddy give you a letter
at twenty five minits to five you left your room again
at ten minits past eight you came back again

it is qorter past eight and i cannot rite any more and i have to go to bed now cos its my bed time
from Thomas

Sean had hoped for something more enlightening. Something useful. The mention of a name or a place. Instead, all he got were inconsequential facts, most of which were of no use to him. They merely confirmed the time he'd left his room to kill again, though he remembered neither that nor the phone call, and since the murder soon after, the rest of his day had been a living nightmare.

He sat back on his bed, despondent, a newspaper lying next to him with a blown up picture of him emblazoned across the front page and the headline in bold print. **THE MUTILATOR**. Only… Sean wasn't The Mutilator. Not really. The Mutilator was a cruel, sick and twisted person hidden deep within him. And only *he* knew where his daughter was hidden. One way or another, he had to find a way to get through to him, and again he thought of doctor Schmidt, thinking about how, under his treatment, he had learned that the conscious mind was responsible for deliberate thought and problem solving, but the majority of what we do stems from our subconscious. It is this part of the mind which is responsible for drawing on everything we have ever learned. It is this, along with instinct, that enables us to perform everyday tasks without thinking. This is what controls who we are. And this, he was sure, was where The Mutilator was residing. If Sean could find a way to trigger his re-emergence whilst maintaining his control, then maybe, just maybe, he could discover what he had done, where he had been, and most importantly, who the accomplice was, and where he was holding Abby.

He racked his brain for an answer, wondering how he could best remember. Wondering how he could tap into his subconscious thoughts and trigger another flashback, his problem being that they only ever occurred during times of violence, and maybe that was what was needed to reach his goal. Maybe he had to kill someone, either as The Mutilator, or whilst in control of himself and aware of what he was actually doing. But then again, did he merely think he was in control right now, or was this how his alter ego would normally behave during his time-lapses, and if so, would he forget ever having these thoughts. Whatever the answer, there was no way of knowing what was going through his mind during the time of the killings, and though the deliberate taking of a life was the worst act imaginable, it was something he was forced to consider. But to the question of whether or not he was capable, Sean already knew the answer. To him, the cost of a stranger's life was worth far less than that of his daughter's, and he would do anything he had to to save her.

He scrunched Thomas's note into his pocket and headed for the boy's room, questions still to be answered.

Quietly, he negotiated the stairs and ventured into the private section of the guest house, stealing his way past the unattended reception desk and along a corridor-come-hall to a nest of adjacent rooms, past a kitchen, bathroom, and the living room where he could hear the opening spit of a can as Thomas's father settled down in front of the t.v. to watch football. Next, he came to two doors opposite one-another, just as Thomas had said. One of which, had his quarry's nameplate. This was it. The boy had told Sean how to find his room so he could slip his reward under his pillow. He would be expecting a payment of £5 in an envelope. He certainly wouldn't be expecting this.

Sean sneaked into the boy's room, thankful for street lights, the glow filtering through the flimsy curtains to shed light into the toy-littered room, the walls adorned with posters of Transformers and football heroes, and in a corner, a computer console stood next to a box stacked with games. But the focal point, by far, was the bed against the far wall.

Thomas lay sound asleep with a look of peace and contentment, almost angelic, and slowly, as he turned in his sleep, a hand drew closer, reaching to cover his mouth. And with the smothering of the hand, Thomas's eyes opened wide with fear.

"It's okay, Thomas," Sean whispered. "It's me. I need your help. Can I trust you to be quiet."

The fear in Thomas's eyes evaporated, and with a nod of his head, Sean removed his hand and put his finger to his lips, "Shhhh."

Thomas sat up with excitement and almost blurted out loud, then corrected himself to a whisper, "Is someone after you, sir?"

"Kinda'" said Sean, "I need you to do something for me. As a spy. Can I depend on you?"

"Yes, sir," Thomas whispered, and gave a sharp salute. "Secret agent Thomas Golightly, at your service."

"I need to know everything you *didn't* write in your note," said Sean. "More importantly, what was said on the phone."

Thomas gave a puzzled look, "I didn't do noffing wrong, sir, did I? Only. You said the times. I didn't know I was 'posed to listen to your calls."

"No, Thomas. You did nothing wrong. It's my fault. I should have asked you to write down everything you could. And from now on, that's what I want you to do. I want you to write down times, phone calls, any names or places you hear me mention, and whatever you can remember from my conversations. Can you do that for me?"

"Yes, sir."

"Excellent. I knew I could count on you. From the moment I clapped eyes on you, I thought to myself; this boy's highly intelligent and has the makings of a real spy. I bet you already know that James Bond isn't real, don't you?"

"Yes sir, I do."

"Like I said, highly intelligent, but you may not have known that he was a character from a book which was then turned into a film."

"Like Harry Potter?" asked Thomas.

"That's right. Just like Harry Potter. You see. You *are* a smart boy. And because you're so smart and I trust you so much, I'm going to tell you a little secret. You already know there are real spies out there, and that I'm one of them. And, just like James Bond, we also have agent numbers. But what I'm about to tell you must remain a secret. My life, and the life of my daughter depends on it."

"I can keep secrets. I'm good at keeping secrets. I won't tell anyone, honest I won't."

Sean looked around as if to check no-one was listening, then whispered, "*I'm* agent number 007."

Thomas took in a breath of surprise before Sean continued, "As a double-o agent, I have been given the authority to promote anyone I see fit to serve queen and country, and as my partner on a top secret mission, I now issue you with agent number 008, if you choose to accept this mission."

"Oh I do, I do," said Thomas, excitedly clapping his hands. "Will I get a badge like the ones the police have, only better?"

"We don't carry badges, Thomas. In case one of the bad guys get a hold of it. But there's no need to be frightened. You are the most secret of top-secret agents. No-one knows you are helping me, and it must stay that way. Do you understand?"

"Yes, sir."

"Good, now, from this moment on, the rules are back in place. Sometimes I may not seem myself, and if that is the case, do not speak to me and you will be perfectly safe. Even if I speak to you first, unless I salute, you must ignore me. This is very important, Thomas. Do you understand?"

"Yes, sir. Only when you salute."

Sean gave him a reassuring smile, "Good. Just keep putting the notes under my door, and because of your promotion, you will now find £10 under your pillow every morning. But, before I go, I have to ask;- is there anything else you can tell me, Thomas? Anything at all?"

Thomas looked up at Sean, unsure if he should say what was on his mind, but Sean saw the hesitancy in his eyes, "There is something, isn't there?"

"Yes, sir. I was trying to be a good spy, sir. Honest. I was listening through your door. But I was only practising. I didn't mean to."

"What is it, Thomas? Relax. You can tell me."

"I couldn't hear everyfing," said Thomas, looking up at him with puppy eyes. "You were on your phone. You sounded funny. You started talking… *different*."

"Tell me, Thomas," Sean prompted, restraining his urge to shake the information from him, "Tell me what you heard."

"You said 'rushing' or 'Russian' or somefing. Then you said somefing about a flower. It sounded like 'remember rose.' Then you said the date, but it was wrong. I thought it might be your birfday."

"What was the date, Thomas. Do you remember?"

"29^{f} of March 1951."

Sean was stunned. March 29th was the day the murders had begun, but the year meant nothing to him. Then he remembered. "1951." The sum of money in the box;- £1,951. And the letter that had been with it had said '*the clues are everywhere*'. But what did it mean? And more importantly; what else had he missed?

Fifty

Schmidt felt as though he were repeating himself. "It is during his lost time episodes that his mind as Sean Edvards has shut down. That is ven he is no-longer himself, and 'the mutilator' as you call him, is in control.

"Isn't there anything we can do to stop him?" asked Meg, "During his calls, if given the chance, aren't there any drugs or suppressants we could persuade him to take to subdue him until we can pick him up?"

"If you get the opportunity to speak to Mr. Edvards as himself, then maybe, but it could have disastrous implications."

"Disastrous, how?" Meg asked.

"If, in defeating his nemesis, he discovers his daughter is already dead, then I fear he vould take his own life."

"Not so disastrous, if you ask me," Ben said, walking into Meg's office to hear the tail-end of the conversation.

Meg looked at Ben, not allowing her expression to give away her annoyance at his interruption as he slipped an A4 sheet onto her desk.

"This is a list of everyone who has had access to the trophy cabinet during the last seven years," said Ben. "And as you might expect, none of them are listed as logging out any items of evidence from the Inkleman case."

Meg looked at the list. There had been five custodians of evidence during the time since the original mutilator killings, any one of which could have taken the knife. And added to that was the chain of custody listing police officers, detectives and lab technicians, all of which had handled the evidence at some point throughout the investigation.

"So we've drawn a blank?" she asked. "The knife could have been taken by just about anyone?"

"Anyone with clearance," Ben answered, "It's simply a matter of gaining access to the lock-up, supposedly looking for one thing, while actually after another. And as you can see from the chain of custody, Morton's on the list, as well as myself and quite a few others."

As Meg ran her finger down the list, Ben continued, "I've got someone going through the reasoning behind all those who have had access to the lock-up and the relevance of their visits, but it doesn't look good. There's the usual backlog of cases, and there's plenty of reasons for all of those listed to have had access." He looked at his watch. It was 9:55p.m. "We're on in twenty. I'm off down to the video technicians before the call comes in. Tony says he has something I should see."

"Something promising I hope."

"I'll let you know," he answered, and with a 'see you later' was gone, leaving Meg to turn her attention back to Schmidt.

"Tell me, doctor. Do you know if Mr. Edwards had any connections to anyone from the station?"

"I am sorry, I do not. We spoke very little of his life outside his family."

"It would seem that Mr. Edwards was an amiable man," said Meg, looking through the gathered statements, "Witty. And charming were some of the expressions used. And friendly too by all accounts. Don't you agree?"

"I myself found him affable," said Schmidt. "Of that there vas no doubt. But during our sessions together, we focused mainly on the problems in his life and the solutions to those problems. I am afraid I know very little of his life beyond that."

"But, don't those problems stem from his personal life?" she asked.

"To a degree, yes. But from a trauma he suffered as a child."

"What kind of trauma?" she asked.

"The death of his father," Schmidt said solemnly, "Which I have already mentioned to detective Miller.

"Indeed you have, doctor. But it puzzles me that an expert such as yourself seems to have had little success, if any, with the outcome of Mr. Edwards' condition."

"Vat are you suggesting?" Schmidt asked defensively.

"Let's face it," said Meg, "You're an old man," she paused, searching for the right words, "Past your best shall we say. Your appointment book isn't exactly bursting at the seams with custom. You have an expensive clinic to run. Bills to pay. And here you have a man willing to pay good money for one session after another." She looked deep into the ailing eyes of the old doctor, "I would imagine that that money would be difficult to turn away, even if you knew he were suffering from something more than a sleep disorder, and regardless as to whether or not you were qualified to deal with his particular form of mental illness."

"Vat are you trying to say?" Schmidt asked, his rising voice becoming hoarse. "You think I took advantage of a patient?"

"I'm saying that you probably knew Mr. Edwards was unstable, and a risk to the general public. I'm saying that you should have diagnosed him as such and made sure that he was monitored, or sought the appropriate help. But instead, you opted for the financial returns from his visits."

Doctor Schmidt stood from his seat, "In case you have forgotten, detective. I am here to assist you. And *this* is my reward." He made towards the door, angry and resentful, "But I do not have to listen to this any longer."

"Oh, but you do," said Meg. "He's still out there don't forget. And you may well be his next target. And besides, I want to know everything there is to know about his alter-ego. And I mean *everything.*"

His pride dented and resigned to his predicament, Schmidt sank back into his seat.

"So tell me of the mutilator," said Meg.

"I did not know he vas the mutilator," Schmidt said moodily. "I only ever saw signs of him in glimpses, and it vas a side I took care to avoid."

"Go on."

"I did not vant to risk making things vorse by bringing him to the fore. You see, we all have an alternate self. Boys, more so I feel. We are all guilty of killing insects as children, throwing stones at birds, or saying something hurtful. But for the majority of us it is a passing whim, spoken off the cuff. It is something we grow out of."

"Mr. Edwards hasn't grown out of it," said Meg. "Why?"

"Cruelty is a caged monster buried deep vithin us all. Sometimes, that cage is opened by the key of jealousy, greed, or vengeance, and goes on to reek its havoc. But in some cases, the cage is not merely opened, it is broken. And as you are only too vell avare, the broken ones kill to satisfy their demons, their appetite, or in some cases, purely for pleasure. Many such examples are displayed in the journals of psychiatric hospitals or on the pages of the daily newspapers. And as I'm sure you are already avare, more times than not, the vorst of those cases have come from a background of neglect or abuse, either mental or physical. I believe that Mr. Edvards could be such a killer. The problem vas, until his alter-ego manifested itself, I could never be truly sure of vat he vas capable of."

"Yet you took the chance with his life and the lives of others."

"I vasn't taking chances," Schmidt said resentfully. "I knew vhat I vas doing. It's just that, venever we seemed close to a breakthrough, his mind vould shut down. He vould go into a trance and I vould have to snap him out of it."

"Snap him out of it before what, doctor? Before he cracked?"

"Let me ask you something, detective. Vat is your first memory as a child?"

Not eager to relinquish her standing, Meg partially answered his question, "First day at school, I guess." (and being left there with strangers by my mum)

"A traumatic day, no doubt, as it vould be for most children. But Mr. Edvard's first memory is of caterpillars." Schmidt peered over his glasses and pushed them higher on his nose before continuing, "He vas a child of about four, sitting in a cabbage patch in his parents garden. His arms aloft. His hands full of big, fat, green caterpillars. And he vas squeezing them in triumph, the green juices from their bodies flowing down his bare arms as they wriggled in the grip of his fists. And he vas laughing, even as he licked their juices from his hands."

"Not what you would call a little angel, then," said Meg.

Schmidt continued. "From that point on, he has no more memories of his childhood until the age of fourteen, ven he first fell in love. Up until then, it is as if he has blocked out all the memories of his life during the time his father vas alive."

"And you're saying his life began anew with this teenage romance?"

"Don't get me wrong," said Schmidt, "I am not saying his falling in love brought an end to his troubles. But, until then, he lived in a dark place."

"And what became of this romance?" Meg asked.

"Ven they met, he vas in care. But they were separated soon after ven he returned to the care of his mother. He and the girl stayed in touch via letters and were in their twenties when they eventually got back together, marrying some six years later."

"She was his wife? The girl was Amy?"

"That is correct," said Schmidt. "His vife and his daughter are both very important to him. He loves them both very much."

"Tell me, doctor. Having killed his wife. Do you think his daughter is also dead?

"Hard to say. Either vay, I'm sure he does not know of her whereabouts."

"Why do you say that?"

"Because if she were dead and he knew it, then I'm sure he vould have killed himself by now."

"And if she were alive?"

"As the mutilator, it is likely he is keeping her somewhere safe. Somewhere she is unlikely to be discovered. Yet familiar to him, and reasonably close. But as Sean Edwards, I feel he vould surrender her to you in order to protect her from himself."

"You said earlier that you had to snap him out of it. Is it possible that you could do that over the phone, in, say," she looked at her watch, "fifteen minutes?"

"Honestly, I don't know. I doubt it. At my surgery I had him under my control. In an induced regression. The mental state he is in during his time-lapses is of his mind's own doing. I can but try."

* * *

The picture grainy, Ben looked at the monitor as the technician slowed down the tape of Sean Edwards seeing his daughter onto the train.

"There, look," the technician said, pointing to a hazy image of what appeared to be an elderly woman following the girl onto the train, her back to the camera. She was hunched over and wearing a headscarf, and a long wishbone-patterned overcoat like the one reported missing from Cordelia Armstrong's home. And she was carrying what was now known to be 'Flopsy'.

"The accomplice," said Ben. "Can't you do anything to clear it up a little?"

Tony adjusted the contrast and tweaked at the various dials and buttons, enhancing the image but with little improvement to its clarity. "That's the best I can do," he said.

"And you say she wasn't on the platform before the train pulled in?"

"Checked and double-checked." Tony answered. "I figure she came from the footbridge over the track. It's the only access and vantage point not covered by the c.c.t.v."

"Can you get a frontal?"

"Already tried. There's nothing. It was only after the train pulled into the station that she came into view."

"What the –" Ben stared at the image in disbelief.

"What is it?"

"Her shoes," said Ben.

Tony's gaze fell from the woman's coat and black trousers to the black slip-on shoes with their broad base and negligible heels.

"It's a disguise," said Ben. "That's not a woman. It's a man."

"Bloody hell. You're right."

"Quickly. Back it up."

Tony wound it back by about thirty seconds and pressed play, the two of them watching the unsub coming into sight from the bridge, his gaze staring downward, his identity still hidden.

"Wind it back again. Further."

Tony did as he was asked and almost jumped when Ben suddenly shouted for him to stop, the unsub not yet in view.

"What is it?" Tony asked, seeing nothing out of the norm, his eyes shooting to Sean Edwards sitting sedately next to his daughter, "What's wrong?"

"David Hetherington," said Ben, recognising him from the picture he'd taken from his flat. He pointed to a tall skinny guy in the corner of the screen, standing on the platform and looking down the track. "What's he doing?"

"Train spotting," Tony answered. "I noticed him earlier, taking photographs."

"Go further back. I want to see if that's all he's doing."

Ben watched the tape play out in real time and saw David Hetherington, apparently oblivious to Sean Edwards, checking a time-table before heading over to the pedestrian bridge and out of sight of the c.c.t.v.

Two minutes later, the unsub came across that same bridge.

Fifty One

There were eight desks spread out around the shared office-space, each with their own telephone and computer monitor or laptop. Some with personalised items. Meg sat at the least tidy of them, a couple of crossword magazines splashed across the left side of the desk and the rest of it covered with loose pens and an open file along with a picture of Ben with his mum and dad perched next to an unfinished mug of tea, his desk cluttered and disorganised, unlike her own. Yet, in some strange kind of way, she felt connected to him as she sat in his chair, her head buried in a book of quotes.

She highlighted the ones used by the unsub' in his letters to Sean Edwards;-

What we see depends mainly on what we look for. Sir John Lubbock.

I close my eyes in order to see. Saint Augustine.

Each was a taunting mockery of their failure to spot something crucial. A hidden clue Sean Edwards' alter ego had backed up with a quote of his own;- *And all closed their eyes to the killer surprise.*

"Still reading the Bills and Moon?" asked Morton, interrupting her train of thought as he commandeered the desk opposite.

"It's Mills and Boon you idiot," she said, angry at his chauvinist assumption. "Where the hell have you been?"

"Botanising," Morton answered with a smirk, "if there is such a word."

With a disapproving glare, Meg asked him to explain himself, and Morton sat facing her, smiling smugly to himself, his arms folded on the desk. "I got to thinking about the flower," he said, "I spoke to a botanist, and some of the stuff he said got me to thinking; what if 'Remember Me' was neither a question nor an instruction? What if it was a hint?"

"A hint?"

Morton was no team player, but sometimes, like it or not, he was forced to share what he had learned, like the tape given to him by doctor Schmidt. But there were also times when he was more than keen to share his discoveries, especially if it served his needs or gave him the chance to show how good he was at his job. "The Inkleman killings of seven years ago," he teased. "They also had a yellow rose. And even then, from the very first of the murders, he was saying 'Remember Me'. But why? It didn't make sense."

"And you came up with?"

"Nothing. At least, not at first. Then I wondered how Edwards, who appears to have had no access to our records, was able to copy the original crimes so accurately?"

"You're running over old ground," said Meg. "We already know he has an accomplice. Possibly on the force. And you yourself aren't exactly above suspicion."

"And again, that got me to thinking." Morton said, acting like the regular Sherlock Holmes. "During one of his calls, Edwards said to Ben that he could have stopped this, and that he could have stopped Inkleman too. He went out of his way to highlight that *Ben* was the one connecting factor in all of this."

"And you think *Ben* is the accomplice?"

"I didn't say that," said Morton. "I'm saying that Edwards wants us to think that, to throw us off track. It's how his mind works. By now, he knows we are aware of the accomplice and that we think it's a cop. And whoever the unsub is, he'll know our every move. He'll keep Edwards informed. And that puts us at a disadvantage."

"So what do you suggest?"

"I don't like Ben. I make no secret of that. But one thing I'm sure of;- he's as straight as they come."

"And your point is?"

"I'm pretty sure our guy knows of our mutual dislike for one-another and is trying to use it against us. Trying to shift our attention from himself;- the *real* culprit as it were. So let's throw a spanner in the works."

Meg was keeping an open mind. "Go on."

"We have to cut the unsub out of the loop. Give him less to work with."

"And just how do you propose we do that?"

"Me and Ben may not be friends, but we *are* allies. We have to put our differences behind us. Even if it's only for the duration of the inquiry. With plenty to keep us busy, it shouldn't be too difficult to keep up the pretence."

"That's a big ask," said Meg. "I don't know if he'll go for it."

"He has to," Morton said, uncompromising. "Next, we have to keep certain information on a need-to-know basis, leaking out only what suits our purpose, even amongst the team. Then, hopefully, our unsub will make the mistake of revealing himself to us and we can use him to find Edwards and the girl. But there's something else."

"What?"

"As I said earlier, from the very start, Inkleman left a yellow rose. He was saying 'Remember Me' even then. So what if the message was never from Edwards, **or** Inkleman? What if our unsub was involved in both sets of murders. What if it's been all about *him* the whole time, and he's been taunting us. Reminding us he's still out there. Telling us to remember *him*, even then."

Meg thought of what Ben had told her earlier about the photos. How he had sworn her to secrecy about his suspicions that the unsub was connected to both cases, and now, Morton had come up with a similar theory. Maybe Morton was right. Maybe it was time to bring him into the fold.

"You think that's why Edwards is able to copy the original crimes so accurately?" she asked.

"I do."

"Possible, maybe," said Meg. "Though highly unlikely."

"Maybe so. But Edwards has to be getting his information from somewhere. And the message in the name of the flower tells us more. Even back then, during the Inkleman killings. 'Remember Me' is telling us that there had to be others;- further back. The question is;- just how far back do we have to go?"

"You think Inkleman himself was a copycat?"

"No. I don't. I think Inkleman, like Edwards, was a puppet. And that the real killer was the unsub all along. And if he *is* amongst us, then we have to draw him out into the open. We have to set a trap."

Meg gave this some serious thought. If Morton was right, this would be difficult. The unsub would know everything they know. He'd have access to all the information he needed. He'd know their strengths and weaknesses. He'd know where they were and what they were doing. He'd know their every move. "You think he is using others to do the killing to mask his own involvement?" she asked.

"Yes," Morton answered. "That's why we have to find a way to break the cycle of events. And that brings us back to Ben. He and I need to talk."

Meg's thoughts raced through the possibilities of who the unsub could be. If there *were* other killings before Inkleman, and they *were* connected to the force in some way, the suspects could be whittled down considerably, simply by checking who was involved in those prior cases. But more worryingly; she wondered how many more murders could be related to the accomplice, and if evidence had been covered up throughout.

She clicked her mouse on the computer screen whilst Morton started searching through the records of all the officers involved in both the Inkleman case and the present one, checking for anything out of place, including work history and case involvement. All whilst Meg searched elsewhere.

'Remember Me' she thought.

Because Inkleman was known to have no criminal history, there had been no search to see if there were any similarities with any past murder sprees, so Meg decided to back-track, and began by linking up with H.O.L.M.E.S, (Home Office Large Major Enquiry System) searching for any other killings with the same m.o. The same yellow rose and severing of limbs. The slashed throat of the first victim and the abduction of a child.

Nothing came up.

She expanded the search from regionwide to nationwide, going as far back as records allowed. If there *was* a link, She wanted to know who, where and when. And as the computer ran its search, she turned to the sound of Ben's voice, "It's time."

Once again, Edwards began with his sickening rhyme. Singing it this time. Badly. His lyrics out of time with the strum of the music in the background;-

"Fingers… and toes… in exchange for my rose.

Hands… and feet… now we're getting to the meat."

"Cut the crap," Ben interjected.

"You could have saved her, Ben. I warned you. I told you *'someone close'*. Didn't you even *try* to stop me?"

"Not everything is as it seems," said Ben.

"My thoughts exactly," Edwards replied.

Ben glanced to Meg, her gaze still fixed on the computer screen as he sought answers to why Edwards had changed his m.o., "So, tell me," he said to Edwards, "how can I be sure this was your doing?"

Edwards skirted the question, "Have you ever seen anyone bleed to death, Ben? The blood, it just keeps on flowing. Around five litres of it in the average adult they reckon, but as you sit there, watching it, it seems so much more."

"Why the differences?" Ben asked again.

"Have you watched it? The way it flows and soaks into everything. Deep red. Coagulating where it pools. And the body getting paler and paler."

"Why didn't you cut off her arms and legs?" Ben asked.

"Such beautiful shades of red. Oxygenated and bright. Darkening as it seeps out. When it dries it's almost black."

Ben kept at it, "Why wasn't there tape over her mouth?"

"It's amazing what an incentive the threat of killing a child can have," Edwards finally answered. "She was a remarkable young woman. For a short while, I even began to think she would resist the compulsion to scream. But, like all the others, she was weak. She *did* scream. Or should I say; she tried to. But by then it was practically pitiful. Hardly enough noise to scare the most skittish of creatures, let alone raise help."

"Is that why you allowed the baby to live?"

"Funny thing about that," said Edwards. "I don't really remember."

"You don't remember? Or you had a moment of guilt?"

"Guilt?" Edwards laughed. "Guilt for what? I felt no guilt. I'm not bothered in the slightest that the baby is alive. He's hardly a witness now, is he?"

"Don't you worry about leaving survivors? Don't you think your friend worries about the fact that you failed to do as instructed?"

"I have no friends. I do as I wish."

"The man who killed your mother-in-law. The man who has your daughter. Isn't *he* a friend?"

"I don't know what you're talking about."

"Oh, but I think you do. You like to call yourself the mutilator. You like to pretend."

"I pretend *nothing!* I *am* the mutilator."

"No. You're not," said Ben. "You're just the shell of a man, under the control of someone else. *HE* has your daughter. *HE* pulls the strings. And *HE* is the mutilator."

There was a moments silence before Ben continued, "I have someone here who would like to speak to you."

Edwards remained silent.

"Hello?... Sean? It's me, Doctor Schmidt. I vould like to help you."

Still there was no sound, and as Schmidt looked to Ben for confirmation that the line was still live, the speakers crackled in response, "I'd like to help you, too," said Edwards, his droning voice sinking to a whisper as he continued the poem where he had left off.

"Elbows and knees… I'm their killer disease."

"Arms and legs… hack them off while she begs."

And with the following line, his last words before hanging up, he spoke with the emphasis of a whispering snake as he lay out the clue to the fate of the next victim.

"Killer's surprise, when I gouge out their eyes."

Fifty Two

As the phone-call ended, Meg's computer screen sprang to life with a list of the known victims, bang up to date, beginning with those of Sean Edwards and working back through time.

Their details given in brief, Meg scrolled down the names looking for a common denominator.

Deceased		Marital Status	Profession	Age	Date Deceased
Olivia	Crompton	married	Housewife	31	1st April
Rachel	Earnshaw	single	factory worker/escort	23	31st March
Cordelia	Armstrong	widowed	Retired	64	30th March
Amy	Edwards	married	Solicitor	27	29th March

With the slightest of breaks, the list went on, again starting with the most recent of the victims, their names preceded by that of their killer. The perpetrator;- Mr. Joseph Inkleman, was aged thirty-seven. A bank manager with no previous history, he had killed his victims seven years ago and committed suicide on the last day of his murder spree.

Deceased		Marital Status	Profession	Age	Date Deceased
Angela	Inkleman	Adolescent	Not Applicable	7	4th April
Jody	Maxwell	Single	Shop Assistant	24	4th April
Sarah	Ingles	Married	Housewife	29	3rd April
Jane	Hargreaves	Single	Unemployed	30	2nd April
Peter	Ashton	Divorced	Window Cleaner	44	2nd April
Angelina	Trovero	Single	Teacher	28	1st April
Hayley	Irvine	Single	Unemployed	27	31st March
Jennifer	Sewell	Single	Physiotherapist	31	30th March
Margaret	Inkleman	Married	Housewife	34	29th March

The names of Inkleman's victims still echoed in Meg's mind, but none more so than those of his wife and child.

Margaret Inkleman had died of asphyxiation and blood loss caused by trauma to the trachea, epiglottis, and carotid artery. Her throat had been slashed; the blade cutting so deeply, it had exposed her spinal cord. Her daughter was to suffer a similar fate, and the story of her murder, Meg had heard from Ben.

Angela Inkleman was only seven years old when she had died. Her body fastened to a table, she had been tortured and sexually abused before her father had held her head down, his hand across her face as he sliced through her throat, Ben arriving at the point of her decapitation, too late to save her. She was the last to die before Inkleman had committed suicide. Not out of guilt, but in some sick and twisted way, giving a slap to the face of authority and rubbing their noses in their failure to imprison him.

His earlier victims Meg knew to have suffered varying degrees of torture and dismemberment. All that is, except one. She highlighted the only male victim on the list and the details of his death flashed onto the screen.

Mr. Peter Ashton, a window-cleaner, had been found on the rear patio with his fallen ladder. A man in the wrong place at the wrong time, the report had concluded that he had most likely witnessed the attack on Miss Hargreaves through her bedroom window, and on being seen, Inkleman had thrown a lamp at him, knocking him off his ladder. The fall causing him to suffer a broken pelvis before he was killed from a separate wound inflicted minutes later; that of a garden fork thrust heavily into his chest.

Meg's eyes scrolled down the screen for comparisons to Edwards, skipping through the obvious. The m.o. The causes of death. The matching dates, etc, had all been followed to a T. And other than Inkleman's daughter and Peter Ashton, the rest of the victims had all been women. *Seven* women to be exact. Followed by a gap of seven years between the last spate of murders and the present one. And to top it all, his daughter was just *seven* years old, just as Abigail Edwards was. '*Still is'* Meg reminded herself.

She looked up from her computer screen to grab Ben's attention, saw he was busy, and instead, beckoned Morton, her gaze returning to the monitor just as it sprung back to life, and one by one, another group of names flashed onto the screen. The worrying confirmation of yet more murders.

"My god," said Meg, "Inkleman *was* a copycat."

Again there was a gap of seven years, and again, the first was dated 29th March, though this time, the killings were in Liverpool.

Meg stood with her palms flat to the computer desk as she leaned towards the screen in disbelief with Morton looking over her shoulder.

"The pattern's the same," Morton said, stunned.

"It's an anniversary," said Meg.

"Anniversary?"

"Seven women every seven years, and a child aged seven too."

"Anniversary for what?"

"That's what we have to find out," she answered. "*That,* and how he chooses his victims."

They both stood staring at the screen, reading through the list of details, starting with the perpetrator. A chemist named Kevin Swinton. Aged 32yrs. Again, with no previous convictions. And again, committing suicide on the 4th April.

Lisa	Swinton	Adolescent	Not applicable	7	4th April
Dianne	Oakley	Married	Secretary	26	4th April
Mary	Hardwick	Married	Housewife	29	3rd April
Beverly	Newman	Single	Florist	23	2nd April
Susan	Iveson	Married	Dental Nurse	31	1st April
Deborah	Yates	Single	Barmaid	29	31st March
Sheila	Preston	Married	Hairdresser	32	30th March
Judith	Swinton	Married	Sales Assistant	27	29th March

Meg highlighted the names one by one, and with a click on the mouse, looked at their details in depth, the horror unfolding before her eyes.

Morton was right. In almost every way, the pattern was the same. First, Swinton had murdered his wife, and then followed with six apparently random women. Some married, some not. Their murders verbatim, each was left a yellow rose. And *'all'* of them were mothers.

"The connection," said Morton. "Between Inkleman and Swinton. Why wasn't it spotted?"

“Because each case was solved in its own right,” Meg answered. “Each from a different area. Each by a known offender with no prior history. And the perpetrator dead in both instances, each drawn a line under and closed.”

Meg dragged the cursor across the screen, and with a few clicks on the mouse, the machine in the far corner of the room rang out a stream of copies, its actions drawing a secondary glance as she looked across, surprised by what she saw.

Standing just a few feet from the printer, Ben was pretending to look over the wall-charts, his occasional glance to his left betraying his sly conversation with a young officer she vaguely recognised. Both of them stood with their backs to the rest of the room as Meg watched them curiously, trying to remember where she had seen him. So many new faces since the day of her arrival and first briefing, and too many to recall in such a short space of time. And then it struck her.

‘Jason Trevors.’

The officer Ben had ejected from the briefing, setting out his stall with an example to the others of his intent. But what was he doing here? And what were they talking about? And then, in an instant, she remembered having seen him somewhere else, his pale young face looking like he was ready to vomit, standing guard on the door of the Edwards house when she had first arrived on the scene.

She saw Ben’s attention stray to the sound of the busy printer and watched as he momentarily browsed through the printouts before passing one of them to Trevors, the two of them parting company as Meg weaved her way towards them.

Fifty Three

Abby shivered against the cold, her faint whimper floating on the damp air as she cried for her mummy and daddy, needing them now more than ever, asking herself why this was happening to her?

Why she was being kept here like this?

Why hadn't her parents come to get her?

Where were they? What were they doing?

Frightened and alone, she was desperate to hear their voices, comforting and reassuring, huggles all around. The two of them making everything right again, there for her always, just as they had always been. Both of them with her on her first day at school, a smile and kiss of reassurance at the gate. Her mum at her first dance class. Her father, the steadying hand on her bicycle as she rode it for the first time without stabilisers. And the three of them together on what had been the saddest day of her life so far, huddled close around a tiny grave in a corner of the garden.

Between them, they had made a little wooden cross for Icarus, the three of them planting it together and saying a prayer to see him safely on his way to heaven.

"Why did he have to die, mummy?"

"Budgies don't live as long as people, hun. That's the way it's always been."

"Why mum? Why don't they?"

"Because god wants them to join him in heaven, dear."

Again, Abby had asked "Why?" and her mum had answered patiently, "There are lots of wonderful people in heaven, darling. And not enough pets to keep all of them company."

"Will Icarus keep granddad company?

"I'm sure he will," her mum had said sombrely. "I'm sure he will."

Satisfied at last with her mums explanation, Abby had made the grown-up decision not to have any more pets until she was older. A few days later however, that decision was to be taken away from her; twice over.

On one of the last warm days of the summer, the fair had come to town and was bustling with life, everyone buoyant and happy. Her mummy and daddy walking either side of her until they had stopped at a stall with a game her father hadn't played since he was a boy, and keen to recapture his youth, took aim at the coconuts whilst Abby had pointed out a huge cuddly rabbit to her mum, "Look mummy, look."

"It's beautiful, hun," her mum had said, "But it would take a magician to win enough tokens to prise *that* away from the fair." And so they had wandered around the various rides and stalls with the sweet smell of candyfloss and fresh doughnuts as they laughed and giggled at her daddy making a fool of himself at the 'stick-a-dart-in-a-card' game (and a few others besides.)

"You girls go on ahead," he had said taking aim with his dart, his tongue sticking out the corner of his mouth in concentration. "I'll catch up with you a little later."

It was almost *two* hours later when they saw him again.

"Abracadabra," he had said triumphantly, holding the biggest cuddly rabbit you ever saw.

"He can never replace Icarus," her father had said, holding the cuddly toy out to Abby. "But he'll never die. And he'll never-ever leave you."

Abby called him 'Flopsy' on account of his huge ears. A rabbit half the size she was and ears to match.

With a creak of the cellar door, Abby wished she were back there now with her parents. Wished that her father had some kind of special power that would help him to hear her and know exactly where she was. A power which would allow him to fly here, even faster than superman, to whisk her to safety and away from this terrible place.

In her head, she cried out 'Please, daddy, come get me. I'm frightened,' her eyes closing tightly under the blindfold as she wished for her wish to come true. Wished it was her father who had opened the door and was coming down the stairs, his footsteps coming towards her, here at last to pick her up in his arms and take her home.

She listened for his cheery arrival and instead heard the cough of the horrible man. The *'rat-man'* as she had come to think of him. A dirty horrible creature, keeping her from her parents, a prisoner in this cold damp place.

She'd conjured up an image of his hands caked in dirt and imagined long skinny fingers with black curly nails, his beady eyes watching her and his grin showing pointy flesh eating teeth, black and yellow and dripping with saliva.

Rat-man made her shiver more than the cold did. The way he spoke to her. The way he combed his fingers through her hair. The way he pretended to be her friend, sounding gentle and kind, making out that everything was going to be okay. But he didn't fool Abby. He was horrible and cruel, she could hear it in the sound of his voice, his tone saying that he wasn't to be trusted in anything he did or said, and the way he treated her making her dislike him more than anything she could possibly think of. Making her think her father would like him less, and given the chance, would hurt him for being so mean to her. For although her father was a kindly man who loved her very much, she had once seen a side of him she had tried to forget. A side that had scared her. And a side that had scared *him too*, truth be told.

They had been walking the green belt skirting Chester Park, Abby holding her father's hand as they crossed a footbridge, just the two of them traipsing along the trail of the river when they had heard a splashing sound off to their right and turned to see a young man, a hoody in jeans, trudging out of the river and running off into the woods, a hessian sack left in his wake, bound with cord and sinking into the depths of the water.

Abby had just stood there, frozen to the spot. Partly as instructed by her father, partly in shock at his sudden outburst. Shouting. The one and only time she'd ever heard him swear, "Hey! You! Come back here you cruel bastard!"

She had seen something in her father's eyes that day. Something she had never seen in him before and hoped never to see again. Her father was furious. Angry at the cruelty this man had shown in the river, though she herself had not understood what was happening or what had angered him so much. All she could see was the hessian sack, its bloated swell shrinking into the river, and bubbles rising in its place as her father told her not to move, to wait there. And that's what she had done as he rushed down the river bank and bounded into the water, dragging out the sack and frantically pulling at its cord to peer inside. That was the day we got *'Lucky'* she remembered. A Golden Retriever cross. The one and only survivor from a litter of pups.

Abby wondered if *this* man was a hoody too as she heard him approaching. Rat-man would make her father angrier than ever, she thought, and she was glad. Maybe her father would put *him* in a sack too.

"Stop your snivelling," he barked.

She wasn't snivelling, she was shivering. The chill slicing through to her bones like a shard of ice, no coat to keep her warm, reminding her of the frost on the morning her nan had taken her to school, her breath like that of a smoker as she stepped out into the cold. And now, in the cold damp air of the cellar, she wondered if the silvery frost had found its way indoors, her blindfold shielding her eyes from the advancing cold of winters end. Jack Frost a friend of Rat-man, invited to share her prison in order to hide from the warmth of the sun.

Rat-man leaned over her and removed her gag, "If you want to be fed, you had better stop your snivelling."

"I want my mum," she shivered.

"Your mum's dead!" he snapped. "And soon, your father will be dead, too. Now, *there's* something for you to cry about."

In the blackness of the blindfold, his words tore through her frightened little heart and curled her into a ball, crying at him, "You're lying! She's *not* dead. My mum's *not* in heaven. She's waiting for me, at home."

Rat-man crouched down beside her and ran his fingers through her hair, "Oh, my sweet, sweet rose. I'm sorry. Did I hurt your feelings. I didn't mean to. Really I didn't."

Still sobbing, Abby's anger burst from a place deep inside, "I *hate* you! You're nothing but a big, fat, horrible, liar." But even as the words left her mouth and his slap struck her face, in her heart of hearts, she feared the worst. Feared he was telling the truth. Because Rat-man wasn't a man at all, he was a monster. And monsters do horrible things.

"Here," he said, thrusting a sandwich into her hands, "eat *this*."

She threw it down and felt his hands grip tight around her arms, shaking her with anger, "You ungrateful little *bitch*!" Then he let go and prised her mouth open, the gag fastened tighter than ever and the tears rolling down her cheeks as she realised no-one was coming to help her. Realised that, soon, *she* would be dead too, with her mummy and daddy in heaven. And over her sobbing, she heard Rat-man pick something up.

"Don't eat," he growled, "see if I care. Maybe you'll be hungry enough to eat them later when they are dry and stale."

He stood over her, quiet for a spell before he dropped something to her side and it fell against her legs. Something soft and furry. "I brought that from your nan's house," he said, his tone slightly mellowed. "Thought you might like it for company."

Tentatively, she reached out into the darkness, and as her hand brushed across its body, she knew instantly it was Flopsy and snatched him to her chest, gripping him close as she sobbed into his cushioning warmth, rocking back and forth and squeezing him so tightly that no-one could ever take him away from her.

"Oh, one more thing," the monster said before leaving. "Your nan's dead too."

Fifty Four

Standing outside the nightclub, two burly doormen watched the group of scantily clad women giving hugs and kisses on cheeks, their eyes flicking between figure hugging skirts, painted on jeans, and flimsy little tops revealing midriffs and the occasional glimpse of cleavage. Five young women in their twenties, tipsy with laughter as they said their goodbyes.

"You going to be alright?" asked one of the girls as the four of them climbed into a waiting taxi.

"I'll be fine," said Naomi. "Just a few minutes walk and I'll be home."

A window wound down as she stood waving from the kerbside, an attractive brunette leaning out of the taxi, "Call me, tomorrow. We'll meet up for a natter before Paul comes home from work."

"About eleven-thirty!" Naomi called out, the taxi impatiently pulling away as the women shouted and waved their goodbyes.

It was only now, come the end of the night, that Naomi wished she'd worn something warmer, the silver glitter of frost sparkling on the paths and the chill in the air bringing out the goose-bumps on her arms, causing her to hug herself as she began her short walk home. Just five minutes of shivering was a price worth paying, she had thought, rather than being dowdy and going unnoticed amongst her friends who were more attractive than she was. Prettier. With cuter smiles, nicer hair, and better figures. Wearing something skimpier was all she could do to keep up; her short white dress making the most of her curvier figure and more ample breasts. And sometimes, if she were lucky, it got her some male attention, though apparently, not tonight.

The bar just a short distance behind, she walked over the pedestrian crossing and past the hospital, taking a short cut through the back streets and past the church, her heels clacking against the pavement as the houses closed in around her and the noise from the throng of people climbing into taxis faded into the distance. Soon, she could hear nothing but the echoing clack of her shoes, the sound of her breathing, and the high-pitched constant of a whistling in her ears;- the after affects of loud pumping music. All making her oblivious to the sound of the following man.

He watched her as she stopped mid stride, her hand pressed against a wall for support as she fiddled with the strap of her high-heeled shoe, twisting to adjust it. The dark line of her cleavage plunging a little deeper and her nipples standing pert as her dress rode a little higher to reveal more skin, the soft sheen of the street light shining on her smooth tanned legs.

He fantasised as he watched her set away again, his focus drawn to the feint line of a G-string through her figure-hugging dress.

'Look at her' he thought. 'Dressed like that, she fucking well deserves to be raped. The things she's wearing, and the things she's obviously not. Well. Maybe it's your lucky night, girlie. Maybe you'll get exactly what you want. Because, if it's penetration you're after; then I'm your man.'

He kept to the shadows as he followed close behind, watching as she struggled in her shoes, her heels scraping across the ground, watching her every step and ignoring his own, before, sharply, he stopped, a crunch like nuts beneath his foot. The shell of a snail giving him away and pissing him off as he stood in the shadows, biting his cursing tongue as her head whipped around in fright.

"What was that?"

She looked straight at him without realising it, her eyes searching the shadows where the street lights failed to illuminate. Her gaze shifting to the cars and doorways, the spatterings of bushes and the crowds of bins. She was being watched. She could feel it. Someone was lurking in the shadows, spying on her as she tried not to panic. Tried not to make a fool of herself by reading into every little noise. Tried not to alert whoever may be following her that she was aware of his presence. Tried to act calm, telling herself; just a few hundred yards and I'll be home.

She turned and carried on walking, her senses heightened and the affects of the drink washed away by the adrenaline as she hurried down the street.

'Oh god.' There *was* someone following, she could hear him. The sound of his footsteps trailing hers. Their pace quickening just as hers did. Some forty yards behind her. Even as she crossed the road she could hear the quiet slap of his shoes against the pavement.

Her strides short and clumsy in her tight dress, she picked up her pace, constantly looking back to the shadows. Her thoughts racing back to the day's newscasts; The Mutilator still free. The things he had done to his victims now prevalent in her mind. Things that only ever happened to *other* people. But that's the way it was with the news. Always someone else. Always a stranger. Only now, she was frightened that *she* was going to be that next 'someone else' and scarcely broke stride as she bent to slip off her shoes, oblivious to the cold of the pavement as she focused on every little shadow, studying the line of parked cars on the opposite side of the street. Wondering if he was hiding there, watching. Her eyes searching as she constantly looked back. Listened for every sound. Constantly looking at the doors she passed just feet away, counting down the numbers as she headed towards the end of the terraced houses. 47, 45, 43. She headed towards number 1, to the turn of the corner and the last hundred yards to her house.

41, 39, 37. When she got there. When she turned the corner, she would run, faster than she'd ever run before.

35, 33, 31. Run for the light from her kitchen window, left on by her father. Run as fast as her legs would carry her, screaming every step of the way if she had to.

29,27,25,23,21. Her countdown grew quicker as she picked up her pace. Rushing past the row of terraced houses, tempted to knock on one of the doors. Glad to hear the complaints of a disgruntled neighbour. Glad of their company. Glad to accept an offer to walk her home.

19,17,15, unlucky for some;-13. She was almost there, under the glare of the streetlight. Its amber glow revealing all that was to be seen in the opening at the end of the houses.

11,9,7. The last of the parked cars were some fifty yards behind, leaving nowhere close for him to hide.

5,3 and 1. At last she could ease up. She needed to catch her breath. Needed to give herself a head-start in her sprint for life once she turned the corner. And with a great force of will, she stopped where she was, standing under the light at the end of the street, and turned to face the way she had come, her eyes picking out shapes in the shadows before fixing on a recessed doorway some thirty yards away and seeing a shadow that didn't fit.

She called out into the darkness, "What are you doing? Why are you following me?"

Her only answer came in the form of vapour escaping his lungs and drifting from the shadows.

"If you don't stop following me, I'll scream."

He didn't reply, didn't move, his breath the only sign he was still there.

She looked up at number 1 and thought about pressing the doorbell. How long would it take to answer? How long to stir the occupants from their blissful sleep?

She imagined the tired mutterings of an old man fastening his dressing gown as his legs carried him slowly downstairs. Too long, too late, she'd be dead before he opened the door.

"My father will be waiting for me," she shouted down the street. "You'd better not follow, he'll hurt you. He's a body-builder."

Still, the shadow didn't move, and frightened to take her eyes from it, she took a deep breath, her grip tightening on her purse and shoes. Her lungs scarcely recovered and her heart still racing as she turned to casually stroll around the corner, then burst into a run;- straight into the arms of her prowler.

His hand clasped over her mouth, he dragged her kicking and screaming into an alleyway. Her eyes wide with fear. Her fingers fighting to prise away the hand that stifled her screams. Her feet lashing out as she was dragged backwards, further into the darkness, further into the shadows of death. A pull to the ground, his hand still over her mouth as he picked up a brick and brought it down on her head. Then everything went hazy, the man a blur as he crouched over her, his gaze pouring over her body and his hand reaching for her throat before he stopped. A sound coming from behind him. His head turning to the blow of a fist making contact with his face.

Naomi lay dazed as the man fell to the ground beside her. A startled pause before he jumped to his feet and turned on his attacker. The two of them like shadows fighting in the darkness as Naomi held her hand to her head, woozy, the blood trickling down her face as she struggled to her feet, staggered, and fell down again. The shadows swapping blows as she struggled to make sense of what was happening. Their whacks and thumps; dull thuds in her ears as she lay crumpled on the ground watching the clash of dark shapes, afraid her prowler would win and then come to finish her off.

A punch from one, a lunge from the other, one of them fell, and the other fell on top of him, a sharp grunt of pain as the lower one slumped, his body sitting propped against the wall as the other man climbed to his feet, still a shadow as he stood over him. Naomi's head pounding as she looked on in shock, in fear, struggling to make out her prowler from her rescuer. Unable to discern which was which as she heard the collapsed man groaning and saw the other man walking towards her, panting as he said, "That's the last time he'll attack anyone on my patch."

In her semi-conscious state, Naomi felt a flood of relief. "Thank you," she uttered, "Thank you. Thank you so much."

Her rescuer helped her to her feet.

"You saved my life," she said.

"Don't mention it," her rescuer said in a breathless, though calm and friendly voice. "There was never any need to panic. *He* just wanted your purse and maybe the pleasures of your flesh. Where as I," he said, staring down at her heaving chest. "**I…** want something a little more valuable."

Light bounced off the blade of the bloodstained knife as she staggered back, her eyes shifting from the blade to the shadow of his face, unable to take her eyes off him. Searching for mercy as she backed away. Backed towards a wall. Her feet unsteady as she stumbled over a kerb. A glance to her sides;- nowhere to run. Just seconds left to escape. And with a smear of light, she saw the glint in his eyes and the smile on his face, the knife held firmly in his grip as he moved slowly towards her.

"It seems you are a very popular young lady tonight," he said.

Naomi glanced to the man behind him collapsed against the wall, hoping he would avenge himself. Hoping he would not allow this to happen. That he would attack this knife-yielding killer in retribution. But his groaning stopped, and as she looked to the crumpled body for assistance, his head collapsed to face her, Naomi letting out an ear-shattering scream at what she saw. A trail of blood running down the mugger's face from hollow eye-sockets; one eye hanging from its optic nerve and resting on his cheek, the other nowhere to be seen.

"Is this what you're looking for?" his killer asked, waving the blade of the bloody knife in front of her face, side to side in the darkness, watching her as she watched the knife and saw the eye on the point of the blade looking right back at her, the madman's smile merging from the darkness, his mouth slavering, "I think he still has his eye on you."

The retch to her stomach was instant, as was the flicker of light from the window above, the glow of the light bouncing off the blade as he held it to her throat and pulled her back into the shadows as someone twitched at their bedroom curtains to see and hear nothing, his voice whispering in her ear, “Make a sound and it’ll be your last.”

Fifty Five

Earlier in the incident room, Meg had approached Ben querying the presence of Jason Trevors, their voices raised and their words heated.

"He's been working this the whole time, *hasn't* he?" Meg had asked.

"I'm sorry. I couldn't tell you," Ben answered.

"So that scene in the briefing, the whole eviction crap, that was a set-up?"

"Yes."

"Why? For whose benefit?"

"He's new. He's keen. I figured I could use him."

"Use him for what, exactly?"

"To keep tabs on someone." Ben's gaze shifted briefly to Morton at the other end of the room. "To check things out for me."

"He's a rookie, Ben. I doubt he even knew what you were getting him involved in?"

"Of course, he knew. That's why I chose him. It stood to reason he wasn't involved in any of the leaked information to the press, or our copycat for that matter. And he's the only one I could trust."

"The only one you could trust to do what? Give it to me straight, Ben."

His voice lower, still firm, he answered, "We've got a leak, Meg. A dirty cop. The stolen weapon. The call to the press. Edwards isn't alone in this. Who else could I trust?"

"You could have trusted *me*," she answered sharply.

Ben saw some of the team taking sideways glances as they pretended not to listen. "You already had your plate full. I didn't want to bother you."

"So you decided to go behind my back."

"It wasn't like that."

"What *was* it like, Ben?"

Ben didn't have an answer and Meg shot another question, "You have him watching Morton, don't you?"

"Amongst others," he replied.

"Does that include me?"

"No… it's. I can't say."

"I want this to stop, Ben. Do you understand. Trevors is either in, or he's out. Either way, you have to leave Morton alone. You're letting your personal feelings get in the way of the investigation. And if you persist with this, I will have no alternative but to relieve you of your duties."

"You can't do that," said Ben, his face flushing with anger as he looked around the faces turned towards them.

"*I'm* leading this investigation," said Meg. "And I'll do whatever I see fit."

"But, I've got him checking something. Something important. Just one last thing. When he's done, I'll debrief him. Then it's over. I promise."

Just as they had intended, their exchange of words had been overheard by everyone, and although Ben still had his doubts of Morton's innocence, he'd had to admit that if Morton wasn't the accomplice, then this ruse to flush him out might just work.

2:08a.m.

Some three hours had passed since their not so private tete-a-tete, and now, Ben and Meg worked alongside one-another, their supposed differences behind them. They had a case to focus on and got on with it, making their calls and checking their facts. Everyone busy. Everything forgotten. An occasional member of the team fighting their tiredness with a stretch or a yawn whilst trawling through the deluge of paperwork.

Meg rubbed her eyes and read through the lyrics of the song that had been playing in the background of Sean Edwards' last call.

What has happened to our town
There's people sleeping on the ground
Cold and lost, they fear the night
Left alone they'll lose the fight

Hadn't we better reach for more than just a dime
Shouldn't we try to talk that boy out of his crime
Haven't you had it knowing nothing's getting solved
Maybe we'd better, better get involved.

The lyrics were from a song by Chicago. Meg knew a few of their hits, but Ben had every album and knew practically every song they'd ever released.

"The bastard knows things about me, Meg. He's taunting me."

"I'm sure that's part of it," Meg said, thinking about how the lyrics fitted with what was happening. "But there'll be a reason he chose this song in particular."

Ben put the lyrics to one side and looked at the other printouts, an obituary of those dead at the hands of Edwards, Inkleman and Swinton.

"Closed my eyes to the killer's surprise," Ben said, thinking out loud.

"What'd you say?"

"Even back then, he was telling me I'd made a mistake."

"You didn't make a mistake, Ben. You did all you could."

"*You could have stopped this from happening* **'again**.' That's what he said. All those people dead, before and since Inkleman. And I could have stopped it."

"Don't beat yourself up over this. There was nothing you could have done about Swinton. And Inkleman was a first time offender. You weren't to know he was a copycat."

Ben's fist came down hard on the desk, "You're wrong, Meg. We're missing something. But no matter how much I look, I just can't see it."

"Because he talks in riddles," said Meg. "No-one could have seen it. Then, or now. Just like Edwards, Inkleman was acting out of character. You didn't have the hindsight we had for Edwards. There were no files. And there was no way you could have known he was copying a killer from another area."

As Ben sat cursing himself, staring at the long list of victims, two support officers were being patched through to Meg from the scene of a reported disturbance.

"It looks bad, ma'am," said one of them. "Looks like some guy and his Mrs had a falling out. Must have been *some* argument 'cos she's left us with a John Doe."

"As if things aren't bad enough," Meg moaned. "Now we've got killers coming out of the bloody woodwork."

"No means of identification?" Ben cut in.

"No, sir. Nothing. No I.D., and no eyeballs either. You want us to send his picture so you can check if he's on file?"

'Killer's surprise, when I gouge out their eyes.'

Within minutes, Ben and Meg had arrived on the scene and were face to face with the officers who had secured the area.

"Looks like there was a struggle over there," said one of them, pointing to the glittery shoes just a few feet away from the body. "The scratches to his face and all, looks more like it was done by a wildcat than a woman."

Ben took notes as Meg looked over the body, saying, "The scratches, maybe. But our man Edwards took his eyes."

Stunned, the other officer said, "But, there's no posing of the body. No rose."

"There never is with the men," said Ben. "*They* aren't the prize."

Even over the fresh odour of death, Meg could smell the victim's cheap aftershave like burnt oranges as she bent down to take a closer look while Ben stood beside her, his gaze fixed on the victim's face covered in blood, an eye hanging loose from a nerve and the other just a dark bloody hole. Four blue ink teardrops trailing from the edge of the socket and down his cheek. And another tattoo on his throat, of barbed wire worn like a necklace around his neck.

"His name's Troy Evans," said Ben. "He's a known felon around these parts. Got a rap sheet as long as your arm. Drugs mainly. And a few relateds."

"He have a girlfriend you know of?" Meg asked.

"Not as far as I know. He's a loner. Lives on the other side of town. Rough area. Wangled his way out of a rape charge last year when the victim failed to testify. Looks like maybe he was guilty after all."

"Scum got what he deserved, then," Meg said under her breath.

One of the attending officers looked to the white glittery shoes, wondering about their owner as he nervously directed his question at Meg. "You think he was the intended victim?"

"No, I don't."

"How can you be so sure?"

"Edwards goes after women. The only time he'll kill a man is if they get in his way."

The officers had stayed with the body, securing the scene of crime, and now felt a pang of guilt for not doing a sweep of the surrounding streets. "So, she's out there, in need of our help, and we missed her?"

"Shit," said the other. "We fucked up and she's gonna die… If she's not dead already."

"For now, she's alive," Meg said, looking at her watch and counting down the hours to 10:15 a.m. "But we have less than eight hours to keep it that way."

Fifty Six

Blackened tears ran like tramlines down her cheeks and mascara smudged the back of her hand. Naomi couldn't speak, couldn't scream, couldn't ask her captor to show her mercy.

"I said, keep walking!"

The point of the knife pricked into her back, and in bare feet, Naomi trudged on, feeling every little stone embedding itself into her soles as she was forced to walk towards the hospital she knew to be closed. *Was this madman actually trying to help her?* He had saved her, then threatened her. He had killed her attacker, and now, having found the entrance to be locked, made her walk the perimeter of the hospital, her eyes looking up to the grate protected cameras on every corner. And with every one they passed, her hopes of someone coming to her aid had dwindled.

"Keep walking!" The point dug a little deeper. "Do as I say and you just might survive this."

In the secluded borders of the hospital, she doubted his sincerity, and looked to his expression for reassurance only to find his patience running low, "You're not listening to me, bitch. I said *keep going."*

She tripped in the darkness and felt his hand grab her arm to stop her from falling. "How many more times. Watch where you're fucking going you stupid slag."

His words dug deeper than the knife into her back. Slag was a name given to her by strangers and some so-called friends. Even her fiancé. All brought about by the boastful tales of conquest by young men showing off to their mates, too proud to admit their failings, too keen to bolster their reputations, and in the process, damage her own.

Crying and angry, she wanted to scream at him *'don't call me that!'* But unable to open her mouth, instead, she took a swing at him, missing as he stepped aside, brushing her slap away with a snigger and whacking her hard across the face. Then again she was marched onwards, crying as she stumbled ahead.

No matter how they had done it, all of the men in her life had been cruel to her, toying with her feelings or playing with her mind in their quest for sex. They had called her names she didn't deserve and given her a reputation fuelled by lies, and because of those lies, the locals perceived her as a loose woman. A slag. A slapper. A tart. A slut. All of which she had heard as taunts or as mutterings behind her back. But now came the grand finale. The torment to top all torments. This man had beaten her and marched her to the secluded grounds of the hospital, punishing her with every stride, his cursing feeding her anger and starving her fears. Turning her from victim to aggressor, lashing out against his jibes, her stray slap spinning her off balance and his whack knocking her to the ground, her eyes looking into his as he stared down at her, probing her clothes and tracing her curves, his dilating pupils betraying his thoughts and his stare making her feel dirty. Making her frightened once more. She looked away in search for escape, knowing it was only a matter of time before he forced himself upon her and took her humiliation to a new low with the ultimate degradation of rape.

He yanked her up by the arm, "Keep moving."

She staggered ahead, questioning whether she had brought this upon herself. Wondering if she had projected the wrong kind of image. But it wasn't sex that made her go off with men so easily, it was her inadequacies, her worries, her fear of growing old, alone the rest of her days. Her parents would not live forever, and she needed someone to be there for her when they were gone. Someone to love, and to love *her* in return. That's what she was searching for. And no matter what men had said about her in the past, most of them had lied. She *hadn't* been 'easy'. *Hadn't* 'put out' as often as they had said. She was a good girl, seen in a bad light, until, eventually, three years ago, one guy had seen her differently, and her life had been turned around.

Almost at once, she had fallen in love with him. A popular young barman named Bradley, he had worked in the cocktail bar at one of the nightclubs, juggling bottles and mixing drinks, serving everyone with a wink and a smile. Too good for her, she had thought, and maybe her friends had thought so too. So she was overwhelmed when he had shown an interest and given her a free drink, flirting with her and making her feel special. Making her feel good about herself with one compliment after another. The mere fact that he had wanted to be around her an ego boost in itself, especially seeing as how she'd liked him for ages. And although at first she had been unsure of his intentions, eventually, she would weaken to his charms, a night spent at his place.

For the next few days however, she had struggled to get in touch with him and worried he had used her. Worried that he was the same as all the rest. Until he had called the following weekend with a list of excuses, one late night after he had finished work. The last night they had spent together. From then on, trying to get in touch with him was like trying to catch a ghost. He was always working or at the gym. Playing football or out with his mates. Always an excuse and never enough time. Then, two months later, she had found she was pregnant and had gone to his home to confront him, standing on his doorstep like an unwelcome salesman. Crying when he had said he didn't believe her. That the child wasn't his and could be anyone's. Told her to fuck off. Told her that he wanted nothing more to do with her, even as she cried for him to stop, telling him that she loved him and that he was hurting her. His final response;- a mere laugh as he called her a slut before slamming the door in her sobbing face.

It was almost a month later when she had heard he'd moved abroad to work the bars of Ibiza. She had told her 'friends' that he was there to make extra money so they could get married. Said they were engaged. Even bought herself a cheap engagement ring and said he had sent it over. All of it in denial of the truth, just as she denied what her friends really thought of her. Knowing she wasn't *really* a friend, she was the *gofer,* the *hanger-on*. Go for this. Go for that. Hang on to this. Her night spent queuing at bars and holding onto drinks whilst the others went to the toilet, danced, or made fun of her. And every time they laughed at her, she laughed with them, pretending it didn't hurt. Now, she wondered why she had ever mixed with them in the first place. The so called 'popular' girls. And with the knife still digging into her back, she faced up to the truth of the matter. That they weren't *real* friends at all, and Bradley was never going to be a part of her life. The only good thing to come out of their relationship was her baby. And that, more than anything, had made her life worth living.

With the birth of her baby, Naomi had lost interest in men, didn't feel she needed them anymore, though occasionally she was glad to get their attention. Happy to flirt and know that men were still interested, even if it *was* for the wrong reason. But one day, she hoped, it would be for the right reason. Hoped that that someone special would see her for who she truly was. Someone nice, who would love and take care of her and her daughter both. But most of all, now more than anything, she wished she had squeezed into the taxi with her friends, taking there offer of a lift, however insincere it may have been, so she could live and be there for her child.

"That way!" He barked, pointing with the knife as she looked around, a push into her shoulder forcing her off to the right, sticking to the shadows.

They walked down the inclined pathway to the neighbouring ambulance station, and at the sight of lights through the opaque windows, Naomi allowed her hopes to soar. Allowed herself to think that, in some mentally sick and twisted way, after having hurt her, he'd had a change of heart and was now trying to seek attention to her wounds, just as she'd heard he had done with his last victim. But with the sound of voices and a flash of torchlight in the nearby streets, he grabbed her hard and pressed her against the wall around the corner from the main doors.

"Do you like living around here, Naomi?" he asked like an interested acquaintance.

Naomi couldn't answer, he'd seen to that. Her mouth gagged with the white cotton belt from around her waist.

"What's the matter?" he asked, "Cat got your tongue? I'll make the question a little easier for you, shall I. Do you like *living*?"

She answered him with a vigorous nod before he pressed her face against the wall and waved the knife before her eyes, warning her to be silent before taking his phone from his pocket and making two calls.

The first was short and to the point. "I'm at the ambulance station."

The next was to the emergency services to report the discovery of a stabbing, his voice panicked and anxious, "Please, you have to help me. The man's dead. But there's a woman, further up the street, hidden in an alley just off Wansbeck road. She's bleeding. Please, you have to come quick." With that, he hung up and switched off his phone.

His call had been taken seriously. She could hear the activity of the police in the neighbouring streets shifting away from them, screeching tyres and people running off into the distance, blue lights focusing their attentions in the opposite direction. Then men's voices nearby and an engine starting, the doors of the ambulance station rolling up and a vehicle speeding out, its lights flashing, and her captor grabbing her from behind and dragging her inside before the door rolled back down to lock them in.

Fifty Seven

Meg went through the possible scenarios in her head. The woman was still alive and had probably been taken to a place where Edwards could perform his tortures, his sickening acts of depravity to be played out in seclusion and over time, meaning he had to have transport, or had made arrangements for his accomplice to pick them up at some pre-arranged location. Either way, she hoped he'd made a mistake and the vehicle had been caught on camera, heading towards his den of torture or the place they were holding the girl. But regardless of how far they may have fled during the past twenty-odd minutes, she could ill afford to take chances, and had to work patiently from the scene of crime, fanning out to gather every little scrap of evidence, keeping herself in check. A sequence to be followed and an understanding to be built up of exactly what had happened.

There were police vehicles trawling through every street within a half mile radius, and here, just yards from the body, officers knocked on doors, lights flicking on up and down the neighbouring streets as people stood in doorways wearing tightly wrapped dressing gowns and tired expressions. Some, like politicians, answering questions with questions of their own.

'What's this all about?'

'What's the meaning of this? knocking people up at this time in the morning.'

Meg stood facing a gathering of around twenty officers, her back to the activity of the forensics team as she dished out her orders.

"I want all c.c.t.v. footage from the surrounding area. There'll be cameras in the grounds of the nearby hospital. There's one on the roundabout at the top of Ropery Lane. And I want full co-operation from the nightclubs on the main street. The bars'll be closed, but staff'll still be clearing up, so see to it that we get full access to their surveillance tapes and all images are downloaded immediately."

Throughout her series of requests, Ben split the horde into groups and directed the pattern of the operation. They had a missing woman, with no idea who she was or where she was being held. And all they had to go on was what they knew from the killer's m.o. and what little they could glean from the scene.

Meg turned back to the corpse to find Chris Bolden walking towards her in paper overalls, the flash of a camera behind him as an assistant took another picture of the body in situ.

"What can you tell me about the missing woman?" Meg asked.

"She's Caucasian, with bleached blonde, shoulder length hair. Her shoe size would indicate she's somewhere between 4' 6" and 5' 8", she had a fake tan and was wearing false nails painted white."

"What about Stevie Wonder?" Meg asked, nodding in the direction of the body.

"He was stabbed twice in the chest and suffered a punctured lung. Looks like his eyes were forced out with the applied pressure of fingers and-"

"Time of death'll do for now. The rest I'll find out later."

"Ten to twenty minutes."

"And the call came in at two-o-eight," Meg thought out loud as she looked at Ben. "The times coincide. We've knocked on every door in the street and so far there's no reports of anyone missing. Plus, if she lives around here, a taxi would have dropped her at the door."

"So she came on foot and probably lives close by," said Ben.

Meg gave a nod of agreement. "She won't have come far. We're only five minutes from the top of the main street, so let's start there." She turned towards the car, then cursed, "Shit!"

"What?" Ben asked.

"Chicago... *'Chicago Rock'*. He wasn't just taunting you. He was telling you where he was going to strike next."

Blue lights flashing and sirens wailing, they raced the short distance to the bar at the top of the street. Less than half an hour ago the road would have been awash with people pouring onto the street, climbing into taxis or piling into takeaways. Now, only a few drunken stragglers spilling kebabs and the fillings from their burgers staggered down the street to the taxi rank.

At Chicago Rock, Ben and Meg were greeted by the bar supervisor and shown through to a room at the back of the premises where Morton was already pouring over the tapes, Jason Trevors on hand to run his errands.

"We have a window?" Morton asked.

Ben answered, "If she *was* here, and allowing for the possibility she went for food, or was intoxicated, she'd have left between 1:45 and two-ish."

Morton keyed in the time-slot and the screen was split into four images of a bar full of people. He highlighted and enlarged the one covering the main entrance, slowly scrolling through it until the punters began to leave in their droves. The time in the corner of the screen showed 01:49 and now played in real time as Ben, Meg and Trevors looked on, their eyes focused sharply on the screen as they studied the stream of people leaving.

"Any other means of exit?" Meg asked.

"None," Morton answered. "Except for emergencies, this is the only exit used."

"Okay, we can't be sure Edwards was on the premises, so focus on the women only. We need to find the missing woman."

There were groups of twos, threes and fours, a hen party and the occasional loner, but amongst the throng of people leaving at two o'clock, it was hard to pick out anyone specific.

"Peroxide hair and white shoes doesn't help much," said Morton. "We need to know what we're looking for."

"Okay," said Meg, "Lets give our girl a description. She'll be wearing light or bright colours rather than dark. Maybe pastels or something white. She won't be wearing trousers and I doubt she'll be wearing shorts. Most likely, it'll be a skirt or a dress."

"How'd you figure all that?" Ben asked, surprised.

Meg remembered the shoes having diamante ankle straps, similar to a pair she had herself. "Those shoes are meant to be seen, not hidden under the hems of trousers. The rest's common sense."

"Yeah, to a woman maybe," muttered Morton.

"There! *Look.*" Meg was pointing to the screen as it was invaded by balloons from the hen party.

"What?" Ben asked, "I don't see it."

Then, as the group of women exited the building and turned off to the left, he saw the young woman Meg was pointing at, kissing her friends goodbye. Maybe for the very last time. He watched as her friends waved to her from a taxi. The only woman who fitted the description, left at the estimated time, and headed in the right direction. And in that instant, Ben was on the phone to the taxi firm as Meg and Morton rewound the tape and searched for the woman in white, the screen now split into eight as they tracked her every movement around the club.

"There!" Meg shouted.

"And there!" Morton pointed.

Moments later, they had both spotted a shaven haired man shadowing her movements, standing in the background, his face half hidden by a glass as he took a sip of his beer. He had shaven his hair, grown some stubble, and was now wearing glasses, but it was definitely Edwards.

"He's tailing her," said Meg.

Meanwhile, Ben had discovered the drop-off addresses; all of them at neighbouring villages. Two of the girls were from Pelton, one from Grange Villa, and the other from Beamish. With another call, he had a car on the way to the nearest. A Sergeant would interview the friend and find out as much as possible about the missing woman.

"Look at this," Morton complained, watching Edwards on the screen. "The cheeky bastard's standing outside talking casual as you like to one of the doormen, just feet away from three PC's. And what's more, we've got a fucking car parked across the street and not one of them have noticed him."

"They were watching for drunks and troublemakers," Meg said, disappointed and annoyed, but accepting that the last thing they'd expect was to see Edwards amongst a crowd of clubbers, and accepting, once again, that he had outsmarted them. "He hung back," she said. "He was quiet and avoided drawing attention to himself. In a crowd of hundreds, what could you expect."

"Fucking road-slappers," Morton said, referring to his low level colleagues.

Meg felt helpless as she watched the woman set off on her journey, not a thing she could do as she saw Edwards pass between the doormen, and with a wink, wave to the camera, his digits spread wide as he mouthed the words '*number five.*'

Meg gritted her teeth, her eyes fixed on his as she felt the vibration of an incoming call, the phone in her pocket set on silent. And without letting on to the others, she let it go unanswered.

"Her name's Naomi Watts," said Ben, his eyes fixed on the frozen image of Edwards on the screen. "Twenty-two years old. Got a two year-old daughter and lives with her parents at number 43 Lavender Crescent."

Meg knew the street and turned to Ben, "She was just a hundred metres or so from home. Quick. Get round there. See if they've heard from her."

Morton improved the image on the screen and with the press of a button, a copy slid into his hand and he passed it to Meg. "Here's his latest mug shot."

Meg looked at the picture then back to Morton, "Take Trevors with you. Check the grounds of the hospital and check their tapes. I'll catch up with you in a few minutes."

Finally, alone, Meg checked the message on her phone.

Fifty Eight

With a rush of fear and excitement, the blood racing through his veins, he had bathed in the thrill of what was happening.

Bar the venue, everything had been unplanned. Every act done spur of the moment. Yet, somehow, in the midst of it all, he had known there was a specific target, his search taking him past the throng of people at the bar and skirting the edge of the dance-floor, thinking on his feet and squeezing between one group of people after another. His actions those of an opportunist, blending into the swollen crowd and mingling with the punters, casually hovering within earshot of their conversations. Searching for a loner. Listening for a name. Until eventually, he had found her; a group of young women stabbing her in the back with their jibes, telling him all he had needed to know. Her so called '*friends*' unwittingly stamping the seal on her death warrant.

Now, she lay in the back of the ambulance, strapped to a gurney and unable to move. Unable to scream as she listened to the distant laughing of ambulance-men in a far off room, passing their time away playing cards as *she* lay close to death, and death whispered in her ear, "Does it upset you, Naomi? The sound of men laughing as you are about to die."

Panting into her gag, her eyes filled with terror as she fought against the straps, pulling and Yanking. The scream from the back of her throat stopped short as the flat of the blade pressed against her mouth and the sharp edge touched against her septum, threatening to slice up through her nostrils. "Scream again, bitch, I'll cut it off."

He trailed the point of the blade from her nose, over her lips, and down her neck, drifting slowly toward her cleavage, beads of sweat standing on her skin as the blade travelled over her dress and down to her abdomen, it's journey continuing southwards, lingering over her groin as his hand reached for her throat to feel the pulse of her heart racing his own. His grip tightening. Her breathing;- shorter.

Faster as she strained against him. The knife pausing at the hem of her dress before slipping underneath and the smooth metal of the blade pressed against her inner thigh, then stopped. "Not yet," he said, his face leaning into hers and his breath falling on her ears, "Not the time or the place."

The knife peeled away and his grip relaxed on her throat, his eyes drawn to the bead of sweat trickling from her brow before he blocked its escape with a lick of his tongue dragging up her face, tasting her fear as he fought to control himself. His craving barely subdued, desperate to feel the high of cutting into her joints. Wanting to start dismemberment now, but having to bide his time and wait impatiently for his partner in crime. His teacher and voyeur, who had made all of this possible, sometimes from the other end of the phone, making the decisions and telling him exactly what to do. And so he sat, like a dog on a leash held back from his prey, locked in the ambulance and staring at the doors. Unable to take her life without consent. Growing frustrated.

This was new territory; a new pattern to the methodical planning that had gone before. Only the choice of hunting ground and the selection of his prey had been deliberate, and he had all but given up on finding her. A woman who ticked all the boxes. His quarry had to have all the relevant requirements, and to find her, he'd had to act on impulse, dealing with problems as they arose, events unfolding before him to throw up their challenges as he wandered the bar, having to go unnoticed and follow his prey without being seen.

He hadn't counted on the mugger and the trouble it would bring. Nor the early call to the police from a woken neighbour or the hurried change of plan when he had failed to gain access to the hospital, hoping to take her to an empty theatre where he could perform his own brand of surgery, surgical instruments lying at his disposal. A life to take rather than save, the sterile surroundings to be smeared with her blood as he sliced into her skin.

He had counted on finding a side door or an emergency exit, unwittingly left unattended by a member of staff busily performing their duties. But as it turned out, the hospital was for convalescence and out-patients only, and all of the doors were locked by 9 p.m.

His forced change of plan had brought him here, to the ambulance station. Manned twenty-four-seven, the remaining crew were in a room toward the back of the building some twenty feet away from the vehicles where he sat with Naomi. He looked at his watch, worried that he was running out of time. The ambulance on the wild goose chase was only a short distance away and could return at any moment. And with the build up of personnel came the risk of being discovered.

"Come on. Come on. Where the hell are you?"

The excitement of spontaneity now gone, he cursed through gritted teeth, beginning to think his accomplice wasn't coming. That there were too many risks involved. Too many police.

He reached into his pocket and pulled out his phone, tempted to switch it on again, weighing up the pros and cons of what might happen should it be traced before slipping it back into his pocket and fixing his eyes on the ambulance doors, waiting for them to open. Feeling uncomfortable with this whole situation. Everything disorganised and haphazard. Too random. Too amateurish. He liked things planned and in order, but his time in Chicago Rock had been risky and unprepared, and this didn't fair much better. If a call came in for an ambulance now, he could find himself in real trouble, and his anxiety growing, he worried that his mentor had been caught. That the police would learn of his whereabouts and were on their way. The result of a lack in planning. His mentor wanting to play games with Ben instead of just getting on with it all; just killing those chosen and being done with it.

He looked at his watch again, and time ticking on, turned to Naomi, the knife pressed to her throat as he heard a click behind him and turned to see the ambulance door swing open.

"About bloody time," said Edwards, before his gaze met that of Jason Trevors.

Naomi looked at the man standing at the doors of the ambulance and was filled with a moment's hope. A policeman, not much older than herself, his gaze shifting from her bindings to the glint of the knife in the mutilators hand, and through closed lips, she screamed for him to help, her captor's knuckles turning white and gripping the knife more firmly, ready to put it to use. Then her eyes filled with terror as she screamed out in fear. Her eyes no longer on the policeman, but behind him, looking over his shoulder… to the fire extinguisher crashing down on his head.

Fifty Nine

The headlights of the returning ambulance swept around the corner to be swallowed up by the brightly illuminated ambulance bay. The doors open, the other ambulance was gone, and in its place, a crowd of police officers gathered around a body on the ground, the female amongst them crouching for a closer look as two of the men stood arguing.

"He was walking the grounds," said Morton, his voice raised. "We had him on camera. I didn't expect him to wander off."

"You were supposed to be partnering him," Ben snapped back at him. "You should never have let him out of your sight. That should have been *you* lying there, not *him*."

Morton didn't answer, didn't argue. His eyes shifting from Ben to the body of Jason Trevors lying face down in a crumpled heap, a fire extinguisher to his side and a pool of blood extenuating from his broken skull. His life cut short by his eagerness to impress a reluctant partner who was now struggling to keep a lid on his emotions, outwardly appearing unfazed, but inside suffering a heavy burden of guilt he felt he'd carry the rest of his days, his thoughts of how he'd shut him out as he registered his own stubbornness and his preference to work alone, set in his ways and void of attachment, his focus fixed on results. And because of it, a young policeman now lay dead.

Ben turned away from him in disgust and spoke to Meg as she stood up, "The other women were all attacked in their homes," he said. "This one was grabbed in the street. Why the change of m.o?"

"It's getting harder," Meg answered. "News is out. People are being more cautious."

"He's adapting, you think? Changing tack?"

"Yes. But what made him choose *her?* She wasn't the only one on her own. And again, she was a mother. How did he know?"

"He followed her," said Ben. "He overheard it mentioned in the bar."

"Too random," said Meg. "We need to look at anywhere there's mention of mothers. Like birth registers. Childcare facilities. Nurseries, etc. We need to find his selection process, and find it *fast*."

"That could take forever," Ben said, resigned to the fact that the search could prove fruitless, but that it was worth a try, and they just might get lucky. "Just two more days and it's the girl," he said, "He'll kill her before we can find what we need."

Meg turned to Morton as he stood in silence, a blank expression of guilt etched into his face, "Morton. I want you to get back to the station and write out a full report. I don't care how long it takes. Then, go home. You're suspended till further notice."

Ben took a call on his radio. The transmitter on the stolen ambulance had given away its location and they'd found it half a mile away. He relayed the message to Meg. "It's empty. They think she was transferred to another vehicle."

Back at the station, the two of them alone in her office, Ben and Meg argued over her decision to pair-up Morton and Trevors.

"Morton was first on the scene," said Ben. "I'm telling you, he *allowed* Edwards to escape. He's our leak, Meg. He has to be."

Meg's thoughts were elsewhere. She had a dead cop on her hands. Questions to be answered.

"What were you *thinking*, Meg," Ben continued.

There was a long pause before she answered. "I… I guess I wasn't thinking straight. I thought Morton might work better with someone not set in his ways. Someone willing to listen to him. I was trying to get us working as a team."

"A *team?...* With a spy in the camp?"

"It was a balancing act, *okay*! A make or break decision."

"Well, it broke, Meg. And what's more, you should have known better."

"Yeah, well, maybe I thought I had other, more important things to think about."

"Like what, for Christ's sake? What could have been more important?"

Meg diverted her gaze.

"Come on, Meg. Tell me. What is it?"

His hands on her arms, he turned her to face him and looked deep into her eyes, "You can tell me anything, Meg. You know that, right?"

She looked at him uneasily, angry that he could make her feel like this. Angry for letting herself get into a situation without knowing which way to turn. And for a moment, she wanted his arms to hold her closer, tighter, and at the same time, to push her away; the safeguard of separation maintaining a barrier between them, unbroken and unrelenting. She returned his gaze, her eyes telling him of hidden secrets and her lips telling him nothing until he pulled her closer and pressed them to his own, a surge of passion travelling between them like a wave of electricity, each of them consumed by the moment before she wrenched away.

"Don't do this," she said. "Don't ever do that again."

"What's wrong, Meg? You want this. I know you do. Just as much as I do."

"Go home, Ben. Go to bed." A moment's pause before she added, "Get some rest."

"You need your rest too, Meg. You're not a machine."

She turned her back to him. "Please, just go."

"Come with me. Let's talk about this."

"I can't. I have other things to consider."

"For gods sake, Meg, *delegate*. You can't do everything."

"No, Ben, you're wrong. I can't do *anything*. Not with you around. Please… Go home. Leave me alone. I need time to think."

His shoulders slumped, he turned to leave, a glance back at her as he held the door open, "This is not the end of it, Meg. This isn't over." And as the door closed behind him, Meg dipped into her pocket for her phone.

"I'm sorry," she said, "I couldn't get away. Tell me. How is she?"

Sixty

It was 8:32 a.m. when Sean pulled up to the B&B, the news on the car stereo telling him of a woman who'd disappeared earlier this morning. A young mother called Naomi, there was a chance she was still alive, the importance of finding her quickly, urgently relayed through the airwaves. And though it hadn't been said, Sean knew as well as any listener that if she wasn't found by 10:15, she'd be dead.

Exhausted and with an inkling of how he'd spent his night, Sean walked through the reception area and passed the dining room where he could hear new guests having breakfast. Foreigners speaking in what he assumed to be a German or Dutch accent, and the proprietor telling them how lucky they were to have booked up when they did. "What, with the big cricket match down the road and now these murders, every hotel and B&B in the area is hiking up its prices to take advantage of the influx."

"Influx?" He heard one of them ask.

"Extra cops," came the reply. "And for every extra copper there's a reporter. Not much room for tourists any more."

"So those two men who left earlier. They were reporters, yes?" asked the other tourist.

"Yes"

"And we are your only guests?"

"Yes. Oh, and of course there's Mr. Waders."

"Mr. Waders?"

"Quiet fella. Been here a few days. Keeps himself to himself pretty much."

Sean picked up his pace as he headed for the stairs and was caught by Thomas rushing out from the kitchen, greeting him with a salute, Sean's stride remaining unbroken as he returned it with a salute of his own.

"What did you win, sir?" Thomas asked excitedly.

Sean stopped and gave him a quizzical look, "Excuse me?"

"What did you win?" Thomas asked again, looking at him with bemused suspicion, curious of what was being kept from him. "Dad heard your car pull up. He said you must have got lucky last night. What did he mean?... Didn't you win somefing?"

"Not exactly."

"So where've you been?"

"I'm not entirely sure," Sean answered, his voice low.

"On a mission?"

"Sssshh."

With a nod, Thomas smiled and whispered, "Was it dangerous?"

Sean tapped his nose, pondering before answering, "It's a secret." A secret even to himself he thought as he dropped to his hunkers, eye level with Thomas, and asked quietly;- "Can you tell me what time I left my room last night?"

"I don't know, sir. I heard your car out front after you left my room. Then I fink I must have fallen asleep."

His memory jogged, Sean vaguely remembered having sneaked into Thomas's room around nine and discovering his mention of a date, the year coinciding with the amount of money he'd found in the shoebox, and the day; the beginning of his nightmare, *29th March, 1951*. The rest of his night remained a mystery up until his return to the B&B this morning, driving along the final stretch of road with a slip into normality, his time-lapses getting worse, and with it, his memory.

"Are you okay, sir?" Thomas asked, his friend looking at him with a distant gaze before his stare melted away and his eyes fixed on Thomas.

"Yes, I'm fine," Sean answered, a smile of reassurance before saying his goodbyes and rushing up to his room to switch on the television.

Naomi's father was already in a conference room making an emotional plea for her safe return and asked for anyone who may have seen her to contact the police. Then came the bombshell as Sean removed his woollen hat and spectacles, brushing his hand over his shaven head as his likeness flashed onto the screen, the voice of the anchorman giving a description of him in his new guise. Sean looking on, mesmerised. The picture had been taken from a security camera late last night, some time after he had left the B&B. The police pleaded for anyone with information to contact them immediately and

Detective Meg Rainer, looking as tired as he himself felt, looked straight into the camera, pleading with him directly as if she were sitting right in front of him. "Please, Mr. Edwards, if you are watching this;- return Naomi to her family unharmed. I know you are capable of this. There have been times when you have shown great constraint, compassion, and sometimes strength. I implore you to show those qualities now. Together, we can bring an end to this." Then, with the blinding flash of cameras, the detective put her arm around Naomi's father and steered him away from the prying lenses.

Sean had had no knowledge of where he had been or what he had done, and now stood shocked with the discovery he'd been to a nightclub of all places. He'd mingled in the crowd. He'd bought a drink. And he had followed a young woman from the bar, the last time she was seen alive shortly before 2:00 a.m. this morning. And he remembered none of it.

He racked his brains, wondering if he had already killed her. Asking himself if her corpse was already lying in state somewhere waiting to be found, and if so, where?

"His accomplice," he uttered, referring to his alter ego's partner. "*He* has her. They worked together on this."

He wondered if, in his altered state of mind, he had spent the early hours with his accomplice assisting in some sickening act of depravity. Wondered too if Naomi were being kept alive somewhere, safe from discovery. Maybe the same place his daughter was hidden. By a man, as sick and twisted as his own alter-ego.

He looked at the clock checking the time, filled with a compulsion to do something, the temptation pulling at him, yanking on his chain, reminding him there was a chance he could find her. A chance he could find them both. Before he or his accomplice committed the final act of murder.

But there were risks.

He was already suffering from parasomnia and time-lapses, and by performing self hypnosis there was a chance he could make matters worse. Make his condition worse. The killer within him becoming more violent, more dangerous, and playing into the hands of his accomplice. And the life of his daughter, almost certainly over if he failed to keep his alter ego under control.

The alternatives racing through his mind, he dipped into his pocket for his pills and took three, then a fourth.

He switched the t.v. off and lay on his bed, closed his eyes and tried to relax, his senses focusing entirely on himself..., listening to the sound of his breathing..., feeling the rise and fall of his chest, his attention focusing on the sound of his pulse, counting backwards with each beating throb of his heart...

One hundred...

Ninety-nine...

Ninety-eight...

Ninety-seven...

His heart-rate slowing, his shoulders slumped; the relaxation travelling through his arms and down his body. His stress dissolving like sugar as a distant blur of images projected onto the screen of his mind.

Eighty-three.

Eighty-two.

The images drew closer and larger as his breathing shallowed, until at last, a sense of calm tranquillity seeped throughout his body and the flashback played again in his head...different this time. The images clearer. In sharp focus and in more detail.

Again it started with the sight of a boy peering from behind a willow tree, still the black-rimmed spectacles and baggy clothes of before, but this time, everything in colour, and it was only now that he realised his first flashback had been a silent monotone of greys; like watching an old black and white movie. But this was different. The details clearer. The images alive and vibrant. And the sound slowly filtering through to his subconscious hearing as his viewpoint shifted to that of the boy, peeking from behind the willow tree.

"I'm going to caaaaaatch you."

"I'm going to huuuuuurt you."

"I'm going to kiiiiiiill you."

He subconsciously skipped forward to his last memory of what had happened. His stalking through the garden to ease the lip of the jar over a bee as it trawled over the yellow rose. The tinny SNAP! of both jar and lid, trapping the bee and decapitated rose within.

"I'm going to pull your leeeeegs off."

"I'm going to pull your wiiiiings off."

For what seemed like ages, he watched this flying tiger of the insect world crashing indiscriminately into the walls of its transparent cell, its futile attempt to escape draining its energy, and its occasional rest disturbed with a violent shake of the jar, until finally, its movements laboured, he removed the lid of its prison.

"Nowwww it's time to play," he grinned.

He turned the jar over and with a few hard slaps to its base, the bee spilled out onto the wooden picnic table, drowsy from its dismal onslaught, the unspoilt rose lying nearby.

He spoke to it like a friend, his tone gentle, almost caring. "Hello there little bee, my name's Sean. Sean Edwards. I thought you should know that before I kill you."

Then holding the head of the rose, he pushed it's stem under the bee's abdomen, coercing it to straddle onto his neighbouring hand. Watching it as it limply explored its new surroundings, oblivious to the threat and its chance to escape. His hand drawn to eye-level, exploring its every detail. Its tiny head, its eyes, its feelers and translucent wings. His piercing gaze flicking over its length, counting black and yellow stripes and noting pollen deposits on its hairy body as it slowly climbed the web of his thumb.

"Aaaaaahhh!"

Sean woke with a start, snapping upright and rubbing at his hand as though he had just been stung, the imaginary pain ripping him from his trance, confused by what he'd seen and his focus gone. Too alert to try again. No wiser than before. And no memories of the past portrayed by the images of him as a boy, though he was convinced they held the key to his daughter's whereabouts. A trail of breadcrumbs brought about by his parasomnia. Or worse still;- repressed memories stretching back through time, absorbed into the mind of his alter ego. A past intertwined with his own, shown to him in fragments, like snippets of a childhood relayed to him as scant recollections from parents not his own. But just as dreams are meant to be a guide through waking life, the images had to mean something too, though he was unable to decipher their true meaning. The images more like a forgotten memory, the boy a stranger. Sean watching, more from the point of view of an onlooker than a past participant, sure he was a witness to an event of some kind, but what?

He looked at the time again, '8:58 a.m.' and feeling like he hadn't slept in days, looked at the picture of Naomi on t.v., his hand reaching into his pocket and pulling out the small brown medicine bottle, thinking to himself, 'If I'm asleep, then I can't kill her.'

He twisted off the security cap and spilled two more pills into the palm of his hand, looking at them doubtfully before spilling out some more and popping them into his mouth, swallowing hard as he tossed his head back.

For now, he would get some much needed rest and find out the answers to his questions when he woke.

And he would need all of his strength to face up to them.

Sixty One

A young life wasted, He thought, and it comes down to this.

More than anyone realised, Morton regretted what had happened to Jason Trevors and the part he had played in his death, but until his killer was caught, someone had to be held accountable, and Morton was the one in the firing line, the finger of his superiors on the trigger. *'I have no alternative but to suspend you till further notice'* Meg had said, *'and I expect a full report on my desk, sooner rather than later'*

Morton had written a first draft whilst everything was still fresh in his mind, alone at his desk, nodding into the early hours of this morning until awoken by the bustle of the following shift.

He now held the finished report in his hands, reading through it one last time and reliving the scene in his head as he did so. He had tried to explain the circumstances;- everything happening so fast and the cause of events forcing them to take action. The two of them standing at the main door of the hospital impatiently waiting for the security guard to answer their buzz for attention, and with no response, Morton had begun banging his fists on the double-glazed doors.

"I'll check the grounds," Trevors had said.

Without argument, Morton had let him go. His banging on the doors incessant as his eyes searched the darkened reception for signs of someone responding, and as Trevors had disappeared around a corner of the building, a dishevelled security guard ambled up to the door, idly tucking-in his shirt.

Morton angrily held his I.D. to the glass pane, "Open the fucking door!"

Slovenly and overweight, the security guard squinted tiredly at his badge, "Is there a problem, officer?"

"There will be if you don't open this fucking door. Where the hell have you been?"

"Erm… toilet break," the guard answered, rubbing his eyes and lazily punching a code into the alarm system, the door sliding open.

Toilet break was about right, thought Morton, his breath smelled like shit. "You were fucking sleeping, weren't you."

The guard yawned, "So I spent a little time in the land of zeds. Where's the harm?"

Morton barged past him, "I'll tell you this once, and once only. Get your fucking arse in gear, now! And don't go wasting my fucking time going on some kind of power trip. I want to see your surveillance tapes, and I want to see them *yesterday!"*

The guard was startled into obedience; answering to Morton's commands like a lap-dog to his master, and within minutes they sat at the screens to the surveillance cameras watching the live feedback of Trevors walking the grounds, his torch shining into corners and delving behind bushes.

"Take it back to 2:00 a.m. and wind it forward, *Slowly*," Morton instructed, looking at the other monitor.

"What're you looking for?"

Morton didn't answer, his gaze fixed on the grey images of a quiet night, the scene unchanging. Only the speed of the quickening clock in the corner of the screen belied the lapsing time. Then, with a movement that made the guard jump, Morton leapt to his feet and shouted, "There! Stop!"

"Well I'll be." The guard looked on, his mouth agape.

Morton got on his radio, "Trevors?... Trevors?!"

"Receiving."

"Be careful out there. He was here. Not ten minutes ago."

Trevors looked around in the darkness, his voice quietly crackling back, "Okay, sir. Will do."

By now, Trevors had come full circle around the perimeter of the hospital and branched off in the direction of the ambulance station, his wanderings unnoticed by Morton as he sat glued to the movements of Edwards and the woman on the other screen, the real-time monitor forgotten.

Morton harried the guard, "Come on, man. Pick it up." The winding motion of his fingers urging him to wind the recording forward, faster. And it was only when he saw the woman and Edwards heading away from the hospital that he looked at the other monitor and realised Trevors was nowhere to be seen. Then came the call on his radio. It was the last time he had heard Jason Trevors speak. "I'm at the ambulance station. I need back-"

As quickly as his legs could carry him, Morton had raced out of the surveillance room and down the corridors, radioing for back-up as he went. Banging on the doors of the hospital exit as the guard caught up with him and punched in the security code, the doors sliding open and Morton rushing out. But by the time he got down to the ambulance station, Jason Trevors was dead, his skull cracked wide open and an ambulance missing, Edwards and the girl gone. And it seemed, the accomplice had played a part in their escape.

Now, his report in hand, Morton was to perform his final task on the case.

He knocked on the door of Meg's office, and with no answer, pushed it open to find it empty. A cold welcome from a room yet to be personalised. 'Of course she's not here' he thought, 'Why would she be.' Regardless of how much he felt he still had to offer, Meg was far too busy to hang around and give him a chance to explain himself or admit he'd made a costly mistake. But this was a crime in itself. There was work to be done. Things he could do to help. How could he be expected to leave an active case before its conclusion.

He wandered over to her desk and hovered there a moment, his report held over the in-tray with an uneasy waver, indignation gnawing away at him. Failure gnawing deeper. This wasn't fair. It wasn't right. He could help bring the killers to justice for what they had done, but without him, the body-count could climb higher. Then, there'd be more arses on the line, and like it or not, *that* bothered him.

'Fuck it' he thought, 'Why should **I** care. If *she* wants me out of the way, then so be it.' He dropped the report into the tray and turned to leave the office, stopping short, not a stride taken, his back to her desk, asking himself who he was trying to kid. He hated this. The exclusion. The not knowing what was happening, even before he had left the building; playing no further part in the investigation whilst two murderers continued on their rampage, both of them responsible for killing several women, a dick-head rapist, a colleague, and effectively, bringing about the end of his career. But there was still an innocent child out there, and as long as she was alive he couldn't let this go. He wanted to play his part in saving her. Wanted a chance to put things right. Or as right as was humanly possible.

Then, with a glance back at the in-tray before leaving, Morton saw paper poking out of the fax machine and walked around the desk to read it.

It had come from the Danish police, apparently, just a few minutes ago. A detective Vandaag apologised for having been unable to help earlier and added that, although they had no record of any serial killings with the m.o. Meg had described, evidence had surfaced connected to the coin which she may like to take a look at. If so, she was to call the above number at 16:30 GMT. That was when a semi-retired old hand called Hans Gruber came in for a few hours each day, and might be able to help with some of their questions.

With the sound of Ben and Meg approaching, Morton snatched the sheet from the machine and scrunched it into his pocket.

"Everything you might need is in my office." He heard Meg say to Ben as she approached the door. "But any major developments, I want you to call me."

"What about the press?" He heard Ben ask.

"I've told the boss, we've got too much on our plates right now to be spending our time in front of the cameras. From now on, *he* has that tiger by the tail, and he can hang onto it for as long as he wants to as far as I'm concerned."

Meg opened the door to find Morton coming from her desk.

"You still here?" she asked bluntly.

"My report's on your desk. But I'm asking you to reconsider the suspension."

"Don't waste your breath," she said.

"You're making a mistake."

"If that '*mistake*' as you call it, means losing no more men, then that's a cross I'll have to bear."

Morton looked her in the eye and blushed red, his angry gaze shooting to Ben before he barged past them and stormed out with a clash of the door.

Sixty Two

3:04 p.m.

Sean had slept for almost five hours and awoke with a start, his arms flailing and knocking the bottle of pills from his side to the floor, a re-run of Friends playing on the t.v. now drowned out by the sound of sirens screaming outside.

He shot to his feet and rushed to the window to peek through the blinds. A fire engine whizzing past in the street below, the Doppler affect of its wailing sirens, closing and fading into the distance. His sigh of relief followed by anxious moments with the realisation a chunk of his day had been lost, and while ***he*** had slept the day away, his daughter was somewhere out there, frightened and alone.

He flicked through the t.v. stations, one news channel after another, searching for news of his daughter. His finger;- press, press, pressing on the remote, from a report of vandalism in a local graveyard, headstones overturned, some of them broken, to another channel, another story. "*Sixty percent of Brits will be classed as clinically obese by the end of the year*." Every narrative pointless, unimportant. He pleaded into the screen, "My daughter, for god's sake. Tell me about my daughter."

He paused impatiently at the next channel, the euphonic introduction of the Tyne Tees News fading out as an anchorman introduced the headliner over a repeat of footage taken earlier in the day; scenes of lead detectives turning up at Aykley Heads police station and getting out of their cars to have microphones thrust into their faces, their repeats of "No comment," echoing down their ranks as they strode through the main doors. The newsreader spoke directly into camera. "For the latest on the tragedies besetting the town of Chester-le-street, we can now cross live to our correspondent Mark Jakes… Mark, what can you tell us about the latest developments?"

"Well Geoff, so far, the police have gone on record as saying they still don't know the whereabouts of Naomi Watts, the young mother who disappeared just yards from her home in the early hours of this morning after a night out with friends. However, police remain hopeful she is still alive and say they have no reason to believe otherwise at this stage."

"And what of the suspect, Sean Edwards?"

"In light of this latest incident, we now know that the fugitive has changed his appearance and police have released new c.c.t.v. footage taken last night, showing him with his head shaven and wearing spectacles."

A grainy image of Sean flashed onto the screen.

"Any news of his daughter?"

Sean turned up the volume and drew his face closer to the screen, holding his breath as he listened intently to the reporter, his voice business-like and disconnected. "No news thus far, but as we now know, there ***is*** mention of an accomplice, and because of this, we cannot be sure as to whether or not Abigail Edwards is being held by her father, the accomplice, or if they are jointly holding her some place yet to be discovered."

The anchorman begged another question. "If it was her father who abducted her, then isn't it likely she is with him?"

"As yet, the police can only speculate on who is holding her and how closely the two of them are working together. But, as has been said all along, by the police and those who knew him, Sean Edwards is acting completely out of character. And there is also the distinct possibility that he himself is being held to ransom;- killing, so that his daughter may live. However, I must add that this is merely conjecture at this moment in time. For now, our primary concern is the safety of the public and the safe return of Naomi and Abigail. Earlier today, I spoke to detective superintendent James Brandt, and this is what he had to say."

The next clip showed Jim Brandt on the front steps of Aykley Heads police headquarters in Durham appealing for the press to be patient as he took their various questions, beginning with Mark Jakes; "Do you believe Naomi Watts and the killer's daughter, Abigail Edwards, to be alive as we speak?"

"Until we have proof to show otherwise, we will proceed as though they are alive and well. And we are making every possible effort to bring about their release."

Jostling for his position amongst other reporters, Mark Jakes fired another question, "Are you any nearer to making an arrest?"

“Enquiries are ongoing, but we have a number of promising leads and we hope to bring this to a conclusion as soon as is possible.”

Another reporter shouted, “You know the killer. You know what he looks like. Why haven’t you been able to make an arrest before now?”

“Sean Edwards is a troubled man. But he is also an intelligent man. Though you have already seen a picture of his change in appearance, you can be sure he has other guises. This makes our task more difficult, and I would appeal to the public to be vigilant. There is also the possibility he is being sheltered by his accomplice or renting a place or room somewhere we have yet to discover. Again, I appeal to the public;- If you see this man or know of his whereabouts, please do not approach him. Instead, call us immediately on 0800 2278873.” He pointed to another reporter, “Last question.”

“Is it true that they have killed a police officer?”

“It is with deep regret that I can confirm we have lost a colleague in the process of the investigation, but I am not at liberty to give specifics on that at this moment in time. I can go as far as to say that the officer who died will be sadly missed by all those who knew him and our thoughts go out to his family in their time of grief.”

As reporters vied for answers to more questions, Jim Brandt gave his apologies and made his escape back up the steps and into the building, the picture rolling with the thump of Sean’s fist on top of the t.v. “You’ve told me *nothing*, god damn it!”

The police had divulged only what they had needed to, but they were hiding something, Sean was sure of it, and wondered if they had allowed him to escape last night for the sake of his daughter. Maybe they knew exactly where he was and hoped he would lead them to the accomplice. ‘If only that were so,’ he thought, then maybe his daughter would have a chance. But there were other possibilities to consider too. *Worse* possibilities. What if he had been allowed to escape by the one person who had been helping him all along, and that person was a cop, right in the thick of the investigation. If that were so, then his daughter’s fate would surely be sealed, and he alone would be left to suffer the debauchery to follow. No-one he could turn to after his heinous crimes. His only friend; a lonely young boy, left by his mother and ignored by his father, his trust in the hands of a killer.

Sixty Three

3:47 p.m.

It was an arm they came across first, torn off below the elbow, the wrist broken, the fingers chewed up, and the limb dirty from being dragged along the tracks. It was some thirty yards further on before they found what was left of the body. A lump of mangled flesh, crushed and broken, part of it eaten by animals and the skin like leather, bubbling with feasting maggots. What remained of the clothing was torn and tattered by the wheels of the train dragging him along the tracks and spitting him out into the thorny bushes.

Head of forensics;- detective Christopher Bolden, had been at the scene for some forty minutes when Ben and Meg came to join him, leaving superintendent Brandt further down the track talking to the maintenance staff who'd found the body.

Up until now, Ben had drawn a blank when trying to find David Hetherington, but he had turned up just a few hundred metres from Chester-le Street train station. The last place he had been seen.

"How long do you figure he's been lying here?" Ben asked.

Christopher Bolden was examining the large creamy-white maggots, which, he figured from their size and shedding skins, were in the late stages of their first instar. "Can't be sure," he answered Ben. "Two, maybe three days. When did yer say he went missing?"

"Friday."

"Seems about right by the looks of these," said Bolden, confident that the entomologist would agree that the maggots were in their first stage of development.

Meg's eyes scoured the bordering grass and fauna for anything out of order. "Why would a guy go train-spotting and then kill himself?" she asked.

"I'm not sure he did kill himself," Ben answered.

"You think it was an accident?"

Ben looked down the track and Meg followed his gaze, guessing at his suspicions. "Murdered?" she asked sceptically. "You think he was thrown from the bridge?"

Bolden interrupted their conjecturing, "We've been here for almost an hour now, and although I can appreciate it's early days, I have to say;- I think yer on the wrong track." He stuttered a little in his embarrassment, "Sorry, I mean… err, well, yer know what I mean."

"You don't think he was murdered?" Ben asked.

"At this point," said Bolden, "suicide's my best guess."

"This wasn't suicide," Ben said, scratching his cheek as he looked down at the corpse. "He *saw* something. Either at the Church Mouse, or later, down at the train station. Something that got him killed."

"Like what?" Meg asked.

Bolden butted in again, looking along the track to the secluded bridge, "He was skinny but tall. If he was murdered, then it's likely there'd have been a struggle. But prints indicate this guy was sitting on the edge of that bridge, and he either fell, or he threw himself off."

"Why wasn't he spotted by the train driver?" Ben asked.

"I'm guessing he mistimed his jump, hit the roof of the train and bounced along the top before falling between the carriages."

"Probably the preferred way to go for a train-spotter," said Ben, still thinking there was a possibility he was pushed. "But why top himself? Especially on the same day Edwards was known to be at the station. It's too coincidental."

"Life's full of coincidences," said Bolden.

"What's his background?" Meg asked Ben. "What reason might he have had to commit suicide?"

Ben had been on the phone to the victim's mother earlier in the day, asking if she'd heard from him. "His parents are working class," Ben answered. "Not well off. I got the impression they were very proud of him. The fact that their son was studying to be a doctor seemed to be something they thrilled in. They were worried when he hadn't been in touch, and more so once I gave them a call. I didn't have the heart to tell them he'd dropped out of university."

"So he might have committed suicide after all," said Bolden, "because he felt he was letting them down."

"I doubt it," said Ben. "We thought he'd gone into hiding because he'd seen something. We've been looking for him for days."

Bolden looked at the mangled body, "No need to look any further."

"Wait a minute," Meg chipped in. "At the train station, the c.c.t.v. showed him crossing the bridge and disappearing from view shortly before our unsub came across that same bridge and boarded the train. Maybe David Hetherington knew our unsub. Might even have spoken to him. And it cost him his life."

"His camera?" Ben asked Bolden, "Have you found it? It's one of those small digital ones, about the size of a mobile phone."

"There's nothing on the body, but in a mess like this, it could be anywhere."

"It could have been taken from him," Meg offered. "Maybe he'd seen something he wasn't supposed to, at the train station. Or some-ONE for that matter. And if he took pictures, then this was his reward."

Ben looked at the victim's right foot facing in a direction it was never meant to, and saw what looked like pieces of metal embedded into the soul of its shoe. "What's that?" he asked.

"Looks like plastic," Bolden answered, bending to take a closer look. "There were similar fragments found on the bridge. Maybe that's what's left of your missing camera."

"He stamped on it?" Meg asked.

"Looks that way," Bolden answered.

"But why?" Ben asked. "Why take pictures and then destroy them. Unless, he was forced to."

"Forced by whom?" Meg asked. "Edwards?"

"By the accomplice," Ben answered. "Maybe Hetherington *did* jump. Not to commit suicide, but to escape. Maybe our accomplice came at him with a knife, or threatened him with the missing gun."

"What gun?" Brandt asked as he came to join them, walking along the edge of the track to where Ben and Meg were standing bouncing ideas off one-another.

"The missing Luger," said Meg. "But right now, that's not important. What matters is that we find out the identity of our unsub. We know he's on the team. He *has* to be. But until we find out who it is, we have to-"

"Never mind that right now," said Brandt. "*I'll* look into that. You two look like shit. And there's not much else you can do here. So I suggest you both go home and get some rest."

"Later, boss," Ben said, speaking for both of them, his mind on the same wavelength as Meg's. "First, we want to-"

"When I say 'suggest', I mean 'that's an order.' If tonight's anything like last night, I want your heads clear, and your minds sharp. I'll see you back at the station later."

Sixty Four

4:21 p.m.

Almost ten minutes early and too impatient to wait any longer, Morton had rang the number from the top of the fax, frustrated he was still forced to wait as he sat in his study, his fingers pattering on the desktop as he suffered the delay of inter-office connections before he was finally put through to Hans Gruber.

His voice that of an old man, he spoke almost perfect English. "Good day detective, how is the weather in England?"

"It's not good," Morton answered, "but the temperature's rising, and as you've seen from our report, so is our body count. We're hoping you can help us."

"I hope so too. And I'm sure you are far too busy to be wasting your time with idle chit-chat, so I will get straight to the point. The coin. You say it was found in the body of one of your victims?"

"Yes. In the stomach."

Hans Gruber spoke slow and steady, with thoughtful deliberation. "Interesting," he said curiously. "As you already know, the coin was dated 1958, but we must go back still further. Seven years to be exact, to 1951.

"1951?"

"The year of an unusual robbery in my country. It was at Landsmans bank in Copenhagen. At 10:15 a.m., the robber, Palle Hardrup, normally a placid man, shot and killed two people before calmly making off on a bicycle."

Already Morton's patience was running low. "Forgive me, but, our man tortures and dismembers his victims. He uses a knife. No guns, no robberies. Just plain and simple murder."

"In my country, detective, murder is *never* 'plain and simple'."

Morton held his tongue, thinking to himself;- 'Just get to the point and tell me what I need to know for god's sake', before respectfully saying, "My country too."

"As I have said already. A very unusual case. You see, the robber was followed home by a boy who witnessed the crime through the bank's window. He tailed him, as you say in your country, for four miles, all the way to his home. Then, the robber turned and aimed his gun at the boy but failed to pull the trigger. The boy then fled to flag down a police car and the robber was duly arrested."

Morton knew from experience that the most ardent of detectives in any major police force, could dredge through case upon case, and would almost always find a similarity or connection, however tenuous, between one crime and another: whether it be real, hypothetical, or unequivocally coincidental. "I fail to see the significance," he said, fidgeting in his seat with impatience and angry that this was going nowhere fast. "The year of the robbery matches the amount of cash withdrawn from our suspect's account, and the time itself is self explanatory, but how does it all tie in with Sean Edwards?"

"Like Edwards, Hardrup was also acting out of character, and he too had an accomplice. But it was only through patience *and diligence* (the terms stressed excessively for Morton's benefit), that we discovered his true identity."

"Diligence is a necessary evil in this job. Patience is a waste of time. So please, Mr. Gruber, just tell me what you found."

"The accomplice turned out to be a Mr. Bjorn Nielsen. An uncaring man, full of his own self-importance. He appeared to have complete psychological control over Hardrup and used it to his own personal gain. When the case went to court, the hearing lasted just three days, after which, Nielsen was found guilty of the crimes and sentenced to a life of imprisonment. Palle Hardrup, on the other hand, was found guilty but not responsible, and after a spell in a psychiatric clinic, was released, then moved to England some two years later, supposedly to start a new life."

"And you think Hardrup's our accomplice?" Morton asked doubtfully, the time-span too great to be believed.

"Don't you read your own files, detective? The copy you sent us. Your first murders. They were in London, in 1958. The victims were Palle Hardrup, his wife, and their four year old son. The first in a long list of killings with the mention of a yellow rose."

Morton stumbled in his response. He was now out of the loop and hadn't seen the extended list of victims that Hans Gruber, a detective from another country, was now privy to, all brought to light by the killer's m.o. and the discovery of the coin. "Are you telling me that the date and origin of the coin lead you to the identity of our accomplice and the year his crime spree began?" asked Morton.

"Yes…I am. It all makes perfect sense."

"You're saying it was Nielsen? That he escaped and tracked Hardrup down?"

"No, detective. Nielsen died three years later, while still serving time in prison. I think your unknown subject is the boy."

"The boy?"

"The boy on the bike. The boy who followed Hardrup." Now, Hans Gruber was the one losing his patience. "Give me your e-mail address and I'll send you the file."

Morton trapped the phone between his shoulder and ear and swivelled in his chair to face his computer as the file was downloaded and the printer began reeling out hard copies, Morton retrieving each sheet as it came through and scanning through the text as he listened to Hans Gruber's simplified account of what had happened.

"I think the boy was mentally scarred by the whole event and had some kind of backlash," said Gruber. "He became withdrawn. He started having nightmares and wetting his bed. Add to that, the fact that his father was sexually abusing the boy's sister, and we have a recipe for disaster. And that disaster occurred within a week of the robbery, with the deaths of his entire family."

Morton looked at the first of the black and white pictures as it came through the printer. A man in his mid forties lay dead. He was wearing a long black robe and lying on his back with an eight inch crucifix sticking out of his chest.

"The boy's father was a priest?" Morton asked, surprised.

"Yes. It was in all of the papers. His father and the boy were in a struggle and the priest was impaled when he fell on the cross he was wearing. The boy must have freaked out."

Morton looked at the next picture. An old-fashioned wheelchair tipped on its side, and lying next to it on the floor, a woman in a nightgown. "He killed his mother too?"

"By now, the boy had been pushed over the edge. In court, he said that it was all his mother's fault. He said that, because of her disability, she had turned a blind eye to what his father was doing to his sister."

"So he killed her," said Morton, remembering the murders of seven years ago. A woman with her eyes gouged out. The connections now obvious. The victims laid cruciform in reference to his father. The disabled mother borne out in the victims, almost all of them mothers, their limbs had been severed and one had had her eyes removed to signify her blindness to the truth. All of it leading to the murder of a little girl.

"What became of his sister?" Morton asked.

"There, we have some confusion."

The last sheet of paper came through the printer. Another black and white photograph. The body of a little girl lying just a few feet away from the body of her father. Her throat cut.

"What do you mean… confusion?"

"The boy and his sister were very close. And the boy's mind being disturbed as it was, we can't be sure of the sequence of events. The boy said he had attacked his father who was at the point of raping his sister. He said that, during the struggle, as they fought with a knife, the girl got in the way and died."

"You don't believe his story?"

"I don't know what to believe. But then, maybe I just don't like to think that a priest is capable of molesting his own child."

"What became of the boy?"

"He was taken into care. They say he adjusted well, though I have my doubts."

"What doubts? Why?"

"It was something in his eyes. He made me feel… uneasy. In his interviews he said he was interested in police work and that he wanted to go to university and study law. Said he might even become a policeman. But I had this underlying feeling that there was something more to it than that. Anyway, at the hospital they said he showed a lot of promise. He was released in 1958."

"The year of the coin," Morton uttered. "The year of our first Yellow Rose murders here in England. The boy killed his parents. And probably his sister too. But his mind being what it was, he blamed Hardrup for making him react the way he did, and came to seek his revenge."

"He should never have been let out," said Gruber. "It was a mistake if you ask me. There was something wrong with that boy from the start. Something strange. We should have kept an eye on him after his release, but, policing being what it was back then, we lost track of him. He fell right off the map. Until, that is, you contacted us."

"So what's the significance of the yellow rose?"

"Look again at the picture of his sister."

Morton looked carefully at the old black and white picture;- a little girl lying on the floor, a ribbon in her hair and a cute little face, angelic, like that of a sleeping child. Only, she wasn't sleeping, she was dead. The graphic picture betraying the horror of her passing, she wore little black shoes, rolled up socks, and a light coloured dress, her head tilted to one side, the thick dark line of the cut drawn around her throat. And in the whites and greys of the picture, her face whiter than white, she lay framed in a black pool of blood.

"I don't see it," Morton said. "Tell me what I'm looking for."

"The dress she was wearing," said Gruber, "it was *yellow*. And her name is the same in *your* language as it is in mine."

"Rose?" Morton asked. "Her name was Rose?"

"Those of us who have been around long enough will never forget it." Said Gruber, his sadness recounted in his voice. "'Death of a Rose' is what they said in all of the papers. Have you ever seen a murdered child, detective?"

"No. I can't say that I have."

"It does something to you. Twists you up inside. And I don't know why, but the fact that it was her birthday seemed to make it feel worse," Gruber said, picturing her smiling and blowing out candles, surrounded by friends, only an hour before they had left and the scene had completely changed. "She was still wearing her dress when she was assaulted," he continued, "supposedly by her father. The boy said he had put up with it for years, but on this particular day, he had built up the courage to confront him, trying to protect her. The boy was a loner, you see. His sister was the only one he ever talked to. Anyway, at the funeral, the whole town turned out, and all of them seemed to bring yellow roses."

"The boy's name?" asked Morton. "What was the boy's name?"

Sixty Five

Reluctantly, Ben and Meg had spent the last few hours at home as ordered by Superintendent Brandt, neither of them keen on leaving the crime scene, but both resigned to the fact they needed sleep. Now, with darkness looming and their batteries recharged, it was time to return to work. Time to pick up the task of closing the net on a sick and twisted serial killer and his accomplice.

Ben gave a toot of his horn as he pulled up to Meg's house and watched her as she strolled to his car. So natural, he thought. Even without make-up and still looking tired, her beauty was undeniable, her hair blowing softly in the breeze and her dark brown eyes, mesmerising, entrancing him as she swept back her hair, making him wonder why he had let her go that night. Things left unsaid. A moments hesitation, unsure of what to say to her as she had screamed her accusations at him and jumped into a taxi, shouting him down the instant he had opened his mouth, no chance to explain before she had left. And the end of their night marked with the end of their relationship;- his life in tatters ever since.

But it hadn't always been that way.

He thought back to a time when they were happy together. A weekend break by the coast at Summerdale hotel, the early light of morning warming his back as he sat up to watch Meg sleeping and brushed the strands of hair from her face to then awaken her with a kiss, his head filled with thoughts of a life together, their future stretching out before them. Thoughts of getting married and having children. Those thoughts stirred during a romantic walk along the seafront and the sight of fathers playing with their little boys, their first clumsy kick of a ball followed by the unfailing trust of a child perched high on a parents shoulders. Parents besotted with daughters, their dainty little girls showering them with kisses and proper-little-madam attitudes. Scenes like those he'd envisaged sharing with Meg, pride etched into their faces as they walked together swinging their little one between them. That vision making him think once again, that, if anyone could look after a child, or indeed, if anyone could love and protect them the way a child needs to be protected, then surely there was no-one more capable than a cop. Let alone;- two cops. But he had kept those thoughts to himself. Afraid to admit them. Dismissing them to the back of his mind for fear of scaring Meg off, their late night talks still weighing heavy on his mind. She was a career woman, she had once said, and that was that.

He stretched to open the car door and she climbed in beside him.

"You sleep okay?" he asked.

"Hardly a wink," she replied, her tiredness evident in her voice and her eyes avoiding his own.

"Me neither," he replied. "The job'll do that to you sometimes, but once we catch-"

"Save it, Ben. I'm not interested. And don't go bothering me with small-talk about needing sleep either. I've got other, more important things to think about."

Ben sat dumbstruck by her response. When it came to work, they had always shared the same convictions. The same passion. The same devotion to duty. And the same unflinching belief that catching the bad guys was more important than almost anything. Their streams of purpose merging together to become a surging river, their sweeping torrent shifting everything in their path and allowing nothing to come between them. Nothing, that is, until the night he had returned home to find her jumping into a taxi, her bags packed and his world turned upside down. A knot in his stomach like the one he felt now, intrinsically linked to her sudden change of attitude since this morning. Making him feel uneasy, worried that history was about to repeat itself. That she was going to leave him again. And wondering why her sudden change of heart, he asked, "Is it something I've done?"

"No."

"Something I haven't done, then?"

"Why does everything have to revolve around you?" she snapped. "Just let me stew for god's sake. It's nothing to do with you."

Her guilt flushing her cheeks, she turned to look out of the window, feeling Ben's eyes, concerned, burrowing into the back of her head. Sensing something was wrong. That she was hiding something.

His eyes traced her slumped shoulders, the exhaustion echoing throughout her body, and even with her back to him, he sensed her tired expression. Her eyes unwilling and her thoughts elsewhere.

"You're not a machine, Meg. You need your rest, just like the rest of us. What could be more important than making sure you're fit enough to deal with this?"

She crossed her arms and continued looking out of the window without answering, her eyes sore with tiredness.

"Whatever it was, couldn't it wait?" he asked. "Until later I mean. When everything's sorted."

"Some things shouldn't have to wait!" she snapped. "I can't go on like this, Ben. I don't even know what I'm doing here. "

"Where else would you be?" What else would you do for that matter? Nine till five in some office? A managerial job? That's not you, Meg. You couldn't live like that, even if you wanted to."

"You think you know me. You think you know what I want. But things have changed, Ben. *'I've'* changed. I should never have taken on this case."

Ben slipped the car into gear and pulled away from the curb, hoping that the act of heading to work would give her the jolt she needed and make her see sense. "But, you did take it on," he said. "You can't quit on me now. I need you."

His words rang out through her head. *'I need you'.* The exact words she'd wanted to hear, but the context completely wrong. 'I need you too', she thought.

Driving faster than he should, he shifted the car up a gear, his foot getting heavier on the pedal. "I can't believe you're talking like this. There's a kid and a young woman out there. They need our help, and you're acting like you don't care anymore."

"Don't turn on me, Ben. I don't need this right now."

"What's going on, Meg. What's wrong?"

"What's *wrong*?" she half laughed. "Do you really want to know."

"I asked didn't I."

"Then answer me this, Ben. If it were a choice between saving the girl or nailing the perp', which would you choose?"

"I'd save the girl. No question."

"You're lying, Ben, and it just rolls off your tongue like it's nothing. But that's how it is with you, *isn't* it. When it comes down to it, you just can't face the truth, can you."

"What does that mean?"

"I know you better than you know yourself, Ben. That's what I'm saying. You'd want to nail the perp. You'd stop him at all costs and forget about the vic'. You wouldn't care, and why should you. To you, this is just another case. You've never wanted a child, and I doubt you ever will."

Ben's mouth hung open for a second before he asked, "Where the hell did that come from?"

Meg looked out to the sun dropping over the horizon of passing fields without answering.

Was that *it*? he wondered. Was that what this was all about? Did she blame *him* for the vacuum in her life? How could he ever hope to understand the angst of being a woman without a child, her biological clock ticking away and her time running out.

"You may be right," he said. "Maybe I won't have children. Maybe I'm never meant to. But that doesn't mean I don't care. And I thought you of all people knew me better than that."

"You don't understand."

"You're damned right I don't understand. And how can I. You won't tell me anything. You won't let me in. When we were together, we agreed we could never bring up a child. Not in today's society. Or should I say;- *you* said we couldn't bring up a child. I just went along with it. We wouldn't want to, that's what you said. And now, *'I'* wouldn't want to."

From the moment the words escaped his mouth he wanted the ground to swallow him up. His foot eased off the accelerator and the car ground to a halt. "I'm sorry, Meg. I didn't mean that. It's just that… I'd be frightened. I'd worry too much. The horrors we see in this job, it's not the adults that hurt you inside, it's the children. Some of them murdered and abused. You've seen it for yourself. It wouldn't be fair to bring a child into this world. I don't know if I could do that."

Meg thought of Abby Edwards; how she had lost her mother and how, if she survived this, she would lose her father too.

"The world's getting worse," Ben continued.

"Okay, okay. You've made your point. Neither of us wanted kids when we were together, and *you* wouldn't want them now."

"When we were together, neither of us were ready. Now, it doesn't matter. You've got your life, and I've got mine."

Meg wanted to ask why that was and what had gone wrong between them. Why *couldn't* they be together? Weren't they grown up enough to learn from their mistakes and talk things through. Wasn't it time they were honest with one another and said what they really felt instead of all this pussy-footing around. She bit the bullet and turned to him, and as she opened her mouth to speak, she was interrupted by the ring of her phone.

Angrily, she snatched it up, "Meg Rainer."

There was a short silence before she continued, her voice dropping close to a whisper as she turned away from Ben to speak discretely into her phone;-

"The hospital, yes…"

Ben checked his mirror and pulled away again, his ears honed on her every word as he watched the road.

"I can't say much right now," she continued, a pause as she listened to the caller before she spoke again, "You are? Good. You don't know how much better that makes me feel."

She shifted the phone to her other ear, further away from Ben. "I wish I could have been there."

She checked to see if Ben was listening, her hand shielding her mouth and her mobile phone, "Yes, okay. I'll try. But I don't think I can make it tonight. You know how things are right now." She paused for a response before adding, "Okay, but don't wait up for me." The delay of a few more seconds before she finally answered, "Yes. I know. I love you too."

Ben tried to mask his irritation as he tried to make sense of what he'd heard. Tried to think of who it could be. Wondering if it was a man, but thinking it could just as easily have been a member of her family. The *only* member of her family. Only, Meg's mother lived alone, some eighty miles away.

Her call finished, he tried to sound nonchalant, "Your mum staying with you is she?"

Picking up on his tone, Meg knew he had other suspicions and remembered a saying she'd often heard from her gran'. *'Love is blind, and jealousy sees too much.'* She turned in her seat to face him. "There's something I need to tell you," she said.

Ben's heart sank, a lump jamming in his throat, "You're seeing someone."

"Give me a moment, Ben. It's not what you think."

"Then what is it? Just a passing fancy? A whimsical fling?"

Meg was also getting angry, "Give me a chance to explain, god damn it."

"There's nothing *TO* explain. You're playing the game in both courts, and I was too blind to see it."

"I'm not playing any game. I-"

"Don't give me that, Meg. Come on. Admit it. You're involved with someone else."

"Okay. You're right! I am involved with someone else. But until you're willing to listen to what I have to say, I guess we'll have to leave out all the juicy bits."

Meg crossed her arms and Ben slammed his foot on the accelerator, a jerk through the gears in his race to get to their destination and separate, a thick air of silence hanging heavy between them for the remainder of the journey. Meg too hurt to speak for fear of crying, and Ben too frightened to open up for fear of being hurt all over again.

* * *

It was after ten when Meg and Ben were able to show some semblance of normality dictated by the needs of circumstance. The incident room was gearing up for the next call and information was being processed through computers, telephonists, and officers bouncing ideas off one-another. Superintendent Brandt had stayed to monitor how things were being handled, and on their arrival, had filled Meg and Ben in on the latest developments.

"The unsub contacted Edwards about an hour ago," said Brandt, "spot on 21:15 as usual. But there was no known contact this morning."

"None whatsoever?" Meg asked, trying to understand why the break in pattern. If Brandt was right, it was the first morning since the murders began that they hadn't been in touch.

"Not even a text," Brandt replied.

"Maybe there was no need for them to get in touch," said Ben. "Maybe they were together, sharing the thrill of the kill."

"Or maybe they are just being more careful," Meg added, thinking it could be any number of reasons.

Brandt had a more worrying concern. "What if they've split up. Or worse still, what if they've gone their separate ways. Branching out on their own so to speak, to make it harder for us to nail them."

"I doubt it," Ben said sceptically.

"I doubt it too," said Meg. "They need each other. But we have to consider all the possibilities. Even killers have their disagreements. And even if they *have* been in touch this evening, there may still be a problem. My main worry now is;- Edwards might not call."

They all looked at the wall mounted clock to see the minute hand click to thirteen, and with it came the ring of the telephone next to Brandt. He answered it then held the phone out to Ben, "It's Morton. Ringing from London."

"London?" said Ben, simply looking down at the receiver in Brandt's held out hand.

"He says he needs to talk to you."

Ben looked at the clock and shook his head, angered by his timing and leaving it to Brandt to bark down the phone, "You pick your fucking times, Morton. What's this all about?" Seconds later, Brandt reddened with anger and held the phone out to Ben again. "He says it's important. And he won't speak to anyone but you."

Ben grabbed the phone, "Make it quick, Morton. You've got seconds to tell me what this is about."

"I want to be included, Ben. After Edwards' calls, I need to know what's going on."

"You've had your chances, Morton. And I'm not the person you should be talking to about this. Especially not now. Speak to Meg."

"I can't. You're the only one I trust. Listen. I have a lead. I can't tell you anything for sure right now until I check it out tomorrow morning, but in the meantime, watch your back, Ben. I think our accomplice is closer than we think."

Another ring, another phone, Morton was cut off as Ben hung up to answer the other call. A quick glance at Meg and she pressed the speaker button to hear Sean Edwards' disjointed singing; "I'm in piece-es, bits, and, piece-es… I'm in piece-es, bits, and, piece-es."

"What have you done with Naomi Watts?" Ben asked sharply.

"Who? Oh, you mean *'Chicago'* girl. Another clue missed, Ben. What would the papers say."

"Stuff the papers. You knew who I meant. Where is she?"

"Ah, Naomi, Naomi," he lamented. "What's in a name. Thing is, Ben; they are all the same to me. Once they're dead, they're dead."

"Where *is* she?!"

"She was hurt, Ben. She needed a doctor. I took her to the hospital. I even got her a fucking ambulance for Christ's sake. And not *once* did she say thank you."

"Listen here, Edwards."

"No, Ben. Just this one last time, *YOU* listen to *me*, because this is my last call, and my last warning. Tomorrow, you will find another body, and the following day, someone else is going to die. Then, it's Abby. So if you really want to save her life, then I suggest you don't go wasting your fucking time worrying about Naomi, and instead, you concentrate on opening your eyes to the fucking clues before it's too late."

"What clues?" Ben asked, hoping Edwards would mention something they might have missed.

"For god's sake, Ben. Every call. Every note. Every victim. Do I have to spell it out for you. You're the detective. Do some detecting."

"Why aren't you calling tomorrow? Are you afraid we're getting too close?"

"Don't rest on your laurels, Ben. Just because *'I'm'* not calling tomorrow, doesn't mean there won't be a call."

"The last victim?" Ben uttered. "Before you kill the girl."

"No, Ben. Let's just say;- the next call will be more... *enlightening*."

"Your accomplice?" Ben asked.

"My accomplice. My associate. My partner in crime. Whatever you want to call it. Tomorrow you will get to know who it is, and then, I'm sure, everything else will fall into place, and maybe, just maybe, you will have a chance to save poor little Abigail. But until then, remember, the clues are right in front of you. Another offering tomorrow and then we will be privileged to have an extra special guest; The last of the clues before the final act of sacrifice. The final act of remembrance."

"Remembrance of what?" Ben shouted. "What's the point to all of this?"

Edwards laughed. "I hope you like surprises, Ben. Because tomorrow's going to be a day *full* of them." He paused as if in thought before continuing, "I think I will enjoy tomorrow very much...

Tomorrow, will be a good day...

A day to remember."

Sixty Six

Most people referred to him as Chatty Old Joe or old Mr. Jacobs. A man who'd do almost anything for anyone, he had been running the charity shop for over thirty years now, and stood behind the same old counter, chatting with one of his regulars. "You treat this place like a library, you do," he said. "Always exchanging, never buying."

Bill removed his cap and scratched his head, "Howay, Joe. Stop yer messin'. Yer know you'll get it back next week. Three for one's the goin' rate."

"Aye, and I hope it doesn't take you so long to get goin' this time."

Bill feigned being hurt. "Is that any way to treat your best customer, come to visit yer on a windy day an' all."

Joe and Bill had gone through the same old banter for years. The swapping of books and leg-pullings. Every Tuesday, between nine and ten. Two casual friends exchanging witty remarks and opinions on the weather.

"That wind's going to turn to rain again," Joe said, taking the books from their plastic carrier. "I can feel it in my bones."

"There yer go again," said Bill, ten years his senior and more nimble on his feet. "Always lookin' on the downside. I don't know why your lass puts up with yer, I don't." He posed like a bodybuilder, "Not when she could have a strapping young bloke like meself."

Joe laughed, "Dementia's setting in fast I see."

"A new lease of life, Joe. That's what retirement does for yer. I keep tellin' yer, yer should pack this place up and join the gang. Become a recycled teenager, like meself. It'll perk yer up a bit."

Unsteadily, Joe climbed a nest of steps to place the dog-eared books on a shelf. "Not just yet," he said, stretching awkwardly. "I've got a few good years left in me yet."

"A few years, maybe," said Bill. "But I think yer kiddin' yerself if yer think they're good'ns."

"You carry on doing your silly poses all you like. We both know who'll be first pushing up daisies."

Bill leafed through the pages of his latest acquisition, *'Six Shooter At Snake Pass.'* "Kidding aside, Joe, you're not getting any younger. It's time yer put your feet up. Time yer spent some quality time with that darlin' wife of yours. Speakin' of which, where is she today?" He flexed his skinny arm and tugged at his jacket, puffing up the material where his bicep should be, "She hasn't seen my muscles."

Joe glanced at the intercom button on the counter, his link to his wife when she was pottering around upstairs or confined to her bed. "She's in the flat," he said, the smile melting from his eyes.

"Not well again?" Bill sighed.

Joe's heart hung heavy in his chest, "Just a bit under the weather, she says, but it's worse than that, Bill. I'm losing her. I doubt she'll see the year out."

"Nonsense, Joe. She's a fighter. She'll see *me* out, she will."

"If only that were true," Joe said sombrely. "I mean… well, you know what I mean. But, it's different this time. She won't rest up. You know what she's like. She can't keep still for one minute. And even up there, you can be sure she'll be putting the finances in order or messing on with something else that needs sorting."

"Yer ought to tell her, Joe. The two of yer, take some time off. Go on a fancy holiday some place. Sell up even. Be a bit selfish for a change, before it's too late."

Joe picked up an old pair of shoes and began polishing them for display, trying to hide his welling tears. "She won't listen. She says she wants to end her days here. Who am I to stop her."

"Most unselfish woman I ever met," Bill tutted. "Yer know she's just thinking of you don't yer."

It was a question that didn't need answering. That was what made it so hard. Joe knew more than anything that she was holding on to this place, thinking it would keep him busy when she was gone. Giving him something to live for and less time to grieve. But it wouldn't change a thing. "I don't know how I'll cope without her."

"I know what yer mean," Bill said, feeling sad for his friend. "She's a good woman, Joe. One of the best. Tell her I'm asking after her, will yer."

Joe nodded and Bill turned to leave, saying, "Think about what I said, Joe. Do something special for her. It'll mean a lot to yer both."

With the tinkle of the bell as the door opened, Bill shouted his goodbyes as he side-stepped an incoming customer, but Joe had turned his back and was oblivious to the stranger in his shop, his thoughts elsewhere and his attention focused on the shoe rack as he continued rearranging the shoes, making room for those he'd polished as the man in black turned the latch of the lock and the door sign to 'CLOSED'.

It was only when Joe had finished re-organising the rack that he turned to see the man sauntering around his shop and apologised for his ignorance. "Oh, I'm sorry, I didn't hear you come in. Can I help you?"

The man didn't answer, his gaze drifting over cheaply framed paintings and poor quality prints as Joe wondered if he were deaf or ignorant, or simply too stuck up to answer. An art collector or antique dealer perhaps, looking for his latest bargain. He watched the man wander in slow deliberate steps, his weight transferring from heel to toe and his arms behind his back. He wore a smart cap, black leather gloves, and an expensive black suit with well polished shoes, one of them with a tan brown lace.

"You looking for anything in particular?" Joe asked.

The man passed the outdated lamp shades on a row of shelves and ran his finger across the bric-a-brac as though checking for dust before flicking at the head of an ornamental cat.

"Could you be more careful, please," Joe asked, trying to sound diplomatic. "What we make here goes to charity."

The man ignored him and his actions obviously deliberate, he flippantly knocked over a vase of artificial flowers before Joe lost his patience. "What do you think you're doing?"

The man looked across to Joe, his eyes studying him, his tone mundane, "What kind of people buy these things?"

"*Nice* people," Joe said, taking offence at his arrogant disregard for other people's property. "People who put others before themselves."

"Are you saying I'm selfish?" the man asked calmly.

Joe asserted himself, "If there's nothing that interests you, I'd like you to leave."

"You don't know me, do you?" The man asked with indifference, pawing through a rail of second-hand clothing and pausing to look at a little girl's dress. He slipped the hanger from the rail and dropped it to the floor.

"What do you want!" Joe snapped.

"I *want!* ... you to be more polite."

The man turned to a shelf and removed the lid from a boxed jigsaw, grabbing a handful of pieces in his leathery fingers and sprinkling them to the floor.

"Is this a robbery? Is it money you want?" Joe's fists clenched by his sides as he wished he were young again. Wished he were as fit and strong as he was just twenty years ago. He'd beat this bastard to a pulp, then haul him off to the police station. But gone were the days of rash behaviour. His thoughts turned to the calming influence of his wife and he opened the till, scrunching the few five-pound notes into his fists. "That's all the cash we have. Take it and get out. We don't keep anything else of value here."

"I can see that," the man said, surveying the shop. "I could buy this place outright, for fuck's sake. Not that I'd ever want to."

Joe picked up the phone on his counter, "Leave, or I'm calling the police."

"You do that, and you're dead before they get here."

There was a menace in his voice that told Joe he was deadly serious. He stood a moment, staring into his eyes and weighing up the risk before returning the phone to its cradle, and watched, quietly, as the man traipsed around his shop, looking at trinkets and baubles, with curiosity rather than interest.

"I think it would be best if I introduced myself," he said casually. "They call me Sean. Sean Edwards. You may have heard of me. If so, you'll know it's not your money I'm after."

"So what then? What do you want?"

"Something you can't give me. Something I will have to take."

"I don't know anyone called Edwards," Joe said defiantly. Though, like most people in town, he was aware of a serial killer from the papers, and, vague though it had been, this man matched the description.

"I much prefer being called The Mutilator," the man smiled, picking up a small brass bell and giving it a shake. "It has a much better… ring to it, don't you think?"

Joe felt vulnerable and wished the wall-mounted swords were closer at hand as the man started walking towards him. Slowly. Deliberately. His voice now a whisper.

"I'm going to caaaaatch you."

Joe wanted to shout for help but knew it would arrive too late. He had to do something. And his hands shaking, he reached nervously across the counter. Reached slowly, so the man couldn't see what he was doing. The button off to his right, just out of reach. The intercom now his panic alarm. He needed to press it. Needed his wife to overhear what was happening and call the police. *Her* safety more important than his own. The man was getting closer. His whisper growing louder.

"I'm going to huuuuurt you."

Joe kept his eyes on the advancing man and took the slightest of sideways steps, closer to the button.

"I'm going to kiiiiill you."

Before Joe could press it, Edwards lunged towards him, fists flying. A thump to Joe's jaw knocking him hard against the shelves and sending him sprawling to the floor, dazed, his mouth bleeding, a pounding headache as he lay where he fell behind the counter, a lump on the back of his head. The pain hurting so much more than he remembered of his fights as a young man, few though they had been.

"Get up!"

"Get up! I said."

"Look at you, so weak and feeble. The sight of you makes me sick."

Edwards looked to the cluttered shop window through hanging hula hoops and an overdressed mannequin, the street getting busier as a throng of people bustled their way past the shop window, no-one noticing the assault. No-one attempting to stop the attack or what was to come.

Joe groaned as Edwards slipped his arms under him, dragged him to his feet, and gave him a hefty push in the back, forcing him through the beaded curtain that lead from the shop to the hallway and stairs. Staggering off balance, his head spinning and his legs unsteady, his arms stuck out in front of him to break his fall; an almighty crack as he felt the snap of his arthritic wrist and slumped to the floor again, praying, in his agony, that his wife had heard the commotion and called the police. But in his daze, Joe heard her frail voice shout from the kitchenette of their first floor flat, "What's going on, Joe? What are you doing?"

"One wrong word and she dies."

Frightened as he was, Joe tried to warn her, his hand pressed to the swelling lump on his head, hurting like a hangover as he weakly shouted up the stairs, "Isn't my ten o'clock brew ready, love?" the tremor in his voice betraying the excruciating pain he felt in his wrist.

"Since when do you have a cuppa at ten?" he heard her shout as they started up the stairs. "Never mind. I'll put the kettle on."

Close to the top, Joe heard the click of a record falling onto the spinning turntable and the scratching hiss of the needle as it lowered onto the spinning disc, the track of the needle following the groove that lead to the voice of 'old blue eyes', drowning out the sound of their approach. Joe stumbling up the stairs as Edwards followed close behind him, the stairway narrowed by the rail of the stair-lift and the chair sitting at the top.

Joe's legs weak and heavy, he tried to resist the force of his attacker hurrying him along. "You don't want to do this," Joe said. "My son's in the next room and he won't take kindly to you threatening us."

"Shut the fuck up, old man. You haven't got a son."

"Yes I have. He's a big lad, and I'm telling you, he'll bloody well knock your block off."

Edwards smacked the back of Joe's head, sending him sharply to the floor. "Don't bullshit me! You have a daughter, not a son. And if you don't do as I say, she will die too. Do you want me to tell you how?"

"If I were a young man I'd –"

"You'd what?!"

Joe stood up and using the banister for leverage, hurled himself backwards in an attempt to throw Edwards to the bottom of the stairs, scarcely knocking him off balance. Too weak and frail, no match for the younger man, who used his strength to barge him forwards and force him hard to the landing floor.

Sixty Seven

Edwards walked around them in a figure of eight as they sat facing one another, Joe on a wooden dining chair, his arms bound behind his back with a belt, and his mouth gagged with a plain blue tie. Yngrid looked into his eyes, her tears running down her face. She too was gagged, another of Joe's ties serving an ulterior purpose. Two more around her wrists, fastening them to the wheels of her chair, and her legs already lifeless, she sat helpless as a quadriplegic, both of them screaming into their gags as Edwards walked between them, muttering to himself. Incoherent babble. A knife tapping against his leg as he walked faster and faster, his words becoming clearer.

"Fingers and toes is how the rhyme goes."

His speech quickened with his pace as he walked between them. "Hands and feet, now we're getting to the meat."

Still the figure eight, his babble getting faster, repetitive, like a stuck record, "Elbows, knees, arms and legs. Elbows, knees, arms and legs. "

His knuckles turning white, he drew the knife to his face and pressed the blade against his cheek as he paced around them, his eyes those of a madman babbling away to himself, and then he stopped. "***OUT!*** with their eyes," he blurted, whipping around and dropping to his knees beside Yngrid, turning her wheelchair to face him and whispering slowly. Clearly. And with a smile, "Tits and cock, nicely sends them into shock."

He held the knife close to her face as Joe looked on in panic, struggling desperately against his bindings, his muffled screams of hatred drowned out by the sound of the record player and the bustle of the street below, the clashing of doors on delivery vans muted by the sound of buses and shoppers, and a busker playing an accordion. Ordinary people living ordinary lives as they went about their daily business, blissfully unaware of what was unfolding in the flat above.

The point of the knife hovered under Yngrid's left eye before he traced it down the crease of her mouth and over her chin, then paused at her dewlap, the loose fold of skin lying over the sharp edge of the blade before it travelled to the buttons of her blouse, sliding between them and cutting them away. Her blouse falling open.

The legs of Joe's chair thumped hard against the floor as he struggled to break free, and his wife turned her head to him, her eyes filled with terror, pleading for help as Edwards grabbed at the flailing material of her blouse and cut it away to reveal the bra of her sagging breasts resting on the paunch of her lily-white belly, a colostomy bag taped to her side.

Edwards looked at her with disdain, then turned to Joe, "Look at the state of her. What good is she to you? What good are *either* of you to *anyone* for that matter?"

Joe looked into his wife's eyes with the glimmer of a smile. A smile of reassurance. A smile that said *somehow, they'd get through this.* A smile accepted with a look of resignation, knowing he was wrong. Knowing he loved her as deeply as she loved him.

"Can you still get it up old man?"

Edwards moved behind her and stood with the knife to her throat before trailing it along her shoulders and cutting through the straps of her bra, her support falling away to reveal her breasts hanging like large white socks with nipples pointing south.

"Jesus, would you look at that. She's falling apart for fuck sake. With tits that keep her belly warm and legs she can't use, it's no wonder you can't get it up, old man. She doesn't even have her own teeth for fuck sake." He stared at her with a sneer of repulsion, as if bewildered that someone could find her attractive. "Or is that it, Joe? Is that what does it for you? Does she give you head, old man?" He ran the point of the blade over her nipples, "Does she suck you dry?"

Joe fought back his tears and stared defiantly into his cold blue eyes.

"No?... Well then, maybe it's time she did."

He grabbed at the waist of Joe's trousers and tugged them down to his ankles along with his underwear, leaving him on full display as he turned and walked to the record player to turn up the volume. When he turned back pulling something from his pocket, Joe's eyes were wide with fear.

"If it's only used for pissing out of, it's not much good to you, *is it.*"

He nipped the end of Joe's penis in the grip of the pliers, slowly twisting and stretching it, the foreskin tearing as Joe and his wife screamed hysterically into their gags, Joe's eyes searching for mercy in those of his torturer.

"You want me to stop? *Already?* But I've scarcely begun. And if you think *that* fucking hurts, you're going to *hate* this."

Strapped tightly into his chair, Joe was unable to defend himself. Unable to avoid the grip of the pliers and the stretching of his foreskin, his eyes squinting closed at the sight of the knife in the man's other hand, anticipating what was about to happen. The blade slicing through the base of his outstretched penis and shuddering spasms of pain surging throughout his body as he squirmed in the growing pool of blood. His torturer standing cruciform beside him; his back arched proud, his arms out wide. The knife in one hand and his prize in the other, still in the grip of the pliers as he shouted triumphantly to the heavens, "Am I not all powerful." Then he turned to Yngrid and laughed out hysterically, "Talk about being dis*membered.* You didn't think I'd forgotten about you, did you?"

He removed her gag and waved the limp lump of flesh in front of her face. "Which is it to be, old girl? Spit? Or swallow?"

She recoiled in horror, shaking her head this way and that as the penis was thrust into her face.

"You've heard of 'Help The Aged' haven't you? Well, that's what I'm trying to do here. Like a therapist giving you advice on how to explore your sex life. Only, I'm making it easier for you. Giving you a helping hand you might say. No awkward positions or lengthy foreplay. It's just there, right in front of you. But if you don't want it, then..." He opened the pliers, watching her eyes follow the lump of flesh to the floor before he stamped on it, squishing it under his foot as though it were an insect. Then he scraped the soul of his shoe along the spokes of her wheelchair and stood behind her, drawing the knife close to her throat. Holding it there for a while as she cried, more for Joe than for herself.

"Well, if he couldn't get it up before, he certainly can't now, that's for sure. Even Viagra can't change that. So... I figure you owe me, seeing as how you no-longer need to pretend you're asleep or that you've got a headache."

He ran the knife around her breasts and leaned to whisper in her ear, "Do you want to live, Yngrid?"

Crying, she answered with a nod.

"Do you want his pain to stop?"

Again, she nodded.

"Good. Because, in my generosity, I'm going to give you the chance of both."

He cut the ties from her wrists and pushed her chair closer to Joe's, then thrust a clear plastic bag into her hands. "All you have to do… is finish him."

She looked down at the bag and sobbed, "I can't?"

"Put the bag over his head, and end it. If you don't, I'll hurt him some more."

Her hands trembled as she held the bag close to Joe's head, knowing she could end his suffering. And her tears streaming down her face, she pulled it away, "I can't."

She felt the blade of the knife slip under her breast as the man looked over to Joe, "Tell her to do it old man, or I gut her, right here in front of you."

Joe gave Yngrid a weak nod and she leaned towards him, crying and shaking so much he could hear the rustle of the bag, even before it was slipped over his head. But it was only there for a matter of seconds before she pulled it away again, "I can't. I can't."

"Do it, or your daughter dies too."

Joe grunted for Yngrid's attention and gave another nod.

She sobbed to him; "I'm sorry, Joe, I can't."

"Never mind *him*!" Edwards barked. "*I'm* telling you, you can. If you don't. I'll be waiting here when your daughter returns. Is that what you want?"

Joe lowered his head so she could reach more easily, submitting his life to her for the sake of their daughter.

"NOW!... Put, it, over, his, fucking, head, and, *smother him!*"

A tender stroke of Joe's cheek, she slipped it over his head again, crying, the bag misting up as Joe struggled to resist the urge to fight for breath. His lungs starving. His heart pounding. But as breaking point came, he instinctively sucked for air, desperately inhaling through his gag and nostrils, the bag pulling tight to his face with each gasp for breath. The blur of his wife's face in front of him, crying, distraught as she was forced to hold the bag closed around his neck, trying once again to pull it free but unable to. And then Edwards released her arms and she yanked it from his head. A moment's sobbing before she felt a hand cover her mouth and the knife slip under the fold of her breast, a quick flash of pain as it sliced through her flesh. Her shriek of agony followed by a high pitched scream as he sliced through the other and the sagging folds of flesh flopped down her belly to land on her lap, her head swooning as Joe looked on in tears, his own pain forgotten. His face flushed red with anger and the hairs stood on the back of his neck like the heckles of a rabid dog. His whole body shaking as his arms yanked at his ties, struggling to break free, his chair banging hard against the floor in his effort to escape. His efforts pumping the blood through his body and out through his groin. Then, almost in unison, as his wife's spasms faded out to a stop and she collapsed, Joe's body jerked and stiffened. His body tight, his heart in a vice-like grip, before he too collapsed into his seat. Dead.

Edwards grabbed Yngrid by the hair and shook her head for a response, her eyes closed as he spoke to her, "Look at what you've made me do," he said. "He's dead, and it's *your* fault. You could have saved him from seeing that."

Her eyes didn't flicker, even as he raised her head with a tug of her hair and spat in her face, angry she'd escaped into unconsciousness. Didn't answer. Didn't stir. Didn't feel him wipe the blood of the blade across her back. And didn't wake to his final act of ridicule. Her colostomy bag ripped from her side and placed on top of her bowed head, then punctured with the knife, its contents flowing down her face as he walked to the door and paused to look at his watch.

10:15 a.m. to the second.

He looked at his distorted reflection in the blade of the knife and tilted it to look back at the bodies;- one a corpse, the other about to join him. The last song on the record fading out with a scratching hiss as the needle travelled down the spiral to the centre of the record before the arm lifted and clicked back onto its perch. And as the momentum of the turntable wound to a stop, he turned for one last look at the old couple and smiled;

"Just one more. And then… it's the girl."

Sixty Eight

Ben's turn for refreshments, he had only been gone two minutes when Meg saw little miss twinkle eyes enter the incident room, remembering her from a few days ago when she had been flirting with Ben in the corridor.

She caught Meg's eye and headed over.

"Is Ben. Sorry, I mean, is D.S. Miller about?"

"He's busy," Meg replied. "Why?"

"I have a note for him. From Doctor Schmidt. He said it was important."

Meg held out her hand for the folded piece of paper and with the briefest of face-offs, twinkle eyes reluctantly let go of it.

"I'll see that he gets it," Meg said dismissively, and watched twinkle eyes turn to leave with her chin held high and a '*look at me, I'm gorgeous*' swagger. Meg's eyes burrowing into the back of her skull, mumbling to herself "Tart," as she slid the note between her fingers, asking herself why Schmidt had entrusted it to a subordinate rather than to a member of the team. And why wasn't he here to speak to Ben himself? And then it struck her that, for the first time in days, she hadn't seen hide nor hair of him. Not since she'd accused him of incompetence and using Edwards for monetary gain. And come to think of it, even before his absence, it seemed that Schmidt had been avoiding her, and it was only now that she realised they'd hardly spoken a word since their initial contact, though on occasion she had caught him watching her. Studying her like she were one of his schizophrenic patients. Sometimes taking notes and speaking into his Dictaphone as he glanced over, a strange look in his eye, like he didn't trust her. Or like he'd discovered something she wanted kept secret.

Shit. Was that it?

She wondered if he'd picked up on something she may have said or done and worried that Ben was about to discover her secret. Sooner or later, he would come to know the truth. It was inevitable. It was only a matter of time before he would find out the reason behind her mysterious phone calls and who was staying in her home. But not yet, she thought. The timing had to be right, and this wasn't it.

She unfolded the note.

I'm at home. Please come alone as quickly as possible. There's something I think you should know. Everything will make sense when you get here.

Doctor Jahn H Schmidt.

She scrunched up the note and threw it in the bin.

Sixty Nine

Meg stood outside the porch of the large detached house, a ring of the bell followed by a knock on the door, her eyes searching for movement through the stippled glass of the inner door, wondering if he had seen her approaching. Wondering if he was ignoring her.

She knew he was home. His car was on the drive and though it was daylight, a ceiling light shone from behind the inner door. But something was wrong, she could feel it.

She turned the handle and entered the porch, trying to define shapes through the stippled glass. Thinking she saw movement. A shifting blur against a light coloured wall. A trick of the light, she told herself, and tapped her knuckles against the pane of glass. Lighter this time. Wanting attention but wary of its source. And with no response, she slowly opened the door, her eyes looking downward for the tell tale sign of feet hidden on the other side.

She called out, "Doctor Schmidt?" The hallway empty and her voice hollow.

"Doctor Schmidt, it's Detective Rainer. I think we should talk."

The hallway dimly lit, it was cooler than outside. On par with the chill of a refrigerator as she edged forwards, wary of what she might find, her skin crawling cold with the pungent smell of death.

She spun to the sound of the door closing behind her and watched it as it slowly creaked shut, the light of day shining through the glass to reveal no-one on the other side. And her nerves on tenterhooks, she turned back toward the closed door at the end of the T-shaped hall, checking left and right as she reached the juncture point and called out again, "Doctor Schmidt, are you home?"

From where she stood she could see that left led to the kitchen, well lit and silent bar the hum of a fridge, and right led past a staircase and on to the adjoining garage, a door open at the far end, the bumper of another car partially visible, though not enough of it to identify its make.

She stayed where she was for a moment, directly in front of the one closed door, her gut telling her that what she was looking for was on the other side. And her nerves jangling, she checked left and right again before slowly pushing it open, her eyes drawn to the trail of blood leading from the door to the centre of the lounge, the trail growing in width and density and ending in a thick red mass with what looked like arms and legs lying in the centre of it in the shape of a cross. And as she stared at it, having taken a few tentative steps into the room, she suddenly realised that the trail had ended behind her and turned to look back at the door, shocked to find herself facing Naomi's body pinned to the other side, the head of a yellow rose sticking out from each of her empty sockets and a heavy duty nail hammered through her throat, the naked trunk of her body hanging below, her shoulders and hips hacked back to the joints, and torn flesh hanging ragged from where a blade had cut through the muscles, tendons and cartilage that had once connected her limbs to her body.

She turned away and leaned against a bookcase to steady herself, fighting off the nausea as she reached for her phone and speed-dialled Ben.

Engaged.

She pressed the letter X to access her file of numbers and contacts developed throughout the case, quickly scrolling down to;-

X Schmidt Home;- 0191 4769479
Mobile;- 07493760947

X Sean Edwards Mobile;- 07485693255

Seeing the numbers together, her thumb hovered a moment. *Which one damn it?* The options racing through her mind along with the scenarios. Schmidt could be lying in trouble somewhere, if he wasn't already dead, but Edwards could be lurking nearby: waiting for his moment to pounce. If either of them had their phones switched on, then the ring-tone would give away their position.

It was at times like this when she wished she were carrying a gun. What good was armed response if you were already dead or being fired at.

Her phone fell from her shaking hand and bounced across the floor, stopping against Naomi's severed limbs. A moment's pause before she snatched it up again, and her decision made, the sound of ringing came through in stereo via the tones through her phone and a higher pitched ringing from behind. And in that instant;- it all made sense. A cold shiver running through her spine as she whipped her head around to see his face and met the dark hole of the barrel against her brow.

Seventy

Ben was getting sick of this. Sick of her sneaking around and the constant secrecy, sometimes unsure of where she was or what she was doing. She was supposed to be running the case, and again she was nowhere to be found.

Again, he worried for her safety.

He sat at his desk in the incident room, the team going about their tasks as W.P.C. Angela Ainsworth sat facing him and he asked her again, his voice a little louder, "Where is she, constable? This is important. We think Meg could be in trouble. She's not at home, and she's not answering her phone." His anger was growing with his impatience as he continued, "I know you two had your differences, but I need to know what was said between you, however trivial it may seem."

Angela was confused and upset, blinking away her tears as she answered, "I don't know, sir. I can't remember."

"You can't remember? Or you choose to forget? Which is it?"

"I've forgotten, sir ….. I mean;- I don't remember." She rubbed at her temple as if to conjure up her memories. "I don't know what's the matter with me."

Like a Nazi-styled interrogator, Ben pressed on. "Tell me about the slip of paper you were seen handing to Meg. What was it? What was on it?"

"I don't know, sir. Everything's hazy. I vaguely remember manning the reception desk and the next thing I know, I'm on traffic duty. Everything else is a blur."

"Don't waste my fucking time here, constable. You were the last to be seen talking to her. Practically everyone in here saw you. So why don't you just cut the crap and tell me what the hell's going on?"

"I don't know," she cried. "I don't understand any of this."

"Are you prone to forgetting things, constable?"

She fought back her tears, a hanky held to her eyes, "No, sir."

"Have you had a bang on the head then?"

"No, sir. I don't think so."

Ben's fist came down heavily on the desk. "Then don't fuck with me, constable! I'm warning you, if any harm comes to Meg, you'll regret you ever fucking crossed me. Now, get the hell out of my sight and report to the superintendent. And don't go *anywhere* without informing *me* first."

Over an hour had passed since his interview with Angela Ainsworth, and although she had sworn she were telling the truth, the evidence suggested otherwise. She was hiding something, she had to be. Something significant.

To make matters worse, the bodies of an elderly couple had been found murdered in their flat, and with Naomi Watts still missing presumed dead, the clues had begun to reveal themselves. This wasn't about *all* of the victims, it was about the women. Only the women had had a yellow rose left on their bodies, and still he was at a loss to what it meant.

'*Remember Me',* he thought.

He drew a line through the names of the male victims and pondered the list again, starting with the most recent.

Yngrid / ~~Joseph~~ Letterman.		62/67	married	charity workers
Naomi	Watts	22	single	shop assistant
~~Troy~~	~~Evans~~	~~26~~	~~single~~	~~unemployed/vagrant~~
Olivia	Crompton	31	married	unemployed
Rachel	Earnshaw	24	single	care-worker/escort
Cordelia	Armstrong	72	widow	retired
Amy	Edwards	27	married	accountant

"What's next, Edwards? What the fuck are you up to?"

Looking at the names, he thought of the taunting jibes dished out by Edwards in his calls;-

'*What we see depends mainly on what we look for'.*

'*Closed your eyes to the killer surprise'*.

Then it hit him like a brick in the face.

'For god's sake, Ben. Do I have to spell it out for you.'

He stood there, frozen, reading back through the names of the victims in the order they were killed and cursing himself for his blindness to the obvious, the clues right in front of him, unravelling with each woman's murder. And as he looked through their names, it all became frighteningly clear to him. His heart jumping from a steady pulse to a pounding race, beating against his chest with the realisation of who was next. The first initial of each woman's name spelling out ACRONYM.

And 'M' was for Meg.

"Quickly!" he shouted. "The notes and a list of all the victims. Project them onto the board."

"What is it?" asked a sergeant.

Ben scattered the copies on his desk, too impatient to wait for the transition of the information to the screen as he relayed what he had discovered and searched for the vital clue. "We're looking for an acronym," he shouted out. "Somewhere amongst Sean Edwards' notes or in his letters. Check the transcripts of his calls. And go through the names of the victims again. See if I've missed anything."

A white square of light shone onto the board at the front of the incident room, the screen split into two. On one side were copies of Sean Edwards notes, and on the other, a list of all the victims, past and present, as Ben had instructed.

"The women are the key," Ben said, looking through his lists then up at the board. "In all cases, the number of men differs. They were victims of circumstance. In the wrong place at the wrong time. But whether we look at Edwards, Inkleman or Swinton, in each there are seven women. I want you to focus your attention on those most of all."

He ran his finger down the list of Inkleman's victims, drawing a line through the names of the one male victim and the little girl, his pen almost tearing through the paper as he did so. He scribbled notes in the margins and toyed with the remaining names. Rearranging the letters. Swapping them and puzzling over them before rewriting them horizontally with only the briefest of details. A list of seven women on a plain piece of paper, unclouded by the deluge of accompanying facts and information. Victims from the past with undiscovered secrets. Some married and some not.

ALL of them mothers.

Margaret	Inkleman	34	married
Jennifer	Sewell	31	single
Hayley	Irvine	27	single
Angelina	Trovero	28	single
Jane	Hargreaves	30	single
Sarah	Ingles	29	married
Jody	Maxwell	24	single

Almost at once he spotted the acronym in their surnames and darted up to the projection at the front of the room, his actions grabbing the attention of all those present. "There's more to this than meets the eye," he said loudly. "This isn't just about Edwards and Inkleman. It's about the unsub'. He was involved in both cases and maybe in the Swinton murders too. What's more;- the cheeky bastard left us a clue, telling us as much."

Ben turned to the white board, and with a thick black marker, drew a line through the men's names and wrote the first initial of each woman's surname. 'I.S.I.T.H.I.M.'

He read it out loud;- "IS IT HIM."

"What does it mean?" one officer asked.

"IS IT Edwards?" asked another.

"It's not referring to Edwards," Ben answered. "Of that much I'm sure. This clue was laid out long before Edwards ever got involved."

"Does it mean Inkleman, then?" asked a sergeant.

"Back then, it may have done," Ben answered. "But there's no way of knowing for sure. My guess is, the unsub was hinting at his own presence, even then."

"Didn't Edwards say something similar in one of his earlier calls?" asked another detective. "*'Is it him'* or *'is it me'*. It didn't seem to make much sense at the time."

"Yeah, like a lot of what he says," said the sergeant.

Ben asked him to explain what he meant by that.

"Well, this quoting lark, and that other thing he keeps saying. *'Closed their eyes to the killer surprise'* and the like."

Ben looked at the list again, thinking out loud. "Closed their eyes... Closed their eyes. He's telling us we are missing something."

"Yeah, but what?" asked a detective.

Ben turned and pointed indiscriminately to a bunch of officers on a nearby desk. "Give me another quote. Anything. What else did he say?"

After a stuttering pause, a constable said "*I shut my eyes in order to see.*" Then one voice after another, the quotes coming thick and fast from various parts of the room.

'*Open your eyes.*'

'*What we see depends mainly on what we look for.*'

Some of the officers made notes whilst others squinted at the board as Ben searched for answers, the black writing on the screen blurring as he stared at the list. He rubbed his eyes and looked at it again in the hope that something would reveal itself, but still the answer remained hidden.

'*You have 2 eyes. Use them,*' came another voice.

Ben wrote it down in thick black marker. **TWO EYES,** and looked through the names again, his attention shifting to the details of the victims, everything hinting towards seeing something. Hinting… to the eyes.

"Bloody hell, that's IT! *You have two eyes. Use them.* Not *eyes,* but 'I's."

He pointed to the nearest officer on a computer, "Only two of the victims were married. Margaret Inkleman, and Sarah Ingles. Quickly, tell me their maiden names.

With a drag of the mouse and a click of the button, the officer came up with their names. "Davenport and Campbell, sir."

Ben changed the letters accordingly in the acronym and a mishmash of letters stared back at him.

DS IT HCM

His eyes lingered over the new puzzle for a mere second before his face flushed with embarrassment and the name of the unknown subject jumped right out at him.

Seventy One

"Enter!"

With memories harking back to his childhood, Morton entered the headmaster's office and stood inside the door, waiting for him to get off the phone. An old man with silver hair and steel-rimmed spectacles, his furrowed brow deepened as he continued his conversation and gestured for Morton to take a seat.

Morton crossed the expansive floor and pulled up a chair, impatiently twiddling his thumbs like an adolescent schoolboy awaiting his admonishment. A landscape catching his eye as he waited, ever the policeman, checking out his surroundings. An old-fashioned wood-panelled room with an antique cabinet full of books off to his right and brass-framed landscapes adorning the walls along with pictures of fox hunts and scholarly portraits. A posh school, he thought, for posh boys. And with an equally posh accent the headmaster wound his conversation to its conclusion and peered over his spectacles, stretching his hand out across the large rosewood desk to shake Morton's.

"How can I help you, detective?"

"This may seem a lot to ask, but I'm trying to trace a student who studied here some forty-odd years ago."

The headmaster's hands resting on the desk, his fingers knitted together, he gave Morton a bemused smile, "I was a student here myself back then. You don't mean me perchance, do you?"

Morton nodded down to the nameplate on the desk. **Professor Levensworth** in bold black letters. "If that's you, then you're not the one I'm looking for."

"Glad to hear it. Now, back to the matter of finding your reprobate. As you can well imagine, the staff from back then are long gone, but if you can tell me his name, then maybe we can find him in the school archives. Or failing that, there's always the possibility I may have known him myself."

"In Denmark he was known as Jurgen Heinrik," said Morton, "but here in England, he went by another name. You yourself may have known him better as Johan Besta."

The professor's smile slipped from his face and an uneasiness crept into his voice. "I'd hoped never to hear that name mentioned again," he said, his hand to his chest as if to steady his faltering heart.

"You know him then?"

"I knew *of* him, detective. This is a big school. There was no way anyone could have known everyone. But everyone knew Besta. Some called him the beast. I was in my first year of study here when he left. Under a dark cloud I might add."

"What can you tell me about him?"

The professor stood from his seat and crossed to the cabinet, digging out an old leather-bound book and flicking through its pages. "There's only so much the yearbook can tell us," he said, his finger tracing down a page. "The fact that he was majoring in English and psychology, for instance, or that he had a good attendance record. But it doesn't tell us about his *other* studies I'm afraid. There's not much *anyone* could tell us about those."

"What studies?"

"Like most boys, I'd heard rumours. Tales of boys who'd experienced the ultimate high. You know how it is. Some kids tried coke. Some: Marijuana. Some tried other things."

"Drugs?"

"Don't look so surprised, detective. They were around in my day too, just as they are now. But I heard Besta was offering them a fix like no other. The sailboat in the sky on a trip to cloud nine was what they were calling it. Cheap too, they said. But they were wrong."

Teaching was in Levenworth's blood and it showed in his explanation.

"The brain is a wonderful thing, detective. A biological computer in charge of our bodily functions, it is the core of our being, but occasionally, it malfunctions, and when it does, strange things can happen. Many of our students studying psychology would use their knowledge to rectify those malfunctions, working in the fields of mental illness, or in some cases these days, with the likes of yourself in the profiling of criminals. But Besta went beyond that. He saw the mind as a plaything. To him, those boys were just lab rats. Things happened. Things that should never be repeated. Everyone knew he was responsible, but no-one could prove it."

Morton leaned forward in his seat, intrigued to hear more. "Please, professor. Explain."

"I'm not sure I can. Even his 'lab-rats' were at a loss to explain what had happened to them. Some of them had fallen ill, suffering from convulsions or irregular breathing patterns and the like. It was only after Besta was expelled that their symptoms improved."

"You think Besta poisoned them?"

"No, detective, I do not. Don't get me wrong here. Besta was a brilliant student, with top grades throughout. I'm pretty sure the teachers were unaware of his meanderings, or if they *were* aware, then they turned a blind eye to it. But either way, there was an ulterior motive behind Besta's so-called 'extra curricular' activities. I'm sure of it. I heard things. Through the grapevine so-to-speak. Things that… unsettled me."

"What things?"

"I think he was experimenting. Some of his fellow students began acting out of character. Quiet students became rambunctious. Introverts became extroverts. And some otherwise placid students began to show violent tendencies. It was all getting out of hand."

"Anyone get hurt?"

"Worse. Two students died. Problem was, nothing could be proven of Besta's involvement. The board found an excuse to let him go and that was the last I ever heard of him."

"But the illnesses. The boy's deaths. How were they caused?"

"It's a dangerous world out there, detective. You don't need me to tell you. But in here," his finger tapped against his head "it is a far more dangerous place. *This* was Besta's playground. A world in which he could bend, twist and manipulate others to do his bidding. You have to remember;- Besta was a loner. He was different from the rest of us. He had other ideas on how to use his new found knowledge and he took it to the extreme. Perhaps he had another agenda all together."

"What kind of agenda?"

"Who knows. Maybe he was a misunderstood genius working for the good of mankind. But somehow, I doubt it. I think professor Hindmarsh doubted it too."

"Professor Hindmarsh?"

"He died. Or rather;- he was killed, just days after he had had Besta expelled. Damned suspicious if you ask me. You see, Henry Fotheringay: another 'lab rat', had never hurt a fly. And then, one day, he just cracked. Gouged out the professor's eyes and slashed his throat, then was found dead himself just a few days later."

"And you think Besta had something to do with it?"

"That was the rumour. They say he had found a way to unlock the dark side of people's personalities. A way to switch off their inhibiting voice of reason if you will. I prefer to think of it as some kind of mistake or accident caused by his unorthodox tampering with the mind, because, if his aim *was* to turn people into monsters," the professor stood looking out of the large sash window, his hands clasped behind his back "then I'm afraid there could be a great many untold crimes going on out there, with all manner of people being blamed for something they themselves can not control."

"Is there anything specific you can tell me about Besta? Any contacts or known associates and so forth?"

"Chinese whispers. Things you hear later. I had heard he'd changed his name, though I can't be sure that's true. Tell me detective;- has he killed someone else?"

"Yes. I think he has. Or played a part in some way."

"It doesn't surprise me. I don't mind telling you, a man like that could do all kinds of untold damage."

"Do you know where he went after he was expelled?"

"To another college I expect, though I couldn't tell you for sure. I had hoped he had returned home, wherever home was. But obviously, that's not the case."

Morton looked up at the engraved plaque on the wall behind the professor. He'd seen one like it before somewhere. '*The body of the mind lies trapped within its cranial shell, yet the mind roams free, inhibited, only by the limitations of thought.*'

"I have to ask you, sir;- were you ever a lab rat yourself? Or did you ever have any dealings of any kind with Besta?"

"No, detective, I did not. Fortunately we mixed in different circles, and I'd go as far as to say that I'd never even spoken to the man. Not that I'd ever wish to mind you. But there was an instance where I heard him speak once. Most uncivilized. And in exceedingly bad taste."

Morton listened without interrupting.

"It was shortly before he was expelled, you see. I was stood close to him in an assembly held for those boys who'd died. He was standing there, next to me, cold and unfeeling. That's when he said it." The professor gazed blankly out of the window, his mind drifting back in time as uniformed students crossed the yard below, rushing to their classes.

"Said what? Morton asked.

Barely audible, the professor uttered ominously, "Closed their eyes."

"What was that?"

"Uhm?"

"What was that you just said?"

The professor cleared his throat and spoke more clearly. "Not the sort of thing you'd expect at a time like that. But that's what he said. Closed their eyes to the killer surprise. And not the slightest hint of compassion in his voice."

"Christ," said Morton. "Tell me sir, how did he do it. To the students I mean. How did he get them to behave in such a way without anyone being able to prove it?"

With disbelief, the professor answered, "My god, man, haven't you been listening? He studied psychology. The books he read. The lessons he learned. It was all there. He invaded their minds using the tools of the trade."

"Answer my question, sir. Tell me; how did he do it?"

"Why… Hypnosis of course."

Seventy Two

Business was normally quiet this time of year, but with the events of the last few days and all of his rooms occupied, Arnold Embleton sat at the reception desk, his face buried in the sports pages of a newspaper when the entrance-door swung open and Mr. Waders stood in the doorway looking distressed, his face pale and gaunt and the collar of his jacket riding high around his neck.

"You okay, sir?"

"I'm fine," Sean scowled, looking around to see the coast was clear.

"If you don't mind me saying so, sir, you don't look fine."

"I'm okay I tell you." Sean walked briskly past him and hurried up the stairs to find Thomas sitting on the floor outside his room, fiddling with what appeared to be a foldaway dinner fork.

"What are you doing here, Thomas? Haven't you got anything better to do?"

Excitedly, Thomas jumped to his feet with a quick salute and a broad smile. "Yes, sir. I mean;- no, sir. I mean, what do you want me to do, sir?"

He snapped another salute and Sean responded likewise. "At ease agent Thomas. Mission accomplished."

Sean turned the key in his door and pushing it open, turned to bar Thomas's way as he followed behind, "I'm sorry, Thomas. Now isn't a good time. There are things I have to attend to."

Thomas's smile dropped to a frown and he turned to walk away. "Grown-ups are *always* too busy."

It was a line Sean had once heard from his daughter, and his door not yet closed, he stopped Thomas in his tracks. "Don't you have any friends to play with?"

"They're all at school."

"And what about you?" Sean asked. "Why aren't you at school?"

“Chickenpox,” Thomas answered, scratching his belly through his t-shirt, unsure of how that could be possible. He hadn’t eaten any lately, and he certainly hadn’t been near any chickens.

Sean breathed a heavy sigh and opened his door a little wider, gesturing for Thomas to come inside. He had dreaded this moment but known it would come. “There’s something I need to tell you, Thomas. I suppose now’s as good a time as any.”

Mr. Waders was sad. Thomas could tell. Whenever a grown-up said ‘we need to talk’ it always meant they were sad or something was wrong. Thomas sat on the edge of the bed and Mr. Waders sat next to him.

“You remember I said I have a daughter?”

Thomas gave an affirmative “Uh huh.” Half listening, half focusing his attention on the fork as he folded it into its handle.

“Well, I have to go find her, Thomas. She’s lost in a bad place somewhere.”

“Where, Mr. Waders? Where is she?”

“I don’t know, Thomas. But I have to go look for her.”

“I can help you,” Thomas offered, excited by the thought of another adventure.

“No, Thomas, you can’t. I have to do this on my own. It’s time for me to leave, Thomas.”

Thomas’s head dropped. “You mean… for always?”

“Yes, Thomas. For always. Whatever happens, I’ll never be able to come back.”

Standing by the bed, his head still bowed, Thomas began to sulk, “Whyyyy, Mr. Waders? Why do you have to leave? Everybody leaves me. And now you’re leaving me too. It’s not fair.”

“Your father hasn’t left you, Thomas.”

“My *real* daddy left when I was a baby, and *he* will too. One day.”

“You know that’s not true, Thomas. He cares for you. I know he does. Sometimes grown-ups forget just how much they care until something happens to remind them. And I’m sure your mum cares for you too. I’m sure she tells you all the time.”

“I guess,” Thomas answered sadly.

“Doesn’t she tell you she loves you?”

“Every morning. Straight after breakfast. She calls and says she misses me, but sometimes I fink it’s just words. If she missed me, she wouldn’t stay away so much.”

"Why do you think she stays away, Thomas?"

"I don't know. She cries a lot. She says she *has* to. She says Nan has cancer."

"Sometimes it's like that, Thomas. Sometimes, people do things they don't want to. Sometimes, they do things because they have to. It doesn't necessarily mean they don't care or that they're bad people. Like playing on the stairs, for instance. You don't mean any harm and you don't intend to get in the way, it just happens that way sometimes."

Thomas turned the lump of metal in his hands, the fork now joined by a blade as he sat prising each of the other gadgets from its handle. "It's like a spy knife isn't it. There's a can opener and a screwdriver and even a tiny pair of scissors and everyfing."

Sean looked down at the multi-faceted knife, bulky in Thomas's hand. A knife not too dissimilar to the one he himself had held just a few hours earlier. "You know that's not a toy, Thomas, don't you?"

"That's what Arnold says. He says it's his fishing knife, but I was only borrowing it. I was going to put it back. Honest."

"I know you were, Thomas. You're a good boy. That's why I have a little something for you in a box under the bed. A special present for a special boy."

Thomas's eyes lit up, his hands clapping together. "What is it, Mr.Waders. What is it?"

"I'll let you discover that for yourself. Let's just say; it's something Arnold, I mean;- your father would like me to give you. But first, I'd like you to give me the knife."

Sean held out his hand and the instant the knife was in his palm, Thomas was rummaging under the bed for his present.

* * *

Arnold Embleton broke the empty silence of the B&B with a shout from the foot of the stairs, "Thomas. Your lunch is ready… It's your favourite."

Thomas didn't answer, and nor did he come running along the landing anticipating his favourite dish. Toad-in-the-hole with thick creamy mash.

"Come on, Thomas, what are you doing? Get yourself down here this minute."

Still no sign of him and his patience waning, Arnold headed for Thomas's room, thinking he must have come downstairs, but Thomas wasn't there. He checked the living room and looked out of the window to the playground across the street. He checked the back yard and the downstairs bathroom, and his anxiety growing, he turned back towards the stairs, intending to check the hallway to the guest rooms but Mr. Waders stopped him short, standing at the reception desk with his holdall over his shoulder.

"I'd like to settle my bill, please."

"Erm, yes sir, okay. If you could just hang on for a moment, I'll be right with you."

"I haven't time to wait, Mr. Embleton. I'd like to settle now."

Arnold flicked through the register, his mind preoccupied with Thomas as he struggled to tally up the bill, balancing parenthood with business. "You haven't seen the boy by any chance, have you?" he asked.

"I have as a matter of fact. He's in my room. He was upset and crying a little. I think he was missing his mother. But not now."

Arnold gave an audible sigh of relief, his pen no longer scribbling out the itemised bill.

"I believe this is yours," Sean said, showing him the knife and placing it on the counter next to the newspaper. A warning in the way he put it down. "Thomas had it. You should take more care, Mr. Embleton. The boy could have hurt himself."

There was a sarcasm to his tone that Arnold didn't like, and as he looked up from the knife, his eyes met those of Mr. Waders, his disturbing gaze making him feel uneasy. "What was he doing in your room?" he asked. "Has he been bothering you?"

Sean dropped a wad of notes onto the newspaper, and with a smile, turned towards the door, "That should more than take care of my bill, Mr. Embleton. And there's a little something extra there, to help towards the cost of the funeral. All I ask is that you remember me."

"Funeral?"

With the subtlest hint of a smile, Sean stood at the open door, the sound of a car passing by as he adjusted his hat and put on his spectacles. "Go check on the boy, Mr. Embleton. He needs you now more than ever."

There was something ominous in the way he had spoken and a look in his eyes that Arnold had seen before somewhere. Then something clicked in his brain. Something he had said. And with a sense of urgency, he swiped away the money and flipped from the sports pages of the paper to read the headline 'REMEMBER ME' emblazoned across the top of the front page. And underneath, the picture of a yellow rose and the victims accompanied by pictures of their killer in a series of guises, the eyes unmistakable. Those same eyes he had seen from his guest just moments before he had left now stared back at him from the page. Edwards and D. Waders were one in the same.

His heart banging hard against his chest, he raced up the stairs two by two and burst into the room to find Thomas lying on the floor next to an open cardboard box, and stood in the doorway, staring for a moment, his eyes filling with tears as he looked at the discarded packaging and Thomas's little face beaming with joy as he marvelled at the silver Aston Martin.

That was why Thomas hadn't answered. He hadn't heard. His mind lost in his own little world of fantasy, oblivious to his father's calls as he scrutinised the car's every detail.

He turned to face Arnold, "Mr. Waders said *you* bought me it. It's fantastic. It's got a trajectory seat and everyfing."

Relief soaked through Arnold's body and his beaming smile matched that of his son's, his arms open wide as he rushed over to him, dropping to his knees and scooping Thomas up in his arms. "You're okay," he cried, hugging him tighter than ever before. "Thank god you're okay."

Thomas was stunned into a moment of surprised silence. Arnold was hugging him. And not just make believe, but a *real* hug. "Mr. Waders. I mean, Mr Edwards, 'cos that's his real name, he's a spy. He gave me the car. It's the one I always wanted, daddy. He said you asked him to get it for me. He said it's 'cos you love me."

Arnold looked into his son's eyes, and for the first time ever, realised just how much Thomas really meant to him. "I *do* love you, son. I'll always love you. And I'll always be here for you, no matter what."

Tears ran down his cheeks as he hugged his son closer and Thomas held him back just as tightly, his arms wrapped around his neck, squeezing him nearer, and all thoughts of the car slipping his mind as he lay his head on his new daddy's shoulder. At last, just like Mr. Waders had promised, his biggest dream of all had come true.

Seventy Three

It wasn't good to scream. If you screamed, he hit you.

Blocking out the angry yells of a woman shouting for attention in the other room, Abby lay on the floor, immersed in her own thoughts, thinking of what her daddy would do to make her happy and what he'd say to change how she felt.

'Corners up,' he'd say, his eyes focused on the edges of her mouth as she fought not to smile.

'Here they come,' he'd point, ignoring her petulant expressions and watching her frown melt away to be forgotten.

'They're bending,' he'd say, his own smile widening.

And no matter how hard she tried to resist, or how much she wanted to sulk, he got her every time.

'That's it. That's it. Here they come.' And inevitably *'There it is.'* Her smile breaking free to match his own.

It was a ploy that worked every time. Even now, in this dark and dingy place. "Corners up," she told herself, her mouth forcing the semblance of a smile for no-ones benefit but her own. *'Daddy's little princess looks so much prettier with a smile'* he would say. *'As pretty as her mum and twice as cute.'*

Anyone finding her now would think her strange, her inappropriate grin broadening, beaming with the mere thought of his smile as she pictured him in her head. And then her smile fading as she saw him crying, sad because he couldn't find his little girl.

"Corners up, daddy," she whispered, trying to change the picture. "I'm here, daddy. I'm alright." And as her daddy stopped crying, the picture melted away to the sound of rats squeaking in a far off corner and the creaking hinges of the door. Ratman back again.

No matter how softly he spoke to her, his voice made Abby shiver, and she cowered as he drew closer.

"Don't be afraid child," he said, helping her to sit up on the floor. "I've brought you a treat."

For the first time since she'd been brought here, she felt his fingers loosening the knots of her blindfold, and like the beating wings of a moth, her eyes flickered open to see his shapeless blur sitting across from her on the floor, a bulb hanging bare from the ceiling, framing him in silhouette. His outstretched hand reaching to stroke her cheek as her eyes adjusted to the glare of the light and she leaned away from him.

"Such pretty eyes," he said, his fingers combing her hair from her face.

Abby pulled away, shaking her head as if to shake his horrible germs from her every strand.

"Such nice hair, too," he said, smiling. "Just like I remember."

Abby didn't speak. Instead, she just looked at him, remembering him from the train. Remembering a time her daddy had warned her never to talk to strangers. And yet, the last time she had seen him, he had picked her up from school during lessons, saying there was a family emergency. Saying little else, regardless of her constant questioning, his pace brisk as they had walked to the train station. And he had just sat there;- quiet. Moody even. Hardly speaking a word until the train rolled in. And then he had put her on it. Telling her that, just this one and only time, she was to go with a stranger. An old woman who would take her to meet her mummy in Durham. And just like that, he had turned away and left her. Frightened. With the strange old woman with half-moon spectacles and a horrible gravely voice, telling her what a pretty girl she was. Everything afterwards hazy, until she awoke where she was now, a prisoner in this rat infested dungeon. That same old face smiling down at her. Not a woman, but a man. Repeating himself. Sounding just like she imagined the wolf to sound in the story of Little Red Riding Hood.

"What a pretty little girl you are."

Abby ignored him, choosing instead to look around the room in which she was being held captive. It had smelled old, and it looked old too. Older than rat-man, she guessed. Everything dusty and black. Not much to look at other than an old wooden stairway off to her right, a door at the top, and a crack of light shining from beneath. No other way in or out. No windows and no more doors. Not much else visible except the source of the dripping water; not a leaking pipe, but a tap over an old-fashioned basin, each drip echoing its crash against the porcelain, the huge cellar come dungeon acting like an amplifier. Just one great big room with a low wooden ceiling and a solitary light hanging from one of its beams.

"Don't fret, my Roeschen," said the old man. "Daddy will be here soon."

"When?" Abby asked, unable to contain her excitement.

"I'm going to call him a little later. Invite him to your birthday party. It's going to be *so…so…* special."

Abby began to cry, "But, my birthday's not till September."

"Nonsense, Rose. It's tomorrow. And it's going to be the best birthday yet. Just you wait and see."

"I'm not Rose," she cried, "I'm Abby. Abby Edwards. I'm seven years old and I live at number nineteen North lodge, Chester-le Street."

The slap to her face knocked her hard against the floor. "Snap out of it, Rosie. We can do this. Tomorrow, when daddy comes;- we can get our revenge."

Seventy Four

Morton rang Ben's mobile from the college grounds and received the cold response he'd expected.

"What do you want, Morton? I'm busy."

"Yeah, well, me too. I'd rather have spoken to Meg, but when I tried to get through to her office, they said she was unavailable."

"Like I said, Morton, I'm busy. Get to the point."

"I'm at Kings College in London. The Danish coin led me here. I'll explain how later, but first, there's something you need to know."

Morton explained the murder of Rose Heinrik and her family in Denmark, her brother Jurgen's change of name to Johan Besta, and his disappearance shortly after the deaths at the school.

"He's controlling Edwards," said Morton, "just like he was controlling Inkleman. That's why Edwards was able to copy the m.o. so fucking accurately. Because it was never *his* m.o., *or* Inkleman's. It was Heinrik's all along."

"And you believe this was all done through hypnosis?" Ben asked doubtfully.

"It's true, Ben. Listen to me. You have to believe me on this. I spoke at some length with the professor and you'd be amazed at what is possible these days. Forget all about that stage hypnotist crap you see on t.v. and the stuff you hear about hypnosis being used to help people quit smoking. The *real* hypnotists. The *specialists*. They can hypnotise you to do absolutely anything."

"Including murder?"

"Why not?" Morton answered, his agitation growing. "I once saw Derren Brown hypnotise Robbie Williams into letting him push skewers through his body. And then there was this other guy on G.M.T.V. who performed self-hypnosis before undergoing an open operation on his hand, *without* anaesthetic. I'm telling you, Ben. This mind control thing's for real. And if they can make someone sit perfectly still whilst they use them as shish kebab, then why not murder. I know it sounds far fetched, but I'm telling you;- Heinrik's our unsub', I'm sure of it. And what's more, I think he's changed his name again, and as unlikely as it may seem, I think he changed it to Schmidt."

With Morton's revelation and now wise to his obvious innocence, Ben felt guilty, almost ashamed. "I'm sorry, Morton. I should have gotten back to you, but things have been hectic here, and I suppose, well, there's only one way to say it."

"Say what?"

"You're right. It is Schmidt. And he told us as much in his selection of victims."

"What are you talking about?"

"He's been playing us from day one. And the whole time we thought we were protecting him, he has been watching our every move. We are looking for him now. We think he has Meg."

"Shit, Ben, we've got to find them. But if he's spent time alone with anyone at the station-"

Ben finished his sentence;- "There's no-one we can trust."

"That's not strictly true," Morton said, armed with his new found knowledge. "He can't hypnotise at will. The professor said the subject must be submissive. There's most likely a visual or verbal trigger of some kind to stimulate the desired response, but it would only work if he had spent some time with that person already, either pre-programming them, or coercing them with the aid of drugs."

"The phenobarbitones," Ben said. "They weren't used to control Sean Edwards' parasomnia. They were used to make him susceptible."

"That's what the professor here told me. He said they're sedatives, generally used to treat epilepsy and insomnia, but they're also used to induce hypnosis."

"Listen, Morton. I'm not saying you didn't get it wrong with Trevors at the hospital, but I'll admit when I'm wrong. And right now, you're the only one I can trust." Ben swallowed his pride, expecting Morton to tell him to stick it up his arse, but telling him nonetheless, "I need you here. And if you're willing, I want you back on the case."

Morton didn't need asking twice.

"I was never off it," he replied, a steely determination in his voice as he added, "We'll make him pay for this, Ben. We'll save Meg, and the girl too. And then, we'll make him pay."

Seventy Five

Feeling vulnerable in the darkness of her blindfold, Meg shuffled around the room until she found a wall, the feeling of it against her back offering her some comfort, some protection. No-longer sitting out in the open with nothing but the floor beneath her and the sound of voices in another room, their muffled words and incoherent babble pouring through the ventilation.

The voices stopped, and instead, she heard feet climbing steps, a door open and close and another door open.

The door to this very room.

Her wrists and ankles bound, her panic set in fast as her heart fought to free itself from her chest.

Who was coming?

Schmidt?

Edwards?

Both of them?– here to share the thrill of the last kill before finally performing their sacrifice of the child?

Only one set of footsteps came towards her.

"Are you comfortable, Meg?" came a voice, his accent unmistakable.

With the memories of Amy Edwards battered face still fresh in her mind, she was almost relieved to hear his voice. Schmidt was an old man, relatively fit for his years but too weak to dish out such a beating. She could expect a quick death. But then, maybe she was expecting too much.

"Tell me, Meg. How does it feel to be trapped here like this, your life at my mercy and not a soul here to help you?"

"Ben'll find me," she answered. "He saw the note. He'll come for me."

"No, Meg. *You* got the note. It vas meant for you all along."

She struggled with her bindings, "Why are you doing this? What do you hope to gain?"

"Don't you see?... It is for Rose. It vas *alvays* for Rose."

He pulled down her blindfold, and with his fingers under her chin, held her gaze, "Closed their eyes to the killer's surprise, Meg. But you see me now, don't you."

"Who's Rose?" she asked.

"Haven't you figured it out yet? A bright girl like you? Rose is my sister."

"*She* put you up to this?"

"Not exactly."

Meg looked around the windowless room; collapsed wooden frames leaning against white alabaster walls and boxes piled high in a corner, some of them filled with cushions and white robes. Others spilling out books. It was important to keep him talking, she thought. Build a rapport and it will be harder for him to kill me. And so, with the ruse of satisfying her hunger for answers, Meg played for time.

"What's the connection between you and Edwards," she asked, "other than the doctor/patient thing that is?"

Schmidt smiled at her. All these years he'd been a listener, but no-one had ever taken the time to listen to *him*. The things *he* thought, or the way *he* felt. And no-one had ever shown an interest in his past either or what he had planned for the future. And even now, he knew Meg was no different. Just another cop trying to join all the dots, he would entertain her whimsical curiosity.

"Patients are like children," he said. "Their minds are merely a vacuum waiting to be filled with a better way of thinking. And that is vat I do. I wipe their slates clean and allow them to absorb every little nuance of information I deem fit."

Meg struggled to control her emotions. "Information, yes. But not facts. Not details. You twist their view on reality and take away the essence of who they really are."

"No, Meg. I clear their minds of their clutter and fill them with thoughts of my own. I replace their memories with my memories. And in time, they think of my past as their own, and with a little auto-suggestion, they can be persuaded to do whatever I ask of them."

"Don't you mean manipulated."

"Oh come now, Meg. That depends on your viewpoint, don't you think? But all in all, what they do is for the greater good. And if that means it is they who take the risks, then so be it. They are expendable. It matters little if they live or die, as long as they have served their purpose. I'm sure it hasn't escaped you that I am no longer a young man. But even now, as I grow old and weak, I am filled with their strength and energy as they do what I will of them. Performing their sacrifices to God in my honour."

"And Sean Edwards is your unwilling disciple?"

"He is my tool of deliverance. All I have to do is call him and you will see for yourself just how efficient he can be."

"And what of Rose? What does she have to do with all of this?"

"She is the reason. The prize. Her coming will signify my redemption."

"Where is she?"

"Look around you," said Schmidt, his hand guiding her eyes to vase upon vase of yellow roses scattered around the room. "She is with us always," he said, smiling. "The flower signifies her presence."

'Remember Me' thought Meg. "She's dead?"

"Not dead. Sleeping. Waiting for her time to return."

"Return from where?" Meg asked, still playing for time.

"One question after another, Meg. Don't you ever tire of it?"

"I just want to understand."

Schmidt crossed to one of the vases, plucked out a rose, and returned to walk back and forth in front of her, his mind regressing to his childhood and a sadness in his voice as he stopped to churn out his memories. "I vas only twelve years old ven it first happened," he said. "My father locked me in my bedroom, and night after night, I'd have to listen to him abusing her. Raping her. My little sister screaming for help, and there vas nothing I could do. Over and over again he ignored our cries, until eventually, we could cry no more."

As Schmidt relayed the horrors of his childhood through distant eyes, Meg continued to struggle with her bindings, her hands feeling around on the floor behind her back, searching for something to rub against the rope. "Where was your mother during all of this?"

Schmidt's response was one of bitterness, his tongue poisoned with the very mention of her name. "In her room," he said through gritted teeth. "She vas always in her room."

"Didn't she know what was going on?"

She'd turn up the music to drown out Rosie's screams, pretending there vas nothing wrong. But she heard the screams as vell as I did, I know she did."

"She did nothing to stop it?"

"She vould not even talk about it. Even ven my father vas out of the house, she'd deny everything. Blocking it out. Acting like we were making it up. Showing more interest in her nails as she lay in her bed, day after day, filing them, and polishing them. Her eyes blind to the truth. Until I forced her to see it for herself."

Suddenly, everything made sense. The revelation stealing Meg's breath away;- The tortures. The mutilations. The dismemberments. Each and every injury signifying his perverse sense of justice. "Your mother, she was disabled?"

"That is no excuse for vat she did!" Schmidt burst out angrily. "She vas our mother. She could have told somevon. *Anyvon!* She could have reported him to the police."

'And what of you, Schmidt? Meg thought. 'What was to keep *you* from calling the police?' But she already knew the answer to her question.

'You will be taken into care.

You'll be split up.

You will never see your sister again.'

Threats his father would have drummed into him as a boy. And as though he had read her mind, Schmidt gave her his answer, sadness in his voice, his eyes dropping to the floor. "I loved my sister. She vas the von person in this world that ever meant anything to me. I'd have done anything to protect her. *Anything*. But my father threatened to kill her. He said if I ever said anything to anyone, she vould die. And I vould be made to watch."

"You mustn't blame yourself," said Meg, her bindings showing no sign of budging.

"I know that god damn it, I'm a psychiatrist. I know that better than *anyvon. He* vas the von hurting her. *He* vas the von making our lives a living hell. A drunk by day and an incestuous paedophile by night. But all of that vas about to be changed the day I asked for help."

"You spoke to someone?"

"I prayed to god. And he answered my prayer."

'Yeah, right,' Meg thought. 'I'm sure if god talks to anyone, it'll be a fucking nutter like you.'

Schmidt continued, "That day vill be imprinted on my mind forever. The day my life changed. The day *everything* changed. I'd sneaked off to buy my Roeschen a present for her upcoming birthday, and as I came out of the shop, I heard shots from across the street. The robber had killed two people and then calmly made off on a bicycle.

And I followed him, for four miles, right up to his door. Then, later, when the case went to court, god showed me the way."

Meg feigned an interested belief in what he was saying, "What did he show you?"

"The robber couldn't help vat he vas doing. He vas hypnotised."

"And he got off?" Meg said surprised. "With a lame excuse like that?"

"It vas the truth god damn it! You know vat I am capable of, Meg. Vat I have done already. Do not underestimate vat you do not understand."

In the angry gaze of his eyes, it was evident that Schmidt thought of the police as inferior, less intelligent, and Meg made sure not to dispel that belief, thinking to herself that, while Schmidt felt in control of the situation, she would seem to pose no threat, and she could use that to her advantage.

"So help me to understand," she said.

"At the hearing, it came to light that Hardrup vas not himself and someone else vas involved. There ver statements and vitnesses to prove it. A manuscript vas found detailing how a man called Nielsen had planned to hypnotise someone to commit crimes in his stead, and, if caught, it vas the weaker man who would be sent to prison, a mindless puppet, pre-programmed to starve himself to death, his secret dying with him. But, as I have already said, during the days before Hardrup's trial, the evidence came to light and Nielsen vas found guilty. He vas sentenced to a life of imprisonment. Whereas Hardrup vas released to psychiatric care, and upon his release, moved to England."

"Hardrup?" Meg recognised the name from the list of unsolved murders dating back to before she was born and following the same m.o. as Edwards and Inkleman. "He was your first victim. In 1958. You followed him here."

"At last we are getting somewhere," said Schmidt.

"But what does this have to do with your sister? How did she die?"

"It vasn't my fault. It vas an accident. *They* killed her."

"Your parents?"

"Nielsen and Hardrup. They made me do it. Outside his home, Hardrup pointed the gun at me. I thought he vas going to shoot."

"But he didn't?"

"No. He didn't. He just kept on staring. Saying nothing. Pointing the gun at my face." Embarrassed, Schmidt continued, "I vet myself. Then I dropped my bike and I ran. I ran for all I vas worth."

"It's alright, Schmidt, you were just a boy. It was brave of you to follow him."

"Don't you fucking patronise me, bitch. There is no way you could understand vat it vas like. There's no way *anyvon* could understand. From then on, it vas different. *'I'* vas different. That day in front of the robber, hypnosis stole my life away. And Rosie's life too. But after the case vas over, I swore I vould never feel that way again. From then on, *'I'* vas going to be the one in control of my life, and no-one vould ever take that away from me."

"You said: they made you do it. What did you mean? How did Rose die?"

Schmidt side-stepped her question, "Tomorrow, it vill be the anniversary of her death." He paused to picture the scene, a brief smile as he pictured her in her yellow dress, then sad at the final image. "It vas the night of her seventh birthday," he said. "It vas god's plan that she should die, so that I could be reborn. Through her, I have reclaimed my life. And tomorrow. At 10:15 a.m. She vill be reborn too."

"You still haven't answered my question. Your sister. How did she die?"

"It vas a mistake. An accident. She vasn't meant to die, and tomorrow I vill put that right."

"But you said;- it was god's plan that she died."

"I vas mistaken. I vas just a boy. God works his miracles through others, and on that April night in 1951, he chose me as his vessel. Only, I made a mistake and she died. But just as I vas reborn, she vill be reborn too.

Then it hit her that, even back then, the psychiatrist was a psycho. "*You* killed her. Deliberately."

"She *isn't* dead. She's asleep." He tapped his finger to his head, "I saved her. And soon, I vill bring her back to join me."

"At what cost?" Meg asked. "The lives of more people. More patients. That was how you chose them, wasn't it. All of your victims. They were patients. They came to you with their problems, and you solved them with their deaths."

With the back of his hand, he slapped her hard across the face and leaned over her, his face red with anger. "Grief! *Despair*.

Depression in all its forms. They all wanted the same thing," he snarled, "Not hope, but escape. And that is vat I gave to them. Just as I vill give it to you."

Their noses almost touching, Meg glared right back at him as he continued, "Haven't you realised why you are here yet, detective? Haven't you figured it out? You know what it's like, don't you. To care for someone else's life more than your own."

Over the rim of his glasses, his eyes searched hers and saw the fear invade her thoughts before he pressed his cheek to hers and whispered in her ear. "Of course you do. Why do you think I chose you. Why do you think I brought you here. Vell, I'll tell you why, Meg…

It is because I know your secret."

Seventy Six

Sean had returned to the security of the B&B to gather his thoughts but had left for the sake of the boy.

It was only now, as he drove to Durham, that he realised he'd left without his pills and worried about the possible consequences. Without his medication he could lose control altogether. The killer within him, free to do whatever he pleased. The murders escalating. His daughter's death becoming more and more imminent. But already too late to turn back, he got to thinking; with all that had happened during the past week, maybe the pills hadn't been helping him at all. Maybe it was an omen he'd left without them, because, for his daughter's sake, he needed to stay alert, and already he felt so much fresher and more energised. Almost felt… *himself* again.

For the best part of a week, Sean had lived in another man's shoes. A killer's shoes, his time spent in hiding and on the run, constantly looking over his shoulder. Constantly fearful of what he might do next. His worrying relentless as the actions of his alter ego forced him into a life of solitude: sleeping in a strange bed by night and searching for his daughter by day, all whilst having to avoid the attentions of the police. And all of it interspersed with time-lapses, murders, and telephone calls from someone as yet unknown. Events conspiring against him, even now, forcing him to take this extended journey in an effort to seek help, having to go the long way around to avoid Durham police headquarters as he headed for Schmidt's home in the hope that his expertise would allow him to retrieve his flashback and bring an end to this living nightmare.

He was almost there.

Further down the road he could see the huge arches of the brick and stone viaduct and cubes of light flashing by overhead as a train headed into the city, the carriages slowing to a stop as he too drew closer to his destination, his foot easing off the accelerator then reapplied almost at once.

Schmidt had visitors.

He drove past the cordoned off road, the heavy police presence at the cul-de-sac's entrance forcing him to take a detour away from the city, and just a few hundred yards from the D.L.I. museum, he turned left up a side road to Wharton park. It was quiet this time of night. No children playing on swings. No sounds of rackets thrashing at balls on the tennis courts. Not even the obligatory tearaways with their two litre bottles of cider and a shared pack of cigarettes.

Now what?

He climbed from the car and stood on the grass bank where he and Amy had had their first picnic together, their blanket smothering the daisies like the clouds now covered the stars. Tonight, the swings hung still, but on that warm sunny day, there had been the sound of children's laughter coming from the nearby rides. Toddlers through to teenagers playing on see-saws and climbing frames, mixing with parents and friends as they ran rings around one-another. All of them happy and having fun. It was a sound he'd grown to love all the more from that day forward. The day all his Christmases had come at once, his heart bursting with happiness as Amy had told him he was to become a father.

Now, Amy was dead and his daughter missing. Soon, he feared, *she* would be dead too. And his time running out fast, there was nothing he could do but wait for the moment he'd hear of her death. Or worse yet, find himself holding the knife, her blood on his hands and her body at his feet. And with that thought, unable to bear the thought of losing his daughter, he dropped to his knees, his trousers soaking up the moisture from the grass as he sobbed to the heavens, begging Amy's forgiveness and praying she was watching over Abby. "Pleaaase, Amy. You have to help me. Tell me. What do I have to do to end it all."

His answer came with the rustle of a breeze through the nearby bushes, his attention drawn to a picnic table like the one in his flashbacks, reminding him of the boy who became a killer. A killer who had to be stopped. And racked with despair, he headed back to the car, his head bombarded with thoughts of Abigail, of Amy, of suicide, of what had caused all of this to happen, his mind running off on a tangent as he sat behind the wheel and wound down the window, the breeze blowing in his face and flicking through Thomas's notes on the passenger seat like a spirit fanning through the pages for a way to find his daughter.

Was that it?

He picked them up and scoured through them, looking at the times he had left and returned to the B&B and how they had fitted around the murders. His time-lapses had resulted in death, but what of his mystery caller? Who was he? And what was his part in all of this?

According to the notes, Sean could expect another call at 9:15, and with only twenty minutes to go, he reached into his pocket to check his phone was off, having seen enough movies and cop shows in his time to know that the police could use it to pinpoint his location, and now wasn't the time for a quick getaway. When the time was right he'd switch it on, and if the call came through, he'd be alert to it, ready to respond at a moments notice, and doing whatever he had to to save his daughter.

He sat rocking in his car, willing the minutes away as the time approached nine and he switched on the radio to keep abreast of the latest news, angry that his life had come to this. Always sitting in his room or the car. Always listening to the news. His decision to take his life now dependant on the information the latter would have to offer and what would be revealed in the call to his mobile.

The bulletin turned out to be pretty much the same as every other but for the mention of the yellow rose. A clue that had been kept under wraps, it was the first time the police had brought it to the attention of the general public. But now, with time running out, maybe they too were clutching at straws and hoped that the rose would bring something to light. To Sean at least, it confirmed that the flashback was important. That the flower wasn't just a part of a nonsensical dream, it had meant something. And with a glimmer of hope, the answer waiting to be revealed, he reclined his seat and readied himself to go under again, desperate to discover its secret and find his daughter before it was too late.

He closed his eyes and tried to relax, struggling at first, until, at last, his mind flowed freely towards the images of before.

The willow tree in the garden.

The boy stalking his prey.

The bee traipsing over the yellow rose.

The metamorphosis?...

And again, he snapped out of it.

With one failed attempt after another, he was finally getting somewhere. The metamorphosis was a first. The bee and rose were at the point of changing into something he felt he wasn't meant to see, and that in itself meant he had to try again.

Weak as he was, his tiredness exacerbated, he glanced around the park to check he was still alone and made one last attempt before the call, again reaching the point of the lid snapping onto the jar, and again spilling the contents onto a bench, the bee trawling over the flower. Only, this time, something was different. This time, the flashback was neither monotone nor vivid, but dark and in shadow, as though drifting into a nightmare.

He felt cold and afraid, consumed by apprehension.

Something bad was going to happen, he felt it.

Was this what had been happening to him shortly before the murders?

Was this how he began to change into the person who would kill his daughter?

The garden and surrounding trees ominously melted away to reveal a child's darkened bedroom and the metamorphosis took a new shape;- the garden bench becoming a bed and the rose growing in size to fill it. The bee still clambering over it. And even in the darkness of the small bedroom, shadows seemed to descend upon them, filling the room with their presence and wrapping themselves around every last dreg of colour. The rose shrivelling and losing its petals, shedding them more and more quickly as the bee grew bigger in size. Then a blinding burst of light and the rose became a girl, the bee a naked man… pawing at her. Trying to undress her as she struggled to resist, his hand covering her mouth as he tore at her yellow dress.

In his trance, Sean wanted to turn away but forced himself to carry on watching, enraged with anger and unable to help, his hand gripping an imaginary knife, desperate for the man to know he was there, wanting him to turn around and see the look in his eyes as he felt the plunge of the blade into his stomach. But still the man had his back to him, the muscles tensing in his shoulders as he writhed over the little girl before he tensed and stopped, screaming out in pain as she bit down hard on the web of his thumb, and his hand flinching away, she let out a high pitched scream, her shrill almost deafening, the man lashing out at her, his hand now dragging a knife across her throat as Sean looked on in horror; the knife the one he himself had been holding, pressed into the girls neck. Her eyes open in shock. Her scream silenced, and the man's hand peeling away, panic stricken, his shape changing again. Leaner. Younger. Metamorphosing into a teenaged boy standing naked in another room, his back still turned to Sean. The scenery chopping and changing with the random inaccuracies of a dream. The boy walking away from the body of a middle-aged man slouched on a couch, a bottle of whisky in his dead hand spilling to the floor.

In his mind, Sean watched mesmerised, desperate to see the boy's face, the knife dripping blood onto the floor as he walked barefoot to another room. A diminutive figure hidden from view. The boy's hand rising high above his head and thrusting the blade into another victim. Time and time again. Blood spattering across the walls with each arching thrust until finally, he stopped, panting from his exertions and stepping back from the body to reveal a middle-aged woman collapsed in her wheelchair. Sean still a reluctant voyeur, feeling sick as the boy turned to face him;- smiling. A face he was familiar with and had trusted. The smile more of a smirk, now laughing at him. Laughing at the things he'd made Sean do. His sick and twisted grin unmistakable, even as a boy. The killer was Schmidt. His family was dead. And the girl he had been raping was his sister.

Sean sprung from his trance with a start, the shock revelation snapping him from his hypnosis, his heart pounding and his fears amplified with the knowledge of who had taken his daughter and what was to become of her, and fumbling to switch on his phone, he dropped it as it rang in his hand.

Seventy Seven

It was almost 10 p.m. when Morton walked through the doors of the incident room and into a sea of mayhem; Ben dishing out orders, phones ringing, and bodies rushing everywhere. 'Organised chaos,' he thought, walking past a detective talking frantically into a mobile phone and dodging another not watching where he was going, dabbing a finger to his tongue and collating papers. Even Superintendent Brandt was working the late shift and stood talking with a technical support officer in a far off corner of the room, everyone immersed in their own tasks and not really noticing him, even as he past between them, stepping in and out of desks as he crossed the floor to speak with Ben.

"What can I do to help?" Morton asked.

Ben's attention was elsewhere, his mind preoccupied with a WPC taking an incoming call. She was still mid-conversation when he turned to Morton and offered a shake of the hand, a new found mutual respect revealed in their grip. "Glad to have you back," said Ben, his enthusiasm curbed.

There was a moment's discomfort, neither of them sure of what to say before Morton broke the ice, keen to play his part. "So what do we have?"

Ben forced a semblance of a laugh, "You mean besides a god damned frenzy?"

"If it was quiet, then I'd be worried," said Morton.

Ben agreed and kept his update to a brief. "We've told the media about the yellow rose, but I'm not sure it was a good idea. We've had calls coming in left, right and centre. Some of them from florists and suppliers. Some from so-called witnesses who say they've seen Edwards. Each of which has to be followed up of course. And then there's the bloody time-wasters moaning about their missing shrubs. Some of them not even roses, let alone the right fucking colour."

"Anything to go on?" Morton asked, looking for a place to start.

"More than we can cope with," Ben answered, looking around the room at the bustling activity and the flustered expressions. "The problem's filtering it out. We've got our fucking hands full as it is, and I've gone and made matters worse by mentioning the fucking rose."

"You did what you had to," said Morton, trying to show his support. "And the way things are going, we need all the information we can get."

"It's not just the calls," said Ben, "it's the manpower. Everything's coming in at once."

Though normally cool under pressure, Morton could see from Ben's expression that he was riddled with worry, clearly stressed out by Meg's disappearance.

Ben continued. "Limbs belonging to Naomi Watts have turned up at Schmidt's place, so we've got a team over there trying to find the torso. And there's another team down at the B&B where Edwards was staying. And get this. The cheeky bastard was only a few hundred yards down the fucking road. We've got a make on his car, though. A grey Nissan Bluebird, registration x-ray, two-four-seven charlie-delta-foxtrot. The plate-recognition units have been alerted and we've got patrol cars keeping an eye out. And on top of all that, I've got every available resource searching for Meg and the girl. We know Schmidt has them. The fucking question is;- *where*?"

"I hate to ask," said Morton. "But, the limbs at Schmidt's place. You sure they belonged to Naomi Watts?"

"Formerly identified," Ben answered. "A tattoo on her right ankle, and an engagement ring on her finger."

"What about the list of victims?" Morton asked, referring to the clues left by Schmidt.

Ben was looking through the photographs of the victims, in each case their limbs posing the sign of a cross. He turned to Morton and nodded to the sheets on a nearby desk, the clues highlighted. And as Morton leaned to read them, Ben's attention was drawn to the glint of a chain dangling from his neck, his fingers idly toying with a crucifix as he studied the clues.

"What's with the cross?" Ben asked. "I thought you were an atheist."

"I am," Morton answered, his focus still fixed on the list. "But I'll take whatever help I can get, no matter how unlikely." And avoiding Ben's eye contact, he tucked the cross back into his shirt, neglecting to say that it was a gift from his ailing mother, his personal life his own, never shared. And now not the time to open up and explain that he took her to church almost every Sunday, just as he had promised before Alzheimers had taken away her memory of him.

"Sir." The WPC put her hand over the phone as she tried to interrupt them, *"Sir."*

"I'm listening, constable. What is it?"

"We've got a report of another body, sir. A torso. They're saying it's a woman's."

Ben swallowed hard, "Find out the details, and tell them I'm on my way."

As Ben turned to leave, Morton stepped in his way, "Hold it, Ben. I know what you're thinking, but this isn't the time for a change of leadership. We need you here to run this."

"*Brandt* can run it," Ben snapped.

"Brandt's a jumped up superior, Ben. He's not a leader. He's not up to this."

Ben tried to keep a lid on his emotions, well aware that the body could be the rest of Naomi Watts, but afraid it was Meg's. Either way, he couldn't bear to hang around waiting to find out. "Get out of my way, Morton. I need to do this."

Morton's voice was considerate, understanding even. "I know you do, Ben. But if it is Meg, then there's only one way you can make him pay. And this isn't it."

"It's a good place to start," said Ben, looking to push Morton aside.

"No, Ben. It's not." Morton stood firm, the death of the young officer still haunting him, reminding him that mistakes can cost lives. "I'm not trying to tell you what you should do, Ben. I'm just asking you to give it a few more minutes. At least… stay until the call. It's what Meg would want, and it could well be our last chance to find him before he kills the girl."

Choking back his emotions, Ben cleared his throat knowing Morton was right. He *had* to stay here. If the call came in, *HE* had to be the one to take it. (*'The next call will be more enlightening'*). He looked at Morton with a fierce intensity, the two of them standing eye to eye. "I want to be there when this goes down, Morton. When we catch up to this son of a bitch, **'I'** want to be there when we nail him. You understand?"

Morton gave him a knowing nod, understanding better than anyone, that, one way or another, Ben wanted Schmidt dead. That same sense of urgency flowing through his veins as he left for the site where the body was found, thinking to himself what he imagined Ben to be thinking too. The thoughts of a man in love, revenge his main objective if Meg had come to harm.

And god help Schmidt and Edwards both if she was dead.

Jim Brandt stood next to Ben when the telephone rang at 10:15 and both looked across to an officer, checking he was ready to trace it, Ben's fingers counting down three… two… one, and with a nod, he picked up the receiver.

Schmidt's voice came over the speaker, a cynical edge to his tone, creepy, like an unwanted guest arriving at a Halloween party, "Surpriiiiise." His voice was a little distant but his accent unmistakable, "You ver told this call vould be special, Ben. And so here I am, making my guest appearance."

"And you think that makes it special, do you?" Ben asked, trying to disguise his annoyance and make sense of the noises in the background.

"No, Ben. Vat makes it special is that, in the past, I have had others do my bidding. I have watched as they have killed for me. And I have watched, as you and those before you have tripped over yourselves trying to stop them. Alvays blind to the truth. Alvays unaware of vat vas really going on. So here I am. My final performance. Von last curtain call before I bow out and take my leave."

"You planning on going somewhere?"

Schmidt gave a half hearted laugh. *'Going somewhere'* wasn't quite what he had in mind. "Not exactly," he answered. "But there'll be no more secrets. No more hidden agendas. And no more subjects acting on my behalf. Tomorrow, it vill all be over."

"You're damned right it will. Because we know what you've been doing, Schmidt. To the copycats. To Edwards, Inkleman, and the others. You hypnotised each and every one of them."

Ben scribbled on a piece of paper; *'What's that noise?'* Passing it to Brandt who motioned for him to keep Schmidt talking (as if he needed reminding).

"They ver never copycats, Ben. They ver experiments. Each von better than the last. Each perfecting the ritual, with me at the helm to keep them right. Guiding them if you like. The puppet-master putting on a show. And you ver the unvilling audience with a front row seat, unable to see their strings. All of it a trick of the mind. An illusion if you will. Building up to this one defining moment."

"So why now. After all these years. Why did you let us in on the act?"

"Because I wanted you to know that, even ven you think it is all over; it is not. Everyvon closes their eyes to the killer surprise, Ben. Speaking of which. I have von more for you. A guest you might say. Somevon I think you might like to talk to."

Ben heard tape ripped from skin and Meg's voice, quiet and calm, "He's just an insect, Ben. Come squish him."

Ben struggled with his emotions, a wave of relief sweeping over him with the sound of her voice, his feelings fighting to break free with things he wanted to say to her, but in his mind he knew that Schmidt would use it against him and his silence won through.

"Oh, you're choked, Ben. Vat's the matter? Did you think she vas dead? You found the rest of Naomi I take it. Sweet girl. And not at all vat you'd expect."

"Let her go, Schmidt. Or would you prefer I called you Heinrik."

"Vell done, Ben. You *have* been doing your homework, haven't you." There was a pause before Ben heard the forceful grunt of Meg being held to the phone again, Schmidt calmly giving her orders, "Speak to him. Tell him vat a wonderful performance he is going to miss and of the show we intend to put on."

"Fuck you!" Meg shouted.

A loud crack echoed into the incident room with what Ben assumed was Meg being struck with the phone, and Ben shouted out, trying to draw his attention away from her, "I know all about you, Schmidt! I know about your family and what you did to them."

"At last," Schmidt mocked. "It took you long enough considering the amount of clues I left. I vas beginning to think you ver never going to figure it out. And now that you have, it is already too late."

"Unless there's been a change of schedule, I still have twelve hours."

Schmidt sounded disappointed, "And there you go letting me down, Ben. Didn't you check?"

"Check what?"

"Think back, Ben. To the time you caught up with Inkleman. Do you think that vas a mistake? Did you really think it vas good detective work that lead you there to vitness him slice through his daughter's throat?"

Ben thought back to that night. The night before Inkleman was due to sacrifice his daughter. Up until then, every murder had been committed at 10:15 a.m. "What are you getting at?" Ben demanded.

Schmidt spoke with an edge of sarcasm, "You must have filed a report, Ben."

Ben stood rooted to the spot as the realisation hit him hard. "12:06" He uttered.

"That's right, Ben. I'm so glad you remember. April 4th, shortly after midnight, at 12:06 a.m. That is ven my Rosie died. That is ven *all* the girls died. You see, you ver meant to be there that night, Ben. Vat good is an execution vithout a vitness. I *arranged* for you to see Inkleman execute his daughter, and ven *'he'* died as vell, you did exactly as I expected. You closed the case. Just like so many others before you. It's like I keep saying, Ben. Closed your eyes to the killer surprise. So you see. There is no change of schedule. In a little under two hours from now, Abigail is no more. And your girlfriend too I think." Schmidt paused, as if picturing the scene in his head. "Yes. That is vat we vill do. We vill make it a twin execution. After all, they do say; two heads are better than von."

Ben's fists clenched by his sides as he spoke through gritted teeth. "So who's going to be there this time, Schmidt?... As you've already said yourself, 'what good is an execution if there's no-one there to watch'".

"Oh, *I'll* be watching, Ben. From the very front row. And I vill have the best seat in the house."

Ben was boiling inside. He wanted to be there with him face to face, his hands around Schmidt's throat, throttling him until his face turned blue. "You want to send me a special invite?" he asked. "You want me to come along for the repeat performance?"

"It would be nice if you could make it, Ben. But somehow, I don't think you vill. Besides, you don't think *I'm* the von performing do you. Good god man, haven't you learned anything?"

"Edwards?"

"He is on his vay, even as we speak."

Meg looked up from the floor, dizzy from the blow, to see Schmidt checking his watch.

'Come on, come on' she told herself. *'Think, god damn it, think.'*

She searched for a clue, her time running out fast and her mind racing through what she knew and what she could see. She had to think of something and quick. A way out of this mess. Something. *Anything.* A way to tell Ben where she was being held, but nothing came to mind. And even if she had known, she dared not blurt it out for fear of reprisal. For fear that Schmidt would kill her and the girl both before Ben ever got here. And as she looked across the room to the collapsed wooden frames and boxes piled high against a far off wall, it came to her; a moment of stunned realisation. This dank old room with its foisty smell was an annex to a bigger building, and the clues were staring her in the face. The dismantled wooden frames and boxes full of books, some of them spilling out velvet and satin curtains. Only, they weren't curtains at all. They were robes or albs. And the other stuff must have been old pews and discarded hymn books.

This was a church.

"Say your last goodbyes, Meg."

Her wrists and ankles bound, she rose to her knees as Schmidt held the phone to her mouth, "I pray to god you can help me, Ben. I pray that whatever happens, you can see your way to forgiving me my wrongs. And I *was* wrong, Ben. It was just like you said. If we ever get through this, maybe we can argue over another meal together and talk about that dream home of yours. If not, then at least you know how I feel. How I've always felt. I love you, Ben. I love you more than you know."

"I love you too," Ben said sombrely.

Schmidt pulled the phone away and pushed her to the floor with his knee. "Ahhh. Isn't that nice, Ben. She loves you. It's a shame Sean is on his vay, because, ven he gets here, he has a choice to make. Meg or his daughter. Which do you think he vill choose?"

Ben shouted down the phone, hoping Meg could still hear him, "I'll find you, Meg. I'll come for-" With a parting burst of laughter, Schmidt hung up the phone, and though the trace had been pinpointed, the expression on Jim Brandt's face didn't look good.

"What is it?" Ben asked.

Brandt had been watching the monitor as the call was being traced. "Something's wrong," he said, the technician behind him nodding in agreement.

"Didn't you get a location?" Ben asked.

"Yes," the tech' answered. "But according to this, he's at the cinema on North Road."

"The noise in the background?" Ben asked. "It was a movie?"

"It could be," the tech' answered. "But he could just as easily be in the foyer, the bar, or in some side room or other. But still, something's wrong."

"Wrong *how* for christ's sake?"

The tech' rewound the tape of the call and replayed the first few seconds.

"What was that?" Ben asked. "It sounds like a ring tone."

"It is, sir," said the tech', remembering what Ben had told him earlier about taking nothing for granted. Reminding him that Schmidt had mislead them throughout the case, and telling him to weigh up every possibility when the call came in.

"What do you make of it?" Ben asked.

"The ring tone," said the technician, "and the echo in Schmidt's voice. The acoustics are all wrong. The background noise is stifled, like he's in an enclosed area, but Schmidt's voice is reverberating. It doesn't fit."

"But he is ringing from the cinema, right?"

"No, sir. Someone else is."

"Then how come we're hearing Schmidt?"

"My guess would be that someone else is at the cinema with two mobile phones. One of them Schmidt's, and the other his own."

"Edwards?"

"There's no way of knowing for sure, sir. But I doubt it. The number we have for Sean Edwards is currently switched off, and if Schmidt was telling the truth, then Edwards is on the move to meet up with him at wherever he's holding Meg."

"Then it's possible we have another unsub."

"Another?" Brandt jumped in. "Who?"

If we knew that, he wouldn't be an unsub. Ben thought to himself, struggling to hold his tongue before finally answering, "Have you forgotten. Schmidt's a hypnotist. It could be anyone."

The technician continued, "Either way, Schmidt called from a different location, and the guy at the cinema is simply holding one mobile phone to the other to establish a connection without there being a traceable link."

"So find the number of the other mobile," Brandt ordered. "And find out who owns it."

"I can't sir. There's any number of mobile phones in the vicinity, and no way of knowing which of them was used as the link."

Ben thought about the Inkleman killings and how they'd ended in Church street, the recording of a screaming child in a burning building; a deception as she was about to be murdered like a sacrificial lamb in an adjacent building. Then, something occurred to him. Something uncharacteristic that Meg had said. An agnostic's clue given along with the mention of his dream home. *'I pray to God you can help me'*

Eager to act but wary of the consequences, he gnawed at his bottom lip, unsure if he should divulge what he had learned. Meg's life was at stake, and desperate as he was, he still didn't know who he could trust. Who he could *really* trust. But with the urgency of the situation forcing his hand, he turned to a bunch of detectives, "Quick. I want a list of every vacant church within a twenty mile radius."

"Shit," said Brandt. "Why didn't I think of that." Remembering what he'd learned of Schmidt's background and that his father was a priest, it now seemed blatantly obvious that he'd choose a church to commit the ultimate sacrifice.

But which one?

Seventy Eight

Sean had thought long and hard about calling the police, but Schmidt had warned him *'Come alone. At 10:20. No sooner, no later, or the girl dies'*.

His headlights dimmed on approach, he had arrived at 10:08. The mid-conversion church standing out like a monumental silhouette against the dark night's sky. A spire and bell tower, black against the heavens, dropped to an arched stained glass window, its warm beacon of light belying the cold intentions within. His daughter was inside, and there was nothing he could do but wait for what seemed like an eternity, watching the clock in the car and checking it against his watch. The minutes ticking slowly by. Second by lengthy second. His thoughts of Abby, of Schmidt, of what was happening, asking himself why he had to wait so long. And his anxieties growing as crunch time approached, he climbed from the car and walked the secluded grounds. Treading carefully. Slowly. Stepping over timber and bags of sand; the churchyard a building site littered with scaffolding and discarded masonry.

'What was that?'

A noise from behind, he turned to the rustle of grass, something small like a mouse, moving away from him, before his eyes flicked back to the church.

He stared along the length of its walls, thoughts of Abby inside, her body lifeless and her clothes covered in blood. Scenes of an untold future. A foreboding sense of urgency telling him he had to act *now*. And moving as quickly as he dared, his eyes delved into the darkness, wary of making a noise as he picked out spaces to plant his feet, tools scattered everywhere, the site apparently deserted some time ago. Abandoned machinery off to his right. A portable cement mixer left standing chained like a prisoner to a wrought iron gate, and next to it, a wheelbarrow lay tipped on its side, its tyre deflated, all within a few short yards of yet more scaffolding piled loosely on the ground next to the vestibule wall.

He headed to the rear of the church looking for a way to tip the balance in his favour, and trudging through the long grass, found an old door hidden in a shadowy recess, locked. No sounds from inside, and no way to see what lay behind.

It seemed that all bar the arched window had been blanked out, and too high for him to reach, no time to search for a ladder in the darkness, he continued around the building and headed towards the large double doors, waiting there until the moment his watch struck twenty past ten, and giving a wary knock, he wandered inside, walking cautiously through the short wide passageway, frightened of being ambushed. Even more frightened of finding Abby…dead.

He squinted as he stepped into the light and was instantly struck by the sweet smell of perfume hanging in the air, his eyes adjusting to the light as he walked just a few short paces and the church opened up into a huge empty shell with bare stonework around dark windows and white-washed walls with a high timber-framed ceiling, the church more like a shrine than a place of worship, with no seating, no font, and no pulpit, the only furnishing appearing to be a sacrificial altar towards the back of the room. And flowers. Flowers everywhere. Beautiful copper-toned hues of yellow in vases, buckets and jugs. In anything that could hold water. Single roses peeping out of jars and long crystal glasses. Bouquets spread about the floor and propped up against the walls. The whole room a sea of yellow. Only the aisle remained bare. A pathway to his tormentor who welcomed him with a beaming smile.

"Ahhh, just vat the doctor ordered," said Schmidt, standing behind the altar as though he were about to give a sermon, his arms spread wide to show off his handy-work, the wall behind him smeared with photographs displayed like snapshots of history, some of them black and white, but the majority in colour. All of them of victims past and present, the timescale belied in the fashion of their clothes, most of them showing women and the occasional man, with only one image looking the same throughout. That of a child like Ben's own daughter. Each picture placed side by side in a straight line through the middle of the display. One little girl after another. Each of them around the same age, with the same blonde hair tied in ribbons and wearing a yellow dress.

"Do you like vat I have done with the place?"

Sean marched briskly towards him and some twenty feet away, stopped short on command, "*Not!* another step."

Sean stood fuming, "Where's my daughter?!"

"All in good time my young protégé. But first, there is someone I vant you to meet."

"I'm not playing your games any longer, Schmidt. I'm here for my daughter. Where is she? What have you done with her?"

"First things first, Sean. How can I expect you to kill someone you haven't yet met."

"If I'm going to kill anyone, it'll be you."

"Not quite vat I had in mind. But you vill kill for me, Sean. If you vant your daughter to live."

"I won't. I can't."

"Oh, but you can, Sean. You have already proven yourself more than capable. And on more than von occasion I might add."

"That's not me any longer. I won't do it."

Schmidt looked him in the eye, and with emphasis, said "*Roeschen,*" expecting him to be more agreeable. But Sean's tone and manner remained unchanged.

"What the hell does that mean?"

"Haven't you taken your pills, Sean?"

"They weren't helping. I guess they were never meant to, were they."

"Oh, come now. I'm your doctor. I vas trying to make things easier for you. But I'm afraid now we vill have to do this the hard vay."

"Do what?" Sean asked angrily. "Why did you do this to me. Why did you make me do those things?"

"It vas all for the greater good, Sean. I suppose there's no harm in telling you, the flashbacks you have been having, they are not your own."

"I know that now. But how? What did you do to me?"

"I altered some of your memories, Sean, and replaced them with a few of my own. As a matter of fact, I even stole von or two. Vithout you I would never have known about this place. You are to be congratulated."

It was only now, standing here looking at the ornamental mouldings and wall tablets that his mind became clearer. This was the church where Abby had been christened. And it could well be the place where she would die.

Schmidt stepped back a few paces to a statuesque figure covered in a white sheet, and grabbing at its hem, pulled it away to reveal Meg standing beneath, her hands and ankles bound, unable to escape or defend herself as Schmidt smiled at Sean before pushing her to the floor. "I vant you to kill her for me, of your own accord. Wilfully rather than under hypnosis. But you do have a choice, Sean. I'm not a complete ogre. The detective or your daughter? Which is it to be?"

Sean looked at Meg shaking her head in protest and yelling into her gag, her eyes defiant.

"But be warned," Schmidt continued, taunting and provoking as he stepped back behind the altar. "Whatever you decide, I vant you to talk me through it. I vant to hear every nuance of emotion. The guilt. The pleasure. The fear and anger. Vatever you feel, I vant you to tell me as she dies at your hands."

Sean moved a step closer to Meg and turned to Schmidt, "Where's Abby? How can I be sure she's alive?"

Schmidt stepped out from behind the altar to reveal Abigail standing before him, his hand resting on her shoulder and his other hand holding a flame-blackened knife by his side, his expression stern. "It is only because of your success rate thus far that she is still alive," he said, a warning in his tone, "Don't spoil it now."

Abby looked frightened but unharmed and Sean choked back his tears, desperate to free her from this madman.

"Please help me, daddy."

"It's alright hun'. Daddy's come to take you home."

"Home?" Schmidt laughed. "Home? Vat home? You have no home. Everyvon is dead."

Abigail was afraid to ask, "Who's dead?"

"Roeschen," Schmidt said softly, the name meaning 'little rose'. "Ask Sean who killed your beautiful dog?"

"Her name's *Abigail*!" Sean shouted.

Abby looked to her father, her tears welling and her bottom lip quivering, "Lucky's dead?"

"I'm afraid so, hun'. He's in heaven."

"But, how?"

"Tell her, Sean. Tell her how you killed her dog."

"Shut up, damn you!"

"Do you see Roeschen? Do you see vat a temper he has."

"I didn't mean to, hun, I couldn't help it." He looked at Schmidt, "*He* made me do it."

Schmidt acted shocked and deeply hurt at the accusation, "Not just a killer, but a liar too. I vasn't even there."

"He didn't have to be there, honey. He tricked me. He hypnotised me. I didn't want to do it, but he made me."

Abigail sobbed, "But why, daddy? Lucky never hurt *anyone*."

"I know, honey. I'm sorry."

Hurt and angry, Abigail turned away from him, stamping her foot in a tantrum, "You're *always* sorry!"

"That's right, Roeschen. He's alvays sorry, but he just keeps on hurting you, doesn't he. And your mummy too. Only, this time, he hurt your mummy worse than ever."

"What do you mean?" she asked, tilting her head to look up at Schmidt and remembering what he had said earlier. That her mum was dead. That her father was going to die too. But her father was here right in front of her, just as she had wished.

"That man you call daddy." Schmidt pointed the knife at Sean, "He sent your mummy to heaven too."

Abigail looked into her father's eyes for denial, and none coming, she turned to Schmidt, her fists beating against his hip. "I don't believe you. Daddy wouldn't do that. He loves my mummy. He loves her."

Her thumping ground to a halt, her tears streaming down her face as Schmidt spun her to face her father and held the knife against her throat, "Time for an answer, Sean. Meg or Abby? Which is it to be?"

Sean looked at Meg then back to Schmidt, "Please don't make me do this."

"Wrong answer," said Schmidt, his hand on Abby's brow and pulling her head back, the blade pressed to her skin. "Maybe you think it seems fitting, that *'Abby'* should die in a church."

"WAIT!"

"Tell me how it feels, Sean. To be both in and out of control. To have to decide which of them dies."

"Okay! Okay. I'll do it! Just throw me the knife!"

"Really, Sean. Do you think I'd be so stupid. I want you to strangle her. And besides, what do you expect *me* to use?" With the knife still held to Abby's throat, Schmidt reached into his jacket pocket and pulled out an old pistol, "*This?*"

Sean froze at the sight of the gun. With a knife there was a chance he could intervene, or that the cut wouldn't be fatal. But a gun. A gun was more… final.

Schmidt smiled and tutted, "It vould be so much easier I suppose. And quicker too. But nowhere near as thrilling." He placed the gun on the altar. "Nothing compares to the feel of your hand wrapped around a knife as it slices into an artery. Do you not agree, Sean. The warm blood spurting onto your skin. You remember how that feels, don't you?" He pressed the blade closer to Abby's throat, almost breaking her skin. "They say beauty is only skin deep, but let's see for ourselves shall we."

Sean rushed forward in panic, his hands held up for him to stop, "*Alright*! I'll do it!"

He turned to see Meg struggling to her feet and attempt to shuffle away, the bindings limiting her movement as he moved towards her, grabbing her from behind and easing her to the floor, not like a killer, but like a nurse with a fainting patient. Not wanting to fell her, but having to. His actions taken against his will, even as he turned her on her back and sat astride her, jamming her between his knees as she fought to resist him, twisting and bending her body as his hands wrapped around her throat. His daughter shouting, "Don't, daddy, don't." And Meg screaming into her gag, choking. Her her eyes watering, imploring him to stop.

"I'm sorry," he cried, his grip tightening with her resistance and tears running down his cheeks as he turned to avoid the sight of her reddening face, her eyes rolling white as they flickered towards the back of her head. And her throat rasping, the vibration felt through the palms of his hands, his grip slackened and broke away, his arms collapsing to his sides as he fought back his tears, "I can't do this."

Schmidt's grip tightened around the knife at Abby's throat, "Don't try my fucking patience, Sean. Kill her! Kill her *now*!"

"I can't."

Schmidt took the gun from the altar and held it in front of his face, staring at it in psychotic wonderment, his voice strangely calm. "My father first showed me this ven I vas a boy. It's a Luger, from the second vorld war. And though it may be old," he said, taking aim at Sean, "I can assure you, it still works."

Sean turned away, expecting him to shoot.

"There are only two bullets remaining," said Schmidt. "Von of them for Meg. And the other, vell, lets just say;- it's a spare." He bent down and slid the gun across the floor to Sean. "How this pans out is up to you. But, unless you do as I say, Abigail is not going to survive this. So why don't you just empty the chamber into her fucking head and get it over with."

Sean saw Meg's eyes fill with horror as he sat astride her, the gun pointed at her face, his hands trembling.

"Do it!" Schmidt ordered. "Kill her, or your daughter dies."

"First, let her go. There's no need for her to see this."

"Look at her, Sean," Schmidt said, running his fingers through Abigail's hair. A smile as he pulled a yellow ribbon from his pocket, pulled her hair into a ponytail and fastened it into a sloppy bow. "Such a beautiful young thing. Is there *anything* you wouldn't do for her?"

"No," Sean answered sombrely. "I'd do anything."

"Then shut the fuck up and put a bullet in the detective's head!... Then. Maybe. We can talk about saving your daughter."

Trembling, Sean wrapped one hand around the other to steady the gun, his finger on the trigger and his shaking more pronounced as his eyes squinted closed and his jaw clenched in readiness for the bang as he began to squeeze.

Seventy Nine

"No! Stop!"

Ben stood at the entrance looking down at Meg, the barrel of the gun still held to her head and her eyes staring into his with a mixture of fear and hope, thankful he had read into her message.

A survivor and an agnostic, Meg had reached out to him the only way she could. *Praying* for his forgiveness and reminding him of their last meal together in the Church Mouse. Each a vital clue to where she was being held, coupled with Ben's memory of what she'd told him of her first interview at Schmidt's surgery. Schmidt having told her that he'd met Sean Edwards in a pub next to a property he was renovating.

"Vell just look at this," said Schmidt. "It is so nice of you to join our little party, Ben. I'm glad you could make it."

With the sign of help here at last, Sean tore the tape from Meg's mouth, his finger easing off the trigger as Ben walked towards them and stood between Schmidt holding Abigail, and Sean sitting over Meg's abdomen.

"Let them go," Ben ordered, his eyes fixed firmly on the gun and his demands directed at Schmidt. "Let *all* of them go."

"Vat's wrong, Ben. You on your own?"

Ben had not dared risk Meg's life by divulging that he had learned of Schmidt's whereabouts to the team. Schmidt had been at the station all week and had obviously performed hypnosis on Angela Ainsworth, but who else was under his influence. Who else might have informed Schmidt that he was on his way. If he were warned, then Meg would already be dead, he was sure of it.

"Back up's on its way," he bluffed.

"Nonsense!" Schmidt shouted, then angrily looked back at Sean. "*Finish* it! This is ***not*** over. Put a bullet in her fucking head or I'll slit this pretty little throat."

Sean looked to Ben for help but seeing none coming, his body tensed and his finger wrapped around the trigger once more, Ben shouting for him to stop as he rushed towards him. But Sean had no choice, and holding the gun to Meg's head, he looked away, averting his gaze from the oncoming shot as she pleaded for mercy, "Please, Sean. Don't kill me. I have a daughter too." And again, Sean's grip eased off the trigger.

Ben stood just a few feet away, his mouth slightly agape as his mind made sense of it all. Her mood swings and disappearances. Her secretive phone calls. All of it because she had been juggling work with being a mother. And with Ben's dumbfounded expression came the sound of Schmidt's voice laced with sarcasm, "Didn't you know, Ben? You have a daughter, and she didn't think to tell you, even ven she vas sick in hospital."

Ben remained silent, his head spinning with thoughts of all that happened between them. Their relationship. Their split. Their time apart when she'd transferred to another branch. She was having his child and he had never known.

"Don't feel too bad, Ben. She didn't tell *anyvon*. That's a career woman for you. She's just like all the others. Always thinking of themselves, every last von of them. Not von of them deserved to have children. And not von of them deserves to live."

BANG!

A shot rang out around the church as Schmidt stood staring down at his shoulder, his face an expression of shock. His mind not yet registering the pain as he looked over to Ben who found himself staring down the barrel of a gun, Sean aiming in his direction.

"No!" Ben shouted, "Don't shoot!" But Sean squeezed the trigger and Ben felt the bullet whiz past him and cut through the air towards Schmidt's head. The bullet penetrating his skull, dropping him to his knees, and then flat to his face. The loud crack of his nose unfelt by his already dead corpse as his face smashed hard against the wooden floor. A stunned silence followed by a moment's confusion with everyone staring at the body, and then;

BANG! Another shot, from another direction, Ben whipping his head around as Sean fell mortally wounded to the floor.

"Stop!" Ben shouted, jumping in the way of the armed unit, his hands up as he shouted for them not to shoot.

Morton and the unit stood in the doorway, three of the team crouched in readiness to fire again as Sean lay on the floor next to

Meg, his breathing heavy and his arm still raised, his aim pointed at Schmidt's body before his shaking hand collapsed to his side and the empty gun fell to the floor, a thick plume of blood seeping through his shirt. And beside him, Meg struggled to her knees as Ben rushed over to help her, kneeling beside her to untie her bindings and then helping her to her feet, looking into her eyes with a gaze that said everything. How thankful he was she was alive. How much she meant to him. How much he loved her.

"How did you find us?" Ben asked as Morton came to join them.

"Edwards left his phone on," Morton replied, looking down at Sean's paling face, and only then, when he saw him manage a smile, did he realise that he had left it on deliberately, the reason blatantly obvious. Sean's grin remaining fixed on his daughter as she came running towards him, crying, "Daddy. Daddy." And draped herself across his body.

"It's alright, honey," Sean uttered. "Everything's going to be okay."

"But, you're hurt daddy. You're bleeding."

His pulse slowing and his strength deserting him, Sean struggled for air as he fought to raise his head, "Abby… Please, remember that, no matter what anyone thinks of me… No matter what anyone says… I love you." He coughed and spluttered, his breathing shallowing and his voice dropping to a croaking whisper, "And I love your mummy too," he said, a tear rolling down his cheek. "You both mean… the world to me."

Abby lay across his chest, hugging him, his blood seeping into her yellow dress as his head collapsed to the floor, and his final gasps for breath growing weaker, she moved closer, pressing her cheek next to his and whispering in his ear, the last thing he'd ever hear before the final sliver of breath escaped his lungs.

"Closed your eyes to the killer surprise, *'daddy'*... My name is Rose."

Epilogue

It's not something you readily admit to people;- the fact that you're seeing a psychiatrist.

In the days since Schmidt's death, the investigation had shown that Schmidt, real name Jurgen Heinrik, had never qualified to be a psychiatrist. His diplomas had been faked, and since coming to Britain he had moved around the country, possibly in his search for the perfect candidate to fill the void left by his sister, or maybe it was to avoid detection for his crimes in other areas. But after the last spate of murders, for reasons known only to himself, he had chosen to remain in the Northeast and build his portfolio; his list of clients steadily growing, ready for the time he would come to make his selection of those who filled his requirements. And in some cases, adding to his list through so called '*chance*' meetings. One such meeting having been with the officer in charge of the lock-up around the time of the Inkleman case. Schmidt had convinced him that he was suffering from depression, just months after the murders, thus gaining access to the items he wanted in his planning for the next killing spree.

Now, finally, it was over.

The loose ends of the case being tied up, Ben and Meg took time out to tie up a few loose ends of their own.

"I'll leave you two alone a while," Meg's mother said, leaving Meg and Ben stood next to a cot on the paediatric ward of Durham University Hospital.

"Is she really mine?" Ben asked, looking down at the baby in his arms.

"You okay with that?" Meg asked.

Ben smiled as the baby wrapped her tiny digits around his finger. 'Course I'm okay," he beamed. "I have a daughter. And she's every bit as beautiful as her mum."

"Not *every* bit," Meg smiled. "She has your ears."

"Do you think she'll be okay?" Ben asked.

"Of course she will," Meg's smile widened, "It's amazing what doctors can do these days. With a little surgery they'll pin them back and she'll be right as rain in no time."

"That's not what I meant," Ben said seriously.

"I know it's not," Meg laughed. "But it's not the big bad world you think it is out there, so let's deal with the present before we worry about her future."

In the last few days, Meg had felt the huge burden lifted from her shoulders now that the case had been solved and everything was out in the open. Before they had come to the hospital, she had told Ben that their baby had been suffering from severe stomach pains. She'd been pale and sick. She'd had a high temperature and begun to pass blood. She had explained how frightening it was to see her daughter so ill, her legs drawing up as she screamed out in pain. And she'd explained that after her daughter was diagnosed and admitted to hospital, she had thought of contacting him, deciding he had a right to know he had a daughter. All of this just days before the Edwards case. Then, the night following her baby's operation, she got a call.

"I was sitting at her bedside," she explained. "Feeling useless. Like there was nothing I could do. That's why I was tetchy that night at the Edwards house. Not because of the murder or the fact that you were there, but because I didn't know what else to do. I felt guilty for leaving her but I couldn't just sit around and do nothing."

Ben smiled, understanding, the secretive phone calls now making sense. "Don't beat yourself up over this, Meg. You did the right thing," he said supportively. "I'm sure your mum was more than happy to spend some time with her grandchild. And what's more, I'll bet she was never away from the place."

They looked into their daughter's eyes. Trusting, innocent eyes. Meg with thoughts of how beautiful she was, and Ben with thoughts of how vulnerable, thinking how much better he would feel if he and Meg were together as a couple, and, just as he was about to ask if that were possible, they were interrupted by a heavy set nurse entering the room and standing next to the monitor, filling out a chart as Ben's eyes drifted to her shapeless legs, finding it difficult to define where her calves ended and her ankles began. A memory of how his mother would jokingly refer to her own similarly shaped legs.

The nurse finished checking the notes on the clip-board and turned to see Ben absently staring at her 'cankles'. She smiled at him, her voice warm and reassuring, “Your daughter’s going to be just fine Mr. Miller. Other than a little discomfort, she’s doing fantastic.”

“What is it, this, intussusception?” he asked, unsure of his pronunciation.

Meg had already explained that it was a blockage of the bowel but Ben needed to hear it from someone else, frightened that Meg may have forgotten to mention something crucial about his daughter’s condition.

“It’s a blockage of the bowel caused by the intestine telescoping in on itself.”

“Is it dangerous?”

“It can be, if left untreated. But you’ve got nothing to worry about Mr. Miller,” she explained. “Though sometimes it can be corrected with an enema by releasing oxygen into the bowel, in your daughter’s case, we needed to perform a relatively minor operation.”

“Minor? But she’s been in over a week. I’ve known heart by-pass patients discharged quicker.”

The nurse’s voice was gentle and reassuring as she attempted to ease his concerns. “It’s standard practice for this type of operation. She had to be fed through a drip, to give the bowel a chance to recover. Then we have to build up her eating habits and make sure everything’s working okay.”

“And she’s okay now, right?”

“She’s fine,” the nurse said smiling. “The doctor said you can take her home whenever you’re ready. But there’s something I would like to ask you before you go.”

“Fire away,” Meg said.

Although the staff generally referred to the babies on their ward by their surnames when talking amongst themselves, it was still the norm to call them by their Christian names when they were with their parents. Baby Rainer however, was an enigma. For although she was four months old and Meg had generally been using one name in particular when talking to her baby, she’d admitted that she may change her mind when it came to the christening.

“Her name,” the nurse asked. “Have you decided yet?”

Meg moved closer to Ben and placed her hands against his chest. “I was hoping we could call her Mary,” she said.

Ben’s eyes welled instantly. Mary was his mother’s name. “I’d like that,” he said, smiling down at his daughter. “I’d like that very much.”

*   *   *

In a corner plot of the cemetery, Thomas stood with his father, just the two of them staring down at the headstone. Arnold's thoughts were of the last words Sean Edwards had spoken to him, '*All I ask is that you remember me*'. And so, he was here, this one and only time. Honouring a killer who had brought him closer to his son.

"Was Mr. Waders a bad man, daddy?" asked Thomas, though they had learned Sean's real name from the papers.

"No, Thomas. I don't think he was," Arnold said, handing him the wreath and standing back as his son laid it against the headstone. A green base of ivy intertwined with yellow flowers, chosen because Thomas thought they were his friend's favourites.

Attached was a card written in Thomas's own hand.

To the bestest spy in the hole wide werld.
Thankyou for been my friend.
I wont ever forget you.
Love from 008.

*   *   *

Elsewhere, a little girl sat in her bedroom at her grandmother's house. She was dressed in her school uniform and fiddled with the dress on her doll, her mind drifting off into a dream of something unreal.

With long blonde hair and milk-white skin, she was sitting in a garden, her yellow dress folded beneath her as she pretended not to notice her brother watching her from behind a willow tree. He was trying to sneak up on her, and she ignored him as he drew closer, the excited glare of her eyes remaining focused on her lengthening daisy chain as he inched closer, like a moth to the flame, the voice in her head imperceptible.

"I'm going to caaaaaatch you."

"I'm going to huuuuurt you."

"I'm going to kiiiiiill you."

"Abbyyy!"

The voice of an old woman wrenched her from her dream, shouting up the stairs, "It's time to come down, Abby. Your friend's here to walk you to school."

"Okay, gran," she replied cheerfully, "I'll be down in a minute." Then cursed her under her breath for calling her that name as she lay her doll cruciform on the bed and crossed to her bedroom door, pausing there a second as she stared down at the waste basket; Mr. Flopsy looking right back at her with fluff coming from the holes where his eyes had been, his head peeping out from beneath scraps of paper.

One piece at a time she had gotten rid of him. Cutting off his arms and then his legs, the head was the last to go.

She smiled; a thought of all those dead including her Nan. Maybe soon, her 'gran' would be dead too.

She closed her bedroom door and started down the stairs slowly, her sentence broken as she paused on every step, whispering to herself;-

"Fingers.. and.. toes.. is.. how.. my.. rhyme.. goes."

A FINAL WORD

Think of how would it feel to wake up from a dream, only to discover you had killed someone.

What would you do?

What *could* you do?

How many times have you heard;- there are two sides to every story. They are like chalk and cheese. Love and hate are but two sides of the same coin.

The list is endless. But ultimately, we are all capable of committing sickening acts of cruelty under given circumstances. It is engrained deep within our every fibre.

The name-calling.

A child pulling the legs off an insect.

One person killing another for nothing more than their own personal gain.

And even the most meek of us may have thoughts of revenge when faced with seeing our loved ones being hurt or killed at the hands of another, our emotions boiling over beyond our control. Actions forcing reactions and faith tested to the limit. And though some of us may hope that the law of the land punishes the culprit accordingly; think for a moment. If it were your mother who was mugged or your child brutally raped, would you not feel so much rage that you would want to take matters into your own hands and dispense a justice befitting the crime, with no regard to the feelings of the assailant or *his* loved ones.

Thankfully, in most of us, these feelings are kept under control. Though in some of us they are not. And in a small minority, they escape to wreak their havoc on the innocents of this world who are left to suffer the consequences of their wrongs.

So as you sit there, analysing your sleeping habits of late and simply putting your tiredness down to working too hard, remember there could be another cause for your tiredness. A lack of sleep perhaps;- your hidden persona running amok, creating havoc. Hurting. Raping. Killing. Keeping you from discovering the truth, even now, whilst you're reading this book, oblivious to the carnage you leave behind, and blissfully unaware of the killer within you, waiting to be set free.

So beware your naps, the tiredness, the occasional lapse of concentration or a moment of wondering where the time went. But most of all;- beware what you dream… *for not everything is as it seems.*

AUTHORS NOTE

It is impossible to do justice to the beauty that is Durham city through words alone. I can only hope that you can forgive my inability to perform such an impossible task and accept any discrepancies in my descriptions which have been included for the purpose of effect in the storytelling and to protect the privacy of the residents of some of the places thereby mentioned.

FACT AND FICTION

The Origins of this story relate back to a bank robbery in Denmark in 1951 and are based on fact. The event, the characters involved, and the circumstances surrounding it actually happened. And although the boy who actually witnessed the robbery did exist;- his name, background, and subsequent events depicted in this story thereafter are a matter of fiction and bear no resemblance to the life he actually led.